THE CONTORTIONISTS

A NOVEL

ROBERT HODGSON VAN WAGONER

SIGNATURE BOOKS
SALT LAKE CITY
2020

For Phoenix and Shae

An earlier version of the chapter "Happy or Sad, It's up to Me" was published in *Weber, The Contemporary West.*

An earlier version of the chapter "It Began Simply Enough" was published in *Clover, A Literary Rag.*

The opinions expressed in this book are not necessarily those of the publisher.

Cover design by Jason Francis.
Cover painting: *untitled*, oil, by Richard J Van Wagoner, courtesy of Van Wagoner Family Trust. Photographed by Angela Moore

FIRST EDITION | 2020

LIBRARY OF CONGRESS CATALOGING-IN-PUBLICATION DATA

Names:	Van Wagoner, Robert Hodgson, 1964– author.
Title:	The contortionists : a novel / Robert Hodgson Van Wagoner.
Description:	First edition.	Salt Lake City : Signature Books, 2020.	Summary: In his second novel, his first in twenty years, Robert H. Van Wagoner explores a family in extremis tottering at the edge of faith: in God and church, in family, and in marriage, in the institutions that promise safety and meaning. Both lyrical and explosive, *The Contortionists* unfolds as a page-turning mystery. Van Wagoner's wrenching narrative propels the reader forward, toward the novel's harrowing climax, while deftly unpacking its major themes—mental illness, sexuality, and substance abuse in a culture that would rather not confront them. Does the truth ever set anyone ultimately free? The stakes for Joshua and his family could not be greater"—Provided by publisher.
Identifiers:	LCCN 2020039472 (print)	LCCN 2020039473 (ebook)	ISBN 9781560852896 (paperback)	ISBN 9781560853886 (ebook)
Subjects:	LCSH: Mormon families—Fiction.	Missing children—Fiction.	LCGFT: Fiction.
Classification:	LCC PS3572.A42276 C66 2020 (print)	LCC PS3572.A42276 (ebook)	DDC 813/.54—dc23
	LC record available at https://lccn.loc.gov/2020039472
	LC ebook record available at https://lccn.loc.gov/2020039473

THE CONTORTIONISTS

CONTENTS

DAY THREE

AFTERWARD

Day One

"Then God bless you!" said Faith, with the pink ribbons; "and may you find all is well when you come back."

"Amen!" cried Goodman Brown. "Say thy prayers, dear Faith, and go to bed at dusk, and no harm will come to thee."

—*Young Goodman Brown*, Nathaniel Hawthorne

In the Garden

The neighbor, Natalie MacMillan, would tell essentially the same story as Melissa Christopher, the missing boy's mother. They would both say the child had been gone twenty minutes before anyone noticed, twenty silent minutes bookended by two telephone calls, the first from the mother to tell the neighbor five-year-old Joshua was on his way to the birthday party, the second from the neighbor to ask the mother if she had sent him yet.

Two hours later scarcely a person in Utah hadn't heard the terrible news. But in the upper Ogden Valley near a town named Eden, Karley did not yet know her nephew had gone missing. Bare-bottomed, she bent to examine her peas and lettuces. They were up, tiny things yet, but up. It was a gift for Hans, this lingering. She could feel his eyes on her.

Smiling, Hans reached to the nightstand for his water. He enjoyed this view through the open French doors, his wife's dark hair still riled from lovemaking. Playful Karley, she was childlike in gardens and skin. He returned the water to the nightstand and rolled from the bed, stretched, then gathered his jeans from the floor. Zipping and buttoning, he wandered through the open doors. At the edge of the deck, he wiggled his bare toes and contemplated the twenty-odd yards of wet grass between himself and his wife. The hard May rain had softened and the interloping mist braced his naked torso. He'd nearly decided to return for a shirt when Karley stood up.

Cocking an ear, she fingered back her hair. Yes, she'd heard correctly, the downshift whine of a vehicle slowing on the highway below. She listened to the car turn up their long drive, the cascade

3

of wheels spinning fast in gravel. Smiling over her shoulder, she primly tugged down the hem of her T-shirt. It barely covered her bottom. She might almost make it to the house if she ran. Instead she turned back toward the highway, her gaze aimed at the gap in the shrub oak and ponderosa. When Caleb's Jeep crested, moving much too fast, she and Hans exchanged a quick glance.

"You're here?" the boy shouted. "We've been calling for over an hour!" Long-legged, he hurried through flowerbeds, over crowning boulders too massive to excavate.

Karley stretched the shirt to her bare thighs and watched her eighteen-year-old brother lumber into the garden, his approach heedless of all, including the young plants he crushed beneath his feet. Karley received him with upstretched arms, hands reaching to still his face.

"Slow down," she said. "I don't understand what you're saying."

Hans started down the stairs. He could hear the boy's voice but couldn't make out the words. Karley said something, and again Hans failed to understand. Crossing the yard quickly, he tried to read lips. Karley stared up at Caleb's face, gave her head an incredulous shake, then touched her throat and took a half step back. Turning—Caleb still talking, doing better now, making sense—she met Hans's gaze.

She was a good athlete, Karley, sure-footed. She crossed the wet lawn at a sprint without slipping, her feet black to the ankles with mud.

Detective Craig's Day Off

Lieutenant Detective Milo Craig rolled up the hill past the Mormon church, its lot already a carnival of police and media. He steered left at the corner around a flashing cruiser, lifted a finger to the uniform who sentried the intersection. A block ahead at the bottom of the boy's street, Jill Grafton's SUV was parked near the corner. Craig pulled in beside it, turned off the motor, then sat for a moment feeling his age. There were advantages, he'd learned, to foregoing retirement, but losing his day off was not one of them. The neighborhood sat high in the foothills above the city, an unobstructed view of Antelope Island and beyond. To the west over the Great Salt Lake, a bright fissure in the tight-fisted sky. He zipped up his jacket and climbed from his rig.

Recovery had pitched a rain fly over the evidence and erected a wall of sandbags to divert the gutter flow around it. The tissue-wrapped book, now obvious in its translucence, lay straddling the concrete and asphalt. One glance at the swollen mass was enough to tell Craig it wasn't likely to help them.

"What a mess," he said.

"Not hopeful," Jill Grafton agreed. "We'll see."

Despite a decidedly feminine presentation, Jill was a gruff, militant wisp of a woman and as capable a criminalist as Craig had encountered. She was married to a Cheryl, a liability in Utah, though the precision of her work largely neutered her antagonists. If the book had anything to tell them, Jill and her crew would find it.

"What should I know?"

"Bleak. Five years old, not even in kindergarten yet. Carrying that"—she gestured at the gift—"to a birthday party. You run the parents yet?" Craig shook his head, though, in fact, he had. Feigning ignorance, he'd found, was the shortest route to learning everything he needed to know. "About nine years ago the father had an alcohol-related accident in the canyon. Went through the retaining wall a mile above the waterfall. Minor injuries. Suspended license. Nothing prior, nothing since. Not on either the mom or the dad. But for that one blip, a good upstanding Mormon family."

Craig nodded. "Repentance is a wonderful thing."

Jill allowed herself a wistful smile. "You've been around long enough to know, I suppose."

Indeed. Craig, at sixty-seven, knew a lot of things, most of them not worth knowing. "Impressions in the grass?" The soggy apron between the curb and the sidewalk appeared steamrollered.

"Who can tell? Neighbors've been all over here."

"Scent sample?"

She thumbed at her SUV. "Kid's pillow. We're just waiting for the dogs."

"Mighty clean scene."

Jill stripped off a glove. "Whatever isn't too clean is way too dirty." From her pocket, she extracted a roll of mints, peeled back the foil, and offered the top mint to Craig.

"What about the kid's house?" He accepted the mint.

Jill excised the next mint with a manicured thumbnail, knifing the foil into a thin little ribbon. She sucked the disc into her mouth where it clicked against her teeth until she got it situated between her cheek and gum. Like an abscessed tooth, the mint bulged beneath her cheekbone. She dropped the roll into her pocket before answering.

"I made a quick once-through of the kid's bedroom then sealed it off. Family seems pretty cooperative, signed the consent no question. I think they'll stay out until we decide if we want a closer look. They released the pillow and a couple hard-surface toys, kid's toothbrush."

Craig nodded. "Later today I may want you to take a look at

the rest of the house. I'm on my way to the neighbor's, then I'll speak with the parents. I'll let you know."

"Sad stuff," Jill said.

"Yes, indeedy."

■

Joe and Melissa Christopher lived in a square brick affair of moderate size, yellow, with mauve trim and false shutters, a fair-sized front porch. The yard was large and well-manicured—mature maples, flowerbeds against the house, tulips tendrilling up here and there, a few late daffodils. The neighborhood was old and staid and built above the riffraff. Here even a modest house like the Christophers' came at an upscale price.

Craig mounted the porch and reached for the bell, and the door swung instantly open. Sally Frye unlocked the storm door and cracked it for Craig who opened it the rest of the way. Sally was an impressive figure, big and broad, dressed down today in blue jeans and a sweater of an intricate floral design. Her weather-scored face was all business, her dark eyes set indomitably against despair. "Milo," she said, stepping back.

"Hello, Sally. Glad you're here." And he was. Though contentious at times, she was the best victim's advocate Craig had ever worked with.

A man, late-fifties, fidgeted behind her.

"This is Curt DeBoer," Sally said. "Joshua's grandfather."

Craig took the man's humid hand. "Milo Craig. I'm a detective with the Ogden Police Department."

Ambushed by emotion, Curt seized his nose and toggled it back and forth. When he released himself, his sinuses emitted a tiny pneumatic pop. *"Ohhh,"* he sighed. "I'm sorry."

"Don't be," Craig said.

The Christophers' living room was like many Craig had seen during his seven decades in Utah, an un-themed hodge-podge of bargain furniture with a quality antique thrown in here and there. The walls were a shrine to family and church—a collage of the boy, Mom and Dad sprinkled in, framed snapshots standing up on various surfaces. But mostly the images were church-related: a framed poster of the Salt Lake temple; prints of the Mormon prophet and apostles rendered in pastel; a big bad reproduction of Christ descending through the clouds replete with heralding angels; a poster-sized document boldly entitled, *The Family: A Proclamation to the World.* One of the end tables sported a stack of the Mormon magazine, *The Ensign.* A collection of old religious volumes lined the lid of the upright piano.

Even without the photos, it was not difficult to identify the boy's parents. The mother sat on the sofa looking through the detective with the vacant affect of a stunned refugee. A somewhat older woman, the boy's grandmother, Craig guessed, sat close beside the mother, her restless hands like nervous birds—touching, withdrawing, fluttering about her unresponsive daughter. The boy's father sat alone in a corner staring out the large front window. He seemed entirely unaware of Craig's arrival.

"Have you found anything yet?" This from a handsome young man, early twenties and clean-cut. Arms folded, he studied the policeman with a clear-eyed confidence Craig recognized. A recently returned missionary or Craig wasn't an aging heretic.

"No, sir, nothing yet. But the search is getting itself organized fast now. We have a lot of good people on the scene." Taking a sociable step toward the young man, he offered his hand. "You are?"

"Jared DeBoer." The kid's muscular grip confirmed Craig's suspicion—a former missionary for sure. He glanced at the woman on the sofa. "Melissa's my sister."

"Who are you?" Melissa Christopher asked.

Meeting her gaze, Craig smiled—he never quite got used to it, the disconnect. "Milo Craig. I'm a detective. I've been put in charge of the investigation. We'll be working together to bring your boy home."

With that, Mr. Christopher began to sob. He wept inconsolably, his whole body shuddering. His wife stared at the floor and gnawed on a fingernail, her features closing in. She shook her head, the movement gaining force until she swiveled toward him, her eyes bright and white against the redness of her rage.

"Stop it," she spat. She lifted her chin and glared at her husband. *"Stop it, now."*

"Sweetheart," her mother scolded. She reached in to pet her

daughter, then instantly withdrew, repelled by the heat of the younger woman's fury.

Joe Christopher blinked up at his wife then looked away. He swiped at his face with the inside of his elbow, but there was no closing the floodgate now. Tumbling from his chair, he stumbled from the room.

Glancing at Sally, Craig was graced with the slightest nod. He couldn't have agreed more.

That Boy in the Corner

"It's true, Melissa." Ezra proffered the engagement ring tweezed between two fingers. "I fasted and prayed and I'm sure of it. God blessed me with a spiritual confirmation."

Melissa had been a little afraid God might do something like this. Leaning in, she squinted at the ring. A dandy—white gold, princess-cut diamond. It filled her with nothing but dread.

"It's lovely, Ezra." She sat back without touching it. She couldn't say she was surprised by this development. They'd been dating five months, a month longer in her experience than the average gestation for a proposal from a newly returned missionary. Her three previous near misses—Colby, Tyler, Steve—had come over dinner at modestly priced restaurants, an approach she preferred to the parked-car thing. She and Ezra were late for a party.

"Put it on," he pleaded. "I bought it on my mission. The best diamonds in the world are mined in Russia."

"Really, it's very nice, Ezra," she said again. Gently she pushed his hand away and adjusted herself in the seat. "In fact, I think I'm going to pray about it."

He let the ring float for another beat then drew it into his lap. He looked down at the thing, dumfounded. It was clear he'd assumed his answer from God counted for them both.

"I didn't say no," Melissa said. She manufactured an encouraging smile. "I just need to think. Certainly you can understand."

"But I love you," he managed. "I was just so sure, I mean, you don't get an answer like I did—" He squeezed the ring in his fist. "I love you is the thing."

Until now he'd never declared his love, and she supposed,

11

under the circumstances, it was time. Four boys in three years, all of them certain she was the divine answer to their matrimonial prayers. Melissa could just see God in his heaven going down that list of diminishing possibilities. She looked at Ezra and tried to imagine what it would be like to be his wife. He was good enough looking in a big-eared sort of way, a decent kisser, temple worthy, ambitious. And he did, she had to admit, have good taste in engagement rings. Nothing much else came to mind.

"Gosh, I'll have to think about that one," she said.

Ezra blinked. "You don't love me?"

"I didn't say that."

Ezra opened his fist and mourned the ring, then reached under his seat where he'd secreted the box. Melissa felt more than a little bad for him. She was a pleaser at heart and wanted to help. But this thing with God and answered prayers, it undermined her confidence. She wasn't entirely convinced she wouldn't wake up one morning married to Ezra Reinholt.

"Maybe we shouldn't go to the party," he said. He shoved the ring box in the glove compartment and slammed the little door.

"Don't be like that, Ezra." She tried to sound cheerful. "It's not like I turned you down."

"That's not what I mean." He glanced past Melissa at his best friend's house. "The party's for me. For us, actually."

Melissa dialed her smile up high. "Well, then. We really shouldn't miss it, should we?"

"It's an engagement party, Melissa. It was supposed to be a surprise. But now …"

Melissa peered at Ezra, then swiveled toward the house. She needed suddenly to void her bladder. A creeping, match-like heat flared at the top of her head. "Wow," she said, fumbling for the door latch. "That must have been some answer to your prayers. Did God appear to you in a blinding pillar of light?" Shouldering the door, she started out.

"Wait!" Lurching across the brake, Ezra grabbed for her wrist and got a handful of her butt instead. She spun back and Ezra blanched.

"Time to party, Ezra."

"Please, we really don't have to go. I can call Matt."

"Call him, if you want." She slammed the door.

"Just wait, please," he cried, throwing his own door open.

Melissa stopped. She turned around and folded her arms.

"*Please* let me warn Matt." He ducked back into the car and emerged with his cell phone. He held it up for Melissa's inspection. She chewed on her lip and watched him pace, his voice hidden beneath a covering hand. Finished with his call, he locked his car then started across the lawn. "I still want to marry you," he informed her.

With a snort, Melissa turned for the house and Ezra quickened his pace to catch up. "I hope you really will pray about it," he plodded on. "I just know it's right. And I believe—I mean I really have a testimony of it—I'm sure you'll know too—"

"*Enough,*" Melissa snapped.

"Don't be mad," he said softly.

"Well, I am."

"I mean don't be mad when you pray about it. That's all I'm asking. And maybe you could fast about it too. Fasting helps."

A micro-pain pinged between Melissa's eyes. "This was not a good idea, Ezra. It doesn't bode well you thought it up."

"It wasn't my idea. It was God who thought it up."

All her life she had imagined marrying someone like Ezra Reinholt, a righteous Priesthood Bearer with a gift for inspiration. And the truth was she and Ezra had enjoyed some good times together. It usually wasn't a chore to go out with him. Maybe she hadn't paid enough attention to whatever signs God was trying to send her? It was not a happy thought that Ezra might be the 2x4 God intended to brain her with. The possibility inspired nothing more than an urgent need to urinate.

"Ready?" she asked.

Ezra rolled his shoulders. "No. But I guess I'm going anyway."

■

"Get on in here!" Matt bellowed.

Melissa liked Matt. She liked him better than she liked Ezra. She followed Ezra inside where two dozen virginal boys and girls did their best to pretend the party poopers hadn't arrived. The room's every molecule felt pregnant with portent, laden with greasy pheromones. What a bummer Melissa had turned out to be.

Matt's girlfriend, Jackie, sidled up. "Hi, Melissa."

Melissa accepted a breasty squeeze and, over Jackie's shoulder, tracked the boys' migration to the refreshment table. Matt restacked a tower of toppled napkins, while Ezra sampled the spread. "I spoiled everyone's fun," she apologized.

"Don't you worry about it," Jackie said. "You have a lot to think about."

"But you went to so much trouble."

Jackie smiled bravely. Her most fervent ambition was a proposal from Matt. Melissa was a mystery she couldn't fathom. Together they watched their dates wander toward the kitchen. "Ezra's lucky to have Matt," Melissa said.

Jackie nodded sadly. "Ezra looks devastated."

Melissa massaged a knot in her neck. "It's not like I said no, Jackie."

"But what are you going to do?"

Most of the kids were engaged in careful conversation, though to Melissa it looked like avoidance. In one corner a boy she didn't know visited with one of Jackie's girlfriends. Looking up, he caught Melissa spying and smiled.

"Sorry?"

Jackie frowned. "I asked what you're going to do?"

"I really have no idea."

"Wow." Jackie shook her perfect tresses. "You two just make such a great couple. The way Ezra's been talking we all figured—" Even she had the good sense to shut up.

In self-defense Melissa drifted back to the boy. She was hoping he'd look her way again. "That boy over in the corner," she asked. "I don't think I've ever seen him before. Who is he?"

"Him?" The question seemed to confuse Jackie. "That's Joe Christopher. He's in the singles ward. Matt's trying to fellowship him. Certainly you've heard about Joe?"

"Heard what?"

Jackie lowered her voice. "He got himself in some trouble a while back. Drugs or alcohol or something. I'm pretty sure it was a Word of Wisdom thing. He's trying to straighten out his life. He started coming to church a few months ago. He's nice enough, I guess, though if you want to know the truth, he makes me a little uncomfortable."

Melissa smiled at Jackie. "Uncomfortable how?"

"You know. He's just not the sort of boy I'd date. For one thing he didn't go on a mission. And then he has all that worldly experience. Who knows what he did when he was drinking or getting high or whatever."

"Does he still do whatever?"

Jackie stared at Melissa, all too aware she'd swallowed the hook. She smoothed her sweater around her shapely hips. "I'm sure he's doing the best he can," she said. "That's why we have repentance, after all."

"After all," Melissa said. "Well, he's certainly no chore to look at."

Jackie blinked slowly, her eyes full of pupil. "He is kind of pretty, I suppose. Too pretty for my taste."

About then Ezra reappeared, and, for the first time since arriving, Melissa found herself glad to see him. "I'd really like to leave," he said, steering her from Jackie. "I don't feel very good. Matt says it'd be okay."

Melissa extracted herself from Ezra's grip. "But I don't want to leave."

"I don't know why you have to punish me like this."

"I'm not punishing you," she lied. "I just think it's rude to leave the party now. Matt and Jackie went to a lot of work."

"It's not my fault it turned out bad."

Melissa laughed. "Leave if you want. I'm staying."

"That—" Ezra's lips formed a thin white line. "That's not fair. You know I can't leave without you."

"Sure you can. Someone will take me home."

Ezra winced. "Had I known you could be so mean—" He stopped himself.

The room hadn't grown still exactly but the voices had assumed a hushed intensity. "Oh, Ezra," Melissa said more gently.

"I'm not leaving without you."

"Suit yourself."

At the refreshment table she poured herself a cup of Sprite and began loading her plate with goodies. She took her time, not quite sure what she'd do when her plate was full.

"This must be tough," someone said. Melissa glanced up. Joe Christopher suspended a bottle half-cocked, waiting for the fizz in his cup to die down. He wasn't looking at her, and then he was, his eyes dark and calm beneath thick brows. Not quite smiling, he topped off his root beer.

Melissa just stared at him. Up close, she understood what Jackie meant. He was more pretty than handsome, those large brown eyes feathered with long lashes. His nose was straight and narrow, though not too narrow, and his flawless skin was better than her own. His brown-blond hair wasn't long exactly but longer than any of the other boys' in the room. It was one length and thick, fingered straight back so it hung loosely over his collar, perfect on him, though Melissa had never before been one for anything but a close-shaved neckline. Tall and broad where it counted, Joe Christopher was pretty indeed, androgynous pretty, at least in the face. Melissa wished she hadn't piled so much food on her plate.

"I guess it is a bit hard," she admitted. "Ezra wants me to leave with him now. Maybe I should."

"Nah," he said. "The party was dull until you got here."

Melissa giggled and wished she hadn't. "Nothing like a freak show to liven things up."

It was Joe's turn to laugh. "You're no freak." He picked up his root beer. "Now Ezra, I wouldn't much want to be Ezra about now."

Melissa glanced over her shoulder. Alone near the front door, Ezra glared at her. "I'm afraid I'm being kinda mean to him. I feel a little sorry about it actually."

"I wouldn't feel too bad," Joe said. "To tell the truth, I almost didn't come. It was the suspense that finally got me. You know, an engagement party for an engagement that wasn't yet an engagement?" He shook his head. "If I were in your shoes, I don't think I'd be so calm."

Staring up at Joe Christopher, Melissa resisted the impulse to lick her lips. "I'm Melissa DeBoer. I imagine you knew that."

"Joe Christopher." He extended his hand. "I'm the current charity project."

He had a nice handshake, firm and unassuming. Melissa could feel the eyes, a roomful of them. She and Joe had quite an audience now. "So I'm told. I'd like to hear more about that. Being a charity case."

"It's sordid. And highly classified."

"Let me guess," she said, smiling. "If you told me, you'd have to kill Ezra?"

To her relief, Joe laughed. He took a sip of root beer and gazed out across the gathering. He was cool, Joe Christopher, but Melissa could tell by the drift of his eyes he'd seen it too. "It would seem we've drawn some spectators," he said. "The dreaded refreshment table assignation. I doubt I'm very good for your reputation, Melissa DeBoer."

The way this guy talked! "At this point, I doubt anyone could do much damage."

Joe leaned in and touched her wrist. It was neither flirtatious nor invasive, a commiserative gesture, and Melissa wondered what it would be like to kiss him. "I really am sorry you had to go through this tonight. If you'll forgive me saying so, it was pretty arrogant, what Ezra did." He withdrew his hand.

"Forgiven." Melissa's wrist tingled.

"Man, check out the vibes in this room." Another shake of his head. "Anyway, I'm really glad I got to meet you, Melissa. For that alone, it was worth coming. Maybe we'll run into each other again sometime. I'd like that." He hesitated then seemed to think better of whatever he'd thought to say. He blinked at her once and turned.

"Curtis DeBoer," Melissa said quickly.

Joe stopped. They were side-by-side now, shoulder-to-shoulder. Close enough Melissa could whisper. "That's spelled D-e-capital-B-o-e-r. Curtis is my father. It's in the phone book."

Joe didn't so much as breathe.

"In a minute I'm going to the bathroom to pee. To tell the truth, I'm going to explode if I don't. Not that you wanted to know that." She rolled her eyes. "What I mean is, after I use the toilet, I'm going to have Ezra take me home. I'd really love it if you called me."

Joe graced her with the merest smile. "When?"

"In about an hour."

"You want me to call in an hour?"

"Okay. An hour and twenty minutes." She was terrified he was going to laugh at her. Instead he loosed those pretty eyes on her. Under his gaze, she rocked on her feet and wondered how long she could hold her water.

"Maybe I should just come by?"

For a breath or two, Melissa pretended to mull this over. "An hour and twenty minutes." She nodded to seal the deal. "Curtis DeBoer. My address is right there with my phone number."

Happy or Sad, It's up to Me

The Christophers' was your standard kitchen, not the newest appliances though neither were they ancient. Seventies-era Formica and linoleum in blazing autumnal colors, cupboards that had seen better days. But it was clean and well organized, and the kitchen table appeared fairly new, a solid oak piece with tasteful chairs. The fridge exterior was a magnetized gallery of Joshua's artwork, a clipped cartoon or two, a few printed scriptures from the Book of Mormon, the kind of thing handed out in Relief Society or Sunday school. Craig took particular notice of one quote matted nicely behind a plexiglass holder:

Happy or sad, it's up to me. I can make the right choice!

"Can I get you something to drink?" Melissa Christopher asked. "Coke, orange juice, water. I'm afraid we don't drink coffee, but I have some herbal tea."

It was an effort, her politeness, a simple gesture of Herculean proportions, and Craig's heart went out to her. It never ceased to amaze him, the gentle courage, the considerate graces, offered by suffering people. Pain did not always bring out the worst in a person. Sometimes it distilled the very best. Mrs. Christopher was composed, entirely present. There was none of the distraction Craig had seen upon arriving, nothing of the fury he'd witnessed in the exchange with her husband only a few moments earlier. It was all gone, and Craig could not tell whether the resolve he saw now was artifice or the real thing. Either way he admired it.

"Tea would be nice, thank you." He slipped his phone from his jacket and brought up the correct app. Showing her the device, he placed it on the table. "Do you mind if I record our conversation?"

She turned away shaking her head.

Craig took the moment to watch her work. She was an attractive woman, late twenties or early thirties, a tad Rubenesque. She wore a loose jumper, her feet bare and white, the nails fire-engine red, a welcome contrast to the yellow-specked linoleum floor. From where Craig sat, he could see the better part of her profile. As she filled the teakettle, she pushed back her hair, lank and tangled now from her time outside searching in the rain for her son. Catching her fingers, she seemed for an instant aware of her disheveled condition, a ghost of recognition manifest in her labored return to a particular snarl. The corners of her eyes webbed with the effort, then she gave it up, her hair no less unruly than before. She shut off the tap and put the kettle on to boil.

Turning, she anchored the heels of her hands on the counter behind her. Gravity weighted her pretty features, and her face seemed cast in wax, plied with a softening heat. Only her eyes were hard, their connection with Craig's unwavering.

"My husband and I, we're suspects, I assume."

Tough, this one. Craig couldn't help it—he liked her. "Yes, ma'am. The parents are almost always suspects at the beginning of an investigation like this."

She seemed strangely satisfied with the detective's answer. Opening a cupboard, she removed a mug and a drinking glass. From another, she extracted a few boxes of bagged teas and set them on the counter. Without looking in Craig's direction, she asked, "Chamomile, apple and cinnamon, orange spice?"

"Chamomile, please."

Head canted away, she wiped beneath each eye with the pad of a thumb, a quick, surreptitious movement. She was not entirely able to suppress the moist hitch of her breath. She dried her thumb on the hip of her jumper.

"It is our fault, of course," she said, not looking at Craig. "Mine anyway. I should have walked Joshua to the party." She selected a bag of chamomile and dropped it in the mug, then returned the boxes to the cupboard.

"There are all sorts of things we'd do differently if we knew how they'd turn out," Craig said.

She laughed tearfully. "Josh loves being a big boy. He turned five two weeks ago. He was so proud of himself. Finally old enough to start school in the fall. It used to make me nervous, sending him to Billy's alone. I got used to it too soon, I guess." She pressed her sleeve to her upper lip, then spread both hands flat on the counter top. "Isn't that what parenthood's all about, learning to live with all the dangers we know we can't protect our children from?"

The warming kettle had begun to tick. Craig waited.

She turned around and faced him. "I'd do anything to bring him back. I *will* do anything. But I want you to know, except for sending Josh to Billy's alone, my husband and I had nothing to do with his disappearance."

Craig nodded. "I expect that's true."

She studied him. The heat was still there, but Craig sensed no hostility. She stepped to the refrigerator and removed a two-liter bottle of Coke. It hissed when she unscrewed the lid. "Do you think we'll find him?"—as though this were not the only question that mattered. She proceeded to fill the glass, then replaced the lid. Finally she looked up, her moist eyes bright with anguish.

"I don't know, Mrs. Christopher. Usually we do. Sometimes when we find them it's too late."

"And then there are times you never find them."

"Once in a while. Yes."

She thought about this. Her questions, Craig suspected, were less about the information they generated than a test of how honestly he would answer. She seemed to be coming to some decision.

"I'm sorry about my behavior in there with my husband." She returned the bottle to the refrigerator, then waved limply in the direction of the living room. "It must have seemed cruel to you."

Craig paid deference with a gentle shrug. "I've never had a child disappear. I can only imagine the emotions."

The kettle began to sigh. Melissa dialed off the flame and filled the mug. "Sugar or milk?"

"No, thank you."

She retrieved a saucer and placed it over the mug, then carried the mug and a spoon to the table. She turned back for her Coke, placed it on the table, and sat down across from Craig.

"He's drunk, you know. My husband. Well on his way there, anyway." Elbows on the table, Melissa lowered her forehead into her hands. At that moment her embarrassment was more palpable than her fear. Finally, she lifted her head. "He has a drinking problem. He binge drinks. Not very often, just once in a while, especially when he gets overwhelmed. No one in my family knows except my sister, Karley, and her husband, Hans. We're usually able to keep it under control. If he weren't drunk now, he wouldn't be such a useless mess. It makes me very angry. I lost my temper."

Craig said nothing for a five count, hoping she would volunteer more. "Was he already drinking by the time Josh left for the party this morning?"

She shook her head. "He started after, when we came back to the house with that uniformed policeman. He always manages to find new places to stash his bottles."

Craig unlidded the mug, releasing a tiny cloud. "Well. I can't say I much blame him. All things considered."

"He's weak," Melissa snapped then, just as unpredictably, she shrugged, her eyes dark and resigned. "I won't deny I saw it coming. And now you know. I doubt he'll be much good for a while."

Craig nodded at the quotes on the refrigerator. "You're obviously very active in the LDS Church. It must be difficult to have a husband with a drinking problem."

"You sound like you're a Latter-day Saint, Mr. Craig. Or have you just lived here a long time?"

"Milo. Please call me Milo. And yes, I was raised Mormon, though I haven't attended church for many years."

Melissa considered his answer. In Craig's not-inconsiderable experience, conscience-heavy Mormons found backsliders safe repositories for confession. "The church is very important to us. Joe would probably be drunk all the time, if it weren't for his faith. We're private about his drinking. We handle it together. He has his bad days, but he manages most of the time."

Craig took a tentative sip. Hot and weak, the faintest tang coming on. "How long have you and your husband been married?"

"About seven years."

"Did he have a drinking problem when you married him?"

Melissa ran her index finger around the rim of her glass. "I don't know what that has to do with finding my son, Milo."

"I'm sorry," he said. "Maybe nothing. You don't have to answer if it makes you uncomfortable."

"It doesn't make me uncomfortable, it just seems a waste of time. The answer though is yes, I knew he'd been a drinker. But he was dry and had been for a year by the time I met him. I knew I was supposed to marry him." Melissa watched Craig closely. "I prayed about it and knew. As a lapsed Latter-day Saint, you probably find that ridiculous."

"Not at all," Craig said. "I'd think your faith should be of real comfort to you now. I'm sure there are many people praying for Joshua. And for you and your husband."

"We're all praying," Melissa said absently, then she swiveled in her chair and stood. She appeared confused for an instant, until, seeming to remember, she dug into a pocket and withdrew a pair of small white pills. There was a willing neurosis in the way she studied the medicine before briskly palming the tablets into her mouth. She washed them down with a long drink of Coke. Distracted, she settled into her chair again.

Craig clicked his pen and watched her. He'd dealt with his fair share of narcotics and, like most veteran cops, owned a working knowledge of those prescription drugs most commonly abused. There were those you saw often, like Melissa's tiny whites. Oxycodone, straight up, manufactured without the extra medicines found in name brands like Percocet. She noticed him watching.

"Bad lower back and neck," she said. "It's worse when I'm under a lot of stress."

"I'm sorry to hear that." He smiled sympathetically. "Must be pretty miserable. Those didn't look like Advil."

Smart woman, Melissa Christopher, too smart to harbor illusions about Craig's meaning. "They're prescribed, and I take them sparingly, if that's what you're wondering. I'm a nurse. I'm very careful."

"I'm sure you are."

She smiled at him—chilly, that smile. "My husband has a substance-abuse problem, detective. I have physical pain."

Craig turned to a fresh sheet of legal pad. "You're a nurse then. Where do you work?"

"I work for my brother-in-law, Hans Nordling. He's a partner in a four-doctor clinic up near the hospital."

"I've heard of him. Do you like your work?"

"Usually." She dipped her head equivocally. "Since Josh came along, I've wanted to be home more, but it hasn't worked out that way. Joe's still building his business. He writes software but makes most of his money as a full-stack web developer. Small-business stuff primarily. He's very good. He works out of the house, well, as much as he can, taking care of Josh during the day. He's a small operator, no employees, which helps. We're surviving this economy better than a lot of folks. Money's tight but we get by."

Craig made notes. "I know you told everything to the uniformed officers, but I guess I need to hear about this morning."

She took another sip of her soda. "Where do you want me to start?"

"Wherever you'd like."

She watched bubbles roll up the wall of her glass. "There was nothing unusual about this morning really. We didn't know about the party until last night. It was supposed to be next weekend, but Billy's father learned last minute he has to be away then. So the MacMillans moved it up to today. I had to run to Walmart for the gift. That put us behind, so I guess we were a little rushed. But beyond that, it was a pretty standard Saturday morning."

"Did Josh go with you to pick out the present?"

"No. I left him here with Joe."

"What did you get Billy?"

"The final Harry Potter book. Nat, Billy's mother, gave me the suggestion."

"I'd think Josh might have wanted to go with you. To pick out the present for his friend."

"He was still asleep when I left at around 8:45." Melissa's tone betrayed no discomfort with Craig's question. "The Riverdale

Walmart's closest, but with traffic I figured it'd still be tight. Time-wise, I mean. I asked Joe to have Josh up and ready when I got back. Josh didn't even know he was going to a birthday party. Nat didn't let me know about the change until nearly nine last night. Josh was already asleep by then."

"What time did you get back from Walmart?"

"Late. Ten-fifteen or so. There was some problem on Riverdale Road—I was stuck in traffic for twenty minutes. I finally managed to turn around and get on the freeway. I came into town across the viaduct. I had to hurry to get Josh ready. He needed a bath, and Joe'd gotten involved in work. He'd completely forgotten. Josh was still asleep when I got home."

"At ten-fifteen?"

"That's right."

"Okay, so you came home, woke Josh up, gave him a bath, got him dressed and ready."

"I also called my youngest brother, Caleb, to cancel a movie date he had with Josh. Because of the party."

"When did you make that call?"

"While Josh was in the tub. Ten-thirty or so. And I fed Josh a bowl of cereal. Fruity Pebbles. He gets sugared cereal on Saturday."

Craig underlined each time—8:45 a.m., 9:00 p.m., 10:15 a.m., 10:30 a.m. He clicked his pen and looked up at Melissa. "I know you've already told the other officers what Josh was wearing, but I'd like to make a few notes of my own."

Melissa wrapped both hands around her glass. "Jeans, elastic waist. GapKids. A white T-shirt and a Harry Potter sweatshirt. It was supposed to be a Harry Potter theme party. Colored socks—I can't remember which color, blue, I think. A little pair of navy duck shoes."

"Duck shoes?"

"You know, the rubber rain shoe with the veins running up the toes. When he left the house, he was wearing a green vinyl raincoat and a matching hat."

"What time did you send him?"

"I called Nat MacMillan a little before 11:00."

"How much before?"

"Ten minutes. I always call before sending Josh. So she can watch for him." Melissa gazed out the kitchen window.

"Then you sent him."

"Yes." She nodded. "I told him to go straight there, just like I always do. 'Don't talk to strangers,' I said. I watched him as far as the next-door neighbor's driveway, then I went downstairs and worked on the laundry."

Craig and Melissa sat for thirty seconds, neither speaking. Melissa had gone somewhere, and, knowing what came next, Craig was loath to pull her back. "Then what happened?"

"Ohhh," she sighed. She removed her hands from the glass and dropped them both into her lap. "Nat called about twenty minutes later. She wanted to know if Josh had been delayed here at the house. He hadn't arrived. Even with his short legs, it's only three or four minutes to Billy's house." Melissa's eyes welled. "It didn't really register, you know. I think I even asked Nat what she meant. And then I dropped the phone and yelled to Joe, and we both took off into the street screaming for Josh. I ran up and down the block, and, of course, he wasn't anywhere, so I started banging on doors like a crazy woman. I panicked. Nat and Brian came out, and then Nat found the book. When I saw it lying there in the gutter, I thought I was going to die. It was worse than finding nothing."

Craig sipped his tea and let the woman compose herself. "Does Josh have any birthmarks, scars, any physical traits we might include in our description?"

Melissa wiped her forehead. Her hand trembled. "He has a birthmark on his right shoulder. A brown spot about the size of a dime. Big dimples when he smiles. Freckles like my sister, Karley, except his are actual freckles, not birthmarks like hers. He inherited his father's brown eyes and light hair. He lost his first tooth last week, his top-front tooth on the right. He was very excited."

"What about health problems?"

"None. He's very healthy. He's a healthy, happy kid."

"We may want his medical records. Dental, too." Craig watched for a reaction.

She nodded. "There's nothing there but the standard kid stuff. I'll sign the HIPAA, whatever you need."

Craig's tea had cooled to room temperature. He hadn't removed the bag and, though it was too late now, he spooned it out and put it on the saucer. "How long have you lived in this neighborhood?"

"Since before Josh was born. Joe and I had been married just under two years. I was pregnant."

"You know your immediate neighbors pretty well?"

"Yes. They're mostly older, many of them retired or close to it."

"Problems with any of them? Disagreements, strange behaviors?"

"No, nothing. Everyone's always very nice. Folks try to get along. They're all—"

A commotion had erupted in the basement directly beneath the kitchen—doors or cupboards opened, slammed closed, something heavy toppled, an unrestrained yelp. Melissa peered uneasily at the closed stairwell door.

"Your husband?"

She nodded.

Craig was tempted to inquire further but resisted, choosing instead to track the woman's reaction. Finally, he said, "Any of your neighbors seem unusually interested in Josh? Maybe someone who goes out of their way to engage him when he's out playing? Someone who's always giving him things, candy or toys or such?"

"Nothing out of the ordinary. Like I say, they're older. Most of them seem to enjoy having a little one around. Every now and again one might offer him a treat of some kind. They usually ask if it's okay first. In any case, unless Joe or I are outside, Josh plays in the backyard. It's fenced."

"But nobody's ever given you a problem? Nobody you've ever sensed you needed to warn Josh to stay away from? No gut reactions?"

"No. I go to church with most of my neighbors. I think I know them pretty well. Maybe I'm just naïve, but I really don't think any of them would do anything to hurt Josh or anyone else."

The noise had relocated to a different part of the basement.

It sounded to Craig like Joe was tearing the place apart. Melissa touched her neck just below the ear and watched the stairwell door. With the tip of her thumb, she absently stroked the pink band where her wedding ring had recently been.

"Should we check on him?" Craig asked.

"No. Please. Just ignore him. He's probably looking for another bottle. He'll calm down in a minute."

Thoughts of fouled evidence crossed Craig's mind chased by the notion that Joe Christopher might be a mean drunk. But beyond the boundaries of the detective's own dis-ease, the interview had produced little that caused him to doubt her. Best for the moment to defer to her wishes.

"I notice you're not wearing a wedding ring."

Melissa placed both hands in her lap again. "The last time Joe went on a bender, I took it off. I was a little more angry than usual. I thought I tossed it in my jewelry box, but now I can't find it." She looked down at her ringless hand. "Joe hasn't even noticed I'm not wearing it."

"When was that, Joe's last bender?"

"I don't know. A week ago maybe. I'm sure the ring'll turn up. Josh plays in my jewelry box sometimes."

Craig drew a circle on his notepad around the time *11:00 a.m.* "Married life sounds a little rough at the moment."

"Married life isn't supposed to be easy," Melissa said. "It's hard to have a husband with a drinking problem. But we love each other. Joe's a good man and a wonderful father. I haven't stopped kicking myself since I misplaced the ring."

"You must have turned the house inside-out."

Melissa glared at the detective, the first genuine anger he'd seen since beginning the interview. "Of course, I have."

"I'm sorry." Craig put the pen on the pad. Melissa looked away through the window above the sink again. The sun had come out. "What about someone who isn't a neighbor? Do you have any enemies? Any encounters lately that seemed strange, even with someone you didn't know? Anything strange at all?"

She glanced at the stairwell door. Joe continued to make noise in the basement. "No. Nothing really comes to mind. I'll think about it. Maybe I'll remember something."

Craig was losing her no thanks to whatever her husband was doing beneath them. "Melissa, when was the last time someone besides you and your husband saw Josh?"

She met Craig's gaze. "Last night. Nat came by. She must have told you."

Indeed, Nat MacMillan had. Craig had interviewed the neighbor after speaking with Jill. But he hadn't mentioned that interview to Melissa. Exhausted, terrified, aggrieved, she'd still gathered the pieces and assembled them correctly.

"She mentioned it," he said.

Melissa held Craig's gaze a moment longer. "Josh was asleep. We went into his room to find a game Billy left. She saw him."

"But no one besides you and your husband saw him this morning?"

She shook her head, her attention drifting back to the door. "Besides us, Nat was the last one—"

There was a large crash below then a plaintive wail. *"Josh? Josh . . . ?"* The muffled sound of it rose through the floor like a summons from the netherworld, and Melissa sprang to her feet, her chair scudding backwards. She yanked the door open and leaped down the stairs, taking them two at a time. She was fast and agile, and Craig followed at a distance, his body unable to keep up. What he found when he arrived did not make him feel any younger.

Cupboards and closets gaped open and empty, their contents pulled haphazardly into the room. Upended storage bins, toppled toy boxes, furniture dragged into the center of the room. An old sofa lay upside down, its cheesecloth all but ripped from its tacking.

Melissa stood over Joe, who sat sobbing beside the entertainment center. She stared down without moving then sank to the floor and cradled his head to her breast. "Stop it now, Joe. You really have to stop now."

"But where is he?" Joe wailed. *"Where is he?"*

Prison Without Walls

"I can't stand this waiting," Caleb said. He stood at Melissa and Joe's large front window watching a small contingency of officers canvass the neighborhood. On a front stoop across the street, a detective interviewed an elderly couple. Wet sunlight warped penumbral, an aura above every surface.

No one acknowledged Caleb's complaint. Even a pause to catch one's breath felt too expensive. The truth was, until but a few moments earlier, the family had been sorting through photographs, finding those most recent, most accurate to Joshua's present likeness. Hans and Karley had arrived in the middle of this treasure hunt, and now the coffee table was an after-storm of scattered images, toppled piles and cast-off stragglers, two open laptops and a tablet playing Joshua. His face was everywhere.

Armed with a thumb drive, Jared had left to make copies.

In the kitchen a detective named Craig interviewed Joe. Melissa lay on the sofa, curled fetal, her head in Karley's lap. Karley stroked her sister's hair and watched Hans pace. Slumped in the loveseat, Curt and Margaret held one another, while outside on the front porch the advocate, Sally Frye, cast animate shadows through the storm door as she conversed on her cell phone.

Hans squatted next to Melissa. "We're going to find him," he promised.

Melissa said nothing, did not even look at him. Tearless and wild-eyed, she stared at some far-off horizon, incapable of any demand, and Hans was struck by the contrast, the dissolution of such a stalwart soul. By the measure of his own fear, he understood her undoing, but it frightened him nonetheless, and not

31

only for her but for Joshua, who more than any of them needed her present and functional. Hans squeezed her hand then stood and resumed his pacing.

"I wish somebody'd tell us what's going on," Caleb complained.

As if to comply, Joe wandered into the room, disheveled and puff-faced, his eyes as glassy and vacant as a stuffed deer's. The policeman—older, short, broad-shouldered—followed.

Hans drew Joe in, and Joe stood motionless against him, listless in old sweats and a two-day scruff, the sour-sweet odor of pore-pressed ethanol pungent on his unwashed skin. Hans put his mouth to Joe's ear. "Let me get rid of the bottles."

Joe shook his head once, his strained expression almost angry, almost fearful, almost guilty. "I don't know what to do, Hans."

Hans stepped back and considered his brother-in-law. "We're all here. We'll figure this out together."

Head down, Joe wandered to a vacant chair in the corner.

"I don't think we've met." The policeman stepped in, hand extended. "Milo Craig. Ogden City Police Department."

"Hans Nordling." Hans shook the policeman's hand. "Melissa and Joe's brother-in-law."

"The doctor." Craig nodded. "If you don't mind, I'd like to chat with you a little later. And with your wife—" He flipped through his notes. "Karley, is she here?"

"I'm Karley," Karley said from the sofa. The policeman paused to take her in. Hans had grown sanguine about the way men looked at his wife. At times he even empathized.

"I'll need to talk to everyone in the family," Craig said finally.

"Of course," Hans said. "Please though, you'll tell us what's happening first?"

Before Craig could answer, the screen door opened and Sally Frye stepped inside. Counting heads, she lingered on Joe before continuing with her tally.

"Come on, Melissa," Karley coaxed. She shook her sister to no response then gripped her by the shoulders and lifted her bodily. "Sit up, now. It's time to talk."

"Yes, sit up, honey," Sally said. She worked her way around the coffee table to the open spot on Melissa's other side. Her body was too broad to fit comfortably in the space, but she wedged herself in anyway, hip-to-hip with Melissa. Like an old friend, she wrapped the smaller woman in her oversized clutch and began to rock. Melissa's submission was boneless.

"Despair's the enemy," Sally said. "There's no room for hopelessness now. There's too much to do. We've got to get your boy back."

"You've helped families get their children back?" Karley asked. "I mean, they've actually gotten them back?"

"I have," Sally said. "Most of the families I've helped have had their children returned to them, usually in the first forty-eight hours. Which is why we can't waste time." Taking Melissa by the shoulders, she leaned her back. "You're a mess, dear, which is understandable. Believe me, I know. But it can't stand. No matter how impossible it seems right now, you have to pull it together. Every cliché you've ever heard on the subject of inner strength applies. Do you understand me?"

To everyone's surprise Melissa nodded.

Sally looked across the room at Joe. "You too, Joe. Anything else is unacceptable."

Melissa shuddered. "What if he's dead?"

Sally cocked her head, her reproach tempered with a smile. "Those thoughts are suspect, honey, and you shouldn't trust them. Statistically speaking, your son's very much alive. Thinking otherwise will only drive you crazy, and you're no good to your son crazy."

"I can't shake it," Melissa said. "The image of him dead."

"He's alive and counting on us to find him. He'll have a better chance if you think so, too."

Melissa blinked at Sally. "I can try. I think I can try."

"Good girl," Sally said, patting Melissa's hand.

"We're lost," Curt said softly. "We have no idea what's going on."

Nodding, she released Melissa, who managed to stay up by herself. Karley took Melissa's hand in both of hers and held it in her lap.

"Here's what we're going to do," Sally said. "First we'll hear what Milo has to say. Then we'll make a plan. We'll concentrate on the media, at least at first. The press is essential and it's free. Once that ball's rolling, we'll start enlisting private agencies. They have lots of resources, money, too, if it comes to that. And, of course, we're going to ride hard on the police."

"Yes," Karley said, fixing her gaze on Craig. "I'd like to hear what the police have to say. I'd especially like to know why you're still here, detective."

Craig nodded. "I know it seems things are moving slowly. The beginning of an investigation like this can be very confusing."

"We're not the least confused by the attention you're giving Melissa and Joe," Karley said.

Craig smiled. "We're looking everywhere, not just inside this house. I'll be happy to tell you all about it." He lingered on Karley another beat before shifting his gaze to Melissa. "But seeing as your sister brought it up, Mrs. Christopher, I should tell you we're going to want to look at a few more things around here. We've been through Josh's room pretty well, but we may want another go at it. I know the first responders made a quick pass through the house, but I'd like your consent to send a recovery team in before the place gets lived in much more. Best to rule out everything we can as quickly as possible. We'd like to go through your cars too, maybe even take them down to the lab. I know it seems intrusive, especially now, but it's for the best really."

The family stared at Detective Craig. Margaret began to cry. "You can't seriously suspect Melissa and Joe," Karley said.

"We suspect everyone." Craig's cell phone had begun to ring. Slipping it from his jacket, he crossed to the front door. "I'll give you a minute to think it over." The storm door whispered closed as he descended the stairs into the yard.

"This is *absurd*," Curt said. "Melissa and Joe had nothing to do with Josh's disappearance."

"Of course not," Sally said. She put her hand on Melissa's knee. "But we have to let the police conduct their searches and ask their questions. The sooner the family's cleared the sooner every resource gets directed where it belongs."

"We're all suspects, aren't we?" Hans said.

"Not all of you, most likely," Sally said. "But Melissa and Joe are, which is exactly as it should be. I know it's rotten. But it won't last long."

"How long?" Margaret asked.

Sally measured Margaret's question before answering. "I'd guess they'll bring the crime scene unit in today. They'll be looking for fresh evidence so they won't want to wait. If you refuse to sign a consent, they'll go after a warrant. If they get it, which is possible given some precedent in cases like this, they'll conduct the search anyway. Only they'll look harder. If they don't get it, they'll likely conclude you're hiding something and waste valuable time trying to establish probable cause. All so they can gain the very access you could have given them by signing a consent. Look, they're as interested in how you react as they are in conducting the search itself. I know it's a damned if I do, damned if I don't, but why waste crucial time, especially when you have nothing to hide?" She paused to let her question do its work. "And then there's the polygraph. Milo will want Melissa and Joe to take one. Maybe some of you others, too."

"This is horrible," Margaret moaned.

"It's an indignity," Sally agreed. "But we have to do everything we can to speed things along. It's the only way to find your boy fast. If you volunteer before Milo asks, he may decide a polygraph isn't necessary. It happens every once in a while. If he still insists, you'll be better positioned to set some of the test conditions. We might even be able to pick our tester. There are some good ones around who can handle it without seeming adversarial. You have nothing to hide, so it'll be okay."

Shadow first, Detective Craig climbed the stairs and opened the storm door. "Okay, folks," he said, coming in. "I'm sorry, we're going to have to hold off on the Q and A for now. I have somewhere I need to be. Sally, I think it might be wise to start working up a statement for the press. It'd be nice to make the early news, which doesn't give us a whole lot of time." He looked from Melissa to Joe and back. "I'm having some paperwork prepared, a Consent to Search. I hope you'll sign the forms."

Melissa wiped her face. She nodded.

"What's happening, Milo?" Sally asked. "Something's going on."

Detective Craig scratched his jaw with the back of his hand, sixty-grit sandpaper on a rough-cut board. "Sally," he began.

"Don't 'Sally' me, Milo." She wagged her head. "You know I don't work that way. If you have it, we want it. This family needs a sign of good faith."

Craig smiled. "I don't know what I have."

Sally pursed her lips.

"Please," Karley said softly. "This is already more than we can bear."

"Milo," Sally pressed.

Craig surveyed the family. Finally, reluctantly, he lifted a cautioning hand. "We just took someone into custody."

In unison, Margaret and Curt cried out. Craig vigorously shook his head.

"But no Joshua," Karley said. "Joshua wasn't with this person."

Margaret and Curt fell instantly silent.

"No," Craig said.

"I don't understand," Sally said.

"One of our officers spotted the guy sitting in a parked car a few blocks from here. When the officer started toward him, the guy took off. We got him before he made it to Harrison Boulevard. Turns out he's on probation for aggravated sexual assault of a child."

Stone-featured, Melissa crossed her forearms between her breasts. Joe straightened himself in his chair.

"But it has to be him, doesn't it?" Margaret said.

"No, ma'am," Craig said. "It really doesn't."

"When it rains, the slugs come out," Sally said.

"Every crime has a fan base," Craig agreed. "I hope I'll know more soon."

"Go," Sally said. "Go, go, go."

Craig opened the storm door. "I'll do my best to make the press conference."

Sally swished him away with the backs of her hands. And as the detective disappeared into the sunlit yard, the Christophers' living room fell silent, the empty minutes expanding like a plague, time nothing but a prison without walls.

"Okay, now," Sally began.

Hardly Dry

"I'm dying to see your place," Melissa said. Of course, what she meant was *our* place. She trusted Joe could fix the pronouns on his own.

They were in his 4Runner driving toward his apartment. Giddy with enthusiasm, Melissa had convinced him to take her to this place where he lived alone. That her motives were mostly innocent, that she trusted Joe to be a gentleman, seemed at odds with the electric frisson that coursed through her body. Perhaps she was still under the spell of the gathering they'd just abandoned. She smiled at his profile, the dashboard just bright enough to light his pretty features. She loved the way he looked in his rented costume, a policeman's uniform replete with handcuffs and a very real-looking pistol.

On principle, they'd vacated the party prematurely, a Halloween bash thrown by one of Joe's bosses, a costume affair to which a handful of women had come in a remarkable state of undress. Melissa had been particularly amused by the abbreviated nurse's uniform worn by one girl—crepe-soled shoes, stockings that started an inch below the hem of her miniature white jumper, the top unbuttoned and protuberant with unholstered flesh. The nurse had made much of bending over as often as possible, showing the world the frilly seat of her pink panties, a style most commonly seen on diapered infants. And then there was the witch with the riding crop. In addition to the requisite black hat, she'd donned patent-leather spikes and fishnet stockings, a black-leather corset and thong. And it wasn't just the women— two young men of narcissistic physique swaggered about

37

bare-chested, Chippendale bowties strapped around their ropey necks, what appeared to be tubers Spandexed to their upper thighs. Melissa had found it difficult not to stare.

Mormon events—the meat and potatoes of her social world—were modest affairs, and Joe's company party was anything but a Mormon event. Her short time as a nurse had normalized the human body in ways her modest Mormon upbringing had failed. But there was more than anatomy on display here, and Melissa found herself in constant suppression of a giggle. The body was one thing, *come hither* an altogether different something. She was puzzled and a little unnerved by how much it all turned her on.

"Had I known it was going to be like this," Joe apologized, "I'd have planned something else for tonight." He surveyed the gyrating crowd, his gaze catching at each pass on the wet bar. The party's host, a single man with a playboy's reputation, stood behind the be-bottled slab gregariously mixing drinks. He was a tech executive, and his manse was impressive, one of the oversized, window-fronted wonders in the foothills above the university.

"Actually, it's kind of funny," Melissa said gamely. "Educational." Joe and she held hands, their wrists joined with Joe's very real hand-cuffs. She was dressed in the pajama stripes of a nineteenth-century felon, a lack of subtlety that pretty well summed up her feelings for Joe. She knew she should be embarrassed but wasn't.

Joe's discomfort with the party was palpable.

"Is it the alcohol?" she asked. The Halloween revelers were imbibing freely, a drink in most every hand, and Melissa, largely ignorant to alcohol's effects, took the party's fervor as proof of lubrication. "It's difficult to be around people who are drinking?"

"No, not really," he said. "Not with you here anyway."

"Well, then, I'm glad I'm here." She squeezed his hand.

"Me, too," he said.

But Joe's discomfort was not so easily abated. Contrary to his sweet claim, her presence here made it worse not better. She could tell. "Why don't we leave?"

Joe turned to her. "Really? You wouldn't mind?"

She smiled up at him. "You could take me to your apartment. I'd like to see where you live."

A ghost from Joe's former life skittered across his face, and in a haze of slattern jealousy, Melissa realized what such a suggestion must once have meant to him. It was a strange moment for them both, aware as they were of the other's thoughts. This was not the first time Melissa had let fantasy get the better of her. Indeed, Joe's certain sexual history had conjured more than a few conflicted scenarios and with them a jealous stew of righteous indignation and blue curiosity. Weird, that combination, quick anger against a slow burning arousal, and Melissa, who'd never felt anything so contradictory, couldn't figure out what to do with it. Glancing away, she found herself eye to cheek with the nurse's butt, its owner making the most of retrieving the little cap she'd conveniently lost to the dance floor. Melissa'd had no idea such people lived in Utah.

"Sure, why not?" Joe said. "I'd love to show you my apartment. Maybe we're still early enough to catch some trick-or-treaters. I even bought candy."

"Candy?"

"The good stuff." Joe arched his pretty eyebrows. "Fun-size Milky Way bars."

"Oooh," Melissa said. "Let's hurry."

■

Twenty minutes later Joe unbuckled his heavy belt and dropped it on the kitchen counter. "It's okay for an apartment I guess. As soon as I finish my master's, I'd like to buy a house."

They'd climbed four flights to the top-floor breeze way, and when he'd opened the door, Melissa had noticed the windows immediately. "Check out these windows," she said. "Check out this *view*."

"Yeah. And no neighbors making noise above me." Joe had tugged his shirt from his pants and was now unbuttoning it. He wore a white T-shirt underneath, and, though he was hardly disrobing, Melissa found the whole thing rather stirring. Joe looked good in tight white T-shirts.

To distract herself, Melissa wandered. Either Joe had recently cleaned (had he anticipated this visit?) or was by nature a good housekeeper. The kitchen was one with the front room, the long counter the rooms' only divider. Melissa noted with approval a dishwasher and a separate laundry room off the kitchen, a washer and dryer inside. Joe's kitchen was smaller than Melissa's parents' but better appointed, with newer appliances and more cupboard space.

"Wow, so much computer stuff." On (and beneath) a heavy folding banquet table Joe had organized an array of computer equipment, the extent of which Melissa had never seen outside an electronics store.

"A buyer's addiction," Joe said. He'd made his way to her side. "I'm still paying some of this crap off."

"Do you use everything here?"

"All the time."

It was a bit daunting, a world Melissa knew next to nothing about. "Will you teach me?" She hooked a finger around his pinkie.

"Anything you want to know," Joe said. Then he lifted her hand and kissed it. On impulse, Melissa took her turn, drawing his hand to her lips. Surprised, pleased, some of both, he laughed.

Smiling, she released his finger and continued her survey. Joe rolled the leather office chair away from the table. He settled in and followed her movements, his attention laced with desire. Melissa felt it, his desire, she liked it. She wanted him to keep looking.

"Gosh, I don't think I've ever been in an apartment with a fireplace." She ran her hand along the mantle, oak like the kitchen cupboards.

"Flip that light switch to the right."

She reached over, flipped the switch, and the gas insert clicked to life, a blue-orange conflagration beneath a fake log. "Snazzy."

"Only the best for me."

Bouncing on her hands, she tried out the sofa. A glass-top coffee table and a pair of matching end tables. No dining set, just three oak stools around the bar. A few liner-framed posters on the walls, the work of some abstract painter. No pictures of people but a single black-and-white of a winter landscape, austere shadows on windrowed snow. In keeping with Joe's electronics fetish, a nice entertainment center graced one wall, a flat screen TV and stereo, fancy-looking speakers at either end.

"What's the bathroom like?"

"Go see for yourself."

Sure enough, it was a bathroom. She was pleased to find a long mirror with an expansive tile counter beneath it, plenty of surface for makeup, curling irons, hair dryers. A tile-enclosed bathtub and a separate shower stall. And clean, not a single bad odor, a phenomenon to which Melissa was wholly unaccustomed, having two younger brothers in residence. She closed the door and situated herself on the commode, noting with some pleasure she didn't have to put the seat down first. Joe's stock was soaring and still going up.

Finished, she washed her hands and dried them on a stylish black hand towel. Before turning off the light, she checked herself in the mirror. A little flushed but not bad. She finger-picked her hair then headed for the living room. Joe swiveled back and forth, right where she'd left him.

"I love it." Bending she gripped the chair by the arms and brought him to a stop. "I have to say, for a geek, you have great taste." Then she kissed him.

If kissing was not uncharted territory neither was it a frequent destination. Much to her dismay, Joe had waited until their third date to launch his first attempt. Chastity was at a premium and enforced in Melissa's world—no premarital sex, no petting, nothing but a little Frenching. Until the wedding night, kissing was the proverbial line in the sand, which was likely why her previous partners had been exceptional kissers or altogether lousy. Melissa much preferred the exceptional kissers both in personality and technique.

Joe leaned his head against the rest, and Melissa followed, her face firmly attached to his. Though heartfelt—and anything but tentative—their kisses so far had lacked much duration. On only one occasion had Melissa been the initiator, but now she leaned forward in a whole new way. Man, but she liked kissing Joe. He had this relaxed, non-urgent way about him, not too wet, not too dry. But there was an intensity, too. He knew his business. Melissa felt his hands touch her thighs above the backs of her knees. He trailed them slowly up, stopping just short of her bottom, then ever so softly down again. She had never been touched there by a boy, nothing like that, and the sensation traveled where Joe did not, flooding her with a sweet familiar heat.

Truth be known, Melissa was easily aroused. So to save her sanity, she'd developed a few skills which she'd mastered through frequent practice. Consider the time her mother discovered her humped over a throw cushion on the basement sofa, coming for the second or third time.

"That's not ladylike!" Margaret yelped, too scandalized to illuminate what exactly she'd found unladylike.

Eleven-year-old Melissa already relished the dulcet aftermath of multiple orgasms. Even then—a tween at the beginning of all new things—she did not know how or when she'd learned her body could do this thing for her. Her mother's response was educational, the first hint her talent was neither unique nor appropriate. Thereafter Melissa was more discrete but just as persistent, a frequency that served to stem the shame she now knew she should feel but didn't. Lucky for her she was a girl and as such was treated to a different conditioning from that reserved by the church for boys—the lessons and pamphlets and diatribes and interviews. She supposed the brethren didn't believe girls had sexual urges, not that Melissa would have confessed either way. Righteousness, the conveyance of its appearance, was far too important for that.

She pushed herself upright, just out of Joe's reach. She'd had a few close calls in her day, make-out sessions that had nearly gotten away from her, but this was something new. Never before had a kiss and a caress unfurled her like a flag in a gale.

"Must be too late for trick-or-treaters," she said. "Maybe we should watch a movie or something."

"Sure. There's probably something scary on."

Melissa was already scared. Just not nearly scared enough. Joe rolled from his chair and kissed her again. The few inches between them yawned like the void, and Melissa closed them by nuzzling into him. Lifting her face, she kissed him on the neck and savored the hard knot he pressed into her abdomen. With a final squeeze, Joe let her go, and she followed him across the room.

"Do you want something to eat?" he asked. He grabbed the remote off an end table and clicked on the TV. He muted the sound. "Maybe some juice, a pop, water?"

"I'm okay," Melissa lied.

"You look hot." He was referring, alas, to the flush in her cheeks, not to the sleekness of her profile.

"I am a little warm," she confessed and Joe reached for the fireplace switch. "Maybe crack a window instead? I kinda like the fire."

Joe stepped away and opened the balcony slider. He raised a window, and the air began to move. Melissa kicked off her shoes and curled her legs into the sofa. "Better?" Joe asked, settling beside her.

She leaned against him. "Much."

"I used to love Halloween night movies," he said. With the remote, he scrolled through the guide. "When I got too old for trick-or-treating I'd stay home and watch all night."

Doomed to her motley desire, Melissa longed to resume what they'd begun across the room but didn't trust herself, not one bit, a perplexing development as she was usually a model of self-control—at least in the company of others. Her current volatility freaked her out. It was ridiculous. She'd hardly even kissed him.

"See anything you like?" Joe asked.

Oh, boy. Melissa shrugged and picked at her lip.

"Check it out," he said. "*Invasion of the Body Snatchers.*"

"I've never seen it."

"*Philistine,*" Joe gasped. "I must save you from your benighted ways."

"I am at your mercy," she said.

Joe turned up the volume. "Get ready. You're in for it now."

The TV's shifting imagery meant nothing to Melissa, dun-colored people in a dark landscape. Another kiss was all that mattered. The trick, she knew, was to prove her self-doubt irrational, her desire not nearly so dangerous as she feared. Both these things had to be true. Less than a month they'd been dating, but Melissa loved Joe. Love had to count for something. If she couldn't abide a little temptation now, she would be lost before they were even engaged. What she needed was to flex a few muscles, build a little stamina. Like developing tolerance to poison by consuming ever larger doses until the poison was rendered harmless. Where had she seen that? *The Princess Bride.* She loved that movie, a love story for the ages. Better than *Invasion of the Body Snatchers.*

"You okay?" Joe asked. "You seem a little distracted. I really don't care if we watch this show."

"Oh, no," she said. "The show's fine."

"Sure? We don't have to watch anything. Maybe you'd prefer to do something else."

There it was.

"As a matter of fact," she said, kneeling up to face him. Joe seemed not the least surprised. Curled like a comma, Melissa wrapped an arm behind his neck and cupped his face in the palm of her other hand. Behind her the TV grunted and groaned. Joe raised the remote and clicked it off blind.

Later Melissa would not remember how long she and Joe kissed in this position, but she would recall it as an escalating season, their enthusiasm speeding them toward a threshold she did not sense until Joe cupped the swell of her bottom. Ever so lightly he stroked her left cheek.

And in that revelatory sensation, Melissa's mind leapt forward, her thoughts clear and magnified as though viewed from afar through a telescope. She knew exactly what she wanted, and this knowing provided her an important clarification: The binding issue was the potential for shame, the fear of being discovered in transgression. Which framed liberation as really quite simple: not being discovered in transgression. Could she abide the guilt? Yes, she could—she had done so through years of self-pleasuring. She did not want much, just a little more than before. As for God's disapproval, she was oddly sanguine. He was patient and would forgive her, if forgiveness was even necessary. It did not seem unreasonable, seemed likely in fact, that this detour had been his route all along. Hadn't God already told her she was going to marry Joe?

Still kissing, she threw a knee over him. She felt him tense beneath her, a parting of their lips that might have been mistaken for a logistical maneuver. She settled on his thighs, a safe distance for now, and met his quizzical gaze. "Okay?" she asked.

"Surprised is all."

"Do you mind?"

"How could I mind?"

Melissa smiled and kissed him again. She worked slowly, determined not to scare him away. Joe's hands were at her waist, entirely the wrong place, but she was patient there as well. When a respectable number of minutes had passed, she reached back and drew his hands to her behind. Joe squeezed her bottom, and Melissa eased in. She could feel him hard beneath her. Her lower viscera were moving quickly now, and it was impossible to feign neutrality. She could scarcely keep from moving her hips. Joe scooted out, a strong move that levitated and repositioned her with better access. She moaned and settled lower.

Joe was no neophyte. He pulled on Melissa and lifted his hips. Had he tried, she would have let him peel off her pants—a finger in her waistband, she'd have done the rest. Eyes closed, she breathed shallowly into his mouth and willed him to mine for flesh. She was rising now, could feel herself zeroing. Far off the first pulse rippled in, a precursor to the tidal movement she was chasing. Moving her hips, she opened her eyes. Joe studied her face—fascinated, curious, concerned?

Nearly frantic now, she humped with precision, kneading her way toward the promised land. Slipping her hand from Joe's face, she inserted it between them and gripped the hard line of his penis. She'd never before held a man's hardness, and the absolute newness filled her with pride. Riding her knuckles, she squeezed and bucked, almost, almost—

"Whoa!" Joe cried. He picked her up and place her lower on his thighs. Gently, he removed her hand. Slumped against him, Melissa ticked and groaned, a hot tin roof in a rainstorm.

"I'm *sorry*," she moaned. Then she burst into tears.

"*No*," Joe exclaimed. "Oh, gosh, Melissa. Look what I've done. Don't cry." He caressed her thighs. It didn't help a bit.

Melissa sat up and covered her face. Still crying she began to laugh. "You *pig*. Why did you stop?" She dropped her hands and glared at him.

Eyebrows together Joe gazed back.

"I mean it," she said, rolling off him. "You shouldn't have stopped."

Joe shook his head. "Talk about whiplash."

Melissa wiped her face with the sleeve of her shirt. "What's that supposed to mean?"

"You know. The rules? The commandments?"

"What about them?"

Joe opened his mouth. Joe closed his mouth.

"What if I told you I was in love with you?" she asked.

Joe's features opened, his confusion drifting. "Is that a hypothetical or are you saying you love me?"

"I love you."

Joe grinned. "Then I'd say I love you, too."

"Then say it. If you mean it, say it."

"I love you."

Melissa kneeled up and kissed him quickly. "Then you shouldn't have stopped."

Joe smiled wryly. "I may be new to this church thing, Melissa, but I have a pretty good grasp of the rules."

"Does it matter so much? We love each other. And it's not like I wanted to go all the way. I know it sounds weird, but I have a good feeling about this. With you it's okay. I can feel it." Melissa noted with not the least alarm that she sounded like a Sunday school lesson on the manipulations of The Deceiver. Fine. She might have played the devil but only because she was on God's errand.

"Sounds like a rationalization to me." He peered at her askance but Melissa could see she was making headway.

"It may be," she agreed. "But I still wanted to come."

Laughing, Joe took her hand. "Wow, what a surprise."

"In a bad way? Are you mad?"

"Heavens, no."

"There's a lot about me you don't know, Joe Christopher."

"I guess so." Amused, Joe assessed her directly. "Am I to conclude you're drawing on some deep well of experience?"

She shook her head. "You're the first."

Joe squinted, unconvinced. "You sure seemed to know what you were doing."

"I'm very talented," she informed him. "But so far just a soloist."

He threw his head back and laughed. "You are something, Melissa DeBoer. How did I get so lucky?"

"At least one of us got lucky," she sulked.

Joe drew her in, and she lay across his lap. She could no longer feel his hardness and missed it. "I've got to think about this." He let his index finger run the contours of her face. "I don't want to mess this up."

"You won't mess it up, Joe. It was my idea."

"But maybe later you'd feel bad. Maybe you'd decide I wasn't worthy of you."

"Is that the way you'd feel about me?"

"Are you kidding? I'm the one trying to catch up."

"Well, then. We'd be even," Melissa said, realizing the notion had merit. It felt true, like a confirmation. Was this what God had in mind?

"It'd take a lot more than that to make us even." Joe curled over and kissed her, an awkward position, but he persisted nonetheless. Melissa combed her fingers through his hair. Eventually he sat back up. "I'm sorry I left you high and dry."

"Hardly dry," Melissa sighed. "Go get me those Milky Way bars, maybe I'll think about forgiving you."

Drawing on the Powers of Heaven

In the little over an hour since Detective Craig had disappeared, there'd been no word, nothing new, and Karley could not help but suspect the silence meant only bad. Melissa and Joe's house had begun to close in, the rooms shrinking miniature under a claustrophobic squeeze. There was no place but memory and speculation to go, nothing to do that offered relief. The family was trapped, and Karley, besieged by a familiar compulsion, resisted the impulse to flee.

Sally had been diligent, her coaching methodical. "You can do this," she told Melissa. "You'll read the statement, that's all. Milo will answer any questions."

Karley glanced up from the piano music she thumbed through. Arms folded, Hans seemed lost in concentration. Karley could not tell what he thought of Sally's plan, but she took comfort in his presence, his long-suffering competence. Hans loved her family, and they loved him. He had won them over with goodwill and by bringing her home to Utah. The contradiction was not lost on Karley, that her family would absolve him of the same trespasses they couldn't forgive her of. With unfailing patience, he had accompanied her through a thousand minefields.

"… notoriously insensitive," Sally was saying. "They'll want to know if you're suspects, maybe worse. It'll be unpleasant. You need to prepare yourselves."

Melissa sat rigid in a wingback chair clutching a stuffed Pooh Bear that belonged to Joshua. To Karley, the grip seemed masochistic, though she could not deny her sister had grown stronger

49

under Sally's tutelage. Melissa had assumed a stoic resignation. Resigned to what, Karley was less sure.

"I can do it," Melissa said.

"Good," Sally said. "Just keep reminding yourself: You're talking to whoever has your boy. Keep that right at the front of your brain. It's an appeal. It can work, but you have to believe it. You have to act like you believe it."

The living room soured in a broiling heat—too many fevered, unwashed bodies, the southwest slap of a post-storm sun. Karley put down the sheet music and crossed to the storm door. As she raised the pane, the loose screen buckled, the house's first suspiration after a long-held breath.

Karley did not share Sally's faith, and the familiarity of her disbelief pained her. She longed to be wrong but, watching the rehearsal, could not convince herself Melissa believed either. Karley, who found it difficult to place faith in anything but her marriage, ached for her sister's failing hope even more than she ached for her own.

She left the room then, to open another window, though mostly she left to be alone. In the kitchen she found a bottle of Coke warming on the counter, an empty glass beside it. There were a few dirty dishes on the table as well, a mug and spoon, a spent teabag in a saucer, another empty glass. Someone had knocked the baking soda from a shelf, spilling white powder five feet into the kitchen. The box was still on the floor, the pantry door open.

Karley cleared the table and threw the teabag away then loaded the dishes in the dishwasher. She returned the baking soda to its shelf then lifted the dustpan and broom from their hooks and swept up the powder. She stowed the Coke and, as the fridge door closed, watched Joshua's stick figures swing into view.

She studied the drawings and tried to imagine. She loved Hans beyond any measure she'd once believed possible. But Hans was not a child, and, no matter Karley's love, he was not her own flesh and blood. The helplessness would drive a mother crazy, the possibility your child might alone face a torment you dared not even imagine. Karley herself could not hold the thought and make herself breathe in and out. If she were Melissa, she would be out of her mind. No wonder Joe had turned to the bottle.

Karley traced Josh's pictures, the waxy surface faintly moist under her finger. She rolled the pad against her thumb hoping in vain for a hint of colored residue, some physical totem of Josh to take with her. She and Hans had told no one they were trying to make a baby. Overnight, it seemed, the *someday* presumption of a distant motherhood had burgeoned into *now*. Her sudden desire had so pleased Hans that she almost regretted waiting so long.

She smiled, thinking of this morning. Hans's lovemaking had assumed a dearness since they'd decided to get pregnant. He had become almost boyish in his pleasure. In Norway the sex had been new and wonderful, but for all of that, it had lacked the freedom she felt of late. There had been the hounding from home and from her mission president, from the church authorities in Utah. The illicitness of their love had intensified everything, the good and the bad.

She took the three stairs to the back door, slid up the pane, then turned and looked down the basement stairwell. The light was on. She descended and, pausing at the bottom, tracked her own breath as she surveyed the damage. Caleb's description was accurate—Joe had been thorough. Books and DVDs had been thrown off shelves, furniture upended, toy boxes emptied. The TV lay screen-down on the carpet, cord and cables stretched tail-like through the gaping entertainment center. Nothing, it seemed, was where it belonged. Karley touched her lips. Poor Joe, he was entirely alone now with Melissa so far away.

The door to his office was open, and Karley picked toward it, stepping over and around debris. There was nowhere in the office for a child to hide, and still the space had been rifled. Only the electronics—the computer equipment, the scanners and copiers—had not been moved. Open cabinets, empty cardboard cartons, their contents dumped on the floor. An uncapped Smirnoff lay on its side in the carriage of Joe's color printer. A sticky rivulet had run down the incline and into the slotted mechanism. Karley ran her finger through the dribble then brought it to her nose. Nearly odorless, the alcohol all but evaporated.

She picked up the empty bottle and dropped it in the garbage.

■

Upstairs again Karley hesitated before Josh's bedroom door. It was closed and marked, the room quarantined by the police for later examination. She reached for the knob then stopped herself, afraid the police might make something of her fingerprints. Paranoid, she told herself, but she did not resist the caution. Stepping back, she considered the collection of framed photos on the hallway wall. Josh was the subject of most every image.

The day's alienation seemed to re-lens Karley's perception, and she noticed how often she too was featured in the photos. Two-year-old Joshua on the 4th of July, Karley smiling from a lawn chair behind her nephew, his bleached curls incandescent in the summer sun. And another, Karley laughing through her tears, scissors snipping, Joshua's beautiful hair like spun cotton on his shoulders, in his lap, floating in the air. That face of his—Joe's eyes and mouth, Melissa's gentle roundness—pinched in protest against the ticklish procedure. His features simply would not masculinize, not even with bowl-cut hair.

They'd cried through the haircut, Melissa and Karley. Joe, snapping photos, had teased them mercilessly.

"You're leaking on my neck," Josh had complained. "Stop leaking, Kollie."

"Yeah, Kollie, stop leaking," Joe said.

So much leaking because of Josh, so many tears shed even before she'd met him. "I'm pregnant, Karley," Melissa told her. "Please come home, I need you here now ..."

And Karley had cried. Oslo, Norway, was so very far from Ogden, Utah.

"I look like a water buffalo. I have to pee every five minutes. I think I'm having sextuplets. If you don't come home you'll miss all the mocking ..."

And Karley had cried.

"Your sister's in labor ..." Eight months since Karley had abandoned her mission to live in sin with Hans—this was the first call she'd received from her mother. Margaret had almost sounded conciliatory.

"He's brilliant," Melissa informed her. "He cries and poops and blows spit bubbles. He sucks so hard, my nipples are four inches long. Next week he's going to write his dissertation …"

Joe: "Log on. No, write this down then log on. JoshuaChristopher. com. Got it? You're not going to believe how beautiful he is …"

And he was—fat and fabulous, more dimples than a golf ball, dark hair that would lighten before darkening again, this time to the color of honey. And there was Melissa, too, a little heavier than before but lovely in a whole new way. And Joe asleep on the sofa, Joshua napping belly-down on his father's broad chest, sucking a tiny fist.

"I'm licensed in the States," Hans reminded her. "I bet they could use a Norwegian doctor in Ogden, Utah."

Chewing her cheek, she'd clicked through Joshua's web page and pretended to ignore Hans's entreaties. She did not doubt her family would adore him, but she was a good deal less certain how he would feel about them. Did her homesickness justify dragging him from his new practice and the country of his birth?

"You missed it," Melissa said. "He rolled over today. I went in to pick him up from his nap, and there he was straight-arming the mattress, trying to get his knees underneath him. He's going to walk before you know it, and you'll miss that too …"

This time Karley had smiled.

"What if you didn't like my family?" she asked Hans. "What if you hated Utah?"

"Melissa and Joe look like nice people. They sound like nice people on the phone."

"You haven't met my mother. As far as she's concerned, you're a kidnapper and rapist, a white-slave trader."

"I'll buy her some nice Norwegian chocolates."

Karley pursed her lips and considered Hans's plan. "You guys do do chocolates like nobody's business."

"How about I make an honest woman of you? Right there in Ogden, Utah, U.S. of A. A big Norwegian wedding. It'll be our peace offering."

Karley smiled. She batted her eyes. Their eventual marriage had never been in doubt. "Will you buy me a ginormous rock?"

He proffered a wistful smile. "Yeah, right. Like you'd wear a ginormous rock."

Joshua was six months old. These were not early negotiations, not really negotiations at all. All that remained were the details, an articulation of what they both already understood. Without telling Karley, Hans put his colleagues on notice. It was as much deception as he was willing to endure. After reaching out to a medical school friend in Utah, he'd confessed the whole dirty deal to Karley. His earnestness had made her giggle.

"Getting a little ahead of yourself there, Mr. Man?" she'd teased.

Hardly.

■

"No, Mom. It's non-negotiable."

"But everyone at church will know," Margaret insisted.

"Hush now, Margaret," Curt said on the other extension. "She and Hans are as good as married already. Our daughter's coming home! Oh, Karley, my heart's going a thousand miles an hour!"

"Married?" Margaret protested. "They'll be living together right out in the open. I don't care if it is only for a few months."

There'd been a time Karley might have hung up on her mother. But she was no longer the girl of such tantrums, and the difference was all the proof she needed. "We're not staying at your house, Mom. And, anyway, you have no say in this. The wedding's a formality. I have no intention of sleeping in any bed but Hans's ever again."

"Karley!"

"Mom!" Karley aped, then she started to laugh. Listening in on his own extension, Hans relaxed into his club chair and grinned. "I'm coming home, Mom. We're going to be together again, all of us. I miss you so much. I miss everyone. Let's not argue over things that don't matter."

"But they do matter," Margaret sighed. Not even she could resist Karley's laughter for long.

Curt was laughing now too. "No, they don't," he said. "Not in the least. Oh, Karley, your siblings will be overjoyed. And Joshua, my goodness, you have no idea what you're in for. The world's a whole new place with him in it …"

Karley located the photo on the hallway wall, the one of her holding Joshua for the very first time. Its frame hung crooked, unsettled by the day's commotion, and she straightened it as she took the image in. An enlarged copy of the same photo stood on her bedroom bureau at home, a gift from Joe. She never grew weary of it.

In it eleven-month-old Joshua points a chubby index finger at the camera. The photographer, Joe, has positioned himself to the side and slightly behind Karley's shoulder. Karley, in profile, marvels at her nephew with a fascination both maternal and ecstatic. In the near background, framed between their faces, Melissa and Margaret look on, their features remarkable in their similarity. They appear stunned, as though they've just been rescued from some terrible fate they'd believed inescapable. Behind them a gaggle of travelers mills around a baggage carousel.

All these years later Karley could still recall the way Joshua smelled that day, fragrant with clean baby, sweet from the juice box he'd been drinking when she and Hans had descended into the baggage claim of Salt Lake City International. The grownups weeping and hugging, everyone talking at once, and Joshua had reached for Karley without hesitation. The heft of him, that astonishing solidity in her arms, was almost too much. All those months of imagining—she squeezed until he wriggled against the confinement. Hans produced the stuffed troll he'd carried through five airports, and Joshua immediately stuck the rubber nose in his mouth. How many times had he dropped the toy only to throw his whole body after it? Karley, who'd thought she understood, finally knew what it meant to hold on.

"Clean dirt," Hans had declared, retrieving the troll from the floor. It became a family favorite, "clean dirt," trotted out whenever the occasion warranted. As Karley had predicted, her family had fallen in love the instant Hans showed himself to them.

"He's gorgeous," Karley had told Melissa and Joe. She reluctantly passed Josh to Joe who waited to secure the boy in the car seat.

"So's he," Melissa whispered. She nodded at Hans who loaded luggage in their parents' sedan. "I think I'm beginning to get it."

Melissa's meaning, her perplexity, was obvious to Karley. Her family was relieved to have her home, joyful in the reunion, but none of them would ever get it, not really. To them, she had jumped off the earth only to come back a green alien.

For you, Josh, Karley had thought. *If for nothing else you're worth it.*

In the next room Sally was still instructing Melissa.

"Try it again," she said. "Only this time make it sound more personal, like you're speaking directly to the one person who can make a difference."

With the back of her fingers, Karley stroked Josh's door then stepped around the corner and slipped quietly into the living room. Nothing much had changed in her absence. Her parents and brothers remained slumped in waiting, half-watching Melissa and Sally work. If they knew Karley had slipped away, they seemed entirely unaware she'd returned.

Melissa read the statement, her voice plodding and false, each word too cumbersome to convince. It took her less than three minutes to read the script.

"Okay, good," Sally lied. "But remember the cameras. You need to look up every now and again."

Karley crossed the room to Hans who stood leaning against the wall. Adjusting his stance, he embraced her from behind.

Sally clapped her hands on her knees then pushed to her feet. "You'll do just fine. We have an hour and twenty minutes until the press conference. Time to rest and gather your strength."

"Couldn't some of us join the search?" Karley asked.

"There are enough searchers," Sally said. "Best to keep the family together right here. The press would like nothing better than to catch one of you alone out there." She stretched, the heels of her hands at the small of her back. "I think I'd like to get my computer set up. You wouldn't happen to have a scanner and fax machine around here?"

Everyone looked at Joe. Joe didn't look back. "All that stuff's downstairs," Karley said. "I'll show you. I know the password for the Wi-Fi too."

She waited while Sally gathered her things, then they headed through the kitchen and down the stairs. At the bottom landing, the older woman stopped. "Dear god."

"Joe," Karley said. "Looking for Josh."

Sally sucked on her teeth and surveyed the room. "He's in trouble, your brother-in-law. Does he drink all the time?"

"Appearances are too important to Melissa for that."

"I gathered as much." Sally shook her head. "Probably lied to the police too."

"What do you mean?"

"This morning. That he hadn't been drinking before Joshua went missing."

"No." Karley shook her head, unwilling to concede a point she herself still litigated. "No, I don't think so."

Sally studied her. "Don't? Or won't?"

Karley refused to take the bait. "He'll be dry for a long time and then—"

"He won't be," Sally said. "For a long time."

Karley nodded. "For days sometimes. I've seen him bad, but even at his worst he'd never do anything to harm Josh."

"Got a brother who's a binge drinker," Sally said.

"It's going to be a problem with the police, isn't it?"

Sally adjusted the computer bag on her shoulder. "Absolutely. Milo's going to pick at it. I sure would. The hiding thing's bad. The possibility he and Melissa are lying about when he started. One secret becomes another. A little guilt here looks like a lot of guilt there. Especially when it comes time for a polygraph."

Unaccountably, Karley's ears began to ring. "Do you think we need a lawyer?"

Sally bent down and picked up a book. She held it at the end of her arm to read the title—*Drawing on the Powers of Heaven*—then dropped it on the nearest shelf. "A little good advice goes a long way at a time like this. A quiet meeting? Probably not a bad idea. But no fanfare, keep the press out of it. I've got an attorney or two I can recommend."

Karley tugged on her earlobe. "I might know someone."

"That's fine, too." Sally considered the room again. "You'll want someone with criminal experience."

"Oh, that sounds awful." Melissa and Joe in need of a criminal lawyer? The irony under different circumstances would have made Karley laugh. For a long moment neither woman spoke. "I keep having these terrible visions of Joe at the press conference."

Sally reconsidered the basement as though reconsidering Joe. "Nothing to do but press ahead. We'll just have to keep him quiet and not let any reporters near him. Everyone expects him to look bad. So long as he doesn't do something outrageous, it might even work in our favor."

Karley knew Sally was right, but she didn't like it. "Seems like a big risk."

Sally nodded. "Given the stakes, we're going to have to take it. This is about getting Josh back. Protecting Melissa and Joe comes a distant second."

Karley breathed deeply. "Here, let me show you Joe's office."

Sally reached out and clasped Karley's hand. "I've been watching you, dear. You're a strong girl. So is Melissa, but I don't know how long she can bear up. A crash almost always comes in these situations, and the timing's never convenient."

Karley studied Sally's face. "Pretty inconsiderate of Josh. Going missing when we all had other plans."

Sally smiled. "We'll have to ground him when he gets home."

Karley out-waited her burning sinuses. "I'm frazzled like everyone else. But of course, I'll do whatever I can. I'm desperate to get Josh back."

"I know you are," Sally said. "But when it comes right down to it, you may have to do more than you can. It's the way these things are." She squeezed Karley's hand then let her go. "Now why don't you show me this office."

■

Karley left Sally to her work and climbed the stairs for the second time in fifteen minutes. In the living room Margaret held court. "But I don't understand," she said. "You've always welcomed a priesthood blessing."

Melissa shook her head.

Jared stood center-room, his hands on the back of a kitchen chair he'd carried in for the purpose of the blessing.

"Please," Margaret pleaded. "Don't you think a blessing would be the best thing right now? You need all the strength you can get."

Melissa buffed smudges from the window with a fold of her jumper.

"Why not, sweetheart?" Karley asked gently. "It might help."

Melissa shook her head again. "No, I don't want a blessing."

It was not like Melissa to resist the ministrations of her faith. She'd dug in, and Karley couldn't help admiring her. "You told me once they comfort you."

"It's not that," Jared corrected. "It's so God's on your side."

Karley spun toward her younger brother. "What kind of God wouldn't help a child because his mother refused a priesthood blessing?"

"The same God," Melissa snapped, "who'd let him be taken in the first place." Karley stepped back, the sting entirely physical.

"What an *awful* thing to say," Jared said. "Like it's God's fault now?"

"Jared," Curt warned from his perch on the sofa.

"Leave her alone," Karley said.

Massaging her neck, Melissa turned from the window and started across the room.

"Please don't fight," Margaret pleaded.

"But she's making a huge mistake," Jared cried.

Melissa slammed her bedroom door.

Karley and Jared glared at each other. Margaret began to weep.

"I want a blessing," Joe said. Jared turned and peered at his brother-in-law, a lengthy sidelong appraisal. "Really, I think a blessing might help." Joe sat up on the edge of his chair.

Jared's face darkened. "All right, Joe."

Joe rose from his seat stiff and halting. He neither stumbled nor weaved, but his crossing was ponderous. He sat down in the chair and bowed his head.

"Dad?" Jared said. Curt pulled himself from the sofa. Jared produced the tiny vial of consecrated olive oil he carried on his key ring. "Should we anoint or just give him a blessing?"

"Anoint," Curt said softly.

"Do you want to do it?" Jared asked his father.

"Why don't we let Joe decide?"

Joe looked up at Jared then at Curt. "I guess maybe I'd like Curt to give the blessing."

It was a nod to seniority and perhaps, Karley thought, a slight earned by Jared's unpleasantness. Jaw set, Jared opened the vial. "I wish I'd worn better clothes." He handed Curt the key ring then tilted the vial into the light to be certain it still contained oil. "A tie at least."

Curt smiled at his oldest son. "I don't think Heavenly Father cares how we're dressed at the moment."

"Still." Jared poured a drop of oil into Joe's hair at the crown. He passed the vial to his father who screwed on the lid before handing the key ring to Margaret. Placing both hands on Joe's head, Jared leaned in close. "What's your full name, Joe?"

Joe turned his head, their faces inches apart, and Karley held her breath. "Joseph Andrew."

Jared winced then righted himself stiffly. He looked up at the ceiling, his expression knowing. Inhaling, he bowed his head and closed his eyes. "Joseph Andrew Christopher," he began. "By the power of the Holy Melchizedek Priesthood and in the name of Jesus Christ, I anoint your head with this holy oil, which has been—"

Jared stopped and removed his hands from Joe's head. "No," he said calmly. "This is wrong. I shouldn't have agreed in the first place."

"Don't you dare," Karley warned.

"What's *wrong* with you guys?" Jared said. "Can't you see he's drunk? Just smell him."

Lurching from his chair, Joe stumbled without falling and fled through the storm door into the yard.

"Joe!" Curt called.

Hans caught the door on the backswing and hurried down the front steps after his brother-in-law.

"What do you mean, drunk?" Margaret said. "Joe doesn't drink."

Karley strode to the storm door and stopped. Head down, she turned back and started across the room. Jared glanced at his father then at his mother. He faced forward and watched Karley come.

"What a fine missionary you must have been," she said. *"You pious little fuck."* Then she slapped him, gave it everything she had. Knocked off balance, Jared stumbled sideways. He swiveled back, his eyes febrile with fury.

Smiling, Karley hit him again before Curt could drag her away.

A Christmas Bride,
A New Year's Missionary

8 YEARS AGO

They had been dating some four months when Joe asked Curt DeBoer for Melissa's hand in marriage. In contrast to the rarefied sacraments bestowed by Ezra and The Seers, Joe's proposal approximated a non-event, which was not to say it lacked excitement. That expansive Halloween evening had primed the pump, and within days they were speaking of marriage. By the time Joe gave Melissa the ring—which she helped pick out and he placed on her finger during a fancy meal at an expensive Salt Lake City restaurant—they were already discussing dates. An aphrodisiac, that ring. Later that evening Joe brought her six times. A banner night as they usually stopped at three.

Of greater suspense was Joe's status as a Mormon, a suspense that might have extended to Melissa had either of them been honest with their ward bishops. Looking back, Melissa was always a little amazed they'd pulled it off, especially Joe, who endured a full course of required interviews with the bishop. So much opportunity to confess under pressure as Joe's bishop was protective of Melissa's purity and inclined to ply Joe with probing questions. But Melissa worried for naught. Joe knew where the real danger lay. He whispered not a word.

Which was not to say Joe lacked conscience. He didn't like to lie, so for deniability's sake, he erected boundaries around their sexual play. Namely, he refused Melissa any contact that required the absence of clothing, a frustrating condition to which she initially submitted. Joe's rules seemed arbitrary and entirely unnecessary. She felt no guilt over the physical intimacy, seeing

63

more clearly with every episode that they'd been granted a waiver by God. Fondling felt right, as right as the bishop's inquiries felt wrong. But Joe alone was required to endure those interviews, so Melissa made an effort to respect his wishes. Joe was a bastion of self-control, facilitating her pleasure while denying his own. Melissa came easily with clothes on, but the same couldn't be said for Joe. She considered it a lucky night when she managed to manipulate him to orgasm through his pants. Among other things, Joe was embarrassed by the mess and wouldn't let it happen very often. Entirely ignorant in the art of pleasuring a man, she pressed on, believing he would succumb when frustration got the best of him. A bad plan. It underestimated his determination to protect what tattered virtue lingered behind her pristine hymen.

She would eventually be inspired to revise.

■

Big changes came with the greening spring of that year and not only because Melissa was getting married.

"I met with Bishop Sutherby today," Karley announced at Sunday dinner. "As soon as the wedding's over, I'm going on a mission."

It was a utensil-freezing declaration. Jared and Caleb, Joe and Melissa gawped at Karley, uncertain they'd heard correctly. Curt smiled mistily, while Margaret fidgeted with her napkin and pretended to be happy. This was not news to them—Melissa could see it in her mother's miserable smile. Both daughters. The abrupt conclusion to an era.

"You've *got* to be kidding," Melissa said. Boorish but the first thing that came to mind all the same. Karley was the last among them she'd have expected to serve a mission. The girl defied the stereotype and not because she lacked devotion. Rather she possessed an *esprit* that contradicted the missionary life. And she was movie-star beautiful. Her mere presence was sure to torment the poor hormonal elders who would find their missions more painful to endure with her in it. For that matter, Melissa had no idea how sexy little Karley would give up her corona of boys.

Karley looked at her coolly. "Thanks for the vote of confidence."

"That's not what I mean," Melissa backpedaled. "It's just such a gutsy thing to do. I'm surprised is all."

Karley put down her bread and flicked crumbs from her fingers. "What, because I'm not gutsy?"

Joe reached for the carrots. "No one's gutsier than you, Karley."

"I just mean you've got so much going on here," Melissa said. "Eighteen months—that's a long time to put everything on hold. School and boys, all those hearts you're going to break." She manufactured a deferential smile. "I think it's wonderful, Karley. Really. Don't listen to me. I never say anything right."

"Nice save," Karley said.

In truth, Karley had, through the years, voiced a desire to serve a mission. But so had Melissa.

"It's an exciting time," Curt declared with emotion. "Our family's growing up."

"Does this mean I get Karley's bedroom?" Caleb piped up. Leave it to him to find the pith.

"Where would your sister sleep when she comes home to us?" Margaret said.

"Our first missionary," Curt said.

"And your first wedding," Karley added. She glared at Melissa. "Unless it's just a never-ending engagement. Folks can't put their lives on hold forever."

Joe and Melissa shared a glance. Ready as they were to tie the knot, they were stuck waiting for Joe's bishop to give them permission. Melissa had been stumping for a holiday wedding, which put them near the year mark of Joe's first interview, the standard probation for new converts and repentant sinners. It occurred to Melissa that Karley's impending mission might provide some useful leverage.

"You can't leave until your birthday," Melissa reminded her. "That's not until November."

"Uh-huh," Karley said. She ate salad without a fork, sucking the dressing off her fingers.

"And then there's Christmas," Melissa said. "I can't imagine you'd want to leave until after the holidays."

"Uh-huh," Karley said.

"We've talked about a December wedding," Joe said. "I think my bishop will go for that."

Karley smiled. "How about I talk to him?"

Joe laughed. "He'd probably *make* us get married next week."

"December will do." Karley wiped her fingers on her napkin. "And guess what? I'll get to go to the temple with you. I'll get to see the wedding."

"*Oh, Karley.* I didn't think of that!" Only adult endowers in possession of a worthiness recommend were allowed to attend temple weddings. Not even Jared or Caleb would see their sister married.

"Neither did I." Margaret for the first time appeared genuinely pleased. "How wonderful!"

"It's perfect," Melissa said.

"A Christmas wedding," Margaret sighed. "Just think of the color possibilities."

"A Christmas bride and a New Year's missionary," Curt added. "My goodness, aren't we blessed!"

Sherm the Sperm

When Craig opened the door to the interrogation room, he was met with the stench of Sherm Stillwell's fear—rank body odor and the nervous gases of a fast-food junkie. An occupational hazard, the smell of interrogation, though Craig had become something of a connoisseur. The riper the stink, the readier the subject. Sherm the Sperm was primed.

Sherm's head popped up, his wide-set eyes round and dark and oddly beautiful. He possessed at age forty the face of a child—confused innocence framed in dark curls. Without a word, Craig placed a carton on the table, removed the lid, and extracted Sherm's file. But for two wet sniffs and the movement of his eyes, Sherm held silent and motionless. Craig had instructed the turnkey to uncuff him.

He studied the arresting officer's report, then brought out his phone and selected the appropriate app. He checked to be sure it was recording then placed the device near the center of the table. Stepping to the wall, he activated the video. Finally he turned and looked at Sherm.

"Howdy, Sherm."

"Hello." Sherm spoke softly.

Craig cocked an ear. "I'm getting old, Sherm. You're going to have to speak up."

"Sorry," he said more loudly.

Craig grinned at him. "Lieutenant Milo Craig's my name. I'm a detective in the Major Crimes Division." He consulted the file again. "Says here you were read your rights. That true?"

"Yes."

"Do something for me would you? Turn your chair this way so I feel like we're having a conversation."

Sherm grabbed the armrests and swung Craig's direction. The chair's rubber feet farted on the linoleum floor. "Sorry."

Craig closed the file. "You understand your rights, Sherm?"

"I guess."

"Yes or no?"

"Yes."

"You know you can ask for a lawyer any time you want?"

"I don't need a lawyer. I don't even know why I was read my rights. I didn't do anything wrong."

Craig grabbed the two remaining chairs and dragged them to the wall. "Sure you do. You ran from an officer. From the scene of a crime. That was wrong."

Reaching out, Sherm touched the edge of the table. He jerked back as though it had burned him. "I wasn't running, I was just going home. And it wasn't my crime. I didn't do it."

Craig put his hands in his pockets. "What crime would that be?"

"I don't understand."

"What crime were you fleeing, Sherm?"

"I wasn't fleeing."

Craig leaned in. "What crime?"

"Someone took a boy I guess. That's what I heard."

"What's the boy's name?"

Sherm's gaze flitted across the detective's face. "Joshua Christopher. It's been all over the news."

"That it has. Everyone's very concerned. People are looking everywhere for little Josh Christopher."

"That's what *I* wanted to do," Sherm said quickly. "That's why I was up by his house."

"So you know where he lives."

"Well no, not exactly. But I figured it had to be somewhere near the search."

"You're quite a guy, Sherm. Child molester with a heart of gold."

Sherm's fleshy chin turned to curd. "Like I said, I was just—"

"The goodness of your heart doesn't interest me."

"I—"

"Sherm."

"I guess I was curious."

Craig smiled at him. "Now that I believe. But you still haven't answered my question."

"Maybe I don't understand your question."

"Oh, come on, Sherm. You're on probation for sexually assaulting a little girl. I think 'curious' is a bit of an understatement."

Sherm shook his head. He rubbed his palms on his pants. "You're trying to make this into something it's not."

"What would that be?"

"You think I took the kid. That's what this is. But I didn't. A person would be crazy to steal a kid then go back to the place. There were cops everywhere."

Craig slid his butt onto the table. His feet dangled at the ends of his short legs. "Look at me, Sherm." Sherm obeyed. "Crazy's a relative term. A person would need real stones to do what you did, but I wouldn't say he'd have to be crazy."

"But—"

Craig waved him off. "It's my turn to talk now."

Sherm closed his mouth.

"See, I think you're basically a good guy. You've got your temptations—Lord knows I have mine—but you've been fighting the good fight, haven't you? I respect that, Sherm. I think you've been giving it your best."

Sherm attended raptly to Craig's lips. His eyes glistened. He swiped his sleeve across his face.

"But it's been tough, hasn't it, son? I think you've been suffering more than usual lately."

Sherm's eyes had gone round. He shook his head, a movement so small it was almost imperceptible.

"Hell, I bet before you spied the boy you didn't even know what you were up to."

"No."

Craig arched his eyebrows. "You're a decent man, Sherm, a man who feels true remorse. I've read your file. Abduction's not your style. I think you were up there trying to figure out how to return Josh to his family."

"It didn't happen," Sherm whispered. "You're making this up."

"Oh, come on. Why else would you go back to the scene? I tell you, it's those stones of yours. I mean it, Sherm. You've got 'em. It takes a lot of courage to do the right thing."

"No. They searched my car. I didn't have the kid. I *don't* have the kid."

"Well, of course you didn't have Josh with you. You left him somewhere safe, tied up maybe, I don't know. You needed a minute to plan his return so you went to your house and watched a little TV with your mom. She says hi, by the way."

Sherm threw his head back and squeaked like a floorboard.

Craig leaned over, put his elbows on his knees. When Sherm lowered his face, they were nose-to-nose. "I'm guessing the news didn't tell you what you needed to know. So you told your mom you were going out and headed for the east bench. Probably drove by the subdivision a few times before you finally turned off Harrison."

"Maybe I need a lawyer. I have a right if I want one. That's what you said."

Nodding Craig sat up. He put his hands behind him and leaned back. "You're right about that, Sherm. You had your phone call but—"

"No, I didn't." Sherm shook his head. "No one said I could make a call."

"Really? Well. You know how it gets on crazy days. But I'll tell you what. You ask, I'll go make the call for you. But if you do that I'll have to assume you're not interested in cooperating. Believe me, if that happens things'll get a lot more complicated. Not everyone out there sees the world quite so clearly as I do. All my help and good will?" Craig shrugged.

Sherm rocked in his chair and tried to think. He looked as though he needed a toilet. "You talk to me like I'm stupid," he said finally. "You're just trying to get me to confess."

"Well, I won't argue about the confession. I do want you to tell me where the boy is. And not just for Josh and his poor family, though I'd be lying if I said my first concern was you. Still, you have to know there's only one way through this. If you cooperate and the boy comes home safely, you've still got a chance for a life. Help me bring Josh home, and I'll tell everyone involved how helpful you were."

Sherm massaged a thumb. Sniffing he wiped his nose with his sleeve again. "That's real nice of you," he said. "But I didn't do it."

Craig hopped from his perch, reached for the carton, and emptied it on the table. An empty shoebox, the last item out, slid off the pile of bagged children's underpants.

"Oh, Christ!" Sherm put his face in his hands.

"Prayer's good," Craig said.

"They're not mine."

"I'm sure you're right about that. But I've got five bucks says we'll find you all over 'em."

Sherm set his jaw and looked up at Craig. "I bought those."

"Come on, Sherm." Craig rifled through the pile of bagged underwear, selecting two worthy examples. "These look a little threadbare, wouldn't you say?"

"I didn't buy them new."

"You're kidding me now."

Sherm stared at the floor. "No, I'm not. I paid a lot for those."

Craig laughed though mostly for show. Few things, he knew, could not be purchased. "So what happens when we strap you to a polygraph?" Sherm's head bobbed up. "Which of course you have to know we're going to do. What happens when we strap you down and ask, for instance, how well you know Joshua Christopher?" Craig waved the two bags of underwear. "And, of course, we'll wanna know how you took these off their owners."

"You wouldn't do that."

Craig laughed at him again. "You know we would."

"No polygraph! I won't do it. Those guys twist—!"

"Where were you at 11:00 this morning, Sherm?"

Sherm looked away. "On my way home from the dog food plant. Check with my boss. I clocked out a little after 10:00. I was starved so I drove to Carl Jr's."

"Which one?"

"By the Home Depot."

"12th Street?"

Sherm nodded. "I got home about 11:15. After that I watched TV with my mom for a while. Ask her."

Craig had. Betty Stillwell had told the same story. "So what happened, Sherm? Why did you take that drive into Joshua's neighborhood?"

Sherm trembled in his chair.

"Tell me, Sherm. I promise, life's going to get better after you do." He peeked at his watch. Coming up hard on the press conference.

"I didn't do it. It shouldn't matter why I was there." Sherm lifted his face. "I have to go to the bathroom."

"Here's the thing," Craig said. "In about five minutes I'm walking out that door. See, I need to help Joshua Christopher's terrified parents go on TV and tell the world some sicko took their kid this morning. Don't worry though, I'll be coming back. And when I do, you and I are talking about some pictures we found on your mom's computer. By then Recovery should almost be finished with your house. Who knows what else we'll have to talk about."

Sherm was squeaking again.

"Let's be objective for a moment, shall we? You're a known offender on probation for diddling a kid. Some two hours after another kid disappears, you're caught fleeing the missing boy's neighborhood. An hour after that, yours truly finds this lovely spunk-covered collection of fetish fodder hidden in the rafters of the same shed you used to diddle your first kid. In the mean-time your probation officer, one Dew Asplund, unearths an ungodly file of kiddie porn on your mom's nice new computer. I think you'd best tell me why we caught you in the Christophers' neighborhood."

Sherm was sobbing now. Chin to chest, he hugged himself and quaked.

"You don't want me to walk out of this room, Sherm."

"I already told you," he pleaded. "I was curious. I just wanted to help."

Craig tugged a clean handkerchief from his pocket and dropped it in Sherm's lap. Sherm used it to smear a thick slug from his lip. Craig checked his watch again—5:30 p.m. "Time's up," he said. One-by-one he tossed the bags in the container. He picked up his phone, closed down the app, and tucked the device in his pocket. Reaching across the table, he retrieved the file. He dropped it in the carton and secured the lid.

Sherm hadn't stopped crying but he'd settled some. "Stand up," Craig said.

"Thank you!" Sherm hopped to his feet.

"Turn around and give me your hands."

Sherm dropped his chin. "You don't really have to cuff me again do you?"

"Now, Sherm."

"Oh, man." He turned. "At least, cuff me in front. How am I supposed to pee with my hands cuffed like that?"

Craig cinched him tight. "Sit down."

"But wait, I've been in here for hours. I gotta go."

"Sit down."

Sherm sat down on the edge of his chair. Craig picked up the carton and started for the door. "It's her fault," Sherm said.

Craig turned back. "Whose fault?"

"You know who. My mother's. Those pictures. She upgraded the computer and everything. You wanna know why?"

Craig's scalp tingled. "Sure, Sherm. Tell me why."

"To keep me from moving out."

"You're telling me she was bribing you to stay?"

Head shaking, Sherm met Craig's gaze. "No. She promised she'd call the police if I ever tried to leave her. Show you guys the pictures so you'd send me back to prison." Craig raised his gaze and peered at the camera. "You don't believe me."

It wasn't disbelief Sherm saw in Craig's face. "This only helps you if your fingerprints aren't all over that computer."

Sherm's waterworks flowed unabated again. "Mom's right, I'm a lousy weakling. Those pictures are just too tempting."

Stepping close, Craig loomed over the man-child. "Where's the boy, Sherm?"

Sherm gripped the rear edge of his metal seat, his face pointed at the floor. "I promise I don't know. I never saw him, I never touched him, I never hurt him at all. You've gotta believe me." He raised his face and blinked at Craig. "I'm telling you the truth!"

Craig crossed to the wall and punched off the recorder then passed his card through the reader at the door. The lock clicked.

"Please," Sherm pleaded. "I need to go to the bathroom real bad."

With a glance at Sherm, Craig closed the door between them.

These Spoils of a Rough Game

The church parking lot was a roiling sea of lens glint and faces. Hans trailed Sally's car through the reporters and gawkers, the crowd parting for the length of three vehicles before collapsing into itself. Waved on by a pair of uniformed sentries, Hans steered the sedan past the barriers and beyond the reach of the pressing crowd. How right Sally had been to insist they drive. They'd have never made the two blocks on foot.

"CNN," Caleb noted from the backseat. "That van says CNN. I didn't know they were even in Utah."

Hans pulled in beside Sally's car. Curt, who trailed Hans's BMW, eased his Camry into the spot next to Hans. Getting out of her car, Sally signaled for the family to stay put, then disappeared into the covered command post. Milo Craig's absence worried Hans. He didn't know whether to think it a good omen or bad.

"I was supposed to take Josh to a movie today," Caleb said. "A matinee." Karley turned in her seat and looked back at her brother. "I keep thinking I should have insisted. Maybe if I'd insisted—"

"Oh, honey," Karley said. She reached between the seats and touched Caleb's knee. "Don't do this to yourself. Melissa would have vetoed you anyway."

Caleb stared out the window at the crowd. Sally hurried from the command post and opened Melissa's door.

"It isn't your fault, Caleb," Karley said. "You're not responsible, not in any way."

"I wish I could believe that," Caleb said. He flailed at the doorlatch and tumbled from the seat then rounded to the front of Sally's car, where Curt and Margaret and Jared assembled.

75

Jared made much of refusing to look at Karley as she hurried to join Melissa and Sally. He nodded at something Caleb said, then glanced back at Sally who was trying to coax Joe from her car.

Pausing between their vehicles, Hans monitored Sally's effort. "I'll get him," he said, and Sally stepped back. "Joe." Hans leaned in. "Come on, now. Josh needs you."

Joe shook his head, his weepy, vodka-veined eyes signaling the misery of impending sobriety. "Josh is dead," he said. His diaphragm hitched. "I'm just sure of it. I can feel it."

"Stop that," Hans said, palming Joe's cheek, his fingers light on the back of his neck. "You have to believe he's coming home. He's alive. He needs us to bring him back."

Pressing into Hans' palm, Joe tilted his head back as if to grasp Hans's fingers with the skin of his neck. It was a tender gesture, pregnant with need, and Hans, who had always liked his brother-in-law, felt utterly helpless.

Sally stepped away, and Joe tracked her retreat. "I don't remember anything, Hans." He looked through Hans, his heavy eyebrows clamped around the fold between them.

"What don't you remember?"

"I don't remember sending Josh off this morning. I don't remember anything about a birthday party. I don't remember any of it."

Hans had learned as a physician to suspend his alarm but found himself weak against it now. "When did you start drinking?"

Blank-faced, Joe closed his eyes and searched. "Yesterday, I think." He opened his eyes but did not look at Hans. "You know how I get when I've been drinking. It's hard to be sure."

"You don't remember seeing Josh at all this morning?"

"I think I did. I must have. Everything's so mixed together. It's like I almost remember but can't bring it up. It's driving me mad."

Hans glanced through the windshield at their waiting in-laws. It was not easy to look back at Joe. "Did you tell this to the detective, Craig?"

Joe shook his head.

"What did you say?"

Joe seemed uncertain now, and Hans feared it was already too late. "I lied," he said finally. "I said I worked all morning while

Melissa got Josh ready. That I kissed him goodbye before the party. I told the police I hadn't started drinking until Josh disappeared."

Hans's relief in Joe's lie startled him more than the lie itself. It was an unaccountable, unabashed relief entirely out of sync with the dangers it defied. He smiled at Joe. "That may be true, Joe. At least, the part about kissing him goodbye. You don't remember."

"I don't," Joe agreed. "I truly don't. Melissa insists I was there. I just wish I could—" Joe went silent, his face averted.

"We've got to do this *now*, gentlemen," Sally said.

Hans withdrew from the doorway, and Sally bent down. "We'll miss the window if we don't hurry, Joe. We need you."

Joe gazed past Sally at Hans. "You can do this," Hans said.

Joe wiped his face, then looked up at Sally who took a step back to make space. "Let's go," Hans said, offering his hand. Joe took it and started out.

"That a boy," Sally said.

Joe came up squinting but steadier than Hans had anticipated. He clutched a framed photo of his son to his chest. "That's the father!" someone cried. Hans could hear the cameras across the distance, the click and whirr of swarming insects. Joe blinked at the masses, his features infant-like in their quickened pliability.

"This way," Hans said, touching Joe's elbow.

"Wow," Joe said. He shuffled toward the family. Hans closed the door and followed.

"Okay," Sally instructed. "Melissa and Joe will stand together in front of everyone else. Joe, you'll hold up the picture of Josh during the entire press conference. Remember to hold it high so the cameras have a good shot of it. The rest of you will make a half-circle behind Melissa and Joe. We want you in close for the cameras. Melissa will read her statement, then Craig will provide a brief update and take questions. Don't give in to the temptation to say anything beyond the statement. That goes for everyone. We're going to keep this short and get out of here as quickly as possible."

"Where *is* Craig?" Hans asked. "What if he doesn't get here in time?"

"He called me as we were leaving," Sally said. "He'll make it, but we've got to hurry now. Everyone follow me. Karley, you stand close to Melissa. If for any reason she can't finish, you'll step up and read the statement."

Karley nodded. They'd discussed all this at the house.

"Let's go," Sally said. She took Melissa's hand and stepped out. Touching the small of Joe's back, Hans guided him after Melissa. The crowd began to stir, someone barked instructions. Craig's unmarked cruiser eased into the lot.

But for the cameras the crowd had fallen silent. Sally led them through the canopy and up a grassy mound between the parking lot and the sidewalk. Hans spotted Craig hurrying from his car.

"Mrs. Christopher!" someone called.

"Mr. Christopher!" a different voice. "Do you have any idea who has your son?"

Melissa and Joe followed Sally's stage directions and paid the questions no mind. When Joe was in place, he lifted the photo, a gesture so boyish it sealed Hans's throat. Sally retreated to the wings, out of camera fire.

"That's not how we're doing things, folks," Craig told the crowd. He'd circled around behind the family to emerge smiling beside Melissa and Joe. A pair of disparate eruptions—a frustrated "Hey!" from the left, a ribald "Haw-haw-haw" from some basso larynx near the center—set the crowd to tittering. Still smiling, Craig held up a hand. "My name's Milo Craig. I'm a detective with the Ogden City Police Department, and I'm heading up the investigation into Joshua Christopher's disappearance. In just a moment Melissa Christopher, Joshua's mother, will make a short statement. Then I'll say a few words and take some questions. The family will not respond to any questions at this time."

"Are the Christophers suspects?" someone called.

Ignoring the outburst, Craig turned around and surveyed the family. "Are you ready?" he asked Melissa.

It was impossible to tell if Melissa had heard him. Face raised, she looked high above the crowd, her gaze anchored on the spire of the Mormon Church house. She seemed oblivious of Craig and the crisis-captive crowd. Karley touched her from behind, and still she stared. It was a preternatural calm, a thing entirely other than her earlier despondence, and Hans's doctor bells began to ring. Slowly Melissa lowered her gaze. She put one hand in the other and began to rub then abandoned that itch to massage her nose.

"Ready?" Craig asked her again.

Melissa seemed to return to herself. Nodding, she withdrew the folded statement from her jumper. She stepped forward and the air came alive with camera sound. Behind her, knees locked, Joe stood fixed in place holding the photo aloft. He swayed, a tall tree in a moderate breeze, and Hans glanced over at Sally. She also seemed to be weighing the dangers. Noticing Hans, she mouthed, *Leave him. He's okay.*

Hans wasn't so sure, but he nodded.

Melissa stood very still and studied the statement. It was an eerie moment, the parking lot silent but for the soft electric hum of technology. If anticipation had a sound, this was it. Melissa seemed not to know what came next.

Painkillers, Hans thought. He knew she had them.

Melissa cleared her throat and squinted out across the crowd. "At a little before 11:00 this morning, our son Joshua disappeared while walking a short distance to a neighbor friend's birthday party."

An explosion of flashes.

Melissa put a hand over her mouth, and Karley canted toward her. Melissa lowered her hand. "Joshua is five years old. We call him Josh. He's a wonderful boy and we love him very much. Though we don't understand why, we believe someone unknown to us has taken him. To that person we want to say you have the power to return our Joshua to us. Please, he must be so frightened. We are, we're terribly afraid. Josh needs to be with us, and we need to be with him. It's not too late. You can do this, you can bring Josh home. It would be so much better for everyone, even for you. Take care of our little Josh. Keep him safe and bring him back to us."

Melissa had grown steadier, her voice firm now, all hesitation gone. Whatever she'd taken was not interfering with her delivery. If anything, it seemed to be helping.

"In the meantime we plead with everyone to be on the lookout for our Josh. When he left the house this morning, he was wearing Gap elastic-waist jeans and a Harry Potter sweat-shirt, a white T-shirt underneath. He was also wearing a green vinyl raincoat, a matching hat, and a type of rubber shoes often referred to as duck shoes. Josh has light brown hair, almost blond, brown eyes, and pronounced dimples when he smiles. He has a brown, dime-sized birthmark on his right shoulder. He recently lost his first tooth, his top-front tooth on the right. Please, if you see our son or have any information about his whereabouts, any information at all, call Detective Milo Craig of the Ogden City Police Department or any other law enforcement agency. The police have assured us they will protect the identity of anyone who provides information. We love our Joshua so much. Please help us bring him home. Thank you."

Melissa didn't move. During her statement, she had gradually tilted forward, a precarious leaning that threatened to topple her into the microphones and cameras. She stared over her script at the crowd. Detective Craig stepped in beside her. She continued to stare at the crowd.

Craig whispered something in her ear and touched her gently on the forearm. She turned her head and gazed at him, then settled on her heels and lifted her shoulders. Stepping back, she took her place beside Joe, the statement clutched in both hands. She and Joe nearly touched, the most proximal Hans had seen them the entire day.

"Okay," Craig began. "A few words, then I'll take some questions. A disappearance like this is very unusual, and we want to assure the public we're utilizing every resource to ensure Joshua's safe return. To the person who has Josh, I want you to hear this one thing: We're going to find you. We won't stop until we do. Your only hope is to return the boy to his family unharmed and to do so immediately. The consequences to you will be much less severe if you release Josh now. Sooner or later we'll catch you. Sooner *than* later."

It was a bold declaration, and Hans was taken by Craig's conviction. The detective's confidence registered like a balm, and by the family's stirring Hans knew they felt it too.

"So where are we now?" Craig continued. "As you must be

aware, a massive area search is underway. So far we've canvassed the victim's neighborhood and are moving beyond it. Police agencies throughout the Intermountain West have been notified, as have missing child agencies."

Craig went on detailing the specifics of the police effort, most of it already known to Hans, who felt himself drifting. Until this moment, he'd not realized how weary he was. The policeman's public reassurance, the illusion of control, was nothing but a ruse, though Hans understood the ploy, the need to guide perception. The policeman revealed next to nothing that couldn't have been observed by any of the reporters who'd been here all day. And yet there was something complicit in his manner, confidential and conspiratorial. He was good, this Craig.

Now he was winding down. "Of course, as important details emerge, we'll be sure to get them to you." He paused. "I'll be happy to take a few questions now."

"Are the parents suspects?" came the same voice as before.

"Hands, please," Craig said. He pointed to a reporter different from the one who'd shouted the question.

"We've received reports you have a suspect in custody. We're told this suspect, a man by the name of Sherman Stillwell, was caught fleeing the scene. We're also told Mr. Stillwell served prison time for the sexual assault of a child. Would you please comment on this?"

"You've been told a lot," Craig said. An appreciative laughter rippled across the crowd. "Mr. Stillwell is not yet a suspect however. We're holding him for questioning, nothing more."

"But he did flee the scene," the reporter pressed. "There was a car chase."

"Like I say," Craig said, "you were told a lot, not all of it correct. Mr. Stillwell was identified in the search area about three blocks from the place we think Josh disappeared. We're questioning him as a person of interest but don't consider him a suspect at this time."

Craig pointed to a different hand.

"You said 'at this time.' Do you expect Mr. Stillwell will become a suspect?" This from a reporter not photogenic enough for TV.

"We don't expect anything except to ask him a few more questions."

"Then you've found no evidence to tie Mr. Stillwell to the boy's disappearance?"

The family watched Craig closely, their faces tense with hope. "It's too early to get into what we have or haven't found." He pointed to someone new.

"In your statement, you mentioned little about evidence and witnesses. Have you recovered any physical evidence suggesting what happened to the boy? Any witnesses?"

Craig thought about this. "We're still evaluating the scene. As I said, it's pretty early yet."

"Wasn't something belonging to Josh found in the gutter a short distance from his house?"

Craig stared at the reporter.

"What was it you found?" someone called.

Craig shook his head. "For the sake of the investigation, we're not releasing any information about evidence right now."

"What about eyewitnesses?"

"So far, we have none. As Mrs. Christopher said, we plead for anyone with any information to reach out to us." Craig pointed.

"It was a gift, wasn't it? That item in the gutter? A birthday gift for the boy's friend?"

Craig smiled, and not a kind smile. He unleashed it directly on the inquisitor, an ambitious looking boy with big hair. "You just don't get it, do you?"

There was something calculated about Craig's reprimand. It was theatrical, and Hans found himself wondering if the detective wasn't secretly pleased by the leak. Craig pointed at someone new.

"Are the parents suspects?"

There it was, front and center, and though Craig had already ignored the question twice, he didn't seem concerned. "There's no indication Mr. or Mrs. Christopher had anything to do with Josh's disappearance."

"But you sent a crime scene unit into the boy's house," a reporter yelled, the same one who'd asked the question the two times Craig had ignored it. "They're there now."

"It's standard procedure in an investigation like this to go through the victim's house," Craig said. "It's a consensual search. The family's cooperating fully. It's not unreasonable to think the perpetrator entered the house recently, even someone unknown to the family. You never know what you might find until you look. Like I say, we believe this was a non-family abduction and we're proceeding on that assumption."

From the back, a face Hans recognized from TV. "Are the parents or other family members going to take a polygraph?"

"I've already stated there's no indication the parents were involved." Annoyance finally and a good deal more sincere than the affected indignation he'd thrown at the big-haired boy. "The same holds true for the rest of the family. It's a little early to be discussing polygraphs." Craig pointed at a new hand.

"Do you believe a vehicle was involved?"

"Believe? Let's say it seems likely." Craig lifted his hand to select someone new.

"Are you just guessing," the reporter hastened, "or do you have a lead on the vehicle?"

"I'd rather not discuss those details. I will say generally that the nature of the evidence so far and the lack of eyewitnesses suggest the use of a vehicle. Which really underscores the need for the public's vigilance. We want people on the lookout for Josh."

A new hand. "Is there any indication this is part of a serial pattern? Could it be someone who's done this before?"

"Impossible to answer that question yet," Craig said. "But it's been many years since we've had a stranger abduction in Ogden. If this person's done it before, it wasn't around here. With that said, there's no evidence indicating we're dealing with a serial abductor." Craig pointed.

"How long will the area search continue? And how far will it be expanded?"

Craig nodded. "Unless we find Josh, the area search will continue until we're reasonably certain he's elsewhere. We'll be pursuing other leads at the same time, of course, and we'll go anywhere those leads take us. As I've said, we're searching door-to-door and canvassing the foothills. Should that turn nothing up, we'll reevaluate. Naturally, we hope to find Josh very soon."

"Are people safe to let their children play outside?"

Craig smiled. "Let's not get hysterical, folks. This is rare. The statistics haven't suddenly changed. Even if this hadn't happened, it's a good idea to keep an eye on small children. Big children too for that matter. Two more questions, then we'll wrap this up."

"Were the Christophers negligent in letting Josh walk alone? Will they be charged with negligence?"

Craig scratched an eyebrow. "This is a quiet neighborhood. The Christophers had no reason to suspect something like this would happen. Josh's destination was close, just around the corner, and he'd previously walked to this friend's house without incident. If that's negligence, most parents are guilty at one time or another. From everything I've seen, the Christophers are excellent parents." Craig pointed. "Last question."

"Is there reason to believe the boy was specifically targeted? Or do you think this was more a crime of opportunity?"

"We really—" Craig stopped. He cocked his head then swiveled and looked behind him.

Hans had heard it too, a high-pitched emission barely audible but gaining volume fast. It took him only an instant to source it. Melissa dropped her statement, a wad now, then followed it down, landing hard on her knees. The crowd heaved forward. Cameras volleyed shots. Karley, who had lunged too late, swooped in and anchored her upright on her knees. Shrieking now, Melissa began to flail. Joe squatted beside her, his dexterity surprising. The photo lay on the grass where he'd dropped it, and Hans snatched it up, afraid the glass would be shattered and cut someone. Absorbing blows Joe wrapped his long arms around Melissa and restrained her against him. And still she fought.

"Get on this side of her," Sally ordered. "Make a wall." She began pulling family members into place between the cameras and Melissa. Craig stood back and watched.

Joe hung on, but Melissa was strong. She hauled him this way and that. Working from the side, Karley tried to brace the couple, while the family closed ranks around them. Though hardly silent, Melissa was no longer shrieking. Rather she had started to laugh, a sound like laughter, though it was not amusement Hans saw. Wide-eyed with panic, Melissa threw her body back and forth, her head buffeting Joe's chest with hard blows. Twisting, she broke loose, and Joe lunged for new purchase. She began pounding her face against him. Hans passed Sally the photo and, bending down, caught Melissa's head and tried to still it.

"No!" she cried. Wrenching free, she threw herself backwards, and Joe landed on top of her. Karley and Hans, like obscene participants, pinned Melissa's arms to the ground. Finally, gradually, Melissa ceased her floundering. Staring at the sky, she breathed heavily, a thick bloody rivulet coursing from one nostril. It pooled at the corner of her mouth before continuing toward earth.

"Do we need an ambulance?" Craig asked. He spoke quietly, addressing Hans.

Hans glanced up at the handkerchief the detective extended and accepted it without answering. He cleaned the blood from Melissa's face. She closed her eyes and didn't protest as he palpitated the bridge of her nose. Though already swelling, it didn't feel broken. He couldn't be sure without an X-ray. Joe reversed himself off her a little at a time. Kneeling between her up-bent legs, he massaged his chest and watched her.

"You're going to be all right," Hans told Melissa. "Take your time."

For all her struggling, she had not begun to weep, not really. A pair of tears welled in the outside corners of her eyes. They released and ran into her ears.

"Can you get up?" Hans asked.

She nodded and opened her eyes. "I'm sorry," she said. "I'm so sorry." She lifted her head, then put it back down. Finally she got her elbows beneath her. Karley and Hans helped her sit up.

"No hurry," Hans said. "Take it slow." He wiped a new issue of blood from her lip, then handed her the handkerchief. She dabbed at her nose, dried her ears and eyes. Curt stepped in and helped Joe to his feet. The crowd behind them murmured, restless in their exclusion. Hans caught movement to the side, the boldest of the camera people creeping up the grassy knoll for a better shot. The family and Sally, even Craig, circled around Melissa.

"Can we go now?" she asked.

"As soon as you're ready," Karley said. "When you can walk, we'll go."

"I'm ready," Melissa said. She gave Hans and Karley her hands and they lifted her to her feet. Half-turned, Melissa leaned into Karley. It was more than a weight-giving embrace or, rather, was an embrace designed to lighten more than the physical. Stepping crosswise, she hid against Karley, refusing to relinquish even an inch of contact. The family parted to let them through, and as they did, the crowd began to applaud. The applause swelled with cries and whistles, a grateful display for these spoils of a rough game. It was sportsmanship of the poorest taste, and Hans was too stunned to be incensed.

"That's all for now, folks." It was Craig speaking loudly above the dwindling cheers. "When we have more, we'll let you know."

Melissa's statement lay where she'd dropped it, now pressed into the trampled lawn. Hans picked it up and stuffed it in his pocket, then stood for a moment watching the crowd disperse. When he could bear it no longer, he turned for the parking lot. The others were under the canopy now, moving slowly, almost to the cars. Theirs was a laden retreat, every shoulder stooped. Amazing, Hans thought, how much nothing weighed. It could atomize you, the absence that lingered when everything else had been plundered.

Silk Panties

At the end of May, the bishop informed Joe that, absent subsequent misdeed, he and Melissa could marry in December. The bishop set a tentative date—October—for Joe's ordination to the Melchizedek Priesthood and, as a show of trust, halved, then halved again the number of required interviews. Melissa's relief could have filled a Mormon temple. She immediately began to plot her defloration. Reaching out to a collegial doctor at work, she got herself on the pill.

■

Melissa also began to collect lingerie. Silk was her favorite, panties and bras and camisoles. Once she began buying, it was hard to stop. Beyond her hope that Joe would find her out, she liked the way the cloth felt against her skin. She liked the way *she* felt wearing lingerie and already dreaded the day she would have to don the temple garment, the knee-length underpants and short-sleeved top required of all temple-endowed members. She should have known Karley would eventually find her out. If only Joe had been so nosey.

"Well, I'll be damned," Karley said. She looked Melissa up and down. Her penchant for John Wayne language made her the frequent object of Margaret's reproaches.

"What?" Melissa said. "Don't you knock?" She had selected a black silk combo for her date with Joe, lots of lace, which was all she wore, when Karley barged through her unlocked door. A wedding dress to get into, that pill weight to manage—she'd stepped up the intensity of her workouts. She was in better shape

87

now than she'd been since high school and was secretly pleased someone had finally found her out.

"Don't give me that," Karley said, circling in. "Since when did you start buying black lingerie?" Hooking a finger in the waist of Melissa's panties, she felt the material, "Wow, silk." She drew back the elastic and let it go.

"Knock it off. You'll stretch them out."

"What could this mean? Sexy underwear is worn to be seen, Melissa. To be unwrapped like a present. By someone else."

"I'm not even going to dignify that."

It was not possible to live in the same house with a sister for nearly twenty-one years without disclosing, or having exposed, a few secrets about one's self. Especially if that sister was Karley. Standard bickering aside, they were very close. Karley alone—make that Karley and Joe—knew the extent of Melissa's sexual preoc-cupation. In masturbation they truly were sisters. In guilt, which Karley suffered terribly, they were two entirely different species.

"You know what they say," Karley said, sinking onto the edge of the bed. She smiled at Melissa, doe-eyed Karley, as delicate and deadly as belladonna.

Melissa poked her head in the closet and began rummaging for something to match her black underwear. "No, Karley. What do they say?"

"A Mormon girl's engagement is the horniest time of her life."

For pity's sake. "You don't say," Melissa mumbled. She and Joe were just seeing a movie, nothing that called for the formality of black underwear. She pulled out a pair of jeans. Jeans went with anything.

"So is it?"

"Is it what?"

"The horniest time of your life."

Melissa smiled her ho-hum cat smile. "What do you think?"

Karley grinned. "I think you're so horny you can't stand it. Tell me. I'm dying to hear."

"No way." Melissa buttoned her jeans and returned to the closet.

"Oh, come on. I can keep a secret."

"There's nothing to tell, Karley." Melissa held up a blouse, replaced it to consider another. Something dark. "All right, fine. Sometimes things get a little heated. But we behave."

"I don't believe you."

"Believe me."

"What if I tell you a secret?"

Melissa glanced back at Karley. "You have a secret?"

Karley reclined on her elbows. "I might."

"What secret could you possibly have?"

Head back Karley studied the stars on the ceiling. "Trade?" she said.

Melissa draped the blouse over a chair and sat down beside her sister. "What is it, Karley?" Karley sat up and shrugged. "You can tell me. I won't tell anyone."

"That's just like you, to be so good." Karley was fighting tears now.

"Oh, honey," Melissa said. She took her sister's hand. "You already know the worst of it. I do that thing. I just like it so much I can't stop. Isn't that bad enough?"

Karley rubbed her nose. "That's nothing. It doesn't hurt anybody no matter what they say."

Oh, but Karley was making it hard to keep secrets. "What's the matter, honey?"

Karley sighed. "I know I'm bad, but I kinda wish these meant something." Reaching cross-body, she poked Melissa's boob. "It'd make me feel so much better."

Melissa smiled. And hated herself.

"Remember Travis Baxter?"

"Of course, he's darling. I had hopes for you and Travis."

Karley nodded. "Well, before he left on his mission—" She covered her mouth.

"Come on. It can't be that bad."

"I wish." Karley took a deep breath. "I guess you'd say things got a little out of control—"

"*You had sex?*"

Karley slapped Melissa's leg. Hard. "Not *that* out of control." She glanced at her sister's face then away. "I let him touch me. I touched him, too. It happened a couple of times actually."

Sweet Karley. "That's it?" Melissa said. "That's all you did?"

Karley peered at Melissa, uncertain of her sincerity. She had begun to cry. "That's all we did, but that's not the worst of it."

Melissa put an arm around her. "What's the worst of it?"

"You know I have these pre-mission interviews with the bishop? Well, we were finishing up—this was last week—when he asked if I had any unresolved sins I needed to confess. I'd been feeling pretty awful about what happened between Travis and me, and I'd been meaning to confess, but I just couldn't get up the nerve, and then, well, he asked."

Mention of bishops and confessions—Melissa's insides buzzed like a beehive in a hailstorm. Joe was quiet about his interviews, and she didn't press, though his silence always left her a little afraid. "Was he shocked?"

"No. He was great, totally laid back. At least, about my part. He didn't even tell me not to take the sacrament for a week. But he freaked when he found out Travis already had his mission call when it happened. He told me he'd have to contact Travis's bishop, and if Travis hadn't confessed before leaving, there could be real problems. He had the Melchizedek Priesthood by then, and he'd gone through the temple too. Oh, gosh, Melissa," she cried. "I just feel so awful. I mean, I was a willing participant. What if he gets sent home from his mission because of me?"

"They won't send him home," Melissa said, though only because she didn't want to believe it possible.

"Maybe," Karley said. She sat up and, finding nothing better, used Melissa's rumpled top sheet to dry her eyes.

"Wipe your nose on that you die."

Karley laughed. "Sure you don't have any secrets?"

"Karley."

"Damn," she sighed. "Your wicked sister could sure use some company about now."

Doing the Florence Nightingale

Hans cracked Curt and Margaret's bedroom door. One of the bedside lamps was dialed on low, its rheostat buzzing loudly. Melissa lay curled on her side facing away from Joe. Stretched out on his back, Joe studied the ceiling. Melissa lifted her head and looked at Hans.

"Hey," Hans said. "I brought a fresh icepack and some ibuprofen." The other Ziploc bag lay on the bed between her and Joe, the ice inside mostly water now.

Melissa pushed herself up. It'd been nearly an hour since they'd come in to rest, and Hans doubted either of them had managed to drop off. Melissa's nose bulged at the bridge, a dangling parenthesis beneath each eye, not much discoloration but suggestive of more to come.

"Headache?" Hans asked, handing her the ice and a glass of water. He opened the bottle and shook free a pair of ibuprofen.

"Since before the press conference." She put the bag in her lap and accepted the tablets.

"Lots of swelling. We may want to have it X-rayed. Let's see what it looks like tomorrow."

"It's not broken," Melissa said. "An X-ray wouldn't help even if it was."

She was likely right on both counts. "How about you, Joe? A couple of ibuprofen might make you feel a little better."

Joe rolled his head back and forth.

"Karley ordered Thai. It'll be here soon. You should both eat something." Hans accepted the glass from Melissa and placed it on the nightstand. "Here, hand me that other bag."

91

Melissa passed him the spent ice, then sank back into her pillow. The fresh bag waited in her lap. "I couldn't eat anything."

"You could give it a try."

Melissa lifted the ice and put it on her face. The bag covered her nose and eyes. "Do you think they'll show my fit on TV?"

Hans didn't answer right away. "It doesn't matter if they do. People understand."

"Mmmmm," she moaned. "Right in front of all those cameras."

"It's hardly a thing to be embarrassed about."

"Oh, yeah. It is. I wigged out."

Above them in the attic, a cooling rafter complained, the pop of a knuckle. The family had assembled here after the press conference to wait for the police to release Melissa and Joe's house.

"Tell me," Hans said softly. "How much have you taken today?" Melissa lay very still. Finally she removed the ice from her face. Lifting her head, she met Hans's gaze then sank back into the pillow and replaced the bag over her eyes. "Tell me what you took, Melissa."

"Ativan."

Hans shook his head. "I don't think so. I've been watching. You don't act like you've taken a tranquilizer. At the press conference, you were rubbing your nose and hands. Ativan doesn't do that."

Melissa laughed.

"You're not telling me the truth."

"You're really something, Hans."

"I don't know what that means, Melissa. But I do know you've taken something."

She sighed. "I took some hydrocodone." Joe rolled his head and looked at her.

"How much?" Hans asked.

"A ten," she said. "I took a ten."

"Where did you get a ten? I only prescribed fives."

"I took two fives," she said.

"Anything else? Muscle relaxants?"

"No," she said. "Just two fives."

"How about earlier today?"

She didn't answer.

"You've only taken the two fives? That's all the entire day?"

"The two fives and the two ibuprofen you just gave me."

Joe ran his hands through his hair. Groaning, he massaged his eyeballs.

"How long ago?"

"Half an hour before we left for the press conference. I didn't think I could get through it, so I took them."

"How often do you take hydrocodone to get through things?" he asked.

Melissa's frosty voice rose through the ice bag. "You don't give me that many, Hans. My neck was hurting, and I had a terrible headache. I should've only taken one. I took the second one for the wrong reasons. I don't make a habit of it."

Cursing himself for prescribing her anything, Hans tried to decide if he believed her. What had possessed him to suspend best practice and common sense? Melissa was family and employee both, which made their arrangement ethical quicksand. "I don't prescribe painkillers for anxiety, Melissa. Take the Ativan next time."

"I *hate* Ativan," she snapped. "I'd rather take nothing than feel like a zombie."

Hans wished he could see Melissa's face. "No more hydrocodone. And you, Joe, maybe it's time you try the Antabuse." Melissa and Joe breathed in and out. More gently, he added, "Let me help you get through this the right way."

"Platitudes," Melissa said. "And a bunch of covering your own ass."

Hans out-waited his anger. "I'll let you know when the food gets here. Until then see if you can drop off. Everyone's tired, especially you two." He turned to leave.

"I won't do that again." Hans turned back. He thought she was speaking of painkillers. "I won't go on TV. I won't speak to reporters."

"You don't have to. Someone else can do it. Karley, perhaps."

"What about Mom and Dad? What have they said?"

"About speaking to the press?"

"About Joe's drinking."

The question, the self-serving underbelly of it, seemed entirely to disregard Joe. He might not have even been in the room. The fading coal of Hans's anger glowed a little brighter. "When things settle down we'll all talk it through."

"It won't help," Melissa sighed. "I wish they didn't know."

"It's better this way."

Melissa shook her head. Joe stared at the ceiling. "Have you told anyone about my pills?"

"No."

"Don't. It'll only make things worse."

Melissa's need to manage information was all too familiar. "You and your secrets."

Melissa sat up quickly, her eyes radiant with anger. "Don't talk to me about secrets, Hans. You're not living my life. You asked about the meds, and I told you the truth. Now honor your oath and keep it to yourself."

Hans stepped to the nightstand, retrieved the water, and carried it to Joe's side of the bed. "You need to drink water, Joe."

From far away, Joe searched him out. "Leave it."

Hans put the water on the table beside him, the bottle of ibuprofen next to the glass. "Someone'll call you when the food arrives."

He closed the bedroom door, then paused in the hallway to calm himself. It was true, there were no rules here, no precedent in his experience to guide him. The darkness of his exchange with Melissa shrouded his perception. His in-laws' home seemed dim tonight, foreign and shadow-laden. More than daylight had given way to nightfall.

In the kitchen he found Karley at the table chewing on a curl of hair. She traced rectangles around three phone numbers she'd written on a notepad. Hans opened the Ziploc bag and poured the contents in the sink then set the bag aside for later use. "Who's that?" He nodded at the pad as he took the chair beside her.

Karley lifted her phone and checked the time. "Theo Evans."

It took Hans a moment to place the name. "The attorney, right?"

"Sally says we need someone good. Someone with criminal experience."

"Wow, Karley. Just wow."

"I know."

"What did he say?"

Straightening her legs, Karley fluttered her feet like flippers, then returned them to the floor. Hans had always loved her talent for releasing tension through the movements of her body. "I haven't been able to reach him. I left a message on his home machine."

"You found his home number?"

Karley smiled. "Cathy Reynolds."

Hans nodded, remembering. "I'd forgotten she works for him. You should be a detective."

"No, thanks." She reached over and took his hand.

"I saw you talking to Jared," he said. "How was that?"

"Bad. Self-righteous little prick. I did, however, apologize for beating the crap out of him."

It was Hans's turn to smile. "So how about you? How you doing?"

"Scared to death." She looked out the window. "It's dark. Joshua's still gone." Hans studied their reflections in the glass. They both looked scared to death. Karley sniffed. She drummed the pencil on the pad. "How are Melissa and Joe?"

"Joe's despondent. Melissa's all over the place. She'll have black eyes come morning."

Karley shook her head. "I guess I'm staying in town tonight."

Hans considered their hands, then began to turn Karley's wedding band on her finger. "I need to run up to the hospital for a little while. I'll meet you at Melissa and Joe's afterwards."

"Why don't you just go home? Sally's spending the night, too, and there's not really room for everyone. One of us should get a good night's sleep. If anything changes, I'll call you."

Though Hans hated to leave her, he knew she was right. "I'll swing by after I finish up at the hospital. Make sure no one needs anything before I head home."

Karley watched Hans turn her ring. The kitchen's large round clock ticked off the seconds. In the living room basketball pundits analyzed the self-evident. "What are we going to do?" Karley said.

Hans had long-since depleted his stockpile of sage answers. "I have no idea."

The doorbell rang, and they both turned their heads. "Dinner," Karley said, her attention already fading back to her wedding band.

"What?" Hans asked finally.

Karley looked up. This close, in this light, he could isolate the gold flecks in her irises. "Did you notice Melissa's not wearing her wedding ring?"

Hans nodded. "I did. I think it's the first time I've ever seen her without it."

"I just can't shake this feeling," Karley said. "Melissa and Joe—" She underlined one of the telephone numbers, then tossed the pencil. It rolled off the pad and halfway across the table. "Never mind. I don't know what I'm thinking."

With the tip of his tongue, Hans plied a tiny split in his lip. He squeezed Karley's hand, then scooted his chair back. "Come on. Let's go pay for that food."

It Began Simply Enough

It began simply enough.

"I must have done something bad," Melissa moaned, this in response to a single sharp slap Joe had delivered to her rump as she came.

As usual they were at Joe's apartment. He lay on the floor, his head propped on a throw pillow. Sitting astride him, she fostering a contact not dissimilar from the one she'd employed the previous Halloween. The position was a favorite and not just for sentimental reasons. Melissa wore a light summer skirt, thigh length, and if her behavior was less than modest, the skirt at least offered the illusion of propriety. Every so often she tried to give him a glimpse by readjusting the cloth around her. White today and silk. She liked skirts—fewer layers and a tempting access for Joe.

"You're always bad," he teased.

Melissa stood up, which surprised Joe as he'd only brought her once. She made much of this dismount, skimming a leg above his face. She paced for a minute, then stopped and looked down at him. "Is that why you spanked me?"

He sat up. "Maybe. Did it hurt?"

Melissa ignored his question. "Really, I have been awfully bad." A wire-thin current threaded right down her center. "Maybe you should have spanked me before."

He stared up at her, his face a shifting cinema of morphing desires. "I'm not a hitter, Melissa." He got to his feet, his eyes never leaving hers.

"Nobody said anything about hitting," she said. "But you have

97

to admit, I've been bad, tempting you when you're just trying to be strong for me."

Chin down, Joe studied her. It was something to watch him register the possibilities. "I suppose you haven't been very helpful."

Melissa traced a tight circle around him, her palm sliding over the bulge in his pants. It had to be painful, confined like that. "You know, I'd let you do anything you want, everything, and still you resist. That's not very nice of me, not when you're trying to be so good." It was the first time she'd articulated her wholesale availability, at least outside her own head.

"No, it's not. Not nice at all."

"I've felt awfully guilty, Joe." She stopped and peered at him sidelong. "Maybe if you punished me, we'd both feel better."

"Huh," he said. His voice was tight, his cheeks streaked pink. Lordy, but he was easy on the eyes, those chiseled bones, that shapely nose, his long hair a little wild. Of late, with regularity, Melissa had encountered his desire, but this was something new. "What are you asking for, Melissa?"

"A spanking maybe. I deserve it."

He looked up at the ceiling, then back at Melissa. She could practically hear his self-control creaking. His pulse pounded against his larynx, a hard little jackhammer. "You have been pretty bad."

"Yes, I have. You'd be doing me a favor. I'm sure my behavior would improve."

They gazed at each other, a goodbye of sorts, a sendoff for Joe's resistance. She'd already realized what he had not. "It's the right thing to do, Joe." Smiling demurely, she touched his hand then bent over, legs straight, and placed both palms on the sofa.

Would it have surprised Joe to learn that Melissa had entertained such a moment in fantasy? Not with him necessarily, but with the nameless, faceless men who sometimes populated her waking dreams. Even as a girl, she had found the notion arousing. She was no pushover, Melissa, yet the warmth of submission drew her in, the loss of control and with it responsibility. Her aggressiveness with Joe had been a matter of necessity. But in the sanctuary of her own bedroom, it was just such a vulnerability she'd longed for. She'd dreamed herself bent over and spanked. Not always, not very often, but sometimes.

She looked back at Joe. "Go ahead. I'm ready." He turned away, then circled back. He ran a palm over her bottom. "Come on, Joe."

"Naughty girl," he said. "You need to be taught a lesson."

"That's right. Teach me a lesson."

He drew back and slapped her. It didn't hurt at all. She spread her legs and pushed out her rump. She could tell she was going to need a broader base. "I'm not a three-year-old, Joe." He slapped her again, and this one stung. It was almost what she'd hoped for. "Ouch. Should I count?" This counting thing—she'd seen it in a movie once. She'd liked it.

"Count, Melissa." He slapped her.

"Three." She glanced back at his trouser tent. "Four. Five." It was beginning to warm up down there and not just her butt. "Six. Seven. Eight."

"Are you sorry yet?"

"No. But I want to be. Ouch! Nine. Ten!" These final two he'd delivered more firmly, one to each cheek.

"What do I have to do to make you sorry, Melissa?"

"Tell me to lift my skirt." Joe turned away and paced a tight circle, his fingers laced in his hair. Coming around he slapped her hard. "Eleven!"

"This is why you need to be spanked." That did it—Melissa jabbed a hand between her legs. "Stop that and lift your skirt. Hold it up with both hands."

Praise the Lord! Reaching back, she scrunched the skirt around her waist. Not exactly how she'd imagined it, but there they were anyway, her white silk panties. She was a two-legged stool in a cool breeze, and the promise of humiliation was a revelation. She could feel herself shedding the accumulated duplicity. Joe's reaction was as good as she could have hoped. Squatting behind her, he enjoyed a long look then nuzzled in for a big kiss on her lips. His face felt cool, even through the silk. He pulled away before she was ready.

"Silk," he said, slipping a finger beneath the cloth. She pressed back, and he gave her a tiny taste. He withdrew too soon and she groaned. "You should see this red against the white. Your skin's on fire. It's amazing."

Melissa was tempted to ask for a mirror. "You have no idea how bad I can be."

"That bad, huh?"

"It's going to take a lot more to punish me for what I'm about to do."

Joe laughed and stood up. It may have been a game to him, but it wasn't to Melissa, not any more. By accident, she had stumbled into a whole new truth. There was salvation in this marvelous pain, forgiveness in submission. With each jolt, she'd felt a flake of culpability shake free and spin away.

"Count," he ordered.

She did, and this time every spank hurt. It was hard to keep her balance. By six the pain was a white happy heat. Little by little she was coming clean. She needed to cry but was afraid Joe would stop. He paused between spanks to caress her bottom. She ached to touch herself, but he'd ordered her otherwise. She wanted to obey but wanted her hand more.

"Hold on." She slipped out of the skirt and let it drop to the carpet. In a rush of fingers, she undid a few buttons and stripped her blouse over her head.

Joe, the lovely boy, fairly shuddered.

"You didn't come, did you?" Without waiting for an answer, she dropped to her knees.

"What if I can't stop myself?" But Joe's resistance had already sailed. He slipped a hot hand inside her bra.

"I don't want you to stop. I'll go crazy if you do." She was frantic, twisting and pulling. It was surprisingly hard to undo a button at that angle. Finally, she lowered his zipper and peeled down his jeans, then returned for his Calvin Klein boxer briefs. Good taste, though they were sad things now, stretched all out of shape and spotted with pre-cum. She doubted they'd ever be the same.

Joe gripped his shorts by the waistband. "This is it, Melissa." Battling for her still. She couldn't have loved him more. "I don't think—"

"*Don't* think." Fisting his underwear, she yanked them from his hands. "Holy crap!" she whispered. She throttled the thing and stuck it in her mouth.

"Ohhh! I'm moving too fast. *You're going to make me come.*"

It was a difficult maneuver, but Melissa pried herself off him. "Now I've really been bad," she said.

Standing on his cuffs, Joe pulled his legs from his jeans. He stripped off the underwear, then stood up and did the same with his T-shirt. He waved like a limb before her fascinated gaze. Reaching underneath, she rolled his testicles. Amazing.

"Get up," he ordered, then took her by the wrists and hauled her to her feet. In a strong, fluid movement, he spun her toward the sofa and forced her over again. He didn't even wait until she was braced.

"One," Melissa yelped. She spread her legs. This was the hardest yet, almost too much. "Two."

"You like being bad, Melissa?"

"Yes," she whispered. Joe had his lines down cold now.

"What?"

"Three," she said more loudly. "Yes, I like it. I'm sorry. Four."

"You want me to take down your panties and spank your bare ass?"

"Please." Like a homing pigeon, Melissa's hand flew to its roost. She was very close to the edge of the cliff. "Five. Six." *The pain was beautiful.* Melissa burned from the backs of her knees to a hand's span above her coccyx. It was a purifying heat, she felt nearly forgiven. She was vaguely aware she was crying. "Seven."

"Three more and down they come."

"Eight. Nine." A hand in the silk, she clenched her thighs.

"Ten," they said together, and she threw herself over the edge.

"Take them down now!" she begged. "Take them down and give me ten more." She planted the crown of her head on the arm of the sofa and tried to look back upside-down. Her panties slid down and caught around her knees. Joe worked a finger inside. *"Oh,"* she said.

"Oh," Joe said, then he struck her with such force it nearly lifted her off her feet. "I'm not going to make it to ten," he exclaimed.

"One more like that, Joe. *Please.* Then whatever you want."

Her knees buckled with the blow, and as she melted to the floor, the final tendon popped. Helium light she lifted off the terra. "You're crying," Joe said.

"It's good. Keep going. Everything's perfect."

"You're sure?"

"I'm positive."

Languid and pliant, she allowed him to arrange her. She was under his control, exactly how she wanted it. Joe was gentle now, his fierceness swallowed by this new desire. Melissa knew it would hurt and couldn't have cared less. She'd earned this and so had Joe. He finished removing her panties and unclasped her bra. He admired her for a moment, then kissed her breasts, one hand gently exploring below. "Oh, Melissa," he said. "You're so beautiful."

"Go ahead, Joe. We've earned it."

"I don't have any protection. I threw my condoms away."

"You don't need a condom. I've been on the pill for months."

"Sneaky girl," he laughed. Then, "I'll try to be careful." Such a strange thing to say given the recklessness that had brought them here.

"Oh, fetch!" Melissa cried.

"Should I stop?"

"No!"

A girl hears first-time stories, most of them fearsome but none detailing the pain Melissa had already endured. This new thing hurt and in exactly the right way. Joe held himself still for ten full seconds. Big eyed, both of them, they stared at each other. Spiraling, spiraling Melissa wept freely.

"Move *now*," she whispered, and as Joe complied, a butt-scratching, back-bending orgasm blinded her. She wrapped her legs around him and squeezed.

Joe kissed her then, his entire body tensing, and Melissa received his breath and sucked it in, his full, stuttered expulsion all hers. His final thrusts notched her across the carpet. "I love you," he cried. "Oh, God, but I do."

Eyes closed, wringing tears, Melissa laughed. Joe relaxed his body onto hers then, misreading her expression, started to get off. "No, stay," she said, pulling him back. He settled on his elbows and studied her face. She wiped a tear from his chin and licked the salt from her thumb. "These are good tears?"

"Good and bad," he admitted.

"Don't say bad, sweetheart. It's okay. I'm so happy. You didn't take it. I gave it to you."

"It was wonderful, Melissa. But what are we going to do now?"

She smiled. "More of the same I hope."

"You know what I mean."

"It was right, Joe. Don't you see? It was absolutely right." He narrowed his eyes, his unwavering gaze utterly attentive. He was trying to see, and his effort alone put him better than halfway there. "I paid for it," she said softly. "And so did you. We paid for it together."

"You mean the spanking?" He shifted his weight and dried his face. He looked at her doubtfully.

"Yes, I mean the spanking. But I also mean our love and your return to the church and how hard we try everywhere else."

Joe shook his head, but there was a smile behind his doubt. "Do you know how strange that sounds, Melissa?"

"I don't care how it sounds. Here, get off, let me show you something." He peeled away, and her damp skin contracted. Shedding her unclasped bra, she rose and turned. "What does it look like?"

"Oh, Melissa, I think I bruised you. You have handprints all over your butt. I didn't mean to bruise you."

"See," she said. "Paid in full."

"This is crazy." Joe touched her bottom, traced the marks. "Can you imagine what the bishop would say?"

"Forget the bishop. We're right with God and that's all that matters. This is between you and me and God. We've done our part. We get to be ourselves with each other. Isn't that proof enough?"

He caressed the welts. He was trying to make it work.

"Will you trust me on this? Please, Joe. You've got to trust me."

"Does it always have to be like this?"

Melissa shook her head. "Not always. Just once in a while. Didn't you like it?"

He sighed. "Too much. But I don't like this." He touched her bruises.

"You'll learn," she said. "I don't mind a bruise or two."

"No bruises," he insisted.

"Okay. No bruises." She grinned. "I'd have to hide them from Karley anyway. Now, stand up."

He did as she asked, and as Melissa kneeled down, a warm tide released between her legs. Her fingers when she investigated came up bloody and slick. "We did it," she said, showing him.

"I guess we did."

It was all the assurance Melissa needed. She reached for his underwear and cleaned herself. Tossing the shorts, she smiled at Joe, then lowered her gaze and launched the expedition. He immediately began to harden. "What are you doing?" he laughed.

"Testing rumor." It was the last she would speak for some time.

Day Two

"Faith! Faith!" cried the husband, "look up to heaven, and resist the wicked one."

—*Young Goodman Brown*, Nathaniel Hawthorne

Seymour the Sea Turtle

Craig found Seymour behind a massive monitor, his translucent purple eyelids at half-mast. Seymour looked asleep because Seymour always looked asleep. Every five or six seconds, his mandible turned a tight revolution. He claimed never in his life to have used a tobacco product but was addicted to nicotine gum all the same. Craig had never seen him without a piece in his mouth. But for Seymour the lab was empty.

"Don't you ever leave this place?"

Seymour's hooded gaze slid up and over the monitor. In some previous life, he'd been a sea turtle—Craig pictured him rising impossibly like a boulder to the surface. "Oh, hey, Lieutenant Craig. You startled me."

Seymour in terror looked like Seymour in slumber. "Name's Milo, remember?"

Seymour selected a Corn Nut from the pile beside his keyboard and tossed it in his mouth with the gum. "I keep forgetting."

Craig smiled. Truth was he dug Seymour. As far as lab nerds went, they didn't come any better. The cannabis he vaped in his van every break kept him sharp on the blade of savant-hood. It slowed his brain to a steerable speed.

"So, anyway," Seymour said. "You're up late, too."

"That I am," Craig agreed. "Jill must have gone home for the night? I was hoping for an update."

"Yeah. She was pretty bushed."

"Had a big day."

"Big day for everyone."

Craig waited. Waited some more. "Maybe you could fill me in."

107

"Oh. Well. Yeah. Maybe I can help. I can try." Seymour rolled his chair aft and stood. He picked another Corn Nut from the pile. "Corn Nut?"

"I'll pass, but thanks."

"Sure, okay." Seymour scanned the lab.

"So what you got there on the screen?"

"This? Oh, fiber. This one's still mounted on the scope. I'm just trying to get a few controls catalogued. Everything's a rush, you know."

Craig walked around the desk. The image stretched across the monitor, the magnified fiber as thick and textured as a cedar fence post. Craig owned a basic understanding of fiber analysis. This one appeared synthetic.

"Poly?"

Seymour nodded. "Petroleum based anyway."

"Carpet?"

"Yup. We took it from the child molester's car."

Stillwell. There were those in the department who still placed hope in Sherm. Craig was not among them. Sherm's boss and time card had corroborated his alibi, as had the security feed at Carl Jr's. His mother, Betty, had told the same story. Sherm the Sperm Stillwell was a molester not a kidnapper. He'd stolen to the scene only to thrill in the living porn. "Anything pop out?"

"One thing maybe." The mouse clicks came in quick succession, the images and dialogue boxes gone before they arrived.

"What am I looking at?"

"Another synthetic. We're still working it up."

"More carpeting?"

"Nah. Tough to say what it comes from, but the material's not right for carpet. Looks more like the nylon canvas used in everything from jackets to gym bags."

"Where did you find it?"

Hard to believe but Seymour smiled. "We scoped the surface of the gift before we fumed it. Found this caught in the weave of the paper. Might have never seen it without magnification."

Craig leaned in and studied the image. It revealed nothing up close that it didn't from a distance. "From the gutter water maybe?"

"Maybe. We found all sorts of crap on the paper, all of it organic except this and a shred of candy wrapper. Leaves, dirt, gutter debris."

"Other theories?"

Seymour studied the screen. "I'd say something off the boy's clothes except the color and the material don't match anything the mother said he was wearing. But look at the top edge. That nice straight line?"

"Cut," Craig said.

Seymour nodded. "Probably. Hard to be positive, small as it is. Jill's gonna send someone shopping, see if we can duplicate what the boy was wearing. I'm not holding my breath."

Process of elimination, technology and luck, all of it older than Abel and Cain. "So we're hoping our guy handled the gift."

"Touched it. Rubbed up against it." Seymour picked up a pair of Corn Nuts and palmed them into his mouth.

Craig smiled. "This fiber's good, Seymour. Nice work."

Seymour hoisted his eyelids a full half-millimeter. "Only if we find the source."

"And the book? You find anything else besides the fiber?"

"A few latents but only on the tape. Thumbs and a couple of index fingers. They all belonged to the boy's mother."

"Fumes gave you nothing? Not even from the mother?"

Seymour shook his head. "Not so much as a smudge. We tried a number of compounds, too. A lot of water in that book. Still, I was kinda hopeful. I've pulled images off wetter paper than that." Massaging an earlobe he gazed across the room.

"What?"

"I don't know."

"What?"

"Maybe you should take a look yourself."

Craig followed the technician across the lab. At the door to Pre-Processing, Seymour paused to don gloves. He offered Craig a pair.

"How about I promise not to touch."

"Suit yourself." Seymour blew into the gloves before snapping them on. He opened the door and flipped on the light.

The room resembled a glorified pantry after an exceptionally tidy looting. Chain of evidence, intake, and analysis. Nothing stayed here long, especially when the lab was backed up. "This is all Christopher," Seymour said. "We've got the molester's stuff next door."

Craig surveyed the collection, pleased and disappointed the scene had produced so little. "We had to prioritize," Seymour said. "Jill had us start with the book and the molester's stuff. We haven't even opened the parents' cars." He pointed at four large evidence cartons. "Those arrived just before midnight. I haven't taken a look yet."

Craig stepped to the table. The gift was laid out like a bloated corpse, the paper split and gaping. Unlike the room's other evidence, it had not been bagged but left exposed on a short rack for drying. The book was a full inch thicker than when Craig had seen it in the gutter. The once-white wrapping was gray now, the splits along the edges detouring around the tape. The wrapping along the spine remained intact. Harry Potter was visible through the tissue.

"Amazing you found anything at all."

"I know. I'm good. Got a ten-cent raise last year to prove it." Like dismantling a bomb, Seymour levitated the book and rolled it over. Careful of every fold and gap, he placed it back on the rack. "Notice anything about the tape?"

It was 1:00 a.m., and Craig's world resembled a 3-D movie without glasses. "Scotch Tape," he said. "Still attached to the paper despite the water. Taped all the way along the seam. One long strip."

"And where's the seam?"

"Off center. Near the spine."

"Right. Not on it but near it."

"Okay. I'm with you."

"The boy's how old?"

"Five."

"How big's a five-year-old?"

"About yay-high, I suppose." Craig hovered a hand a yard or so above the floor.

The gold hoop Seymour had looped through the cartilage of

his auricle flapped about as he scratched his ear. "And a kid that size, how big would you say his hands are?"

For a half second, Craig didn't get the question. "I'll be."

"Yup."

"He couldn't avoid the tape. A book this big, he'd have needed both hands to carry it. He couldn't have missed."

Seymour smiled again. A banner night. "Not unless his hands were covered. Gloves. Mittens. But the mother didn't mention his hands, right? And it wasn't cold."

No, the Christopher woman had not mentioned gloves or mittens. Not to Craig, not to the responding officer. "There's got to be a simple explanation. Maybe he pulled his hands into his sleeves and hugged the book to his chest."

"Still, you'd think he'd've had it in his hands at the beginning. At least to pick it up."

"You'd think." Craig and Seymour stared at the book. "What if he was carrying it under his raincoat? Maybe the mother tucked it underneath, zipped it in, and he never touched it. He gets grabbed and the book falls out."

"That would solve the mystery." Seymour seemed disappointed by the possibility. "That mystery and another. But it does beg a question or two."

"How so?"

"Think about it. At 11:00 this morning, it was raining hard. If you were the mother, would you wrap a book in tissue paper then send it into a downpour with a five-year-old?"

Short-sighted but not impossible. Craig himself had done more careless things. Still, Melissa Christopher did not seem the type to bundle her kid in rain gear but neglect a paper gift she'd just purchased. Craig could see her sending Joshua unaccompanied before he could see her sending the book unprotected. Statistically speaking, the gift was at exponentially greater risk than the boy.

"A plastic grocery bag at least," he said.

Seymour tugged a thin sleeve of gum from his jeans and peeled the backing off a blister. He popped the cube in his mouth and chewed twice. "Inquiring minds."

"No bag at the scene. No mention of a bag from the mother."
Seymour chewed.

"Could have dropped out during the snatch. Could've still had the bag in his hand."

Seymour chewed.

There was something Craig wasn't seeing—there was always something he wasn't seeing. "Begged what question?"

Seymour blinked. "Huh?"

"Book under the coat. Solved a mystery. Begged a question."

"Oh, yeah." Seymour slipped a metal tool from the breast pocket of his lab coat. Tapered-tipped, the tool resembled something a dentist might employ. Leaning close, he slid the flat edge under the wrapping and lifted the tissue until the cloth board beneath was exposed. "Check this out." He ran the tool around the edge to the first corner.

"What am I looking for?"

"See this corner?"

Like the rest of the book, it was swollen but otherwise appeared unremarkable. "Is it different from the others?"

"Nope. Now look at the edge of the board." Seymour lifted the paper, exposing the edges where the tissue was torn.

"What am I looking for?"

"Nothing."

"I don't think I understand, Seymour."

Seymour withdrew the tool and pointed at each corner in turn. "Paper wasn't torn at a single corner. All eight were sound, even after the book took on water."

Craig closed his eyes and smiled. "No dented corners."

"No dented corners."

"No dented cloth board, no torn tissue."

"No abrasions whatsoever. No dents or tears on the cover or the back."

"You'll duplicate the drop?"

Seymour nodded. "I'll try. We've got a bundle of new copies coming tomorrow."

Craig massaged his eyeballs. "Hard, wet cement and not a single mark."

"That gutter wasn't in good shape either. Old and cracked. Lots of rough edges. Loose gravel on the edge of the stream."

"At what height would that be possible?"

Seymour shrugged. "Depends on how it landed. If it came down on a corner, even a very short drop, six inches, would ding it. If it landed perfectly flat or on the spine, say, and if it was dropped straight down, no lateral motion, and if the gutter where it landed was clean and smooth, well." He nodded. "It might be a pretty decent height. Conditions would have to be perfect, of course. We'll see how perfect when we toss a few books."

Craig imagined the book falling from Joshua's hands, from beneath his coat, pictured it slipping from a plastic grocery bag. Eight corners and not a single ding. "The boy put the book down. Something or someone compelled him to put it down. Gently."

"And without leaving a single print."

Craig squinted at the tech. "You're worth a twenty-cent raise, Seymour. Not a penny less."

Seymour peeled off his gloves as he turned for the door. "Cool."

The Morsel

Funny how one thing became another, how the best luck could arrive so massively emblazoned with warnings. It wasn't as though Karley hadn't noticed the handsome young doctor who lived downstairs. Even her missionary companion, Beth Jorgensen, that naïve, earnest, righteous girl, had articulated considerable enthusiasm for The Morsel in 1A. Hans Nordling, *The Morsel*. The nickname delighted Karley, though mostly because Sister Jorgensen had chosen it. And Beth was right. It was not easy to marshal apathy for the charming Norwegian, though Karley worked hard at it, an effort that demanded an oversized concentration. Hans's friendly incursions would have been harmless had she not so anticipated them.

"I'm a ski bum for a few months," he apologized. "An extended holiday to recover from my fellowship." If you were going to be a ski bum, if you had the money, Lillehammer was the place. The natives would complain the Winter Olympics had ruined the local bonhomie. Still, you couldn't contest the world-class skiing.

"If I were to speculate," Beth would opine, "I'd say The Morsel is a man of independent means."

Indeed. Hans Nordling's mother owned the apartment they lived in. The twenty-unit building, Karley would eventually learn, was one of the woman's minor investment properties.

A ski bum, perhaps, though Karley hadn't missed a certain aside Hans had made about the days he donated to a downtown clinic. Real life awaited him in Oslo, but first he'd catch up on all that skiing he'd missed studying medicine in the United States. Karley was not sure what this said about him. He liked to ski. He

115

was civic-minded, socially conscious. But was he a playboy, too? That she found herself constructing a Hans Nordling backstory annoyed her more than a little. He was definitely pleasant to look at. Sweet too, in an unassuming way. If she weren't a missionary, if he were a Mormon … But of course, she was and he wasn't.

"I'm replacing a doctor who's retiring in April," he later clarified. "I had a window so I took it." He shrugged, clearly embarrassed by his life of semi-leisure. "I've been pretty busy these past years."

Such exchanges had become frequent and personal, the three of them visiting in the hallway or at the entrance, on the side-walk in front of their building. Beth had even broached religion, a subject Karley avoided with the neighbors.

"Agnostic," he confessed. "But I'd be happy to hear your message sometime. Maybe I could cook you dinner."

Whoa. Beth's fervor was no less than Karley's and probably as ill-advised. This Hans was crafty. It was nigh impossible for a Mormon missionary to refuse an invitation to preach.

"Maybe so," Karley hedged. "Sometime." She felt righteous in this feat of self-discipline. She might have farted, the way Beth glared at her.

■

Hans opened his apartment door wearing shorts and a sweat-shirt, his face wind burned from days on the slopes. He clutched a beer by the neck, though it was his legs Karley noticed—strong legs, lightly downed, well defined from skiing. She blinked up at his face, horrified she'd looked, and he took a half step toward her. "Is everything okay? Where's your friend?"

"I'm very sorry to bother you," Karley said. "But she's sick and I'm quite worried. I'm hoping you'll look at her. If it's not too much trouble. We don't know any other doctors."

Hans stood his beer on a small table in the entry, depositing his languid bearing with it. It was a subtle transformation, the opposite of self-conscious, and it made him seem wholly new to her. Her radar pinged without sounding his desire. The resistance was gone, and Karley, unbalanced, pitched headfirst off her bat-tlement. To knock her down, he'd merely stepped aside, revealing the man behind the boy. Few things in Karley's experience were sexier than competence.

"Describe her sickness."

Karley struggled to focus. "Fever. She's a little feverish. She's been coughing for days, close to three weeks, but it's turned into something else. It's a deep cough now, croupy. She hasn't been out of bed for two days. She aches like the flu, but I think it's something worse. She seems to be getting weaker."

Hans nodded. "Let me throw some clothes on, and I'll be right up. Will you wait inside?"

"*No.*" Karley shook her head. "But thank you." She'd landed hard and was scared now. Strange, she'd later think, how the fright in falling so often arrived after you were already down. "I shouldn't be away from Beth too long."

"Give me five minutes."

"Sure. Five minutes." But she didn't move and neither did he. They gazed at each other, the neutrality of their expressions insufficient bulwark against this unexpected privacy. His features softened and she felt a deep stirring. The gametes had unified in the open chamber, the zygote rich with flourishing DNA.

"I'm glad you asked," he said.

Such an effort to turn away. Pausing, she peered at him over her shoulder. "Me, too. Thank you."

Upstairs again she checked on Beth. "Hans'll be up in a few minutes."

"Nuts," Beth moaned. "*Poo.* Get me my hairbrush."

"Oh, stop it," Karley said. "He's a doctor for heaven's sake." But she retrieved Beth's brush all the same. She hoped Hans took longer than five minutes. She needed a moment to marshal her defenses. She needed to brush her own hair.

■

Hans stepped into the sisters' apartment possessed of an easy purposefulness. "I may need to run to the clinic for a few things."

"We hate to inconvenience you."

"No inconvenience," he said. "But I somehow left my apartment without washing up. Could I use a sink real quick?"

Karley showed him to the bathroom wishing she'd cleaned

it before inviting him in. The cupboard stood open, its contents a showcase for feminine hygiene. She and Beth menstruated together but were between their periods. The wastebasket contained nothing more revolting than tissues and Karley's hairbrush castings.

"Let me get you a fresh towel," she said. She slipped a clean towel from the shelf and closed the cupboard.

"Thank you." He dried his hands and watched her.

"This way," she said.

He draped the towel over the doorknob and followed her into Beth's room. Beth smiled miserably as they entered. "Now you're going to have to let *us* cook *you* dinner." She'd been rehearsing the line. It came out stilted.

"Now, there's an idea." He placed his bag on the bed beside her. "You look like you don't feel very well."

"I don't," she admitted. "I hurt all over."

"I'll be in the kitchen doing dishes," Karley said.

"You're not staying?" Beth's alarm surprised Karley. Did she believe it a violation of the mission rules to be examined by a male doctor unaccompanied?

Then, again, maybe it was. "I can stay if you prefer. If it's all right with Hans."

Hans opened his bag. "Whatever makes Beth most comfortable."

"I guess I'd like you to stay," Beth said.

Karley sat down at Beth's desk and hardly resisted: While Hans felt the girl's neck for swollen nodes, Karley imagined him touching hers. Hans looked in Beth's ears, in her nose, down her throat. With his stethoscope, he listened to her lungs from the back. When he slipped the device down the neck of her top, it was Karley who took a deep breath. A hand on Beth's breast, Hans was far more circumspect than Karley who let the hand have its way with her.

As for Beth, she did not share Karley's enthusiasm. Looking pained, she stared at the wall and endured. Hans laid her back and, first asking permission, rolled her pajamas and garments to her pubic hair. He asked her questions as he plied her viscera. Some sinus, Beth answered, though it was mostly in her chest.

Yes, there was some discharge, particularly when she coughed. No, Hans's prodding didn't hurt.

Karley only half listened. What would she do if he tendered an advance, if he sent words into the space between them?

"Congratulations," he said. He rolled up Beth's pajama bottoms and tugged down her top. "I believe you're the proud host of a pneumococcal bacteria. Without lab work and an X-ray, I can't be a hundred percent sure, but it's a good enough bet to start you on antibiotics. I'll run to the clinic. I can probably scrounge up a full course. Have you had pneumonia before?"

"Once, when I was a kid," Beth said.

"Are you allergic to any antibiotics?" Beth shook her head. She appeared on the verge of tears. "We'll get you feeling better. You'll be down for a bit but you're going to be fine."

"Just think," Karley said. "No bonking for a while."

Beth sighed. "I should get pneumonia more often."

"Tracting," Karley explained, meeting Hans's inquiring smile. "Stumping for new members door-to-door."

"Bonking," he said. "Knocking. I like that."

"We detest it," Beth said then she started to cough.

"I'll be on my way then. But expect me back in a half hour or so. We'll make you inhospitable yet."

"Thank you, Hans," Beth said. "You're very nice to come to my rescue."

"My pleasure." Reaching down, he squeezed her hand. "You'll be feeling better before long."

All that intimate handling during the examination and it was this final touch that sent Karley reeling. She showed him to the door. "I guess we really will have to cook you that dinner."

Hans seemed reserved now. "I'd like that. I really would."

His unexpected shyness gave Karley courage. "I could throw a sandwich into the offer. I can have it ready when you get back."

"I hate to put you out."

Karley opened the front door and followed him into the hallway. "You mean, like we've put you out?"

He smiled. "Sure, okay. A sandwich would be nice. I was about to grab a bite when you stopped by anyway."

"It'll be waiting."

Hans turned fully toward her then hesitated. Balanced precariously between hope and dread, Karley felt the tightrope quiver. They had returned full circle to that moment downstairs, though this time it was his turn to telegraph. He looked away, through the apartment's open door.

"During medical school, residency, and my fellowship, I spent a decade in the States." He met her gaze. "But I never took the opportunity to speak with your missionaries." Karley watched him and said nothing. He was so serious. And oddly nervous. She wanted to help him. "I don't think it's in me to believe in much but science. Maybe once but not anymore."

Karley nodded.

"I tell you this because I don't want to mislead you, or Beth for that matter. I'd be lying if I said I was interested in your church. But there's something about you, Karley. I think of you all the time. Forgive my saying so, but it's true. I know you have your service. It's unfair of me to burden you with such a self-serving admission. But if I don't say something now I might never get the chance. And then I'll never know if it's just me. You and Beth, you're always together and now, because I can, it seems necessary to tell you. I'm sorry. I'm sure this puts you in a terribly awkward position."

Karley closed her eyes. Here it was and Hans was right—it was unfair though the unfairness, the burden, did not reside in Hans. Karley's desires and fears had fused.

"I made a mistake," he said. "I should have kept my mouth shut."

She looked up at him quickly. "You didn't mean what you said?"

"I meant it," he said evenly. "But I can see I've upset you—I shouldn't have said anything. I've made you unhappy."

"Unhappy?" She laughed. "It's not what you said. I'm a missionary, Hans. It's all wrong. I shouldn't even be alone with you talking."

Hans watched her for a moment. "But you are. Alone with me. Talking."

"Yes."

"And what I said didn't make you unhappy?"

"No. It's not that."

He seemed less satisfied than relieved by her answer. "I don't want to make you unhappy. I would be angry with myself if I made you unhappy."

"You don't need to be angry with yourself, Hans."

He stared at the floor. Karley could not read his face. "I should go now." Glancing up, he turned and started for the stairs. "I'll be back in a few minutes."

Karley spoke softly. "It's not just you."

He stopped on the stairs and looked back. "Pardon?"

With the apartment door open, she dared not raise her voice. She stepped to the top of the stairwell. "It's not just you."

Hans reached out to touch her, and she withdrew her hand. "Of course." He nodded. "I didn't mean to offend you."

"You didn't offend."

He grasped his bag with both hands, awkward now, unsure how to proceed. He had only an inkling of the covenants by which she'd promised to live her life. There was no way to explain, not even to herself, what bound her to the letter of laws whose spirit she'd already abandoned.

"I shouldn't be away from Beth much longer. She'll wonder where I am."

"Can we discuss this when I get back?"

"I don't know," Karley said then she hurried into the apartment and closed the door. Only later, when Hans returned with the medicine, would she realize she'd not turned the locks.

The Anti-Christ

There was nothing worse than an empty house after the Devil's Hour, especially when exhaustion had razed all the barriers. But by 4:30 a.m., Craig had spent his last coherent sentence and daylight was approaching fast. He required nourishment and a bath and a new coat of armor.

The temperature had dropped since he'd arrived at the station. The chill, always deeper during the pre-dawn hours, exerted itself. The cold air felt good. He was glad to be outside. An unusual pressure, high or low, pushed the lake inland on the breeze. Sea brine and something else, the stink of life and death, shit and sex, an odor fat with relentless wildness. If the gods sweat, it was sure to smell like the Great Salt Lake.

Craig lived below the university in an area far more affordable than the one above it. Theresa and he had purchased the house a few years after he'd joined the force. In an upstairs bedroom, they'd conceived their daughter, Kim, nearly a decade after they'd accepted a barren marriage. They'd raised her in its middle-class neighborhood, and not once had they considered selling. But in the two and a half years since Theresa's passing, Craig thought about it every day. He chased the idea like he chased his retirement—like a greyhound who knows the lure is fake.

He entered his house through the back door, turning on lights as he went. Weary as he was, he'd not come home to sleep. From the fridge he retrieved some leftover takeout and threw it in the microwave. In the bathroom he waited for the water to run hot before stoppering the bathtub's drain. He placed his phone on the toilet then wandered down the hall. Pausing in the kitchen,

123

he stirred his food then continued on to his bedroom. By the time the microwave beeped, he was naked. He placed his breakfast on the floor beside the tub and shut off the spigot.

The water was almost too hot. He eased into the tub and sat for thirty seconds before reaching for his food. He swallowed a few bites and put down the container then settled back and closed his eyes. His aching body flashed and needled.

Joshua Christopher. The idea of the child overwhelmed the fact of him, the flesh and bone and blood of him. It was a hazard of the profession, an artifact of pragmatism, this weaponization of hopelessness. Sitting up again, he dried his hands on a towel then fingered his phone from the toilet. He brought up the file, pushed the play button, and placed the device on the ledge near his ear.

Joe spoke first. "Is that really necessary?"

Craig closed his eyes and concentrated.

"The recording bothers you, Joe? May I call you Joe?" Even now Craig could smell the man's despair. "It'll help if you answer with your voice."

"Yeah, go ahead, call me Joe."

"You were telling me why the recording bothers you."

"I don't know. It just makes me uncomfortable."

Pause. "Why is that?"

"Why? Because I've been drinking. But you knew that, right? Melissa told you I don't do well when I drink? I get confused?" Joe laughed. It sounded as though he'd caught a wad of meat in his throat.

"Are you drunk?"

"Do I seem drunk?"

"When did you start drinking?"

"Didn't Melissa tell you that, too?"

"Maybe she doesn't remember."

"Believe me. She remembers everything. And she knows everything too. Just ask her."

"Will you answer my question, Joe? Do you remember it?"

Long pause. "Yeah, I remember. After we came back to the house with that uniformed officer—"

"Hansen."

"If you say so. We came back, and I went down to my office. That's when I started."

"Hansen didn't interview you right away?"

"I don't think so. No, it was later, after he finished searching the house and the garage and the backyard."

"How much did you have?"

"This is all wrong."

"I'm sorry, Joe. But it's important."

"Right. I took a few belts so I must be guilty. You Mormon?"

"Why do you ask?"

"Mormons jump to ignorant conclusions, especially if the sin smells bad."

"Settle down, Joe. I know you're upset, but I need you to settle down now."

"Upset?"

Craig's recorded self cleared his throat. "What's a few belts?"

"I don't remember. Four or five. Enough for a quick bump."

"How much have you had since then?"

"This is bullshit."

"Enough, Joe! You need to get straight now. Your five-year-old son's missing."

After a long silence Joe sighed. "I finished the pint."

"So you've had a whole pint. This morning?"

"That's what I said, isn't it?"

"Then you are drunk." Pause. "I'll take that as a yes."

"You have no clue," Joe said.

"Why don't you fill me in."

"Do you have children?"

"I have a grown daughter."

"Was she ever abducted?"

"You're sure your son was abducted?"

"Aren't you?"

"I have no idea."

Joe laughed again, another chunk of meat. "Our tax dollars at work."

"Okay, Joe. How often do you drink?"

"You're just not gonna leave it alone."

"No."

"You're wasting *time*." A chair creaked, someone shifting. "All right, I drink every now and again."

"Your wife says you're a binge drinker."

"She would."

"Every now and again? Be specific."

"Once a month maybe. Lately it's been more often, I suppose."

"Once a month is more often?"

"No. Things have been shitty these past few months. It's been more like once a week."

"Once a week. That doesn't seem like such a problem. Lots of responsible people drink more frequently than that."

"Maybe you're not Mormon after all. And you're certainly not married to my wife."

"We're not just talking about a drink or two, are we, Joe? I'm guessing once you start you can't stop."

Joe said nothing. His breath was loud and wet.

"Shitty how?"

"What?"

"You said things have been shitty lately."

Joe's elbows hit the table, the sound of a body dropped to the floor. Face in hands, he'd begun to massage his head. Craig could hear it, the vigorous friction of whiskers and palms, fingers and scalp. "Melissa and I have been fighting a lot."

"About the drinking?"

"About that. About the church. About money. About Joshua. You name it, we fight about it."

"Why do you argue about the church?"

"Is that really any of your business? Do I really have to answer a question like that?"

Pause. "Fair enough, Joe."

"Thank you."

"Did you argue this morning?"

Sigh. "She was mad at me for not having Joshua ready when she got home."

"Why didn't you have him ready?"

"I guess I got involved in work. I forgot about the party."

"And you hadn't started drinking by then?"

"I told you. I didn't start until after."

"All right, Joe. Why don't you tell me what happened this morning."

"What do you want to know?"

"How did the morning start?"

Long pause while Joe tried to pull the memory through the fog. Craig recalled the man's eyes, a hint of panic, maybe just confusion. "You've already asked Melissa about this morning?"

"I have."

"What did she tell you?"

Drunks, stoners, tweekers, trippers, cokeheads, pill-poppers, junkies of every stripe—Craig had communed with them all. Hundreds and hundreds of chats, a thousand loaded addicts. He'd come to expect their belligerence, their fragmented, non-linear mental processes, their paranoia and sexual come-ons. Which is why nothing Joe had said so far had given him much pause until now.

"It doesn't work that way, Joe. If I tell you what she said, I'll never find out which one of you is lying …"

Craig drew a hand from the water and ran it down his face. Baiting Joe had been a reckless move, probably a mistake. In an instant the man's features had hardened, his sober gaze impenetrable. It had left a dent, Joe's sudden composure at the instant Craig had hoped to shake him loose.

"Josh was still asleep when I got up." Joe's voice was steady now, cool. "I figured I could get a little work done before he woke up, so I went down to my office. I'm the primary caregiver. It takes a lot of time. I steal every minute I can."

"What were you working on?"

"I'm writing a program for a manufacturer out in West Weber. It has to do with the way their machines speak to each other during a certain phase of the assembly process. It's fairly technical. Do you want me to elaborate?"

"That won't be necessary. I wouldn't understand anyway."

For as much alcohol as Joe claimed to have consumed, he'd scarcely slurred once. And it wasn't just that. Listening to the recording, Craig was struck by the clarity of the man's responses, something he'd missed in person. Joe's affect during the interview, the smell and weave of him, had formed an impression that no longer seemed quite accurate.

"Melissa came downstairs and said she was going to the store to buy a gift for Billy MacMillan."

"Did she tell you which store?"

Pause. "I don't recall. She might have. I was distracted."

"Is that when she told you to get Joshua ready for the party?"

"Yes. And I said I would. It was the first I'd heard of the party."

"You hadn't heard about the party until that moment?"

"No."

"Why is that?"

Pause. "I don't know."

"So you didn't see Billy's mother the previous evening?"

"What do you mean?"

"Mrs. MacMillan stopped by your house yesterday evening to invite your son to the party. You didn't know that?"

"No. Melissa didn't tell me. Like I said, I didn't even know the party was today until Melissa told me this morning."

"Where were you?"

"When?"

"When Mrs. MacMillan came."

Pause. "I don't know. What time did she come?"

A rustling of paper. "Somewhere between eight-thirty and nine."

"I watched a movie in bed last night. I fell asleep before it was over."

"You don't remember?"

"I don't remember finishing the movie."

"Okay. This morning, when did Joshua get up?"

"When Melissa woke him. A little after 10:00."

"Does he always sleep so late?"

"What's that supposed to mean?"

"Just that, Joe. Is it normal for him to sleep late?"

Pause. "It's not a regular thing, but it happens."

"Okay. So you were supposed to have him up and ready, but you forgot."

"I got involved in my work. I didn't remember until Melissa got home."

"Which is when you fought."

"That's right, we fought."

"Did you fight in front of Joshua?"

Long pause. "Maybe he overheard us. We didn't fight long. I don't know."

"Do you often fight in front of Joshua?"

Joe's hostile gaze was still vivid in Craig's memory. "Why?"

"Was Joshua upset when he left for the party?"

There was a hitch, an expulsion, and suddenly Joe was weeping. It had happened so quickly Craig hadn't seen it coming. A full minute passed before Joe could speak again. "It's hard on Josh when we fight. It bothers him a lot. Melissa and I try to keep our voices down. We try to speak civilly. We leave the room. Sometimes, though, it gets out of hand."

"What happens when it gets out of hand?"

"We yell. We say ugly things."

"Do you hit her?" Long pause. "Do you hit her, Joe?"

"No."

"Does she hit you?"

"No."

"You didn't answer my question. Was Joshua upset when he left the house this morning?"

Sniff. "I can't see how that would make any difference."

"Think about it. If he was upset, he might have done something unexpected. He might've disobeyed you and Melissa. Maybe he took a different route or went off to hide somewhere he could cry or sulk or feel safe. It does make a difference."

Joe's crying had picked up again. "I really don't think he was upset. I don't remember him acting upset. We didn't fight long."

"Did you fight yesterday? The day before?"

"There hasn't been a day in the past few weeks we haven't fought."

"Did your arguments get out of control yesterday or the day before?"

"Did Melissa say something? She must have told you something."

Craig didn't answer. "I can't believe she'd tell you about our fighting. That's not her."

"But you're telling me." No response. "Why don't you think she'd tell me?"

Pause. "Forget it. It doesn't matter."

"Your son's missing, Joe. Maybe Melissa decided the circumstances warranted some honesty." Craig recalled the intensity of Joe's gaze as he tried to figure out what the detective had just told him. "Recent fights?"

"The day before was bad. We didn't speak to each other yesterday. Because of the day before."

"Is Joshua obedient? Does he ever act out?"

"He's obedient. Very obedient. He doesn't act out."

Child of an alcoholic. Predictable at home, not always so predictable everywhere else. Still, the book had been found on the expected route. Had Joshua set it down in the gutter to spite his parents? Had he realized his mistake and run off to hide? How upset would a five-year-old have to be to destroy a gift? To run away and miss a birthday party? In Craig's limited experience, five-year-olds didn't miss birthday parties for anything short of the apocalypse.

"You're sure nothing happened before he left for the birthday party? You didn't notice anything in his behavior to suggest he was upset or unhappy? No strange behavior in recent days?"

"No. He seemed normal. He's always been a happy kid."

"And you're sure you saw him when he left this morning?"

"Yes. Of course. He came down to my office and kissed me goodbye."

"So you didn't help get him ready?"

"No way. I wrote code and stayed out of Melissa's way."

An eruption of new noise, movement, Joe pushing his chair back and standing. The squeaky hinge of the pantry door, the clank of glass followed by a thump, a box of baking soda hitting the floor. The cap to the new pint he'd withdrawn from the oatmeal snapping as he broke the seal. By the time Joe had taken his seat again, the vodka was in the oatmeal, the oatmeal in the closet, a third of the bottle gone.

"Go ahead." He coughed. *"Say it."*

"I have nothing to say."

"Where the *hell* is my son?"

"Tell me, Joe. Why did you get so upset when I asked if Josh was distressed when he left for the party?"

Joe moaned. "He's such a good boy." His speech had already gone languid. "We fight and fight. What if he doesn't come home? How will we tell him we're sorry?"

"For what? What are you sorry for?"

"For the fighting. For the mess we've made of this family. For my drinking."

"Addicts get clean every day, Joe."

"Ha. You think I'm the one with the addiction? I just drink to stand my life."

"Addiction? You mean Melissa."

"Let me tell you, she's a lot easier to take after I've had a few drinks."

"Addiction to what? What do you mean?"

"To the *church*. Her drug of choice." Long pause. "She used to be so … free and open minded. Now—"

Craig waited. "Now what?"

"Now she's a zealot." The words came out round, soft where they should have been hard. "And I'm the anti-Christ."

"Joe, do you know what happened to Josh?"

Joe answered, but Craig could not make out his words. He sat up in the tub.

"Joe, tell me what happened to Josh."

"He got sent to the wrong family. That's what. He got the wrong father and mother."

"That's not what you just said. What did you say? Say it so I can hear."

"I didn't say anything. I do not know what happened to my son. I've told you everything I know."

Craig stared at his phone.

"Did you do something to Joshua?"

He snorted. "You mean besides sire him?"

"Joe?"

"I didn't protect him when I should have."

"Protect him from what? From Melissa?"

"Don't be stupid. I let Melissa send him alone. I *never* send him alone, only Melissa does that."

Craig picked up his phone.

"You never send him alone?" The speaker vibrated in Craig's wet hand. "Did Melissa know how you—?"

Pressing the tiny icon, he tracked the progress as he rewound the recording ninety seconds. He slid to Play, confusing the wet screen, and the app refused to respond. He reached for the towel, shifted the phone, and it squirted from his clasp. He glanced up at the pre-drips shimmering on the ceiling, then leaned forward and fished the device from beneath his knees.

Ghosts in the Gloss

5 YEARS 9 MONTHS AGO

Karley slipped from her bed, sleepless as always. Beth, well for weeks now, slumbered in the next room, oblivious. Karley glanced at the clock. Twenty minutes to midnight, forty minutes late for her call to Hans. She'd never been more than five minutes late, and she knew he would be worried. But tonight she needed to be certain Beth would not awaken. For Hans and for herself, she would do this on her own without his bidding or approval.

She did not turn on her light but dressed in the dark, jeans and a large, loose sweater. Tonight she was not a missionary. She wanted no reminder of that life.

On her way to the bathroom, she paused at Beth's door. Her companion's pale skin reflected streetlight—one naked arm curled over her head. She snored lightly, an inoffensive, Beth-like burble, and Karley proceeded around the corner into the kitchen, glancing in passing at the phone. From one day to the next, it had outlived its usefulness. She closed the bathroom door before turning on the light. When her eyes had adjusted, she washed her face and again brushed her teeth, ran a brush through her hair. She had never been one for much makeup—a good lotion and a little mascara.

Mission life had weaned her from mirrors, but she studied her face now. Large hazel eyes, feline in the right light, the right mood. Heavy dark eyebrows neglected at the moment, in need of a little attention. She noted with neither relief nor concern that the absence of sleep did not show in the skin beneath her eyes. A straight nose with a tiny cleft at the tip, a slight upturn that left her self-conscious, particularly when she had a cold. Full lips over

133

white teeth that might have benefited from some minor ortho-
dontia. Character, she'd told her parents, when they'd made a bid
for braces, and in truth she liked the irregularity of her smile, the
way it seemed to balance her face. Slender neck, small ears not
pierced. After a life of wearing her auburn hair long, she'd cut it
above the shoulders. A constellation of birthmarks spilled across
her cheekbones and the bridge of her nose like freckles.

She tried to imagine what Hans saw when he looked at her.
Did he know her well enough to recognize in her gaze the accre-
tion of stress and weariness? Of all her features, these, her eyes,
seemed most altered. She stared at them knowing it was not just
a difference in appearance but a difference in vision she perceived.
Through them, everything looked new.

She turned off the light and, when her eyes adjusted, hurried
back to her bedroom. She couldn't decide whether to stuff the
bed in the fashion of tired adolescent movies. Did such theatrics
actually work? Giving up the idea, she considered closing her
bedroom door, but that as well seemed too much. Mission law
was legislated under suspicion of moral weakness, and moral
weakness demanded opened bedroom doors. If Beth got up for
the bathroom or a drink, she would investigate a closed door.
Covers down, door open, Karley returned to the kitchen and
lifted the key from its hook by the icebox.

She eased the front door closed, then locked it from the
outside. The unheated hallway was well-lit, the tile floor cold
and faintly moist beneath her feet. Karley had never liked the
confinement of shoes, preferring texture, the confidence of flesh
on earth. Moving quickly toward the stairs, she glanced back at
the floor behind her. Ghosts in the gloss, her footprints, fading
from the edges like breath on glass. Her toes had already begun
to ache, and she savored the tiny pain—it felt real at a moment
when so little else did. She was rushing now, her purchase on the
banister tight as she slung through the turns. By the time she
reached the first-floor landing, Beth was a distant memory.

She knocked on Hans's door, both hands on its surface, the
palm tempering the urgency of the fist. Was it possible only two
months had passed since she'd come here to ask for Hans's help?

She pounded again, then glanced down at the threshold, and the door swung free on its hinges.

They stood very still studying each other. Hans was dressed much like Karley, in jeans and a sweater. Closing his eyes, he released a long exhalation, and Karley waited, content just to love his face. He backed into the room, and she followed him inside. She closed the door quietly, then hurried across the distance and met him with a force meant to rivet. Slipping her hands beneath his sweater, she absorbed him through her fingers.

Hans brought her head back and studied her face. With the pads of his thumbs, he traced her birthmarks.

"Scared yet?" she asked.

Karley Awoke

Karley awoke to the brittle alarm of a telephone ringing just behind her head. A pale morning light leached through the slats of Melissa and Joe's living room blinds. She sat up quickly. Her face felt tight and swollen, her heavy head two sizes too large. With painful efficiency, a pinpoint of frisson expanded through her center mass. On the third ring, she stretched to the end table and picked up the landline. "Unknown Caller," said the readout.

"Christopher residence."

"It's a terrible thing what happened to your boy." Male, a bass voice Karley did not recognize, slow and deliberate and resonant, affected. Only half awake, Karley felt her torpid instincts shiver to life. Had she missed something? She could hear traffic through the caller's phone.

"Who is this?"

"No parent should have to go through such an ordeal."

Karley was wide awake now. Two sentences and she understood the caller's intent was cruel. His malice pierced her like an ice pick through the ear. "What do you want?"

"But, of course, some people deserve what they get. Sending that boy out alone? Not very smart."

"I won't listen to this," Karley said. "If you don't tell me who you are I'm going to hang up."

"No, you won't. You won't hang up because I might just know something you need to hear. Maybe I have your boy."

Karley pulled her knees to her chest and shifted the phone to her other ear. The caller was right. She would not hang up. "What could you possibly know?"

137

"Oh, I know a lot. I know, for example, you Mormons bring these things on yourselves. A deceived people, you God makers, so imprisoned by your blasphemy you can't see your own corruption. Prayer only works if you pray to the real God."

Anger always clarified Karley's thoughts. "You have nothing I need."

The voice laughed. "You Mormons, you're not even Christian."

"Christian?" Karley hissed. "Is that what you are?"

"Your boy's never coming home. Lost forever. He's not even in heaven."

"You twisted piece of shit."

"Oops. There you go. Such language from a Latter-day Saint. If I hang up, you'll never know I'm the one."

Karley laughed. The man was soulless but he knew nothing about Joshua. "You're not the one. If you were you'd prove it."

"Oh, aren't you smart? Are they listening? Hello? Hello out there!"

"If you have something worth saying, say it. Otherwise I'm hanging up."

"You'll never know …"

Karley rolled to her knees and planted the phone in its base station. She snatched it from the charger and slammed it back in place.

The Contortionists

She lay face down, her bottom elevated with pillows, Joe plowing her from behind. Melissa's rump was hot and tender, a little furnace that warmed them both. Pinned as she was, it was not easy to reach her cell phone. "Let it ring," Joe ordered.

But disobedience was an important part of their game. It justified a harder punishment. "Hello?" Joe unleashed a crisp slap to both cheeks. Melissa sucked air and pushed back.

"Melissa?" the caller asked.

Melissa turned her head, gave Joe her profile. "Karley!"

"What was that sound? Is everything all right?"

Melissa grazed Joe's thigh with the tips of her fingernails, though by now the warning was unnecessary. He rolled to his back on the bed. "Karley? Is that really you?"

"Can you hear me all right? There's a delay."

Melissa kneeled up and sat back on her heels. "I can hear you fine. Is everything okay, honey? What are you doing calling me? Isn't it against the rules?"

"I'm so glad you picked up. What time is it there?"

Melissa consulted her phone, returned it to her ear. "Nine-thirty a.m. What about there?"

"Seven-thirty in the evening. Have Mom and Dad called you?"

"What? No, not this morning. Why would they call me?"

The transcontinental delay did not account for the time it took Karley to answer. "Maybe he hasn't called them yet."

"Who hasn't called them? What is this?"

"I need your help, Melissa. Something's happened."

Melissa scooted off the mattress. "Are you in trouble?"

139

"Please promise me you'll help Mom and Dad through this."

"*Through what?* Tell me."

"It's a good thing, Melissa. It's a wonderful thing, but I'm so afraid. Especially for Mom and Dad."

"Karley, you're scaring me."

"Please try to understand."

"*Karley!*"

From four thousand miles away, Melissa heard him speak, his voice calm and soothing and too close to her sister. "It's okay, *kjæreste.* Tell her."

Melissa closed her eyes.

"I'm in love, Melissa. I quit my mission. I'm with him now and—"

Melissa thumbed off the phone and threw it on the bed. Propped on his elbows Joe peered at the device. "Tell me you didn't just hang up on her."

"Shut up, Joe! Just shut your big mouth!"

Joe ran his tongue very slowly along his bottom lip. He turned his head, his gaze holding Melissa's, and picked up the ringing phone.

Melissa turned away and faced the mirror. She unzipped her skirt and let it drop to the floor. There she stood, naked and sweating, her hips and thighs stenciled red with Joe's handprints. Joe let the phone ring as he studied her reflection. She raised her hands to cover her breasts, then stopped and returned them to her sides. For the first time in their marriage, her nakedness embarrassed her, and she stood very still giving Joe his due. The skin above her breasts was mottled and blotched, and she could feel the heat in her face.

Looking away, Joe answered her phone. "Karley. Are you okay?" He studied his feet and listened. "No, it's fine. She'll be all right. It's you I'm worried about. Are you sure you're safe?"

Melissa covered her face with her hands. She'd donned play clothes for their game—matching bra and panties, tartan skirt and kneesocks, white blouse, necktie, the whole silly bit—but now she only wanted her temple garments. She lowered her hands and opened the dresser.

"Of course, we will. We'll do whatever you need."

Melissa stepped into the knee-length underpants. The material chaffed her sore bottom.

"No, Karley. I think you should. You'll both be sorry if you don't."

Melissa pulled the top over her head and flipped her hair from the collar.

"I know it wasn't. It had to be really hard. I think you're incredibly brave." Melissa looked up. Joe smiled but not at her. "He sounds wonderful. I'm sure I would like him. I *will* like him."

Melissa turned toward the bed. Joe ignored her.

"I love you too, Karley. We all do." Pause. "No, she's right here. She wants to talk to you." Pause. "Okay. Of course. Anything at all. Hang on, I'll hand her the phone." Joe slipped off the bed and passed her the phone. Melissa wanted to say something, to win a glance, at least, but Joe was already leaving. When the bathroom door closed, she put the phone to her ear.

"I'm sorry." That was it, that was what she'd wanted to tell Joe.

"Me too," Karley said. "I would've never done this to you except—"

"I know. You're in love."

"I don't see another way, Melissa, at least one that doesn't take me from Hans. I know what this means."

Joe had turned on the shower. Melissa sank to the floor. "People make hard sacrifices every day, Karley. We're all contortionists living one lie or another. Sometimes it's the only honorable thing to do." The shower door closed on its magnetic strip.

Karley was silent for a long time. "Fair enough. It's not that I don't see another way; it's I don't want another way. I won't live my life as a contortionist."

"Even if it means putting your family through hell?"

"Yes. Even if it means that."

"Couldn't you just leave your mission and come home? Bring this man with you. You'd have a better chance here. Oh, Karley, honey, *please* just come home. Maybe they won't excommunicate you."

"His name is Hans, Hans Nordling. And you know it's too late for that. We need to be alone for a while. Everything would be too confusing there anyway. And besides, he starts a new job in a few weeks."

"Let him get a job here!"

"He's a doctor, Melissa. Norway's his home. It wouldn't be fair to him."

Fair? "Where are you?"

"We're at an inn. Hans has an apartment in Oslo. It'll be a few days before we get there, but that's where I'll be."

"At his apartment? *At his apartment?*"

Karley was silent.

"Jeez, Karley."

Karley sighed. "This is so bizarre. How can something so good seem so terrible to the people I love most? It's like I've been yanked out of some trance. One minute everything's solid and permanent, the next it's all hollow and arbitrary."

"There's nothing arbitrary about the commandments," Melissa hissed. "You made promises. *Sacred covenants.* You've been through the *temple.* You're wearing garments."

Karley's silence was vacuous.

Melissa knuckled an eyelid until her eyeball ached. "You've taken them off."

And still Karley did not answer.

"Before or after you screwed him?"

"For good, Melissa. *I took them off for good.*"

The line echoed. Melissa groaned. Maybe she'd deserved that. "All right, Karley. What do you want me to tell Mom and Dad?"

"That I'm all right. Tell them I'm all right and I'm sorry for hurting them."

"You'll have to tell them that yourself."

"I know. I will. I'll call them in a few days when I get to Oslo."

"They're gonna be sick with worry."

Karley laughed. "You and Hans."

"What's that supposed to mean?"

"He said the same thing. He thinks I should've called them instead of you."

"Well," Melissa said, "at least he's not a moron."

"I'll think about it. I promise."

"Tell me how to get hold of you."

"Not now. But I'll think about that, too. By the time we get to Oslo, maybe I'll feel differently."

Neither sister said anything for a long time. Joe had recently resigned his job to start his own business. Things were tighter financially, but today especially Melissa was glad to have him near. She felt terrible about her earlier rudeness.

"Promise me something. Promise me, if you change your mind, if you decide you've made a mistake, if this Hans turns out to be all wrong, you'll call me. I'll be on the next plane out. No 'I told you so' either. I'll just come and bring you home."

Karley laughed again. "I promise," she said. "Thank you. I love you, Melissa. But this isn't a mistake. It's the best decision I've ever made."

■

Curt's car was parked in her parents' driveway. "They know," Melissa said. It was Wednesday morning. Her father was not a man to miss work for anything.

"That should make things easier."

Joe was right, of course, which made Melissa's disappointment all the more puzzling. She had dreaded breaking the news to her mother so had tried to reach her father at work. Still, part of her wanted to be the messenger. Joe parked on the curb, and without another word, they got out and crossed the lawn. Melissa opened the front door, and Joe followed her inside. The living room was empty.

"Dad? Mom?"

Joe dropped his keys on the sideboard. "Maybe they took your mom's car."

"No, the house is unlocked. And that's Dad's phone by your keys." Melissa led them into the kitchen. "Dad?" No answer. She opened the door to the basement stairwell. "Mom?"

She closed the door and returned to the hallway. Jared, who'd commandeered Melissa's bedroom, had hung a poster on the door featuring an over-muscled youth from the Book of Mormon. It proclaimed *A Stripling Warrior lives inside.* She continued down the hall past Karley's bedroom. Margaret's sewing machine now resided against one wall, but otherwise the room appeared ready for Karley's return.

At the far end of the hallway, the master bedroom door stood closed. Melissa glanced at Joe then put an ear to the door. She could hear her father's voice. She knocked lightly and when no one answered turned the knob and let the door swing open.

Margaret and Curt knelt side by side, their elbows propped on the bed. Margaret stared at the far wall, her round eyes tearless, while Curt begged God to spare Karley. Melissa did not want to see this, did not want to hear it, but she watched and listened anyway. When she could bear it no longer, she reached for the knob. Margaret turned her head and looked right through her.

■

It was Curt who finally came to find them.

"Daddy."

The word puzzled Curt or perhaps it was his daughter's tone. He'd come from the bedroom to tell them the terrible news. "You know." He nodded. "Of course, you know. Why else would you be here?"

Melissa pulled herself from the sofa and faced her father feeling much as she had standing naked before her bedroom mirror. She was not the daughter Curt wanted. "Yes. Karley called me."

Curt took a step into the room. *"When?* When did she call?"

"About nine-thirty."

He checked his watch. "An hour ago? Why didn't you call?"

"I did. I called your office, but your secretary said you were unavailable. You didn't answer your cell phone, so we came here. I didn't want Mom alone when she found out. I couldn't tell her over the phone."

Curt saw his mistake. Loosening his tie, he wandered to the recliner. He touched Joe's shoulder in passing. "Forgive me." He sank into his chair. Melissa sat down on the sofa, tense on the edge. "Did you talk long?"

"No, not long."

"How did she seem?"

"Determined." Curt nodded with recognition. "She seemed okay, I guess. She laughed a few times."

Curt smiled. He shook his head. "Where is she? Did she say?"

"She wasn't specific. But she's with him."

"With him," Curt said, testing the phrase.

"She said she loves him."

"Nothing gets in the way when Karley loves." It was a succinct assessment. Karley's love was not fickle, the opposite of fickle. Hers was a love that discarded nothing, which was why her defection seemed such a betrayal. "Still, why hasn't she called us?"

"Cowardice," Melissa said, and Curt glanced up, stung by the notion of Karley afraid of him. "She said she will. In a day or two, when she gets to Oslo."

"A day or two?" He thought about this. "She's not thinking clearly. Are you sure she's okay?"

"Yes. She's selfish but okay."

"Did you tell her she's selfish?"

Joe nodded. "You could say that."

Curt smiled again. "Good." Then after a moment, "What do you know about this man?"

"He's Norwegian. He's not a member of the church. His name is Hans Nordling."

Curt nodded. "He lives in Karley's apartment building. That's all the mission president could tell us."

"Then he didn't tell you he's a doctor? American trained."

"No." A tiny flame previously absent flickered in Curt's eyes. "A doctor."

"He's in his early thirties. Karley says he's beautiful."

"Karley's beautiful. She attracts beautiful people. Did she tell you her intentions? Does she mean to marry this boy?"

"She didn't say."

"But what's she going to do?" Curt worried. "Where's she going to live? How is she going to get by?"

The way Curt posed the questions, mostly to himself, Melissa didn't think he expected an answer. Perhaps he didn't think she'd know. "She's going to live with the man," she said evenly. "I expect he'll take care of her."

Curt stared at her. On the other end of the sofa, Joe shifted. He popped a knuckle. "Sorry," he said.

And still Curt stared at Melissa. Finally, he closed his eyes. "She's broken her temple covenants?"

Melissa longed to look away only a little less than she longed not to miss a thing. "Yes. She slept with him. She's taken off her garments."

Bit by bit, Curt rose from his chair. Melissa wasn't sure he was going to make it. Upright at last, he touched his loosened tie, then slowly finished stripping the knot. "The mission president didn't … I didn't think she'd go that far." He looked down at the tie surprised to find himself holding it.

The pain Melissa suffered was almost pleasurable. It filled the chasm between them.

Curt nodded slowly. "They'll excommunicate her. The mission president thought there was a chance she could be spared. If we could convince her—" He lowered himself into the recliner again.

Joe cleared his throat. "Curt." Curt lifted his face. "You know what a good person Karley is. Maybe we're looking at this the wrong way."

Had Melissa actually married this idiot? "What about Mom?" she asked.

Curt's nostrils whistled on the intake. "She wishes Karley was dead. Given the alternative."

Melissa glanced at Joe hoping he understood now. "Whoa," he said.

Curt swept a hand through the air. "I'm sorry. I shouldn't have told you that. I'm sure she doesn't wish she was dead. She was here alone when the mission president called. By the time I got home, she was in shock, I think."

An apt description. Melissa had seen Margaret kneeling in the bedroom. "The boys don't know anything yet?"

"No. They're both at school."

"Have you spoken to the mission president?"

It took Curt a moment to translate her question. "I called him back when I got home. He said Karley's companion tried to stop her from leaving with this Hans."

God and family hadn't slowed Karley down. What made

anyone think her companion could do better? "What does the president intend to do now?"

"He's looking for her. We hoped she'd have called home by now. If she calls, maybe we can talk some sense into her."

Intended or not, this last was an indictment of Melissa, of her failure to talk some sense into Karley. Karley had set her up to fail, but there was no way to explain this to Curt. He might have been their father, but he did not know Karley like Melissa did. Karley had shifted the responsibility, and Melissa despised her for knowing she would take it. "Should I go to Mom? Should I try to talk to her?"

Curt shook his head. "No, I guess not. Not yet. I'll go check on her." But he didn't move. None of them moved. "Your mother will settle down," he said at last but he was talking to himself. "It'll take a while, but the shock will wear off." Nodding to his thoughts, he got to his feet and started across the room.

"We'll stay," Melissa said. "We should be here when the boys get home."

Shuffling like an oldster, Curt passed into the hallway.

"Whoa," Joe sighed again. The bedroom door closed, and as it did Curt's cell phone began to vibrate on the sideboard. Melissa and Joe exchanged a glance then together peered down the hallway. It vibrated again. "What if it's her?" Joe asked softly.

Melissa reached the phone on the fourth ring. "Curt DeBoer's phone."

"Melissa?" Karley said.

"You're spineless," Melissa said. "I hate you."

"Is it bad?"

"What do you think?"

"Are they there?"

"Yes."

"Both of them?"

"Yes." Melissa tasted the bile of her bitterness rising—Karley was about to give their parents something they desperately wanted. "Ready?"

"No."

"Don't you hang up."

"Thanks for being there, Melissa."

"Save your gratitude for someone who wants it. I'm not doing it for you." Without knocking, Melissa opened her parents' door. Margaret and Curt sat side by side on the bed. "It's her." She held out the phone.

Leaping up, Curt snatched the phone. "Karley?" he said, hurrying from the room. "Oh, sweetheart, where are you? Are you safe?"

Margaret considered her eldest with funereal detachment, then lay back on the bed, hands clasped like the dead, and gazed at eternal damnation.

The Bluff

If you were a devotee of the local news, you had heard of Theo
Evans. You had likely seen him surrounded by reporters, pro-
claiming the innocence of some scoundrel whose guilt seemed
a foregone conclusion. As often as not, you would later learn
all charges had been dropped. If the case went to trial, which it
seldom did, the accused was acquitted more often than not. You
admired or despised Theo Evans, but either way you respected his
abilities. He'd championed the state's worst with an impresario's
panache, and Karley suffered deep misgivings about bringing him
in. She was loath to send the wrong message.

When he finally returned her call, he required much less
convincing than Karley had anticipated. She explained and Theo
listened. He explained and Karley listened. Not once during the
conversation did he mention guilt or innocence, and Karley could
not stem her cynicism. She suspected the overwrought media
coverage incentive enough to hook the notorious attorney.

"About nine o'clock now," he said. "I'd say eleven's about the
soonest I can break away. I can come there to the house or meet
you somewhere else in Ogden. Say, noonish? Or you could bring
the parents to my office here in Salt Lake around eleven."

For privacy, Karley had stepped onto the back porch. Melissa
and Joe's cars were gone, confiscated by the police, and she found
it odd and a touch pathetic that no one in the family could bring
themselves to park in the driveway. "What do you think?" she
asked. She wasn't hopeful she could convince Melissa and Joe to
leave the house. She wasn't sure she should even try.

"Well," Theo thought aloud. "I guess that depends on the

149

media. It may be easier to keep them out of the loop if we don't meet there at the house. Of course, if the parents are implicated it's not going to matter. Everyone will know."

"The parents are innocent," Karley said. Theo floated without comment in the wake of her bid for … what? Reassurance? Fisticuffs? His silence made her feel foolish. "But they're not in very good shape either. I'm not too keen on the media finding out, but I'm not sure I can convince Melissa and Joe to leave."

"Do they even know you've called me?"

Karley was tempted to lie. "No."

Theo mulled this over. "On second thought I should come there to the house. See what's going on, take my bearings. The press thing isn't that big a deal. We may need to use them anyway."

Exactly what Karley hadn't wanted to hear. "Let's not get ahead of ourselves."

Theo cleared his throat. "Tell me, Karley, how are the police treating your sister and her husband? Do you think they're suspects, Melissa and Joe?"

What was that lawyerly dictum? Don't ask a question unless you already know the answer. "Of course, they are," Karley said. "The police searched their house. They've taken their cars. The detective left a list of things they removed."

Theo Evans expelled a sharp *"What?"* his anger like wind under a drafty door. "Was it warranted? Please tell me no one signed a consent."

Alarm had never served Karley well. "Melissa and Joe have nothing to hide. We were told it was the best thing to do."

"Who told you that? The *police?*"

"A victims' advocate from the district attorney's office. Sally Frye. She's an expert in missing-child cases."

"It was bad advice," Theo hissed. Karley said nothing, too rattled to contest the point. "All right, let me think about this. When was the last time you saw the police?"

"Someone just left," Karley said. "A detective named Picknell. He came yesterday, too, to take everyone's fingerprints."

"Yeah, I know Picknell. Big guy. Did he tip their hand at all?"

"What do you mean?"

"Did he say they want to go through the house again?"

"No."

"How about a polygraph? Did he ask Melissa or Joe to take a polygraph test?"

"No. Sally Frye mentioned it might happen, but no one's asked yet."

"Did he tell you anything about this suspect, what's his name, Stillwell?"

"Nothing. He just came to give us an update on the search. He left ten minutes after he arrived."

"Means they aren't ready to charge Stillwell. It's unlikely they'd say anything unless they were."

"But it's good, isn't it? If they have a suspect, won't they stop investigating Melissa and Joe?"

"I don't know, Karley. I'd be more hopeful if the cops had said they're charging him."

Karley did not want to talk about this. A man was in custody, but Joshua was still missing. The more she thought about it, the more certain she was a confession from Stillwell would do them all in. "The detective in charge of the investigation is supposed to come by for an update at one."

"Milo Craig," Theo said. "I caught him on the news last night. He's smart and he's patient, meaning he's only slightly less dangerous than if he were stupid and impulsive. This search of the house bothers me a lot. Milo Craig isn't shy about exploiting weakness."

"This all sounds wrong to me, Theo."

He sighed. "Maybe there won't be a problem. We'll deal with it if there is." He already seemed calmer, and Karley found herself doubting the authenticity of his earlier outburst. "Tell you what," he said. "Why don't you have someone pick me up somewhere there in Ogden. A family member who's come and gone a few times since all this started. You have a connected garage there at the house?"

"No, the garage is separate. But the backdoor's mostly protected from the street. And the police are still limiting access to residents." Act or not, Theo had frightened her. She felt manipulated but by whom she didn't know. Had taking Sally's counsel been a terrible mistake? Or had Theo closed the deal by distorting the risks?

"It'll have to do. I'll sneak in and out. We'll make it work. Where should I meet my ride?"

"You know Ogden?"

"I grew up there."

"My husband has an office on the professional campus at the new McKay-Dee Hospital." She gave him directions to the correct building. "He'll be there at noon. He drives a navy blue BMW."

"I had a BMW once," Theo said, apropos of nothing. "I'll be waiting. And Karley?" She gnawed on a hangnail. "No one says anything else to the police or the press without my okay. Completely innocent people get hung out to dry for trying to do the right thing. When it comes to distorting truth, you should never underestimate the police. You might think they're on your side, but they're not."

"On our *side?*" Anger in an instant had subsumed Karley's fear. "The police are the ones looking for Josh. We won't find him without them. I'm warning you, Theo, if you do anything that gets in the way of finding Josh—"

"You can fire me."

"You will not play chicken with my nephew's life."

"Don't confuse the issues, Karley. Finding Josh and finding out what happened to Josh are only related so far as they shed light on each other. The police have a vested interest in finding the boy no matter who's responsible for his disappearance. They look incompetent if they fail. Consider all the attention this case has already generated. Poor self-esteem under a microscope tends to look a lot like overcompensation. So believe me, nothing we say or do is going to diminish the cops' yen for finding your boy quickly." He paused. "I'll be waiting in that parking lot at noon."

■

Karley preferred the back porch to the house but knew she had to prepare the family for Theo's arrival. She palmed the phone into her sweats and withdrew from the same pocket a narrow strip of paper. A receipt, partly disintegrated from a trip through the wash. The paper's plastic content had preserved what remained, a receipt for gas spit out at the pump. The faded lettering was barely legible, and Karley stared at it absently, plotting the encounter that awaited her inside. She wadded the slip and stuffed it in the pocket, then opened the storm door. And stopped.

She released the door and fished out the receipt. Careful of the fragile paper, she picked it open and smoothed it flat. The writing was difficult to read. She tilted the slip into better light. The words and numbers made no sense to her. Bluff Chevron, Evanston, Wyoming. Yesterday's date, 2:17 a.m. Forty-five dollars' worth of regular unleaded. She checked the other pocket, then stood very still rereading every word.

A large black fly landed on her wrist. It regurgitated, scrubbed, and buzzed away.

Karley shredded the receipt into tiny pieces and crammed the bits in her pocket. Like falling, she squatted and rolled back on her heels, her shoulders catching hard on the brick exterior. Bluff Chevron, Evanston, Wyoming. She knew the station well. Once a mom-and-pop, it was now a sprawling truck stop, the place her father always refueled after weekends at the cabin. Margaret owned the structure, a drafty log affair near Manila, a short drive from Flaming Gorge. It had been in her family since long before the dam had swelled the Green River miles closer to the property. Karley and Hans often stopped at The Bluff. Everyone in the family stopped at The Bluff.

Okay, Karley.

Breathe.

What did the receipt tell her anyway except Melissa or Joe, maybe both of them, had passed through Evanston early yesterday morning? Perhaps they had fought and one or the other had driven to the cabin. It was plausible. They had keys. Theirs was a tumultuous relationship. Perhaps Melissa had stormed off because Joe had been drinking. She would not have left Josh, not after a fight, not if Joe was drinking or primed to begin.

Karley tugged the bunched pant cuffs off the tops of her bare feet. The sweats were long on her. She'd had to cinch the waist. When she'd taken them from the dryer, she'd suspected they were Joe's. He and Melissa had fought, and he'd raced off into the night. Melissa had once admitted Joe took long drives when he drank. They had fought, and Melissa had run to the cabin or Joe had driven there drunk. These were logical explanations. Good enough to believe. Karley touched the phone through the cloth of the pocket. She could not feel the bits of paper.

"You all right?" Hans asked through the door's open screen.

"Yes." She frowned up at the screen. "No, actually."

He stepped outside and let the door close. "Are you hiding out here?"

"Recovering," she said.

Hitching his trousers, he took a catcher's stance in front of her. A flake of torn receipt lay at the toe of his shoe, and Karley pressed it beneath her index finger. She rolled the paper into a tiny ball and flipped it into the bushes. Hans absently followed its flight. "From?"

"I just spoke with Theo Evans. He agreed to meet with Melissa and Joe."

"That's great. Isn't it?"

Karley shrugged. "A lawyer like Evans? It's going to look like they're guilty." Hans stood up and offered her his hands. He lifted her to her feet and she groaned and flexed her knees. "We're slipping him past the press. You are actually. At noon. Theo's meeting you at the clinic."

Hans smiled. "How sneaky of me."

Karley pressed her forehead to Hans's chest and studied her chipped toenail polish. Her feet had long-since gone numb on the cold cement. No paper shreds in sight. "What's everyone doing in there?"

"Finishing up that new poster. Jared'll go run a couple thousand and get them to the bishop."

"Like a lost dog." Hans combed his fingers through her hair. "I need a shower," she apologized.

He pulled the rest of her against him. "You look clean enough to me."

"I'm kind of gross. I haven't changed my underwear in two days."

"Ooo. That *is* gross." Slipping his hands under her clothing, he cupped her bare bottom. But even with Hans's hands in her pants, Karley was conscious of nothing so much as the shredded receipt. Hans cranked his head back and squinted at her. "What?"

"Nothing, really," Karley sighed. Toeing up, she kissed him lightly on the lips. "I just can't keep my head straight is all."

Dirt

The office was not much to speak of, a human storage container with four desks, a telephone and computer for each detective, the requisite filing cabinets. It did, however, have windows and a coffeepot, a bottled water cooler empty more often than full. When Craig dragged through the door, Picknell was in his chair, a telephone pressed to his ear. Feet on his desk, he glanced in Craig's direction.

"Yes, ma'am," he said. "I understand. The timing's a bit of a problem is all. We're looking at something after 11:00 a.m."

A bloody scab of toilet tissue fluttered on the abutment Pick called a chin. Ham-fisted, big as a heavyweight, Picknell puzzled his police pals by maintaining a lucrative interest in an upscale salon where two days a week he coiffed wealthy women. Rumor had it his clients waited months for a turn in his chair.

"Uh-huh," Pick said. "No, I can see what you mean. A scruffy old man with a young boy tends to raise alarm. Especially in Davis County." Pause. "Yes, I got the part about the earring and the facial hair. It's all right here in my notes."

At his desk, Craig deposited his new phone and collected his mug, then continued to the coffeepot. His mug was half full of day-old coffee, and, apologies to the janitor, he dumped the dregs in the garbage liner and poured himself a fresh cup. He shook a dozen Advil from the community silo, then returned all but three to the bottle.

"I don't think so, really." Pause. "Well, because 9:45 is more than an hour early, that's the main reason. You said the child's raincoat was red, that's another." Pause. "So the boy seemed distressed?"

157

Craig threw the pills back and scalded them down with an oversized hit of coffee. With so little sleep, it was difficult to parse his various miseries, but he was quite certain he'd caught a bug.

"I'd have been disappointed too. In my experience, most kids don't want a McMuffin."

Craig settled back in his chair and studied his new phone. It was two generations newer and a different brand from the one he'd drowned in his bathtub. Margo in I.T. had updated his contacts and downloaded his apps and files from the cloud, but he didn't yet know how to find them. He dropped the device on his desk and closed his eyes.

"Absolutely. I've got all the information right here. We sure do appreciate your help." Pause. "So do we. We'll do our best." The phone hit the cradle.

Craig didn't open his eyes. "You shouldn't've signed in."

"Didn't," Pick said. "I forgot and parked where Dispatch could see me." He lifted the phone off the hook and dropped it on his desk. After a moment it began to complain. He put the handset in a drawer and shut it on the cord. "You catch the mayor's presser?"

That got Craig's attention. "The mayor? About the Christopher case?"

"Thirty minutes ago. He wanted to assure the public we've got the bad guy in custody."

Craig shook his head. "And where was the chief during this press conference? *Where was I?*"

"Chief was there, off to the side. Kinda looked like he'd swallowed a turd."

Craig was too surprised to savor Pick's description. "This is what happens when the captain takes a vacation."

"Politicians," Pick agreed, his big face condensing around his broad nose. "My two cents? It's the Mormons. Mary and Joseph misplace sweet Baby Jesus and the Romans are on the rampage. The national media's having a field day so the old boys in Salt Lake have decided to throw some shade."

Craig thought about this. "Pretty heavy-handed, even for the Brethren."

"Did you know the mayor is also a Mormon stake president, the Christophers' stake president?"

"You're shitting me now."

Pick smiled. "My friend at City Hall waxed unequivocal. God's law always comes first in Mayor Benson's world."

Craig had policed the theocracy for over four decades, long enough to know Pick wasn't selling bridges. "The chief was actually at the presser?"

"Of course, he was. His contract's up for renewal this year."

"Ah."

Pick shook his head and stared out the window. "Which brings us full-circle to our own tiny troubles. How sure are we Stillwell's not our guy?"

"Did you see the interview?"

Pick nodded.

"How about his jacket?"

"Yeah, I read it."

"Except for thirty minutes, his alibi checks out. And thirty minutes just isn't enough time. Not for anyone but especially not for Sherm. His IQ barely crests 70. This is a guy who delivered his victims to their mothers after he molested them."

Pick chewed on these arguments, his gaze steady on Craig. "Maybe so, but he's still more palatable than Mary and Joseph."

Craig studied Pick. They'd talked frequently during the past twenty-four hours, but this was the first time they'd spoken face-to-face. Pick was Craig's friend, perhaps his best friend, and after a day with the enemy it was good to see him.

Dropping his legs off his desk, Pick collected his mug, then crossed the room to the coffeepot. It never ceased to amaze Craig how huge he really was. Mug replenished, he started back then detoured around the desks. For a half-second, Craig thought he meant to strike him. Instead, he pressed his palm to Craig's forehead. Flipping the hand over, he tested Craig's cheek. "You've got a fever."

Craig rolled unsteadily to his feet and tucked the new phone into a pocket. He hadn't been touched with goodwill since his daughter's last visit and wasn't sure what to make of the tenderness he felt. "Thank you."

Pick nodded. "Go do your thing. And Milo?"

Craig turned back, his hand on the doorknob.

"Nobody wants the parents. Especially not you." In one motion Pick dropped into his chair and swung his legs onto his desk, then pulled the receiver from his drawer and returned it to its cradle. It immediately began to ring. "Detective Picknell," he said.

Craig closed the office door and turned toward the Cave.

■

He stuck to the hallways the chief didn't haunt and exited through the north-side employee entrance. He rounded the building and using his keycard swiped himself into the Cave. Jill poked her head from Melissa Christopher's Outback. "Naughty, naughty," she called. Her words echoed in the vast bay.

It was a busy day in the Cave. Joe Christopher's 4Runner was parked beside the Outback. An ancient Nissan Sentra sporting hand-painted racing stripes and a homemade spoiler cooled at a remove from the others. Who said Sherm Stillwell lacked taste and culture?

Jill emerged from the Outback wearing a recovery suit. Hooded and bootied, she resembled an Oompa-Loompa. She wielded a cordless evidence vacuum, a handy device that provided endless entertainment for the likes of Seymour. Tugging back the hood, she unveiled a sweaty oval the elastic had channeled in the skin of her face.

"Took me a little longer than I expected," he apologized.

"Insubordination always does." Balancing on each foot, she peeled off the booties and tossed them on a rolling cart.

"That's a big word, insubordination. Sounds like someone paid you a visit."

"Indeed." She placed the vacuum beside the booties and waved Craig to follow.

"And how was the chief?"

"Cordial as always." She opened the 4Runner, the driver's door, then stepped back and pointed at the footwell.

"What am I looking for?"

"Dirt."

Sure enough. The carpet beneath the brake and accelerator was caked with what must once have been mud. Here and there in the thickest accumulations, the dirt still appeared damp. The wet spots were the color of ox blood, the dry a salmon pink. "Not local," Craig said.

"And the chief says you're past your prime."

"Yeah, well. The chief would do well to pull his head out."

Jill peered up at him. Anger was not a regular piece in his repertoire. "You don't look so good, Milo. In fact you're looking kinda awful." Forgetting himself he leaned against the doorframe. Jill's features sharpened for flensing. "Are you simple?"

He took a chagrined step away from the rig. "Did you show this to the chief?"

She nodded. "And to his honor the mayor who accompanied him. But as you know it's not the parents. A sweet Mormon couple like that?"

Craig studied the floor of the 4Runner. "Talk to me about dirt."

"Fresh. How fresh I can't be sure." She stepped close and squatted. "The distribution suggests it was wet when it entered the vehicle—as opposed to dry then constituted. The car was parked in the garage which got warm but not hot. Given the dampness in those wet spots, I think we're looking at twenty-four to forty-eight hours."

"Footprints? Impressions?"

"Nothing but smear on the brake and accelerator. But here—" She indicated left and deep then moved out of Craig's way. "Driver was wearing boots. We got some good images. One of my guys is going through the tread manual now. Measures out a ten."

Craig dug out his penlight and leaned in, careful this time not to touch. A single sharp print, heel and ball, near the back of the footwell where the carpet was mostly clean. "Ten. Male?"

Jill nodded. "Or one big woman."

"What about elsewhere in the car?" Craig elevated slightly and looked into the back. "That booster seat? Anything there?"

"Nope. Only what you're looking at. We did, however, find similar soil on the undercarriage. Quite a bit in fact, particularly on top surfaces. Much less on the bottoms of things. A little in the wheel wells. This vehicle was off-pavement for a while. Not a long while probably. But a while."

"What about the mother's car?"

"No. Nothing."

Craig righted himself and circled the rig. In passing he peeked into the Outback and found a booster seat identical to the one in Joe's rig.

"Paint and wheels look clean," he said. "Mud on the undercarriage. Mud inside."

Jill wandered after him, less following than pacing. "We're analyzing some trace residue, but you're right. There was nothing obvious on the paint. Nothing on the tires or the exterior rims. A little on the interior rims and the brake assemblies."

"Somebody washed it?"

Joining him near the truck's open door, she considered the 4Runner's side panels. "Maybe. But you'd think they'd go after the interior too."

"Unless it was still too wet to mess with."

Jill licked her teeth. "I thought of that, but I'm more inclined to blame it on the storm. Better explains the patterns on the undercarriage. So long as the mud never dried, prolonged exposure to rain would probably do the job. Road water did the rest."

It took Craig a moment to peel the days apart. "Storm came in Thursday, right? Mid-morning. But for a few short breaks, the rain didn't really stop until yesterday around noon."

"I checked the Doppler. Oregon and Nevada into northern Utah. Southern Idaho got its share too. Easterly flow into Wyoming and Colorado."

Craig let his gaze drift over the paint job. "So where did it come from?"

"You're the Utah native," Jill said.

"Red rock country. A gazillion square miles of it in southern Utah alone."

"And how does that work for you, southern Utah?"

Craig felt a little dizzy, a little sick to his stomach. He wished he'd taken four Advil. Or maybe no Advil at all. "Not well," he said. "Timeframe doesn't work. Not unless we're talking a Thursday trip. Even then it's what, a three-, four-hour drive one way to the nearest red mud? That makes for a big day on the road. Parents claim they were in Ogden all day Thursday and Friday."

"Three hours if you go south. And not so much as a drop of rain in southern Utah for over a week." Facing herself east, Jill signaled like an aircraft marshal. "But plenty of red mud less than an hour and a half east."

Craig nodded. "I-84 to I-80 and on into Wyoming's Green River Valley. Would southern Utah dirt be different from western Wyoming dirt?"

"Absolutely. But then there'd be a difference between the soil in one part of southern Utah, say Bryce Canyon, and the soil in another, Zion National Park for example." Peeling off her nitrile gloves, she walked to the wall and picked a towel from the rack. She dried her sweaty hands.

"Soil analysis?"

She nodded. "In the works. Got that geologist at the U. Courier's headed to her lab right now. She may not be able to pinpoint the precise location, but there's a good chance she'll get us in the general area."

"How soon?"

"Lots of dirt in this world, Milo. She'll start in close and move out from there." Jill draped the towel over the rack and donned a fresh pair of gloves, then scooped a set of keys off the rolling cart. At the back of the 4Runner, she powered down the rear window. "Might be an easier way to get your answer though."

Craig met her at the rear of the vehicle. "Like asking the folks maybe?"

Jill batted her eyes, then dropped the tailgate.

"Did you see any boots when you searched the Christopher residence?"

"We live in Utah, Milo. Everyone owns boots. Had I peeked in the cars before I closed the scene, I'd have paid more attention to footwear."

Craig could tell he'd caught her tender. "We may have to go back. If the parents don't talk, we won't have a choice."

"It's all interesting, Milo, the mud and the fiber, the boots. But I don't know if it'll pass muster for a warrant. And I got money says those folks will insist on a warrant this time."

Craig studied the truck's rear hold. "You found a match to the fiber back here, the one Seymour discovered on the gift?"

Without touching, she pointed to various locations around the compartment. "A strand here on the carpet, another on the rubber near the hinge. Two on the gate itself."

"Does it look cut?"

"All of it."

"So the source was back here at one point."

She snorted. "There you go, jumping to conclusions."

He smiled, enjoying her act. "Mother bought the book and wrapped it herself. The footprints in the front are a man's, which maybe supports her claim she drove her own car to buy the book. If the gift was never in the 4Runner, why did we find the same fibers back here we found on the book?"

"Now you're playing games with me. Transference, either that or the book was back here at some point after it was wrapped. Both of which probably mean nothing. Stuff starts one place and ends up another, sometimes lots of places. I think the fiber's a weak investment, Milo. We're talking about the kid's environment. There are a hundred good arguments, none of them nefarious."

It was the illness or the exhaustion, their pound of flesh, but he could not stem his recalcitrance. "All the same, I'd really like to know where it came from."

"Good luck with that warrant." Bending her knees she hefted the tailgate home.

"Any interesting prints?"

Jill unzipped her recovery suit and ran two fingers around the collar of her sweatshirt. "Dad's prints, mom's prints, kid's prints, one set of unidentified prints on the front passenger's side, just above the exterior handle. No matching prints inside. When you inquire about the dirt, you might also ask about recent passengers."

"Steering wheel?"

"Both parents. No kid."

"So they drive each other's cars."

"Most couples do."

The hard concrete floor was not helping Craig's system. "I want you to run those unidentified prints to be sure."

"Now you're wasting my time. Ask the parents. Get a name, and we'll track it backwards to confirm." Craig turned fully toward her, his lidless gaze flat. "Yeah, yeah, yeah," she grumbled.

"And should the chief and the mayor come courting again?"

Jill sighed. "Oh, please. Give me some credit. When I have something I'll call you. And nobody else but you, my dear. We can meet in a dark park for some black-op Deep Throat action."

Craig hoisted his eyebrows.

"*Tchaw,*" she scoffed. "Dream on."

Days of Perdition

"It was excruciating," Margaret said. "Half the people at church wouldn't look at us. The other half couldn't stop."

It was Monday and Melissa had dropped in before her shift at the hospital. Since Karley's betrayal, she'd visited or called her mother every day.

Margaret got up from the table, returned with a dishcloth, and polished away a jam smudge she'd missed after breakfast. She draped the rag over the faucet. "And then there was the bishop."

"The bishop?"

Margaret's face sloughed loose on her skull. "He called us in during Sunday school, just your father and me. Thank heavens the boys weren't included."

"What did he say?"

Drying her fingers on her slacks, Margaret wandered back and sat down. "Oh," she sighed. She swiped her sleeve across the damp tabletop. "Apparently, he and the stake president have been in regular contact with the mission president. Or maybe it's the other way around. I don't know how these things work." She scratched at the table where the jam had been.

"And?"

"The mission president is proceeding with a disciplinary court."

A tiny lasso caught Melissa's fleeing heart. She had anticipated this news but not so soon. Church courts were shrouded in secrecy. On occasion some angry excommunicant went public about the process, but one was loath to trust an apostate's venom. It was easier and safer simply not to pay attention.

Courts of Love they were called, a phrase that chilled the faithful Mormon heart. The brethren claimed they were a blessing to the repentant. The sinner paid for her betrayal with disfellowshipment or excommunication, then could begin the humbling process of crawling back to the fold. But at the grass-roots level, a Court of Love seemed little like a blessing. Word seemed always to get out, which Melissa suspected was largely by design. Even more than a public shaming, however, excommunication was an execution, a spiritual execution. It portended an eternal separation from God and family that could only be overcome through abject prostration. And it wasn't merely the sinner who paid this price, but the helpless mother and father, the brothers and sister living in Ogden, Utah. Melissa was no bean counter, but her own quick-and-dirty had never shown much reanimation among those who'd faced that firing squad.

She took Margaret's hand, mostly to still it. "Where will they do it?"

Margaret sniffed. "Norway. Her mission president has authority over her now."

Unmoored as Melissa was by the mission president's haste, she was also relieved they would not have to wait. "It's only been a few days. It just seems so fast."

Margaret slipped her hand from Melissa's and started scratching again at the non-spot. "The mission president located her in Oslo at this Nordling man's apartment. She's living there with him. We have to assume she's sharing his bed."

Clearly, Curt hadn't disclosed all the facts. "The mission president himself went to see her?"

Margaret nodded. "She answered the door but wouldn't invite him in. She made him stand outside like the Fuller Brush man."

"How did she seem? What did he say? Was Hans there?"

Margaret met Melissa's gaze. "Rude, he said she was rude. She told him to leave and never come back. She told him he had no authority over her and she didn't care what the church did to her. That's what she said."

No wonder the mission president was so anxious to ax her. Melissa had always envied her sister's physical beauty, the looks Karley received from men and women both, regardless of their age or station. But now she envied her defiance and conviction, was breathless with the impossibility of such terrible freedom. Somehow Karley had escaped the prison of never achieving the mark. "Did she seem okay?" she asked softly.

Margaret's eyebrows disappeared into the sweep of her coiffure. "How could she possibly be okay? She's lost her mind and everything else with it."

Melissa got up and filled a glass at the tap. She wasn't thirsty but stood at the sink and gulped it down anyway. She refilled the glass and returned to the table. "Did the bishop say anything else?"

"Apparently, Karley's allowed to have witnesses speak on her behalf. He wants us to consider it."

"He wants you to go to *Norway*?"

"Wants?" Margaret considered the word. "I'm not sure I'd go that far."

The unfairness angered Melissa all over again, and not just the unfairness of Karley's cruelty. The institutional demands, the terrible emotional and material costs, it all seemed insult to injury. "Are you going?"

Margaret waved the question away. "Do you think it would do any good? After what Karley said to the mission president, do you think she'll even show up in her own defense?"

No. Karley would never show up. "I don't understand why they can't just do it here."

"It doesn't matter," Margaret said. "The bishop doesn't think we'd make much difference anyway. Karley spit on her temple covenants. She abandoned her mission. Honestly, I wouldn't know how to defend her." Margaret studied the backs of her hands for a moment, then reached for Melissa's water and took a sip.

"You'd get to see her though," Melissa said. "Maybe you could convince her to come home."

Margaret dismissed the idea with a brisk shake of her head, conviction or its opposite, Melissa couldn't tell. "Your father and I have discussed that at length. Karley will come home when she's ready. We're not going after her."

Melissa might have shared her mother's dismay, but she was

also the woman's daughter. She had a vested interest in the limits of her love. "That's it? We just wait for it to happen?"

Margaret sighed. "We're writing letters to be read at the trial. We want you and the boys to each write one too. The bishop agrees it's a good idea."

"Me?" Melissa sat back in her chair. "What could I possibly say?"

Margaret met her gaze again. "Tell the truth. Tell how she ruined our lives."

■

That it took her so long to suspect she was pregnant was a testament to the extent of her emotional disarray. She turned toward the mirror and tried to remember when Joe had last been rough on her breasts. The ache compelled her in a loose-tooth sort of way. She fondled one and then the other, convinced of a foreign heft. Studying her profile, she passed a hand down her abdomen. Her boobs *had* changed. They were fuller, the nipples darker. In the chaos, she'd forgotten they were trying to make a baby, and now she'd lost track of her period. The app on her phone would give her a clue.

Wrapped in a towel, she padded to the kitchen. Joe stopped rooting in the mayonnaise, his mid-morning sandwich on the counter half-made. "What's with the towel?" He tossed the knife in the sink and manufactured a scowl. "I thought we had rules about that sorta thing."

Very sweet and very courageous. He thought he was playing their game. Not seeing her phone, she turned for their bedroom. "New jar of mayo in the cupboard," she told him.

Quick as a snake, Joe stripped off her towel and slimed her butt with a mayonnaise backhand. Melissa spun toward him, already swinging, and landed a strike as resounding as Joe's. Her palm and four fingers welled red on his face. But in all except body, Joe had disappeared. She touched his cheek praying he would hit her. She needed him to knock her down.

Joe dropped the towel and stepped around her. He took a seat at his table and stared at the monitor. For a full sixty seconds, Melissa watched him ignore her, then she turned for the bathroom, unable to recall why she'd left it in the first place.

■

Days of perdition. See Melissa on the sofa chewing her nails. Note Joe scrolling furiously to the top of the document. "No," he moans. "*Please* tell me you didn't really send this!"

These were not Joe's first words to Melissa since she'd slapped him. On the morning of the third day, he'd broken his silence. "I'm sorry," he'd said. "I shouldn't have closed you out."

Perhaps by no coincidence, Melissa had just emerged from her shower. She could tell he'd been watching the bathroom door. She did not want him to claim the moral high ground. There was something cloying about his apology.

Dropping the towel, she crossed to him. "You should have hit me," she said. "I deserved it. I would have preferred that a thousand times to your silence."

Joe peered at her, his dark eyes unreadable. "No. I will never hit you like that. Never."

"Like I hit you?"

Joe lifted his chin.

"Come to bed. Let's skip church. Someone else can give my lesson." Taking his hand, she pressed it to a tender breast.

"No," he said, reclaiming the hand. "I'm not ready for that. Not yet."

Like so much else during that period, Joe's refusal was a first. With time, Melissa would learn to predict this too, but on that day, she tingled with the shock of rebuke. His apology, she realized, had been nothing of the sort, and this knowledge flooded her with affection. She touched his cheek, traced his lips with her thumb, then withdrew her hand and knelt down before him. She undid his belt and he did not resist. When she took him in her mouth, he was already hard.

Joe could stay when he chose, but this time he didn't—he came in less than a minute. He didn't move, didn't touch her with his hands, didn't make a sound. He just stood there looking down, his gaze reeling her in.

When the throbbing ceased, Melissa slowly released him. "I'm sorry I hit you. I won't ever do it again."

He bent over and Melissa thought he might kiss her. But he'd only reached for his pants. Cinching his belt, he rounded into the living room and settled behind his computer. And how did Melissa feel kneeling naked and abandoned, Joe's baby in her womb, his seeds in her stomach? Like a castaway on a float toy in the middle of the ocean, an oddly beautiful sensation in that way even war and disaster can be beautiful.

Three days later she still hadn't recovered. Sitting on the sofa, fingers bleeding at the quick, she studied Joe's reaction and felt the cold roll in. He short-stroked the keyboard and a printer hummed to life. He had the letter in hand before the rollers released it. "It was a *confidence,* Melissa, what Karley told you about that boy before her mission. You betrayed her trust."

"Don't be so melodramatic," she said. "I didn't tell them anything the bishop didn't already know. I'm sure he and the mission president have chewed on it plenty."

Joe stalked in, the letter like a machete. "That's not the point."

"What is the point, Joe? Please tell me what the point is." Opening her face she gazed up at him.

"The point is you torpedoed Karley. You didn't defend her at all. You *pushed* for her excommunication."

"It's the only way, Joe. She has to be excommunicated before God can forgive her."

"That's utter bullshit!"

"I hate that language. And it's no such thing. And that's not all. The church has to cleanse itself. That's the way it's always been."

"What, like blood atonement? Chop off her head and bleed her dry?"

"Don't be ridiculous. Blood atonement's for murder not fornication."

"Not always," Joe snarled. "Only lately, since the church discovered PR."

"Say what you want. I prayed about the letter, then I did my duty."

Joe dangled the letter in the space between them. "You call this an answer to prayer?"

"That's what I call it."

"That's some God you got there, Melissa. The two of you make quite a pair."

"Don't be blasphemous."

"*Blasphemous*? *Blasphemous* is what you did to Karley."

"Stop, now. I'm the best friend she's ever had."

"Oh, yeah," Joe crowed, scanning the letter. "'As you are well aware,'" he read, "'if a sin is repeated, the previous guilt is returned to the sinner even if the original sin has been confessed and once forgiven.' That's just cruel and wrong. I can't believe I married someone who believes such nonsense."

Melissa chose to ignore the bit about marrying her. "It's not nonsense. It's in the scriptures."

"Show me."

"I'm not gonna show you. Find it yourself." Melissa had no idea where to locate the passage, but she knew it was written there somewhere.

Shaking his head, Joe snorted. "You're a hypocrite. You make me sick."

Melissa laughed. "A *hypocrite*? Because I think Karley should have to pay for her sins? Because I think she's a disgrace and deserves to be punished for dragging her family through hell?"

"No!" He tossed the letter. "You're a hypocrite because you want Karley punished for the very sins you got away with."

Melissa's lungs felt pinned to her ribcage. How had two strangers gotten this far? "You thought we were *sinning*? You didn't believe God had given us permission?"

"Listen to yourself."

Melissa's sinuses burned, but she knew the welling would not deliver tears. Rage never made her cry. "I paid for us both. That was the deal God made. I paid. And all that time—" Her diaphragm spazzed and she covered her mouth.

Joe leaned in. "You loved paying. You've always loved paying. It was hardly a sacrifice."

"You thought we were sinning and you did it anyway!"

Joe studied her, his fury and her own sucking like a black hole between them. "I have no illusions about what I am, Melissa. Believe what you want. The sex was good. Who was I to complain?"

Melissa could scarcely hear for the blood in her ears. And she'd been wrong about the tears. "You don't even believe it, do you? All of this—the church, our temple marriage—it's a big joke to you. You're living a lie at my expense!"

Melissa and tears were old news by now. All she got for her effort was contempt. "Like I said, I know what I am. I do the best I can with what I have but I don't live a lie. And I know what loyalty is. You want faith? Here it is—I would never betray someone I loved no matter what she did."

"You betrayed me!" Melissa yelled. "You took me to the temple and you didn't even believe it!"

Joe laughed. "Oh, that's rich. I don't believe exactly the way you do so I don't believe at all. Fine, Melissa, have it your way. At least I didn't lie to myself about all that premarital sex we had."

Melissa had no response. In minutes this man she'd married in the temple *For Time and All Eternity* had exposed himself as a stranger and a fraud. She couldn't have said whom she hated more, Joe or herself.

"What about me, Melissa? Compared to me, Karley's a saint. You have no idea what my life's really been. How could I ever tell you now?"

Melissa gaped at him. She'd fabricated his past with prejudice to cover the holes he refused to fill. How dare he do this to her? Mouth and nose in the crotch of her elbow, she hiccuped and moaned and wheezed.

"What good's a church that won't have Karley? She's the best person I know. You should be proud of her. She won. But instead it's all this weeping and wailing and gnashing of teeth. I don't know what you guys get out of this misery shit, but it must just turn you on."

Melissa had heard enough, more than enough. Howling, she leapt from the sofa and scurried for the bathroom.

"It does, doesn't it!" he yelled at her. *"It turns you on."*

She spun back. "You ruined my life! All I ever wanted was a temple marriage to someone who believed like me. You're a liar. *I'll never forgive you!"*

"Take a number!"

"You lying sack of poop! *Get out of my sight!*"

Delighted, laughing, Joe said, "Thank you." He crossed the room, passing so close she could smell the bitter pong of his fury. He gathered his keys from the ceramic bowl, then counted the cash in his wallet. He opened Melissa's pocketbook and removed all her cash then, an afterthought, lifted the checkbook, too. He slipped his wallet in one back pocket, the checkbook in the other. His cell phone he left in its charger on the bar. Turning for the door, he twirled his keys and caught them in a fist.

"Wait!" Melissa pitched herself across the room and grabbed his belt from behind. "Don't!" she pleaded. She planted her feet, but who was she kidding? Joe was the horse, she the plow. He dragged her into the breezeway.

"Let go," he said.

"Please, Joe!"

"Let go."

So she did.

God's Will

A cry rose through the floorboards, chased by a thundering on the basement stairs. Standing at the storm door, Melissa glanced over her shoulder. Sally swiveled in her chair and looked toward the kitchen.

Caleb shot from the hallway. "They might know who did it! The mayor's making an announcement after a commercial break!" He twirled away and was gone.

For a breath, no one moved. Then Joe bolted and Karley darted after him. Margaret sprang from her chair, followed by Jared and Curt. Hans watched Melissa stare through the window.

"It's okay," Sally said, touching her from behind. "You don't have to see this."

"Please. Leave me alone for a minute."

Hans and Sally exchanged a glance then followed the others to the basement. The segment was just getting started.

"... late breaking developments, the search for Joshua Christopher, the five-year-old Utah boy who disappeared from his suburban street yesterday morning, was recently moved to this Ogden, Utah, neighborhood ..."

The announcer disappeared, his newsroom image replaced by an urban streetscape overrun by police personnel and volunteer searchers. It took Hans only a moment to recognize the location. Once a month he donated a half-day to a homeless shelter less than a block away. The camera settled on a deteriorating house, the identifying text writ large: *Suspect's Residence*.

"In a news conference earlier this morning, Ogden City Mayor Hyrum Benson announced that this man, Sherman Stillwell, the

177

convicted child molester who's been in police custody since yesterday, is now considered the primary suspect in the Christopher boy's disappearance."

The scabrous house had been traded for a mug shot, front and side, of an elfin-faced man of indeterminate age. Margaret and Karley groaned. Joe lowered himself to a crouch. The next frame featured a silver-haired man of considerable height and girth. Against the backdrop of a defunct and boarded building, the man's serious face and tasteful suit seemed entirely out of place. The words *Ogden City Mayor Hyrum Benson* appeared at the bottom of the screen.

"… of these new developments," the mayor was saying, "I've encouraged law enforcement to concentrate its search on the suspect's neighborhood. We plead with anyone who might have relevant information regarding Mr. Stillwell or his mother, Elizabeth Stillwell, to contact the Ogden City Police Department immediately …"

The announcer returned to the screen and with him an insert featuring a candid photo of an elderly woman, the pall of her anger conspicuous. "… *News* has learned that this woman, Elizabeth Stillwell, mother to Sherman Stillwell, was questioned yesterday. Sources could not confirm whether she is considered a suspect." A telephone number replaced the Stillwell woman. "Those with information are asked to call the authorities at the following number. As additional information becomes available … *News* will be there to bring it to you. In other national events …"

Joe switched off the TV and sank to the floor.

"This is *unconscionable*," Karley said. "Are they really so cruel?"

Sally shook her head. "What in the world is Milo doing?"

"But it's good, isn't it?" Margaret said. "They'll stop harassing Melissa and Joe. They'll focus on finding Joshua."

Karley tilted her head, the slightest movement, and cut her gaze to Hans. Jabbing fingers at her phone, Sally stormed up the stairs.

"But they have the man," Margaret persisted. Hands throttling a hankie, she sat down on the sofa. "Certainly, he'll tell them where Joshua is now."

"No, he won't," Joe said softly. "It's too late for that."

"Yes, he will," Margaret said. "Too many people are praying."

"Joe's right," Melissa said, and everyone turned. She hovered serenely on the bottom stair.

"What are you saying, sweetheart?" Curt asked.

Melissa gazed at her father for an eon before answering. "I'm saying Joshua's dead." She nodded at the TV. "That man's not talking because he knows what they'll find."

Karley exhaled audibly. Joe stared at his wife.

"I do *not* believe that," Margaret exclaimed. "*I will not.* We have to have faith Heavenly Father is protecting him."

"Test or punishment," Melissa said. "You've told me a thousand times. God's plan for us seldom resembles our own."

Karley threw her hands into the air, then fisted them tight to her abdomen. "I am so *sick* of this crap!" She started for her sister or maybe for the stairs, and Hans caught her by the arm. Jerking free, she fled to the opposite wall.

"What would you know?" Jared said. "You don't believe in anything."

"Would you guys just stop," Curt said. "We all need Heavenly Father, now."

"You can have the bastard," Karley informed him.

"*Please*, pumpkin," Curt pleaded. Karley turned and faced the wall.

"But Heavenly Father," Margaret cried.

Joe lifted his face. "He allowed it, didn't he?"

Karley spun around. "Joshua's been gone one day." She glared at Joe then at Melissa. "One day!"

Melissa proffered a placid smile. "Stop, now. All of you, please, just stop." She crossed the room and sat down beside Margaret. Back straight, hands in her lap, she was nothing if not composed. "I haven't stopped praying since this started, and I'm telling you, Joshua's dead. I don't know if that man's responsible, I don't know anything about that. But I'm Joshua's mother, and God answered my prayers, and as difficult as His answer is, I have to accept it if I'm going to survive. I'm telling you all because you're going to have to face it too. Sooner or later you'll know the truth, and I want you to be prepared."

Caleb, who'd said nothing since sounding the alarm, strode across the room and turned up the stairs.

"You don't really believe this, sweetheart," Curt said.

Melissa smiled at him "I do, Daddy. With all my heart."

Joe started silently to laugh. Head down, he quailed with the effort to subdue it. Karley and Hans watched him for a moment, then shared notes with a connubial glance.

Melissa drew Margaret into her arms. "Josh wasn't even frightened."

"But that man," Margaret sobbed. "The things he does to children."

Melissa rocked her mother. "Josh didn't know. Heavenly Father had taken him home by then."

Squatting beside Joe, Hans leaned in and whispered. "What is it, Joe?"

It took Joe ten seconds to compose himself. "Honest to God, Hans, I loathe this Mormon mystic shit."

Hans was hardly surprised. He had long sensed Joe's discomfort with his faith. "You don't really believe her, do you? You don't believe Joshua's dead."

Smiling bitterly, Joe peered at his wife. "If I knew how, I'd get out."

Hans glanced over at Karley who watched intently. He could tell she was trying to read lips. "Get out of what, Joe?"

"If it hadn't been for Josh—" Stricken anew, Joe lowered his gaze. "When she gets like this it's all I can do not to puke."

"Like what?" Hans pressed.

"… don't cry, Daddy," Melissa was saying. "It's God's will …"

Joe shook his head, then raised his face. "Like that, like the Holy Ghost. Like the fucking Angel of Death."

An Insect from Its Hole

Theo Evans emerged from the BMW like an insect from a hole, each long limb with a brain of its own, hands and feet like grapnels. It was a lot of getting out, and once upright he towered above the sedan. Clutching a leather document bag, he surveyed the street, then turned and considered the backyard. Karley opened the storm door and stepped onto the back porch. Theo smiled and lifted his hand. "Hellooo," he called.

"Thanks for making the trip, Mr. Evans. I hope the traffic wasn't bad."

Theo rested a forearm on the open door. "Sunday morning freeways. Getting through the neighborhood was the hardest part."

"Has something changed?" Karley asked Hans.

"They're shooting a David Lynch movie," he said. "Cars parked up and down the street, folks wandering to church in their Sunday finery. Very pastel."

"Surreal," Theo agreed. He did not sound displeased. "Person could sneak an aircraft carrier past that command post."

Hans came up the stairs and kissed Karley who felt a good deal better now that she'd showered and changed and flushed the receipt down the toilet. "I think we're all set inside," she told Theo. "Melissa and Joe are expecting you."

Until now, Theo had seemed disinclined to approach. He took a tentative step away from the car and closed the door. Transferring the bag to his other hand, he started for the porch, a frail figure compared to his robust TV image. At least six-foot-six and rail-thin, he less wore his clothes than provided them scaffolding. His was a knobby, misshapen structure, and Karley realized his body

181

was, in fact, twisted. Scoliosis, she guessed, his posture and move-ments hallmarks of surgical correction. But once started, he moved with the practiced grace of a dancer who'd mastered a limited repertoire of motions. His hand when he produced it was large as a baseball mitt. Two steps above him, Karley was close to his height.

"Theo Evans," he said.

"Karley Nordling." Theo's handshake was firm, his hand warm and soft. "I recognize you from TV. You're much shorter in person."

"Hah!" The hide of his big face lifted and dimpled, a mag-nificent velvet curtain with misaligned pulleys. Theo seemed genuinely pleased by Karley's deadpan and not the least bit flat-tered. She put him near fifty, though it was difficult to tell. His black hair, an unruly fomentation, was an uncontestable middle finger to the fashion police. With his crazy hair and hangdog face, Theo Evans was just ugly enough to be handsome.

"I'm afraid we may have wasted your time," Karley said. "They're saying it's Stillwell. There was a press conference."

Sidling against the handrail, Theo placed one foot on the bottom step. "I heard."

"You may have made the trip for nothing. I'm very sorry if that's the case."

Lips pursed, Theo shook his head. "I hope you're right, Karley. It's a good thing when my services aren't required."

"If it weren't for the news, we wouldn't know anything. The police aren't talking to us."

"That fits."

"That the police aren't talking?" Hans asked. "Or that we don't know what's going on?"

"All of it, I'd say."

"Don't be cryptic, Theo," Karley said. "We get enough of that from the cops."

Theo smiled, his crow's feet more like raven's feet. He leveled his forthright gaze on Karley. "Fair enough. You're right, the police are playing games. Mind you, they have no legal obligation to tell you word one. That doesn't make it any less ethical that they haven't."

"You still haven't answered my question."

Theo shrugged. "This has turned into a national spectacle,

Karley. The police are under intense public scrutiny, and the chief's getting hammered by the mayor. Are you aware the mayor is also your sister and her husband's stake president?"

"I had no idea," she said, genuinely alarmed. Utah politicians rarely saw conflict unless their interests made it necessary to deny their religious motivations. It suddenly appeared no authority could be trusted to do the right thing for the right reason.

"So, as you might well suppose," Theo continued, "the mayor's on a crusade to see them cleared. But the detective in charge, Craig, he's not the sort to roll over. If anything, he'll press harder, hoping to break something loose fast. This Stillwell character looks like a finger in the dike. The police haven't charged him, not for your nephew's abduction anyway. They've got him on contraband and for violating the terms of his probation. They found some child pornography in his house. Unless something changes in a big hurry, I expect tomorrow he'll be arraigned for possession alone. Believe me, possession does not abduction make."

"How do you know all this?" Hans said.

"I've been around a long time, Hans. Lots of friends, lots of enemies."

"Are you saying the police don't have anything more than that?" Karley asked.

"If they do, they're being very quiet about it. My pals didn't know a thing."

Karley stared at Theo's huge face and waited out the crush. How tired it made her, losing faith. "There's something you should know," she told him. "Melissa and Joe are convinced Joshua's dead."

Theo didn't immediately answer. "I wouldn't think that's so unusual. They're under a lot of stress."

"God told Melissa. He answered her prayers. She doesn't doubt it a bit."

Theo cocked his head and studied her. "Maybe he did."

"Please don't tell me you believe that."

"It doesn't matter what I believe," Theo said. "It only matters what your sister believes. Or what she wants people to think she believes."

Karley could not tell whether Theo's response was adversarial or some perverse attempt at advocacy. She glanced at Hans who gazed past the attorney at some horizon hidden from her.

"Why did you tell me that?" Theo appraised Karley narrowly, but there was no rancor. "Why did you think I might want that information?"

"Melissa's not herself," Karley said. "She may be difficult. I guess that's why I told you."

"Actually," Hans said. "Melissa *is* herself. That's the problem exactly."

No matter how much she wanted to disagree, Karley could not deny the precision of Hans's assessment.

"And Joe?" Theo said. "Is he himself?"

"Yes," Karley said, watching Hans. "They're both themselves, just a little more so than usual."

Theo shifted his stance, then settled against the railing again. "You're not my clients," he said. "And even if you were I wouldn't inquire after your innocence. Or your guilt. I don't ask and not because I need to maintain illusions. I refrain from asking because there's no utility in it. Few of my clients are entirely innocent anyway. Defending folks, prosecuting folks, it all has astonishingly little to do with truth or reality. It's about getting judge and jury to believe your explanation of the evidence. I'm in the business of damage control. Cynical as that sounds, it's the way it works."

Karley threaded her fingers through Hans's, her hope like a torched bloom.

"Why did you choose me, Karley? There are a lot of good attorneys out there. Why me?"

Karley stared at Theo and didn't answer.

"I only ask because I want us to be completely clear. I'm in no position to make judgments, not that I make many of the sort I think we're alluding to. I haven't even spoken to my clients yet. However, if someone near Melissa and Joe knew something that might help me protect them? I'd want to know. And, of course, the police would certainly want to know if someone had information that might help them catch their man. Understand, it would be unethical for me to encourage anyone to suppress that kind of information even if it potentially hurt my client. It's all a tricky business, especially when a loved one's involved. In that case, a person would have to look real hard at himself, then do what he thought was right."

Karley tucked a dark curl behind her ear. "It's getting late," she said softly. "Detective Craig will be here before long."

Theo nodded. "After you."

■

"You are mistaken if you think the police are trying to help you." Theo lowered the list of items seized by the police. "Milo Craig and company will do everything in their power to make a case against you. They're out to prove what they already believe."

"That's nonsense," Margaret said. "They've already caught the man. He's sitting in a cell down at the police station."

But for Jared and Caleb, who'd left to distribute the latest posters, the family was present. Hovering in a doorway, Sally looked warily on.

Theo raised his unruly eyebrows. "Do you always believe what you see on TV?" He shot a cuff and checked the time. "The mayor held that press conference nearly three hours ago. Why haven't the police come to give you the good news?"

"Because they have no good news to give," Melissa said. It was the first she'd spoken since greeting Theo. She met his appraisal with one of her own.

"I tend to agree," he said. "But I doubt we're talking about the same news."

"Why don't you just say what's on your mind," Sally said.

Theo ran a long finger around the inside of his watch band, the skin underneath like tank tread. "Oh, I will. In just a minute I'll tell you exactly what's on your mind, Sally. But first I think Melissa and Joe need to understand that the police are far from finished with them."

"How do you know this?" Curt asked. "They haven't said anything to us."

"Just listen, Dad," Karley said.

"Detective Craig's under pressure to focus his energies else-where. It's pressure he'll resist."

"What?" Sally barked.

Ignoring her, Theo addressed Curt. "I know this because someone close to the investigation told me. Milo Craig does not think Sherman Stillwell had anything to do with Joshua's disappearance."

"Damnit to hell," Sally said. "What's going on in this town?"

Karley watched her family absorb these new details. In order to save them, Theo had made no effort to spare them. Karley could not help but feel sorry for Sally. Theo in five minutes had provided more information than the advocate or the police had in twenty-four hours.

"So." Theo looked from Melissa to Joe. "If you think you're not suspects, think again. Milo Craig is just getting started."

"And if you're wrong?" Sally asked.

"If I'm wrong," he said, nudging his half-glasses up the bridge of his nose, "Melissa and Joe should fire me." He returned his attention to the paper in his hand. "This was a mistake. A big mistake."

"You're out of line," Sally said.

"Am I?" He peered at her over the frames of his glasses. "Both cars. A Toyota 4Runner and a Subaru Outback. Who drives what?"

"I drive the Subaru," Melissa said. "The 4Runner belongs to Joe."

"Strange they'd want the cars. Expired tags you think?"

Melissa studied Theo, her expression unreadable. "I have no idea why the police took our cars but if—"

Flapping a hand to silence Melissa, Theo glanced at Sally. "Best not to discuss details until we're alone. What you say isn't protected otherwise." Lips pursed, he returned his attention to the list. "A pill, as yet unidentified. Taken from the floor of the master bathroom."

As instructed, Melissa and Joe kept their own counsel. Joe watched his wife. Melissa watched Theo. "No matter. We'll know soon enough. And look at this—two empty vodka bottles, one removed from the office garbage, one from the outside bin. And another, half full, tucked in with the oatmeal."

Melissa looked away. It did not matter that the secret was out. The pain in her expression was fresh and immediate.

"They're mine," Joe said. "The bottles are mine. Everyone knows, even the cops."

"Pills and booze," Theo observed. "Not a healthy combination. Not if taken together or mixed on a seizure sheet. Especially if that pill's something—"

"We can do without the sarcasm," Sally interrupted. "And we can do without the judgments, too."

Theo lowered the paper and removed his glasses. "Sarcastic, perhaps, judgmental, no. At least, not of Melissa and Joe. And if you think I'm unpleasant wait 'til the police get started."

Unmoved, Sally folded her arms. "Melissa and Joe don't need this right now."

"I couldn't agree with you more, Sally. Which is precisely why I don't understand what you're doing here."

Having presaged this collision, Karley suffered an off-kiltering vertigo. She was no longer convinced Theo was wrong about anything.

"That's just plain wrong," Curt scoffed. "Sally's been nothing but wonderful."

Sally acknowledged Curt's chivalry with a nod. "You're not much of a team player, are you, Mr. Evans? For your information, I'm the one who suggested they retain an attorney. Though, I admit, you wouldn't have been my first choice."

"I like that," Theo said. "A team player. And which team are you playing for, Sally?"

Sally laughed through her nose, a long windy gust. "I'm an old hand, Theo, and that's a ridiculous question. If I were working for the police, I'd know a lot more about what they're doing."

"I'm not sure you don't, Sally. I'm not sure I believe much of anything you say. You do, after all, answer to the district attorney."

Sally laughed again, this time out loud. "You know as well as I do what a judge would do if the DA used me like that."

Theo smiled, all teeth and good nature. "Did you advise the Christophers to consent to the search?"

"Of course, I did. Strategically, it was the right thing to do.

Melissa and Joe have nothing to hide and everything to lose by stonewalling. The police would've secured a warrant. They'd have taken what they wanted."

"A warrant on what grounds?" Theo spoke so quietly everyone in the room leaned toward him. "There's no probable cause. Even the talented Milo Craig would've had a hell of a time convincing the judge to sign a warrant." He showed them the seizure sheet. "And nothing to hide? Just look at this list. You don't have to commit a crime for the cops to prove you have plenty to hide. You've given them reason to look more closely and, believe me, they'll find something damaging. It was a colossal mistake. I can hardly wait to see what they do with the cars."

Karley felt oddly vindicated and not the least relieved. She surveyed her horrified family. Glaring at Theo, Sally held her tongue.

"You make the police sound like villains," Margaret said.

Theo gaped at her. "Do friends treat you like a criminal? And what makes you so sure the police are competent and trustworthy? After all these years, I still don't understand why folks feel obliged to help the cops ruin their lives. Does it not seem perverse that demanding your constitutional rights is considered proof of guilt?"

"We're not stupid," Sally said. "We just don't have the time or luxury to stand on principle for its own sake. While you wax cynical, some monster you'd defend still has Joshua."

"Attempting to insult me is not going to bring the boy back."

Joe shivered to life in his chair. "That's the first time you've mentioned helping my son."

Theo's big ugly face softened. "I haven't forgotten about your boy, Joe. Not in the least. I understand why we're here. Better than you think." He paused to let the family breathe. It was a little after one, and the room was warm. Craig was late, much to Karley's relief. "Here's the bottom line: If you want my help, you're going to have to trust me on this thing with the police. Protecting you is the best way I know to help Josh."

Abandoning the doorway, Sally crossed the room and sat down on the coffee table opposite Melissa. "Don't do it, dear." She leaned in and took the younger woman's hands. "I know what Theo says is frightening, but if you give in to fear, the consequences will be terrible. I've seen it before. You'll be fighting the police the whole time. I promise, you do not want that. At least wait and see what they come up with. The shortest path now is right down the center. Show the police you have nothing to hide. Cooperate. It's the only way to bring Josh home."

Melissa withdrew her hands. "Josh is dead. He's never coming home."

"Melissa—"

Melissa shook her head.

Outside, a car pulled up to the curb. Karley heard it before she saw it, an unmarked cruiser, Detective Craig. Theo had seen him, too. "Looks like you have a choice to make. From here forward, I'm in charge. That's my offer. Take it or find yourselves another lawyer."

Sally and Melissa still gazed at each other. Neither seemed aware of anyone else. Craig came up the stairs and raised his fist to the doorframe. Seeing the assembled, he touched his fingers to the screen.

"Come," Karley said.

Craig stepped inside, and Karley watched him count heads, impressed by his composure when he recognized Theo. The detective's face was pasty and drawn. He didn't look well at all.

"Hello, Milo," Theo said.

"Mr. Evans."

Without turning, Sally said, "Tell us something good, Milo. Melissa and Joe need good news."

"I'm afraid this isn't a good-news call."

"Here we go," Joe blurted.

"I was under the impression you were finished here," Theo said, drawing his gaze from Joe to Craig. "Mayor Benson changed his mind?"

At mention of the mayor, Craig smiled with half his face. It might have been a grimace. "I'm sorry, I know this isn't what you'd hoped for. We have a few more questions we need to ask the Christophers."

Raising her gaze, Melissa assessed the policeman. Taken by

her loveliness, Karley studied her sister's face. Not even the slight bruising beneath her eyes diminished her heartbreaking beauty. "What kind of questions?"

"Really, I think we should speak in private."

"Do we need a lawyer?"

"That's a question better asked a lawyer."

"Think of what you're doing," Sally warned.

Melissa rolled from the sofa, then bent down and kissed the older woman on the cheek. Facing the detective, she smoothed her blouse. "Will you be speaking with us alone or together?"

"One at a time," Craig said. "I'll need to speak with you separately."

Melissa turned her head and met Joe's gaze. He seemed to have been waiting for just such a meeting. "If you don't mind," she told Craig, still communing with Joe, "we'd like a few moments with our attorney first."

The table scudded backwards with the force of Sally's retreat. She hurried from the room.

Craig smiled. "I don't mind a bit." He took out a handkerchief and dried his forehead. Karley wondered if they'd all get sick.

Theo slid forward in his chair and began to assemble himself. "Make yourself comfortable, Milo. This is going to take a while.

Holding Vigil

What do you do, whom do you call, when your husband doesn't come home all night? Not your parents, that's for sure, not when they're awaiting a missive from a mission president announcing the execution of their second child. Had Karley been near, Melissa might have turned to her. But Karley was in Norway fornicating with a heathen.

So Melissa did what she could: She called in sick, then dragged herself to the sofa. When she could no longer endure the empty apartment, she donned Joe's trench coat over a pair of sweats and drove herself to the pharmacy.

■

"You've reached Melissa and Joe," the answering machine announced. Stumbling into their apartment, Melissa snatched up the phone. "Joe!"

"It's your mother. Don't you know what day this is? Why aren't you two here?"

Melissa had completely forgotten. She and Joe had promised to hold vigil with the family. "Oh, Momma, I've been throwing up all morning. I called in sick."

"I thought you'd already changed your shift."

"I did change my shift. I called in sick."

Baffled silence on the other end of the line. Then, "Why are you throwing up?"

Who said Freud was wrong? "It's not morning sickness, Mom, it's intestinal flu. The squirts, too. I've been hugging the toilet all morning."

"Don't be crude," Margaret scolded.

191

Melissa shrugged Joe's coat off her shoulders and, shifting the phone, let it slide to the floor. "I'm not going to make it."

"Well, what about Joe? Certainly, he can join us."

Melissa wandered into the breezeway and retrieved the bag she'd flung trying to get to the phone. "An important client had an emergency this morning. We couldn't afford to say no."

"You could've called us."

"I should have. I've just been so sick."

Margaret sighed. "We just got off the phone with the mission president."

"It's finished?" Melissa swung the bag onto the bar and pulled out a stool.

"No. He called to say it was about to start."

Melissa checked the clock. A little before noon. "They're doing this at 9:00 at night? Shouldn't they wait until a minute after midnight?"

"Don't make light. They have their reasons for starting when they do."

Melissa was a little dizzy. She wished Margaret would hang up. The phone was reserved for Joe alone. "How long will it take?"

"President Olesund didn't say. Your father thinks it depends on whether Karley shows up."

"Does the mission president think she will?"

"He sent her a registered letter. He hasn't heard back."

"How about you guys? Have you heard from her?"

Margaret blew air. "No. Has she called you?"

"No," Melissa said. "I would have told you if she had."

"Would you?"

Melissa's left eyeball felt suddenly harpooned. She massaged it through her eyelid. "Totally unfair, Mom. You know I'd call. I'm not Karley."

"Thank goodness for that," Margaret said. "You didn't come by last week."

Melissa emptied the bag on the counter and arranged the two pregnancy tests side by side. "I'm sorry. I've been very busy with work and church assignments. And now I'm sick. Speaking of which, the cramps are coming back. I'm gonna have to run to the bathroom."

"We're all fasting," Margaret went on. "You remember we were all going to fast today? Are you and Joe fasting?"

Melissa tried to remember which test had cost most. She was glad she'd circled back for the second one. "I'm more than fasting. I'm throwing up. I should get extra points for that."

"You're sure you're too sick to join us?"

"Oh, boy!" Melissa said. "I think I'm gonna blow."

"Hold on, hold on!" Margaret barked. "Stay by your phones. We'll call as soon as we hear anything."

"Gotta go, Mom!"

Melissa put down the phone and picked up the prettier of the two boxes, fuchsia and lavender lettered in green. Reading the box, she wandered across the room and kicked the front door closed. Simple as one, two, three the box said. She opened the flap and poured the device into her hand. Fuchsia and lavender just like the box, sealed in a clear plastic wrapper. Where the heck was Joe?

In the bathroom she arranged the pee sticks on the floor, then read each set of instructions. It was painful work. She really had to pee. Mid-stream the instructions said. She removed her bottoms and settled on the toilet then bent over and picked up a test. Curled like a horseshoe, she saturated the first, then withdrew it from the commode and followed it with the second. It was no easy task to stem her flow. She closed her eyes and relaxed.

When she opened her eyes, Joe was teetering in the doorway. She dropped the test in the bowl. Joe took a halting step into the room. His filthy clothing was wrinkled and damp. He'd misplaced a shoe and his hair was a nest of twigs and leaves. Squinting at Melissa, he managed another step. She could smell the vomit and located it quickly, still fresh in the laces of his remaining shoe. She closed her legs and studied his puffy face. Taking one final step, he melted to his knees and laid his head in her lap.

The phone began to ring.

Melissa picked a leaf from his hair and wiped cold sweat from his nape. Joe's head shot up, and he scanned for the garbage, his body already clenching. Scooting back on the seat, Melissa guided him in, and he vomited between her legs. The phone rang and rang, and Joe retched and retched, each seizure as violent as the last. Melissa pressed his face hard to her open thighs to keep his skull from bludgeoning her pubis.

The answering machine picked up. *"You've reached Melissa and Joe. Leave a message at the beep."* "Melissa? Are you there? It's your father." Curt breathed into the phone. "I know you're sick, pumpkin, but please pick up. I think your cell phone's off."

Melissa dragged her fingers through the flora in Joe's hair and mourned the test at the bottom of the toilet.

"It's over, Melissa. The mission president called. Please, if you're there pick up."

Monitoring the wall clock, Melissa checked in with her test, the one that had survived Joe's arrival.

"I'll try your cell phone again," Curt said. "But call me as soon as you get this."

"Ohhhhhh," Joe groaned into the chilly bowl.

Melissa's moist bottom puckered right up.

Trojan Horse

The sister and her parents sat watching Craig, their collective distrust feathering the room like a molting murder of crows. Theo had clearly worked his magic.

"You look ill," Karley Nordling finally said.

A striking woman, Karley, and it wasn't just her lithe lines. She possessed a *something*, a magnetism, that unified the unique elements of her unusual beauty. Her animated face eluded easy labels. Yes, her eyes were large and dark, her cheekbones bold and high, her complexion naturally olive. But none of these, not even the freckles, did justice to the whole. For Karley Nordling was an ensemble piece, and behind her aura of post-virginal innocence, Craig saw a force to be reckoned with. A beauty like hers was a Trojan Horse, and he doubted she lost many battles.

He grinned like a schoolboy. "Yeah, I'm pretty sure I caught a bug."

Karley's smile was less than sympathetic, but her imperfect teeth were just perfect. "And how is Sherm Stillwell?"

"Not good," Craig said. "It seems he's going back to prison. Do you mind if I sit?"

"Please do. Why is Mr. Stillwell going to prison?"

Craig rounded the coffee table and settled on the sofa. Karley occupied the piano bench, Margaret and Curt the loveseat across from Craig. He turned himself to address her. "He violated the terms of his probation."

"By having child pornography in his house?"

Trojan horse indeed. "That," Craig said. "And perhaps by having

195

a collection of children's underthings, most every item stained with semen. I guess it all depends."

"On whose semen?" Karley said.

"On that. And on whose underthings and how he procured them."

"But he's not going to prison for taking my nephew," Karley said. "You don't think Stillwell did it. That's why you're so obsessed with Melissa and Joe."

Craig considered his options and settled for honesty. "Our investigation into Stillwell is ongoing. We have a dozen cops and over a hundred volunteers canvassing his neighborhood, interviewing residents, going through abandoned houses and buildings. So far we've found nothing to link him to Joshua."

"What makes you so sure you're looking in the right place? He could have hidden Josh anywhere."

Craig shook his head. "We're not sure about anything when it comes to your nephew's disappearance."

"Then why did you hold that press conference this morning?"

Again, Craig shook his head. "I didn't. That was not my doing. Had I known in advance, I'd have tried to stop it."

"Because you think Stillwell's innocent and Melissa or Joe is guilty."

"Because we don't have any evidence or witnesses tying Sherm Stillwell to your nephew's disappearance."

Karley looked Craig over with a casualness that skirted contempt. "Why are you here? I mean really. Why?"

"Because your nephew's still missing. And because I meant what I said yesterday. I won't stop until I find your boy." Craig nodded in the kitchen's general direction. "You hired Theo Evans because you wanted the best. I assume it was you who hired him, wasn't it? He's an interesting choice and probably not easy to retain. He'll certainly take care of your sister and her husband, but he won't get Joshua back. That's what I do. That's what I'm best at."

Karley allowed herself a glance down the hall, but Craig could not read her face. "What evidence do you have against Melissa and Joe?"

Margaret DeBoer produced a hankie and fiercely blew her nose.

"What makes you think we have evidence?"

Karley smiled. "That's the first stupid answer you've given. And you knew it was stupid when you gave it."

Craig conceded the point with a smile of his own. "Why did you hire Theo Evans?"

"I asked my question first. You think you have something, don't you? Evidence."

"That's enough, Karley," Margaret said. Karley barely acknowledged her mother.

"Evidence?" Craig said. "We found a few oddities we'd like to have clarified. But no, I wouldn't say we have any evidence against Melissa or Joe."

"See," Margaret told her daughter.

"What oddities?" Curt asked.

"Probably nothing. Once I interview Melissa and Joe, I'm sure it'll all make sense."

"Maybe we can help," Curt said.

"No," Karley said. "We wait. Theo will know what to do."

"That's fine, too," Craig said. "It's not much anyway. A little mud we found on Joe's 4Runner."

"What sort of mud?" Curt asked.

"Dad," Karley warned.

"That's just what we're trying to figure out. It's red like something you might find in southern Utah."

Laughing, Margaret pressed a palm to her breast. "*That's* your mystery?"

"Yes, ma'am. Not very sexy but that's it. One of them anyway."

Margaret smiled. "The cars in this family are famous for their red dirt, detective. They'd probably fall apart if it wasn't there to hold them together."

"Mom," Karley pleaded.

"Stop now," Margaret scolded. "You're the one who made a fuss about evidence."

Karley rocked forward on the piano bench. "*Think*, Mom."

Curt had seen it, too. He looked down the hallway wondering perhaps if he could hail Theo before Margaret opened her mouth again. "Meg," he said softly. "Maybe Karley's right."

She glared at her husband. "Since when has Karley ever been right? About this or any other affair?"

Karley stood up laughing, her face dark with a fury even Craig could tell was ancient. "It's only an affair if you're married, Mom, or if the person you're screwing's married. When you screw your kids, it's called something else. Now close your mouth and keep it shut!"

Margaret turned to Craig. "We have a cabin near Flaming Gorge, just on the Utah side of the border. It's been in my family since before I was born. You can stop worrying about that mud, detective. I know exactly where it came from. Melissa and Joe took Joshua there two weeks ago for an overnighter. The kids all have keys. I do the scheduling, so I know when it's being used. Mystery solved."

Karley sank onto the stool, her expression fraught, and Craig saw she had known all along.

Margaret did not understand the room's sudden stillness. "It's the truth," she insisted. "They were there two weeks ago. That red dirt gets all over everything."

"We'll need to visit the cabin," Craig said.

"I don't know why you'd need to do that," Margaret said. "I told you that mud's two-weeks old."

Craig shook his head. "No, ma'am. I don't think it is. I believe it's much fresher than that."

"I don't understand. How could you know how old—?"

"Our attorney will never allow it," Karley interrupted.

Craig cleared his throat. "Mrs. Nordling. You knew the 4Runner made a trip to your parents' cabin sometime Thursday or Friday, didn't you?"

Karley clasped her hands and thought about the question. She did not avert her gaze. "Why would you think that?"

"Because you knew what I was searching for when I asked about the mud. I could see it in your reaction." Studying Craig, she neither confirmed nor denied. "I know you think you're protecting your sister and her husband. They're worth protecting. But I'm trying to find your nephew. That's all I'm trying to do right now. I really wish you'd tell me what you know."

The weariness in Karley's eyes only intensified her gaze. "We shouldn't be talking to you. Theo gave us strict instructions."

"Yes," Craig said. "I'm sure he did. But Theo's not your attorney. And I think you may have information that might help me find Joshua."

Curt peered at his daughter. "Is this true, sweetheart? Do you know something?"

Karley chewed on her cheek and gazed through the storm door.

"I'm going to ask Melissa and Joe about the mud," Craig informed them all. "Mr. Evans may refuse to let them answer. I hope not but perhaps. Either way we've got enough for a warrant. It'll slow things down, but we'll get one if we must. We have to see that cabin." To Karley, "I really wish you'd answer my questions."

Margaret had proceeded to shrink into the loveseat. "What should we do?" she asked her husband. "Can we just let them do this?"

"Maybe we need our own lawyer?" Curt said.

"No," Karley answered. "You don't need a lawyer." She met Craig's gaze. "I found a receipt in the sweats I was wearing this morning. I needed something to sleep in last night so I took them from the dryer downstairs. The receipt was in the front pocket. It was for gas, credit card, the kind spit out at the pump. It'd been through the wash, but I could still read it. It was dated yesterday morning, 2:17 a.m. Bluff Chevron, Evanston, Wyoming. We always stop there when we go to the cabin. I tore it up and flushed it down the toilet."

Curt DeBoer stared at his daughter. Margaret, a husk, stared at nothing.

"I suppose what I did is against the law."

"No one's interested in that, Karley," Craig said.

Karley studied his old face for thirty long seconds. He could scarcely bear the brightness. Finally, she glanced away at her parents, then returned her gaze to Craig. "There are a thousand reasons Melissa or Joe might've driven to the cabin, none of them having anything to do with Joshua's disappearance. Ask

Melissa and Joe your questions. After that, if you still want to go, I'll take you to the cabin myself."

■

"Nothing like asking a question to get an answer," Jill gloated.

Craig had taken up residency on the Christophers' front porch. Near the bottom of the street, Seymour and a colleague prepared to toss some books. Hans Nordling's BMW turned the corner and accelerated up the hill toward the house. Otherwise, the neighborhood was quiet. It wouldn't last for long. An hour from now, when the restrictions expired, the circus would move to the curb. "Any word from the soil expert?"

"Not yet but this'll speed things up. I'll call her as soon as you let me hang up."

Nordling parked across the street. "How about the pill?"

"Secobarbital," she said. "Generic Seconal, just like you thought."

"Dare I hypothesize?"

"Why would you?" Jill said. "Mormons abhor recreational drugs."

"Play nice."

"It's not the father's, I'm guessing. All that booze, he'd be dead."

Hans crossed the asphalt and started up the driveway. "You have a minute?" Craig called. He showed Hans his phone. "I'm nearly finished here."

"You talking to me?" Jill asked.

Raising a hand, Hans angled his direction.

"I need you to pack your bags."

"Wait," Jill said. "Who are you talking to?"

"You. And gas up your rig. You'll need to pick up a credit card from Financial."

"I don't like the sound of this."

"You're going to the cabin. I've got Picknell making the arrangements now."

"Shit. I hate Evanston almost as much as I hate Rock Springs. Can't we just have the locals do it?"

Hans, who'd stopped a polite distance from Craig, watched Seymour and the tech drop a book and make notes. "I'm not inclined to outsource this one, Jill. Besides, all the keys are here."

"That's why god invented locksmiths." She sighed. "Fine. At least beg a plane."

"I'll see what I can do. In the meantime, let your guys know we're working on a warrant for those boots and that fragment."

"You didn't ask the parents." He'd failed her yet again.

"Oh, I'll try," Craig said. "But I doubt Theo Evans will be too receptive."

"Theo *Evans?* Are you kidding me?"

"I wish I were."

"My, oh, my," Jill said. Then, she whistled.

∎

Craig remained where he was, consolidating energy, while Hans climbed the lawn and mounted the porch. "You look feverish today," the doctor said. "You didn't seem unwell yesterday."

"Just a touch of the flu, I suspect."

Hans sat down in the chair next to Craig's. "You've not had it checked, then?"

The detective shrugged. "If it's the flu, there's nothing to check, is there?"

"Not necessarily. If it's early enough, we might push it back with an antiviral."

Craig could see what Karley saw in the man. In his blond Nordic way, Hans was as handsome as his wife. Blue-eyed, heavy-boned, broad-shouldered, trim-hipped. He looked like an athlete and moved like an athlete, but his demeanor was reserved and gentle. "I haven't thought much about it," Craig conceded.

Hans brought his chair around so it faced Craig. "I'm happy to make a guess, if you'd like. I can do that right where we're sitting." His accent was faint, non-existent, at times. "Are you coughing, congested, a sore throat maybe?"

Craig shook his head. "Just generally achy all over. But I wanted to ask you something."

Hans brought his hands into the space between them. "May I? I haven't washed my hands." Craig assented, and Hans leaned forward and palpitated his neck and throat. "I'm guessing you haven't slept much since this started."

"What I was wondering is whether you might have prescribed Secobarbitol to Joe or Melissa."

Hans sat back in his chair. "I lied. I can't make much of a diagnosis without a few of my tools. We could run up to my office right now. Or I could go grab a few things and bring them back here. We keep a supply of antiviral at the clinic."

Craig chuckled. They were quite a team, Hans and Karley Nordling. A car the detective didn't recognize eased around the corner and motored up the street. Seymour and the tech stopped what they were doing to watch it. Craig wondered who'd let the vehicle through.

Hans stood up. "I'll do that, I'll run to the clinic. It shouldn't take me long."

The car eased to the curb behind Hans's sedan.

"I'm grateful," Craig told Hans. "But I wouldn't waste your time. I don't know where I'll be when you get back anyway."

The storm door opened, and Karley stepped onto the porch. Hans glanced at his wife, and Craig noted the transformation, heard it in the softening of his voice. "If you're too ill, detective, you can't find our nephew. I'm not guaranteeing the medicine will help, but it'll certainly make us feel better."

Across the street a man and woman had emerged from the car. The man wore a suit, the woman a dress. Together they rounded to the trunk.

"Theo wants to talk to you," Karley told Craig.

He nodded. "About before?" he asked Hans. "The matter of that other medication?"

Hans smiled. "Get yourself a subpoena, Milo."

Karley studied the men, trying to suss their exchange, then turned and watched the couple on the street. The man passed the woman a box, then extracted his own from the trunk. "Do you know them?" Craig asked.

The Nordlings shook their heads. The visitors crossed the street and moved up the drive, their ascent a labor, particularly for the woman. Karley hurried down the stairs. "Heavens, thank you," the woman said, relinquishing her load. "I wasn't sure I was going to make it."

"Bishop Furthington," the man introduced himself. "And this is my wife, Andrea." The bishop, bless his heart, peeked at Karley's posterior as she mounted the stairs with her load. He deposited his box on the edge of the porch. "We wanted to stop by sooner," he said. "But what with all the trouble, we weren't sure it was appropriate."

Mormon manna. The boxes were loaded. No wonder Andrea Furthington had struggled under the weight. "We didn't know when you'd be hungry," she said. "Everything but the salads can go right in the oven."

Karley, who'd arranged both boxes beside the front door, descended the stairs again. "I'm Karley Nordling, Melissa's sister. I don't think we've met."

The woman pulled Karley in and gave her a squeeze. "I'm so very sorry for all your troubles."

"Thank you," Karley said. She stepped back and took the bishop's hand. "Bishop Furthington."

"We're all just devastated," the bishop said. "Have there been any hopeful developments?"

Karley glanced over her shoulder at Craig. "I'm afraid not."

"What about that man?" Furthington asked. "The one on the news?"

"It's true, we have someone in custody," Craig said. "But we still have no idea where the boy is."

"I simply do not understand this world," Andrea said. "These are truly the last days."

"We'd hoped to see Melissa and Joe," the bishop said. "Do you think that would be possible? We promise not to stay long."

"I'll ask," Karley said. Hans opened the door and waited for his wife, then picked up the second box and followed her inside.

"You're the detective, Craig?" Furthington asked.

"Yes, sir."

"Then I'm glad I ran into you. We have fresh volunteers if you need them. Everyone wants to help."

"That's a generous offer," Craig said. "Let's see where we are at the end of the day."

Karley opened the door. "They'll see you. But only for a moment if you don't mind."

"Of course," the bishop said. "Should we come inside?"

"Please."

Craig stood back while the Furthingtons climbed the steps, then trailed them into the living room. Melissa and Joe were just emerging from the kitchen. Theo, behind them, did not look pleased.

"Oh, you sweet thing." Andrea Furthington threw her arms around Melissa. Bishop Furthington gave Joe a long, hearty hug.

"Thank you for the food," Joe said.

"Everyone's praying for you," Furthington said. He released Joe. "The whole stake. President Benson called a special fast for Joshua. All eight wards."

"Oh, how wonderful," Margaret said.

Fingers laced at her front, Melissa seemed calm but aloof. Craig noted a slight discoloration beneath her eyes but none of her previous day's panic.

"There's more," Furthington went on. "President Benson made a call to Salt Lake. This one time the Brethren are letting us direct the entire stake's fast offerings into the effort. It was announced across the pulpit, and money's coming in. We'll open an account tomorrow. As long as the funds last, they'll be there to help bring Josh home."

"I don't know what to say," Joe said. "Thank you."

Sister Furthington touched Melissa's arm. "The Relief Society sisters are organizing meals. We'll bring dinner in as long as this goes on. Breakfast and lunch, too, if you think it'll help. But we don't want to be in the way. Just the bishop or I will make the deliveries, at least, until you're ready for visitors. Everyone's been asked not to call. For the time being, the bishop thought that best."

"We don't want to intrude," the bishop agreed, "but we do want to help. Anything you need. Anything at all."

And still Melissa said nothing.

"It's all very confusing right now," Joe said.

"I'm sure it is. It must be unbearable. But you don't have to do this alone." Furthington glanced at his wife who took her cue.

"We should be on our way," she said.

"Yes," Furthington agreed. "We've taken enough of your time. But before we go, perhaps I could offer a blessing? Would that be all right?"

Craig watched Karley watch her sister.

"Of course," Margaret said. "We need all the prayers we can get."

"Joe?" Furthington asked.

It took Joe a moment to nod—like Karley he was studying his wife. Furthington folded his arms and bowed his head, and the family followed suit. Arms crossed, Theo Evans squeezed his eyes tight. Karley lowered her head but kept her gaze on Melissa who continued to stare straight ahead.

"Our Dear Heavenly Father," Furthington began. "At this difficult time we come to thee in prayer to beg thy blessings and help. One of thy precious ones, little Joshua Christopher, has been taken from us. We don't know where he is, Father, but we know Thou hast the power to return him to us safe and sound. Bless little Joshua with peace and courage. Protect him from whatever evil holds him. Please bless the police and the search-ers. Inspire them, guide them to Joshua. Soften the heart of this evil man. Open his mouth and give him conscience. Time is so important. Give haste to Joshua's rescue.

"At this time we ask a special blessing on this house and the people gathered here. Comfort especially Melissa and Joe and the members of this family. Give them courage and strength and clarity of thought. Keep them safe and let them feel thy love. We dedicate our lives to thee, Father, and we ask these things in the name of thy holy son, Jesus Christ. Amen."

"*Amen.*" Theo's big voice resonated above the rest.

Bishop Furthington extended his hand to Joe. "Have courage," he said. "Your son's coming home to you."

It was an effort for Joe to meet the bishop's gaze. "Thank you."

"Melissa." Furthington proffered his hand, but she appeared not to notice. She stared at him coolly until he withdrew it. "It's just a matter of time and faith," he managed. "I can feel it."

Melissa's smile was a bestowal offered in pity. "You pray," she said. "But you don't listen."

"Melissa!" Margaret exclaimed.

Laughing nervously, Furthington glanced around the room. "Well. I'll certainly try to do better."

"You do that, bishop," Melissa said. "Because whatever you're hearing, it isn't from God. Joshua's dead."

Drinking While Driving

5 YEARS 9 MONTHS AGO

When Joe thought he could move without vomiting, Melissa helped him out of his clothes. The silage stink of him—raw, sweet, rotten—was like nothing she had ever smelled. As the bathtub filled, she fished the test from the toilet, then stuffed both sticks in the drawer with the extra soap. She loaded Joe's toothbrush and, steadying him from behind, brushed his teeth. She had to help him spit in the toilet. Not for the last time she marveled that he'd made it home without killing himself or someone else. Six years of binges would follow, six years of blackouts, entire days lost, and still he was never in an accident. Not once was he pulled over.

"Come on, Joe," she said. "Get in the bath, now." With some encouragement, he crawled to the tub and, one appendage at a time, worked his body over the side. The contents of the tub sloshed over the gunwales. Melissa stripped off her wet top and tried to mop the floor with it. She pulled both towels from the rack and finished the job.

Joe groaned. The telephone rang.

She gathered the wet items and padded to the laundry room, leaving a trail of wet footprints on the floor. She loaded the washer and started the machine. On the sixth ring the answering machine picked up. She stopped in the kitchen to listen. "She's still not picking up," Curt said.

Back in the bathroom she retrieved two new towels from the cupboard and hung them over the rack. Joe stared slack-jawed at the ceiling. Pushing hair from her face, she kneeled down beside the tub. The diminished bathwater tested tepid, so she opened the spigot, then reached for the soap and the washcloth.

207

"Where were you?" She wetted the washcloth and rolled the bar in it.

Joe turned his face toward her and squeezed his eyes shut. "Hmm?"

"Where were you, Joe?"

"You don't wanna know."

"Yes, Joe. I want to know." She started with his neck. An ingrown whisker bubbled white above his Adam's apple, and she tried to scrub it away.

"Drinking."

"That's not what I mean. I want to know exactly what you did." She rinsed his neck and reloaded the washcloth, then stretched across him and lifted his arm from the water. "Over your head," she said. Joe's hot breath cooled the side of her damp breast. She washed his underarm, the left side of his torso.

"I started at the liquor store."

"Which one?"

"The one behind the mall. The others close at seven. That one stays open until nine."

Melissa tapped his arm, and he dropped it in the water. She ran the washcloth down the length of it, from the knob of his shoulder to his wrist. "What did you buy?"

"Vodka. A fifth of vodka."

"Why vodka?"

He squinted. "I thought I might come home. The smell of vodka hides. Sorta."

She tapped his right arm, and he flopped it over his head. Water streamed onto the floor. "Why didn't you come home?"

"Because I started drinking."

"The vodka?"

"No."

"What then, what did you drink?"

"Bourbon."

"What's bourbon?"

Soap foam pooled in Joe's navel. He washed a wave over his abdomen but somehow missed the foam. "You really don't know what bourbon is?"

"You know I don't."

"Whiskey. From Kentucky. Or Tennessee."

"Where did you get the bourbon?"

"From Kentucky. Not Tennessee."

"Come on, Joe."

"At a club down on 25th Street."

Melissa stopped scrubbing. "You went into a bar?"

He nodded without meeting her gaze. "I sat outside in the parking lot for a long time first."

"Why?"

"Because I knew what would happen if I went in."

Melissa turned off the water, then sat back on her heels and rested both forearms on the ledge. "What would happen?"

Joe tried to smile. "This."

"I don't know what *this* is."

Joe sighed. He still didn't look at her. "I was so angry, Melissa."

"I don't want to talk about that now. I want you to tell me what this is." She waited.

"I went inside and ordered bourbon. Neat."

"What's neat?" Joe glanced at her. "Please. This is all new to me."

"Straight up. No ice, no mixer. Just bourbon."

"Room temperature."

"Yes, and strong. A shot's worth. That's the law in Utah. One shot per serving."

"How much is a shot?"

Joe shrugged. "An ounce or so. Sometimes bartenders fudge a little. Fudging fosters loyalty."

"You drank the shot. Did you throw it back like I've seen in movies?"

Joe snorted and shook his head. "No. I sipped it slowly. I wanted to enjoy it. I pretended it was my last."

"Why did you pretend?"

"Because when I walked into the bar, I already knew what would happen."

"What happened?"

"I felt better."

"After one drink? Were you drunk?" Kneeling up Melissa rinsed the washcloth.

Joe lifted his hands from the water and kneaded his face. "No. It takes a lot more than a shot of bourbon to get me drunk."

Leaning over the water, she washed his far leg. "So you felt better. What does that mean?"

"I stopped being angry. Music was playing, people were enjoying themselves. The club had a nice feel. I've had a lot of good times in bars. I started to forget."

"Did you see anyone you knew?"

Water dripped from the faucet. "I don't think so."

"How can you not know?"

Joe leaned his head back and lifted his chin. "There were a few familiar faces. From before. Nobody you would've known if that's what you mean."

It was. "So you ordered another drink."

He nodded. "And another after that."

"How many?"

"I don't remember."

"A lot?"

"I don't remember, Melissa. If it's that important, I can try to figure it out from the Visa receipt. I'm pretty sure I put it in my wallet."

"How much did it cost?"

He shook his head. "That's what I'm telling you. I don't remember."

"Were you drunk after all those bourbons?"

Joe closed his eyes. "Yes."

"What's it like to be drunk?"

Joe seemed to be expecting this question. He answered without opening his eyes. "Depends. At the beginning it's warm and comfortable. You don't worry about anything. Later, if you drink a lot, you just feel sick."

"Were you sick or warm and comfortable at the bar?"

"Warm and comfortable."

Melissa started in on Joe's nearest leg. "What then?"

"I paid my tab and left the bar."

"But you were drunk. Did they call you a cab?"

"No."

"They're supposed to call you a cab. I read about it in the newspaper."

"They only call a cab if you act drunk. If you slur or you can't walk right. I only slur after I've been drinking for a long, long time. I was steady on my feet. I didn't slur. I can drink a lot of alcohol without anyone knowing. Some things don't change. Like riding a bike."

"But they knew how much they'd served you."

Joe shook his head. "It doesn't work like that."

The phone rang. Joe opened his eyes and glanced through the bathroom doorway. "Am I dreaming or does the phone keep ringing?"

"It keeps ringing."

"Who was it last time?"

"My father."

It rang.

"Mmm." Joe rolled his head back and forth against the tile. "And how is Curt these days?"

"Not good. They excommunicated Karley today."

Joe's head stopped rolling. "They excommunicated Karley? What day is it?"

"Thursday, Joe. You were only gone one night."

Joe puffed his cheeks and flapped air through his lips. "We were supposed to go to your folks'." He winged his knees, and water sloshed around the tub. "Your parents must be freaked."

"I couldn't say for sure. I didn't answer."

Joe peered at her. "Your dad left a message on the answering machine?"

"No."

"Then how do you know?"

"Because I do." The phone fell silent.

Joe relaxed his legs and his knees dropped open. His penis flopped like a drunken little sidekick. Melissa studied it for a moment, then dropped the washcloth over it. She returned the soap to its tray and rinsed her hands in the bathwater then stood up and dried them on a towel. She closed the toilet and sat down on the cool lid.

"What did you do after you left the bar?"

Joe scratched his thigh. "I got in my truck. I started driving."

"You still had the bottle of vodka?" He nodded. "Did you open it?"

"Yes."

"Where did you go?"

"Here and there."

"Please, Joe," Melissa said softly. "I need to understand this."

"I headed for the canyon."

"Ogden Canyon? Where you had your accident?"

"I know," he sighed.

"Why, Joe?"

"I don't know. I don't remember. I woke up this morning parked in a campground near Porcupine Reservoir."

"You don't remember getting there?"

"No. I don't remember much of anything after leaving the bar."

"So you don't know how you lost your shoe?" He shook his head. "Or got dirt all over you?" He shook his head. "Did you sleep outside?"

"No. The next thing I remember is waking up. I was in the truck."

"Did you still have the vodka bottle? This morning I mean." He nodded. "Was the vodka gone?"

"No. There was some left. Maybe a third of the bottle."

"But it's gone now?"

"It's gone," he said softly. "I finished it. To kill—"

"I'm pregnant," Melissa said.

Joe wrapped his arms around his chest, then sat up and curled himself against his knees.

"I've known for over a week."

He turned his head and raised his eyes slowly, pausing on her breasts. Only now did he register her nakedness. "Pregnancy tests. I thought I was hallucinating."

Melissa peeled herself off the toilet. "You're done seeing things that aren't there, Joe. We both are." Then she turned off the light and closed the door behind her.

Bread and Butter

"There won't be any interview, Milo. Read Joe his rights, put him in the box, he's still not answering any more questions. You'll have to wait until tomorrow to hear the same from Cynthia Armstrong."

"Cynthia Armstrong?"

"Melissa's new attorney. She's not available today, which means Melissa's not available either." Theo and Craig sat in the Christophers' kitchen, the attorney's thin leather bag on the table between them. Theo tapped it with a gnarled talon.

"I suppose that means no polygraph."

Theo smiled. "You look like shit, Milo."

"I feel like shit, Theo. You'd think the parents would want to clear themselves."

"Don't go amateur on me. I have no sympathy for your predicament."

"Spare me," Craig sighed. He could hear the family in the living room, their voices rising and falling with the intensity of their debate. Gas receipts and cabin visits. Good intentions betrayed as often as malice.

"What's next?" Theo asked.

It was Craig's turn to smile. "What choice do you give me?"

Sitting back in his chair, Theo ran a thumb along his jaw, from the hinge of his mandible to the cleft in his chin. "If you use the press you'll lose. But you know that."

"When parents don't cooperate, they look guilty."

Theo rolled his eyes. "You underestimate the public's ability to be educated." He glanced at the fridge door, all those crayon

213

monuments to a happy childhood. "I'm a good teacher, Milo. And so is Cynthia Armstrong. That's why I picked her. Melissa and Joe Christopher are poster children. I couldn't have assembled a better cast."

Craig, sick, had been at it with no rest for thirty-plus hours and Theo Evans could just go to hell. "The parents are lying. We have a gas receipt placing at least one of them in Evanston around 2:30 yesterday morning. Eight and a half hours before the boy disappeared."

Theo shrugged. "Credit cards get hacked or stolen. They get borrowed."

"We've got mud in the 4Runner. Still wet. Red mud. Our soil expert's going to tell us it came from somewhere near Flaming Gorge."

"Like I say, things get borrowed." It was difficult to tell whether Theo was pretending to be bored or pretending not to be. "You're a smart man, Milo. Even if what you say is true, even if one of the parents was driving, there are plenty of benign explanations why that 4Runner might have been in Wyoming yesterday morning."

"And still you're not going to let them explain themselves. Looks bad, Theo. It'll take some higher education to make that one go away." His cell rang, and he checked the screen. Smiling, he looked up at Theo.

"Go ahead." The attorney gestured magnanimously. Craig turned off the phone and placed it on the table—he didn't know how to silence the ringer. Theo touched the device with a fat-knuckled finger. "And how is Chief O'Neil these days?"

"When did you call him?"

Theo tugged back his sleeve and checked the time. "I didn't, I called the mayor. Like forty-five minutes ago." The debate in the other room was getting louder, the voices less civil. Theo adjusted his cuff and listened. It was all but impossible to make out the words.

"Dissention in the ranks," Craig said. Theo gazed at the detective. "You should probably know we're headed to Wyoming. Turns out the family owns a cabin near Flaming Gorge. We'll have to go through Evanston on the way. Maybe stop at that gas station."

But for a slight narrowing of the eyes Theo's placidity held. "Warrant?"

"Nah." Craig shook his head. "Consent. Grandma and grandpa are all for it. The sister agreed to give us the tour. Very helpful, Karley. She also found the receipt."

Ah, Theo's expression said. He granted this new development a tiny nod. "I want to see the receipt."

"Discovery comes later. You know the rules."

Theo grinned. "Discovery comes *if* there's a case, Milo. And if this is the best you've got, I'm guessing my services won't be required for long."

"You may want to hang around a little longer." Craig checked his watch—2:40 p.m. "You saw the seizure sheet?"

Theo nodded.

"Secobarbital. Schedule two. We didn't find a prescription for secobarbital anywhere in the house, just a pill on the bathroom floor behind the toilet. Actually, we didn't find any prescriptions anywhere in the house, which is puzzling because yesterday I watched Melissa take what appeared to be oxycodone. We need that secobarbital script, Theo. Otherwise, we may have to invite the folks down to the station."

Theo niggled his chapped lips with an incisor as he considered Craig's threat. Even if the parents refused to cooperate, both men knew what the press would do if the police hauled them in.

"And then there's Joe's drinking," Craig said. "Certainly you know he's an alcoholic. Poster children, I'm afraid, just aren't what they used to be."

Theo's pupils finally flickered hot. "Anything else?"

"Plenty. But that's all you get. Your clients are each other's alibi. Nine p.m. Friday until they claim the boy went missing. They behave like people who have something to hide. Prove me wrong, so we can move on."

With effort, Craig got to his feet. The argument in the living room had dialed down, the exchange of voices mostly female now and temperate compared to a moment earlier. Theo watched the detective and played out the odds. "How long 'til you drop the dime?"

"How long 'til I get some answers?"

"You don't get answers. Remember, my clients are no longer suspects."

Craig stared at him.

"Give us until tomorrow, I'll see what I can do. I'm making no promises. None. We both know you gain nothing by leaking this to the press. I'm not opposed to trying this in the media. I'm good at it."

Craig rooted through his pockets until he located a handkerchief. He'd learned to keep a number on his person at all times. "The boy's still missing and I'm running out of time." He wiped his forehead and then his lips. "No promises here either, but I'll try to give you a few hours. If I change my mind, don't expect a courtesy call."

Unfolding his limbs, Theo levered himself upright. "You're a reasonable man, Milo. Makes me a little sad I called the mayor."

Craig opened the door. "Do it again, all bets are off."

He passed into the hallway, then slowed to a stop, struck by the lilt of Melissa's eerie calm: "... of course he doesn't remember." He glanced over his shoulder into the kitchen. Theo was zipping his bag.

"But you lied to the police," Curt said. "I don't understand why you'd lie."

"Because it's none of their business, Dad. And when they asked, I didn't know anything about the mud and the receipt. But you're right, I guess. I lied. I didn't tell them he'd been drinking all afternoon."

"He drove to the cabin drunk?" This from Margaret.

"But I don't remember that," Joe protested. "You're telling me I was gone all night? To the cabin?"

"How many times do we have to go over this, Joe? I have no idea where you went. When you got home at five, you hardly knew your own name. You blacked out. You always black out."

Craig felt Theo step close behind him, his presence a gravitational force.

"Blacked out?" Margaret asked. "How could he drive unconscious?"

"Not unconscious," Melissa said.

"Enough!" Theo bellowed, brushing past Craig. "Enough!"

Craig trailed the attorney to the living room doorway. Here it was, the bread and butter of police work, serendipity to misfortune like a match to white gas. The room was a diorama of startled faces—Curt and Margaret, Jared and Caleb and Joe. Only Melissa seemed unaffected by Theo's entry. Sally stared out through the big front window, her profile full of jaw-clench.

"I told you not to say anything to anyone!" Theo raged. "And who gave consent to search the cabin?" Curt and Margaret cowered on the sofa. "Did you sign anything?"

"Well, no," Curt said. "We haven't been given anything to sign yet."

"You're not signing! You hear that, Milo? They're not signing a thing!"

Craig had pulled out his phone and was booting it up. "He's not your lawyer," he said from the doorway. Everyone but Melissa turned.

"I didn't think we needed a lawyer," Curt said.

Are you children?" Theo ranted.

In the short time his phone had been off, Craig had missed nine calls, all from Picknell and the chief. He crossed the room and hurried outside, the phone ringing in his ear. "Jesus H. Christ!" the chief answered.

"You're interfering with my investigation."

"Shut up, Milo." Todd O'Neil sounded as ill as Craig felt.

The sun was hot and Craig was sticky. Hitching like a sick man with a phone to his ear, he jerked his way out of his jacket. "We need a plane. We're flying to Flaming Gorge. The family has a cabin there."

"Listen to me."

"I want a plane, Todd." Craig opened his cruiser and tossed his jacket on the seat.

"You're not going anywhere."

Craig wanted sleep like the parched want water. He imagined diving into it, a large cool pool of slumber. "The parents are lying. The father drunk-drove into Wyoming sometime Friday and home again early Saturday morning. No one seems to know why, including him."

"Milo—"

"We found Seconal in the house. I watched the mother take two oxycodone tablets. We have yet to find a prescription for either."

"Enough, Milo. Shut up and hear me. Elizabeth Stillwell showed up at the station about twenty minutes ago. We've got her sitting in a room waiting for her court-appointed attorney to show up. She says she knows where the boy is."

In an instant the earth stopped revolving. But only for an instant. "I don't care. I want Jill on her way to that cabin, Todd. And I want her to fly."

"You'd leave the boy out there? Walk away from a confession? I don't think so, Milo."

A news rig turned the corner, its transmission fork like a double-barreled Howitzer. A second truck followed at a distance. "My team's searching that cabin. And they're leaving now. We don't have much daylight left."

"You're asking a lot," O'Neil said. The first transmission rig crept in like a stalker, the second rig right behind it. "All right. I'll see what I can do about a plane. I know some folks. But travel only. Nothing happens until we hear what the Stillwell woman says."

Craig settled into his cruiser and closed the door. "You're going to have to pave the way with the sheriff up there. Jill and Picknell can arrange the rest—"

"Yeah, okay, fine," O'Neil cut in. "Just get your ass down here."

Red Lake Frothing

Joe's mother, Julia, missed her only child's wedding. She couldn't make it. She was dead. Joe's father, Melvin, who happened to be alive, sent his regrets with $1,000. Out of the country, Joe explained, doing geographical surveys for some foreign government. Joe was not a proficient liar, but Melissa accepted his claim though she suspected it to be false. Much later—after his drunken night away—she would learn the money was an advance on Joe's credit card, Melvin's regrets a forgery made on expensive cardstock. Fourteen months of courtship, fifteen months of marriage. One would think Melissa might have skewered such deception.

"But it's so strange," Margaret fretted. "What kind of father doesn't attend his son's wedding?"

"He sent $1,000 and a very nice note," Melissa reminded. "We're going to use it for the wedding."

"And you say his mother died?"

"When Joe was very young."

"How?"

"Cancer," Melissa said, though she had no idea. "It's a tender subject. Please don't bring it up unless he does."

■

While Joe slept in the bathtub, Melissa called her parents. Margaret wept on one extension, Curt on another. "Opened and closed," her father said. "He thanked us for our letters."

Pleading nausea, Melissa ended the call quickly. She made soup. She folded laundry. She negotiated with God. When Joe emerged from the bathroom, she sent him to dress, then ladled soup into a bowl.

219

A few minutes later he returned wearing lounge clothes, and she drew back his stool and helped him scoot in. "Tell me about your parents."

Eyeing the soup, Joe nodded. There was no resistance this time from either of them. Joe didn't stop until he'd told her everything.

"Before the accident everything was all right."

Indeed, until Joe's eleventh year, his childhood was unremarkable. While Melvin ran field studies for the National Forest Service, Julia stayed home and raised Joe. "She was a great mom. Patient. Never raised her voice. We were good together."

"What about your dad?"

"He was gone a lot. But I remember being glad when he came home. He could be stern, but he was fun in an outdoorsy way. He'd take me skiing and hiking and hunting. When he came back from his trips, he usually brought gifts. I didn't know him like I knew my mom. But I liked what I knew."

Julia and Melvin had married during college, not a temple marriage, as Melvin wasn't religious, but a good marriage it seemed to Joe. They rarely fought, and when they did, it was Melvin, not Julia, who most often diffused the arguments. When Melvin was away, Julia took Joe to church, when he was home, they all played hooky. Melvin never complained about her religious proclivities, he simply didn't share them.

"It was a regular childhood," Joe said, his untouched soup cooling on the bar. "I didn't have any complaints."

∎

Fast forward to Joe's eleventh year: The environmental movement is carving new inroads and a garden of legislation has begun to bloom. Timber interests, mining companies, petroleum superpowers, Big Ag—hungry money is crying foul, and Melvin Christopher is overworked.

"We never saw him. Even when he was home, he was working."

But Julia does the best she can. She cooks and cleans and helps Joe with his homework. She tucks him in at night, then goes to her own bed where she sleeps alone. She never complains, but Joe knows she's lonely. Joe misses Melvin, too.

Melvin comes home for a week, and the negotiations begin.

By Friday they have reached a fevered pitch. "Please, Dad," Joe begs. He has waited until dinner to launch this bid.

"You know I can't take civilians, Joey. I could lose my job."

"Would that mean you could stay home more?"

Julia laughs out loud. Melvin looks a little wounded then he laughs too. "You're working alone next week," she says. "Who would know?"

Melvin scowls at Julia, but there's nothing behind it. "Did you put him up to this?"

"Nope."

"It's summer vacation," Joe points out. "I wouldn't even miss school."

Melvin considers his son, who is small for his age, then looks at his wife and sighs. "If I get caught, this little lawyer of ours may just have to save my tush."

And so it begins, the ending, with a green government truck pulling a National Forest Service boat down a highway through treeless Ashley National Forest. Northeastern Utah, a chunk of Wyoming. Pretty country despite the barren landscape, red rock and sagebrush and antelope. Three-plus hours from Ogden, Utah, a long trip for a ten-year-old. But Joe doesn't ask how long until they get there. Young as he is, he understands the tenuous nature of opportunity.

"Hopefully, the boys'll be busy with the tourists." Melvin means the local rangers. He doesn't want to get caught with his family in the boat, though, in truth, he's not too concerned. This is a return trip, a monitoring mission, and Flaming Gorge is huge, ninety-one miles long. He'll run his tests and take his samples. The rangers will likely never know he was there.

Melvin foregoes the Forest Service bunkhouse and checks them into a pine-paneled motel room near Dutch John, a handful of miles from the Flaming Gorge spillway. It's hot outside. Joe changes into swimming trunks and a white T-shirt.

Fast forward again: Two glorious days in, three to go. Joe can't believe the size of the lake. While Melvin takes samples, Joe is free to explore so long as he doesn't leave Julia's sight. If the water is deep, he must swim in a life jacket. Julia watches from the boat, sometimes the bank, and every so often jumps into the lake. When Joe gets hungry, she feeds him his lunch or the snacks she's packed in the cooler. Melvin drinks RC Cola until they're headed toward the launch, then he cracks a beer. "It's a slippery slope," he jokes with Julia. "Break one rule and everything comes tumbling down."

Behind her sunglasses Julia smiles. She has a beer of her own, which pleases Melvin. It happens so very seldom.

That night they take a long drive into Rock Springs to eat at what Melvin calls "a cowboy restaurant." The booths resemble covered wagons, wheels and canvas and all. Little lights in the ceiling twinkle like stars. Centered amidst the circle of wagons, cowboy mannequins tend a campfire while stuffed coyotes yip at the ceiling. The floor around the cowboys is duned with sand, foliated with plastic sagebrush. Melvin and Julia order steaks from a pretty waitress dressed in a cowboy hat and chaps. Joe's hamburger arrives with a side of fries slabbed thick as his father's fingers.

"Nothing like a Wrangler butt," Melvin says as the waitress sways away. Julia backhands Melvin, but Joe can tell she's happy.

The next morning, back to the boat. Joe loves to sit in the seat near his father. The trips are getting longer, the sites more distant, and when Melvin opens the big motor, the bow rises then settles as he adjusts the trim. Joe must hold down his hat to keep it from flying off, but the wind feels cool on his sunburned face. Julia sits in the stern, her tapered legs stretched brown across the bench seat. Joe wants to drive but knows better than to ask. He alone wears a life jacket when they're all in the boat.

By mid-afternoon Joe is tired. He's tired by mid-afternoon every day. Only today is hotter, and besides being tired he doesn't feel very well. Julia breaks out the Aloe Vera and slathers him thick. She makes him pull on long pants and a shirt. She sits him on the bench at the back of the boat and cinches him into her own floppy hat. When she isn't looking, Joe loosens the knot and puts the annoying string behind his neck.

Which is how it happens. That and a hard left, the sort of unexpected cut Melvin makes on occasion because it thrills his wife and son.

First, however, the hat. Joe drops his hand to scratch an itch, and the thing spins away like a flying saucer. Panics converge, and Joe lunges at the hat just as Melvin makes his hard left. Julia's scream causes Melvin to turn in his seat—what he sees is her rump and the soles of her feet as they disappear over the gunwale.

Rewind: It's quite a sensation to be thrown from a speeding boat. Joe pinwheels over the water and, when gravity prevails, splats into a lake made of concrete. He surfaces limp but mostly conscious, in too much pain to cry.

Meanwhile, Julia has entered the water with a good deal more grace than Joe. Melvin swings the boat around and prows in through its wake. Julia must swim quite a distance; she grabs Joe's lifejacket and turns him toward her.

"He's bleeding!" Treading water, she frantically examines him.

Melvin cuts the propeller. "Where?" He leans over the side for a better look. Exhaust froths the water near the back of the boat.

"His nose and right ear! I think he burst an eardrum!"

"Settle down," Melvin says. "It'll be okay. Let's get him in the boat."

"Joe," Julia says. "Can you move your arms and legs? Do you think anything's broken?"

"My eardrum," he croaks. "Something in my nose." His voice sounds as though it's coming from the lake.

"Wiggle your arms." Joe wiggles his arms. "Kick your legs." Joe kicks his legs.

"Here," Melvin says. "Bring him closer."

Julia floats Joe to Melvin who dips over the gunwale. The boat turns in the breeze and bobs on the waves, but Melvin manages to snare Joe's lifejacket.

"Sit here," he says, placing the boy between the front seats. "Your mother needs a little help." With pain and some difficulty, Joe gains his feet—he's worried about his mother. Melvin is gesturing over the side near the bow. "The ladder," he tells Julia. "At the back."

The boat rocks, and Joe, his inner-ear damaged, flops sideways into the captain's chair. There are buttons involved, a small hand on the wheel, a lever and a large propeller. The motor roars, and

Melvin tumbles backwards, striking his head on the cooler. He crawls to the bow, throws Joe off the seat, and the boat decelerates as though bungeed from behind. Turning slowly, Melvin scans the milky water. He locates his wife and re-engages the propeller. By now, Joe has managed to get himself sitting. The boat sweeps through the turn, and Melvin disengages the propeller. The craft coasts in, and he reverses the drive train, then kills the motor completely.

Julia's lifeless body bobs face down in the lake.

Melvin looks at his son, then together they peer down at Julia. Her right arm floats higher than the rest of her body, attached by a thin strip of tissue. A wave lifts her gently, and the elbow sinks and the arm rolls bonelessly over. But for a lapping against the hull, it is silent on Flaming Gorge.

Melvin staggers to the stern and rolls the ladder into the water. He toes off his boat shoes and strips off his shirt, then steps onto the ladder and backs into the lake. Before his head sinks below the gunwale, he glances again at his son.

Melvin is not a large man, not as tall as his son will be, but he is fit and strong. All the same he can't carry his wife's body into the boat. First, there's his fist then the side of his face, a shoulder and the back of Julia's floppy head. He falls into the water, and it all starts again. The boat rolls and rocks with Melvin's exertions.

"Get over here and help me." Joe doesn't move. *"Get over here now!"*

Joe takes a step and loses his balance. He crawls the rest of the way. When he peeks over the ladder, he finds Melvin clinging, Julia's back pinned to his front.

"Lean over here. Hold her while I climb in."

Joe stretches long, his chest anchored on the gunwale. Melvin brings Julia around, and her head flops back, her lifeless eyes and too-white face framed in her seaweed hair. Melvin lifts her good arm and extends it from the water. Joe takes it by the wrist with both hands. There's not a blemish above her neck.

"Don't you dare let go," Melvin says.

Joe doesn't let go, not even when the weight threatens to pull him over the edge. Melvin mounts the ladder and hauls himself topside. He sits for a moment shedding water, his face hidden between up-bent knees. Joe holds Julia's arm while the other floats free. The body rolls slowly, and Joe sees his handiwork, propeller-sawed rib-tips like fingers pointing up. Cheek pressed to his biceps, he squeezes his eyes closed.

"Out of the way," Melvin orders, taking Julia by the wrist.

Joe crawls around his father and scurries mid-ship. When he finally turns around, Julia is mostly in the boat, the small of her back arched over the gunwale. The top of her head dangles an inch above the deck, the soft of her chin fine and smooth.

Melvin moans.

Joe looks away.

Melvin lays Julia out and shrouds her with a beach towel, then steps over Joe and toddles to the bow. He tumbles into the helm and slides behind the wheel. The boat rocks, water laps the hull. A minute passes. Five minutes pass. The boat turns in the lake, and Melvin stares straight ahead. Joe registers pain in his ear and nose, a cable-like headache threading the gap. Not five feet away, his mother lies dead.

Finally, Melvin flips on the bilge then cranks the last National Forest Service motor he will ever start. He engages the propeller, and the bow rises sharply. Adjusting the trim, he swings them around, the launch still two hours away. Red lake frothing, the vessel speeds through the pitch, its rooster's tail fat with prismatic light.

The Clinic

The clinic was quiet, its shadows deep in the dim illumination cast by the few lights Hans had switched on coming in. In the supply room, he opened the leather bag Karley had given him in Norway. It was an ornament really, a prop, heavy black leather with a spring-loaded mouth and bold hardware, a gold swivel-latch that fit through the flap eye. He rarely used the bag but loved it anyway because Karley had given it to him. She was on her way to the clinic now, and he wanted her to see him using it.

He assembled the few pieces of equipment he would need to examine Craig, checking batteries before placing the items in the bag. He closed and secured the cupboard, then stepped across the room to the sample lockers. He stood staring at the locks, resisting the direction his brain had been trying to send him since Craig's question about the secobarbital. It was not the cupboard's contents that troubled Hans but accessibility, availability. There was neither Seconal nor hydrocodone in the clinic, no narcotics whatsoever anywhere on the premises. Patients frequently sought them, especially the opioids, even when their pain was not physical. It was easier to say no when there was nothing at the ready. And it was easier to avoid employee abuse when there was nothing to steal. Which was precisely what troubled Hans. He had neither prescribed secobarbital for Melissa or Joe nor seen any indication or heard any complaint that warranted its presence in their house.

He unlocked the cupboard and began to sort through the cartons. Products came in, products went out, a steady rotation that required constant reorganization. He located the antiviral and, counting packets, dropped a full course in his bag.

In his office he placed the bag on his desk, then stood lost in argument with his own better instincts. He was not a distrustful person, he reminded himself, and Melissa had never given him cause to doubt her. This last was a lie, of course. In the past two days she had given him plenty of cause to wonder. He stepped to the doorway and surveyed the nurses' station, not yet ready to look any closer.

The lobby door swung open and Karley hurried through. Even across the distance, Hans could see she'd been crying. She smiled bleakly and shook her head. *No end in sight,* her dark eyes said. She had borrowed Caleb's Jeep to meet him.

Hans said, "That pill the police found in Melissa and Joe's bathroom? It's called secobarbital. Do you know what secobarbital is?"

Karley halted in the middle of the hallway. "No." Head tilted, she turned the diamond in her right ear, the set a gift from Hans after she'd pierced her ears in Norway. Stepping out again, she moved toward him, closing the distance slowly.

"It's a downer. On the street they call it Red Devil, Red Birdie, a few other things."

"It's a street drug?"

"Prescription, but it's more popular on the street than in the doctor's office."

"Did you prescribe it?"

"No. I never prescribe secobarbital. Few doctors do anymore. It's far too dangerous."

"Red?"

"Orange. Generics are various colors, but the name has a way of sticking."

"And you're sure that's what the police found on the bathroom floor?"

"Craig asked me if I'd prescribed it."

Stopping a few feet from him, she watched his face closely but did not otherwise enter the space between them. "What's it used for? As a medicine?"

"Insomnia. Anxiety. Muscle tension. Epilepsy. Side effects sometimes include euphoria."

"So it's addictive." He nodded. "And you think Melissa or Joe's using it?"

"I don't know that." He hesitated. "But I'm quite certain Melissa's misusing opioids."

Karley continued to search his face. She seemed less resistant, and less surprised, than Hans had expected. "How do you know?"

"I spotted it yesterday at the press conference. That was the first."

"And you didn't tell me?"

"I'm sorry. I wanted to be sure."

"What made you wonder? At the press conference?"

"Her calm initially. Then her hysteria. The way she was scratching and rubbing herself."

"How bad is it?"

He shrugged. "Not so bad I can't wean her, if she's willing."

"But that's not the problem is it?"

"No."

Karley wandered away, going nowhere. Reaching over the nurses' counter, she picked up a framed photo of Josh. Hans had seen it a thousand times. "I'm going crazy," she said.

"I like crazy. I almost did my residency in psychiatry."

"Liar." She returned the photo to its place. "I can't make it work. They wouldn't hurt Josh."

"No. Not intentionally."

"Something's missing."

"I think so."

"Something unrelated to Joshua. But something they don't want anyone to know."

"They're both getting high. People tend to hide that sort of thing, especially Mormons."

Karley touched her lips. "I don't want to go to the cabin with the police." She turned around, put her back against the counter. "Theo was right. Craig's going to get it all wrong."

"Say no."

"They're waiting for me to decide. I'm supposed to meet my

ride to the airport back at the house. I told Craig I wasn't so sure anymore. He called just before I got here."

"Don't go."

"You should have seen Melissa's face when she found out about the receipt. She's never going to forgive me."

Karley's misery, Hans's own culpability, the fact that he'd prescribed Melissa the hydrocodone in the first place—it was more than enough. He rounded the long counter into the station. Most of the drawers and cupboards were shared by the staff though the doctors, at least, in theory, reserved a few compartments for their own use. In practice, however, even those drawers and cupboards belonged to the nurses and, like her colleagues, Melissa used Hans's for her own equipment and supplies. The narrow closet-like lockers in the employee lounge did not lock, so the nurses kept their purses here too and anything else they wanted safe or close at hand. Hans pulled back Melissa's chair and opened the drawer.

Karley watched him over the counter.

He sorted through Melissa's items—her stethoscope and an old pressure cuff, tissues, tampons and pads, a bottle of ibuprophen, lipstick, mascara and eyeliner, a tube of hand lotion, a mirror. He opened the bottle and dumped the pills into his hand. Nothing but ibuprophen. He returned the pills to the bottle, the bottle to the drawer, then withdrew a stack of blank script pads. Stepping to the wall, he flipped on an extra bank of overhead lights. The pads looked new, no pages missing, but he held them at an angle under the light anyway. The nurses the clinic employed were LPNs. But Hans and one colleague employed their own RNs, and it was not uncommon for both doctors to pre-sign a number of blank scripts a day. Under the doctors' direction, the nurses filled out the scripts, a time-saving practice that improved efficiency, particularly on busy days. Hans turned each pad under the light. None of the leaves was signed, and the top sheets showed no impressions. He returned the script pads and closed the drawer.

Karley rounded into the station. "She wouldn't hide meds in her drawer."

"Probably not." Hans took a knee and opened his cupboard. Appointment cards, boxes of the pens he preferred. He opened each box—nothing but pens and cards. A case of Coke, un-opened. Two bags of pretzels, a box of protein bars still sealed in plastic, a bag of the cinnamon bears Melissa favored. Two reams of carbon forms, a pair of medical volumes, a layman's prescription reference. One by one, Hans fanned through the pages. He put the books back exactly as he'd found them.

"She's too smart to choose a place someone might stumble across," Karley said.

Hans gazed down the hall at the dark employee lounge. The nurses' station was public domain, their lockers anything but. Reading Hans's reluctance, Karley hurried from the station. Hans followed at a distance.

The locker, when Karley opened the door, gave off the gentle scent of Melissa's perfume. A set of flowered scrubs still in plastic lay at the back of the top compartment behind a stick of antiperspirant, a toothbrush and toothpaste. On the floor a well-used pair of Dansko clogs. An umbrella hung from one hook, a light sweater from the other. Melissa had adhered three photos of Josh to the inner door—Josh as a baby, the other two more recent. A fourth photo, this one of Melissa and Joe and the Ogden Temple, the couple looking young and happy in their wedding finery.

From the second shelf, Karley extracted a leather volume, bumping the top shelf in the processes. Melissa's deodorant toppled to the floor, and Hans picked it up and returned it to its place. Karley unzipped the case, Melissa's Book of Mormon, Doctrine and Covenants, Pearl of Great Price, all of them bound together. "I remember when Mom and Dad gave us these. It was such a big deal."

"She reads it on break sometimes."

Karley leafed through the tissue-thin pages, pausing to read an occasional line. She closed the book and zipped the cover.

"May I?"

Karley drew back the zipper and passed Hans the book. He fanned through the pages, and a paper fell out. Karley retrieved it from the floor, a tithing receipt, a record of Melissa's monthly payment to the church. She studied the figures, each one printed in Melissa's careful script. "I had no idea you paid her this much."

"Don't tell the other nurses," he said. He inserted the receipt between the pages, then zipped the book closed and handed it to Karley.

She rubbed the worn leather cover, Melissa's maiden name embossed in gold along the bottom. She ran a finger across the lettering, then unzipped the volume again and opened the front cover wide. The outer shell was not bound to the book but was an aftermarket casing meant to protect the volume. Working a finger between the shell and the pliable cover, Karley bent the flap and slipped it from the pocket, then withdrew the book from its leather sheath. Four scripts fluttered out.

Hans sank to his knees and gathered the papers, then one by one examined his signatures, the only words penned on the scripts. He moved to rise then fell back on his heels, suddenly uncoupled from the tractor of his will. Finally, he seized the open locker door and pulled himself to his feet.

Karley stared at the carpet where the scripts had been. She released the book, and it landed open, its pages facedown and crinkled. Dropping the cover, she slid her phone from its pocket and scrolled through her recent calls. She selected Craig's number and, phone to her ear, fastened herself tightly to Hans.

Nursing a Disposition

Forgiveness was not in Joe's future, not from his father, not from himself. By the time Julia was interred in the Ogden cemetery, Melvin was no longer employed by the National Forest Service. By the time Joe was fourteen years old, Melvin boozed to maintain and Joe was a ghost in his father's house.

And how did Joe endure his father's silence?

"Stop watering down my Stoli," Melvin told his son. He swirled the bottle he'd just pulled from the freezer, ice crystals like diamonds in the viscous fluid. "It ruins my martini."

Joe glanced up from his homework, his own blessed buzz a balm to his free-floating panic. A beaded glass of vodka Sprite sweated on the table beside him. Melvin picked it up and took a sip, then poured the drink in the sink. "If you're gonna do it, at least do it right."

He removed from the fridge a jar of pickled peppers and a bottle of dry vermouth. The shaker was on the counter from the night before, and he pried off the lid and dumped the old water. He opened the freezer, snatched a fistful of ice, and tossed the cubes in the stainless steel silo. Less than a minute later, he placed the martini on the table. In the spangled vodka, the pepper shimmered, a dimpled little heart in a halo of swirling stars. Joe stared at the conical glass. Three whole sentences—Melvin hadn't used so many words in as long as he could remember.

"Go on, then, thief boy." Melvin thrust his chin at the drink.

The calm that descended as Joe reached for the martini was wholly separate from the vodka already coursing through his veins. For the first time in years, Melvin had given Joe something

233

better than a gutful of dread. Antarctica, that martini, Antarctica on fire. Like a boy sipping water, he took a second swallow, then set the glass on the table.

Melvin considered Joe for an unusually long time, which was to say he considered him period. "How old are you?"

It was not an odd question. Since the accident Melvin had forgotten Joe's birthdays. "Fourteen."

"Fourteen. What grade are you in?"

"Ninth."

"Ninth grade," Melvin mused. "You failing any classes?"

"No, sir. I'm getting good grades."

"Good? What's good?"

"A's. One B. In history."

Melvin wrinkled his nose as if he'd whiffed something bad. "History." Pivoting to the counter, he reached for the shaker. "Unless you're drinking a martini, stay out of my Stoli. It's not made for soda pop." He glanced over his shoulder. "And if your sneaking my booze ends up causing me problems, I'll kick your scrawny ass."

The next day a magnum of cheap vodka appeared in the freezer, wedged in with a new fifth of Stoli.

■

Extra-curricular activities were never really an option for Joe. If he couldn't walk to an event, he had to bum a ride. And he couldn't bum a ride on a regular basis without explaining Melvin's frequent travels. Joe did not like questions, especially from adults, and he did not like to be a burden. There was housework and yard work and homework to do. And alcohol to keep him company.

On this day, however, Joe arrives home later than usual. Melvin is supposed to be away on a trip, so Joe has lingered at school to watch a girls basketball game, to admire a girl he likes. Rigid as a post, he stares at Melvin's pickup, his breath smoking signals in the cold December air. If Melvin is home, something is wrong.

Joe enters the house sober, every nerve firing. Melvin is in the kitchen hipped up to the counter downing the drink in his hand. Joe notes he has decided on Scotch tonight, his weapon of choice when nursing a disposition. He doesn't look up, so Joe starts for his bedroom hoping he's been given a pass.

"Gone three days, not so much as a hello."

Joe turns quickly. "How was your trip?"

Melvin hefts facial fat and bares his teeth—he's put on quite a load since his boating days. He holds his tumbler two inches from his lips. "Hah." He swills a sip, clacking crystal and ice, then places the tumbler on the counter. "Look at my manners." He opens a cupboard and removes another tumbler, a mate to his own. Ritual is important. Melvin likes his accoutrements. He lifts the tumbler to the light, blows in the glass, then checks it again and nods. From the freezer, he extracts a handful of ice.

"Damn." He fishes a few cubes from the glass, tosses them in the sink, then uncorks the Glenlivet and pours three fingers. "Lose the backpack, stay a while." He proffers the tumbler.

Joe doesn't much like Scotch, not at this point in his life, but he is sufficiently schooled in his father's malice to know he had better take it. He sheds the backpack and accepts the tumbler.

"A toast," Melvin insists. His own drink freshened, he throws out his chest. "To bachelorhood and unemployment."

Confused, Joe raises his glass, the very first toast of his life. Eyebrows aloft, Melvin monitors him over the rim of his tumbler. Joe takes a second sip and then a third, each larger and smoother than the last.

"My, my, my," Melvin says. "A man after my own heart."

Joe breathes fumes and smoke through his mouth. "I didn't expect you for a couple of days."

Melvin sets his tumbler on the counter and leans back, his arms spread wide on the surface behind him. "I'm early and you're late."

"I stayed for a basketball game." Joe takes another sip.

"Didn't know you liked basketball."

This is beginning to resemble an actual conversation. "It was a girls basketball game. I stayed to watch a friend play."

"Ah." Lips tight Melvin nods. "Lots of leg. A little jiggle. Next it'll be naked mud-wrestling."

Joe stares straight down at the ice in its amber. Melvin is

seldom blatantly mean, preferring a subtler sort of destruction. You have to care to be mean, and if his silence says anything, it is that Melvin does not care. What, Joe wonders, is Melvin caring about now?

"You must like this girl."

Joe shrugs. He swirls the cubes, then lifts the glass and takes another pull. He is beginning to understand what his father sees in Scotch. He feels more impervious with each sip. "She's just a friend."

"Every man needs a woman." Melvin pushes off the counter and picks up his drink. "A woman or a stiff drink."

Nose in his tumbler, Joe inhales the Scotch. "Is everything okay? Did the project end early?"

"Speaking of women," Melvin says. "Wouldn't your mother just be freaked by how you're growing up? What are you now? Sixteen?"

Joe gapes at Melvin, mention of Julia like a hammer to his skull. "Fifteen."

"Fifteen and drinking single malt with the old man. Got the crystal tumbler, got the look in the eye. By god, boy, I hadn't noticed—you're already tall as I am."

All these years Joe has been waiting for Melvin to mention Julia. And now that he has, Joe feels nothing but disgust. He turns for the Glenlivet, and Melvin steps in his way. They face each other, neither of them giving until finally Melvin grins.

"Allow me." He produces the bottle, still uncorked, and pours four fingers into Joe's glass. "To freaking your mother out." Melvin tinks Joe's glass with the bottle. "So you fucked this girl yet?"

Joe looks away. "No."

"I only ask because your mother would have wanted to know. She was into that kind of thing. Romance. Flowers. Candles. Fucking."

Now Joe looks at Melvin. He must release his jaw in order to speak. "You said unemployment. Is that why you're home? Did you lose your job?"

Melvin stares at Joe. "You should bring this girl of yours around sometime. I'll let you know if she's worth fucking."

Like a single headlight on a faraway horizon, Joe sees a pin-prick of luminosity speeding toward him. He takes a big sip, then sets his tumbler on the table and unzips his parka. He hangs it on the back of a chair and picks up his Scotch again. "Why now?"

Melvin crunches an ice cube, chews open-mouthed, the sound of a dog crushing bone. "Why now what?"

"Mom. Why are you talking about Mom? I didn't think we talked about Mom."

Melvin stops chewing. Cheeks between his molars, he sucks on the shards. He does not swallow for a very long time.

"You lost your job, didn't you?" Joe says.

"You know we almost didn't have you? I had to talk your mother into it. That's right, your mother didn't want kids. For a Mormon, she sure had her own ways."

The light is getting closer. Hot and white. "I don't want to talk about Mom."

"You know what changed her mind? Hmm? Me neither." Melvin shakes his head. "What the hell were we thinking?"

"You're a drunk," Joe says. He strides from the room.

"Looked in the mirror?" Melvin asks, following.

Joe stops in the living room, his back to his father. How much alcohol has he consumed? Hard to say, but he feels it all the way to his fingertips, in his lips and toes, behind his sternum like a thick leather plate. When he turns around, he is smiling. "They caught you drinking on the job. That's why they fired you, isn't it?"

"That a boy," Melvin tells him. "Tough as nails."

"You're not the only one who wishes I'd never been born."

"Boo-hoo-hoo." Melvin rotates a fist under an eye.

"Why don't you just say it?" Joe says evenly. "Tell me I killed Mom. That you hate me for killing Mom. Why not just say it?"

Melvin sips his Scotch. He winks. He grins. He takes another hit.

"Okay, I'll say it. You hate me. I chopped her up, spit her out, left her dead in the water." Joe winks. He grins. He empties his glass. "I ruined your life. I lost your job. I made you a fat alcoholic."

"Oh, boy," Melvin laughs. He rubs his belly. "Now you're getting personal."

They stare at each other. The light is close now, and there stands Melvin, a silhouette in its glare. "So, fat man. Did I lose this job for you too?"

Melvin peels his lips off his teeth. "You know what I remember? I remember her arm. You remember that arm? A little more snip, and we'd've had ourselves one hell of a dandy cup holder."

"You're not my father."

The possibility seems to please Melvin. "You may very well be right, boy, but I'll tell you what. I'd rather have a whore for a wife than you for a son."

Melvin is too drunk and too slow to duck. Joe's glass tumbles through the air shedding watery ice and catches him high on the forehead. It opens him deep then bounces right and shatters against the wall. Melvin's head snaps back, and a bloody arc follows like paint flicked from a loaded brush. Melvin catches himself without going down, then bends over, a palm to the gash. Blood seeps between his fingers and runs down his forearm. He peeks at his Scotch. It would appear he's not spilled a drop.

"Head wounds," he observes. He rights himself and takes a drink, then sets his bloody tumbler on an end table. He mournfully surveys the crystalline wreckage. "Give a boy a man's tumbler and this is what you get. I'm afraid you'll have to pay."

Joe in the throes of something like elation doesn't move until Melvin starts slowly toward him. Stepping backwards apace, Joe keeps his distance. Melvin flicks blood from his fingers, then mashes the hand over the wound again. Passing the sofa, he swipes a throw pillow embroidered long ago by Julia. The small teddy bear on the front is framed by the words *I love you beary much*. He presses it to his forehead.

Joe backs into the hall and turns the corner. He is not afraid, the opposite of afraid—he would bottle this moment, elongate time just to make it last. Melvin follows him into Joe's bedroom, the pillow like a goiter misplaced on his forehead. Joe stops by his bed, distracted by two cartons on the floor beside his desk. Melvin halts and looks at the boxes too. A computer and a monitor, quality gear.

"A little parting gift from the outfit," Melvin says. "The least they could do." He pops Joe close-fisted, and the boy spins onto the bed, the pain weirdly refracted to the other side of his face. Tossing the pillow, Melvin grabs Joe's shirt and hauls him off the bed. Joe comes up swinging and cuffs Melvin's ear, but Melvin doesn't notice. He launches the boy through the open doorway, and Joe bounces off the wall and drops to the floor. Melvin stumbles into the hallway and boots him in the solar plexus, then stoops and snatches a fistful of hair. "You've got a mess to clean up," he tells his son, then he drags him down the hall.

Joe struggles for his feet, his knees at least, but Melvin is moving too fast. They turn the corner, and Joe's shoulder catches. "Oops," Melvin says, changing direction.

Joe grabs the door frame with one hand, Melvin's ankle with the other. The whole house shudders as Melvin bounces on the floor, a tuft of Joe's hair in his fist. Joe staggers to his feet and kicks wildly at Melvin, glancing a blow off his head. Hands on knees, he pauses to breathe. Melvin's blood is all over Joe's new white Vans.

Melvin rolls over grunting. Bent, still panting, Joe watches him get to his feet. Less steady now, Melvin raises his bloody hand and looks at the hair still stuck there. He turns the hand over and a few strands release. Father and son watch them feather to the floor.

"What's the last sound before a pubic hair hits the ground?"

Joe answers by spitting on Melvin.

Nostrils flared, Melvin comes at Joe who this time refuses to move. Melvin's huge college ring, when it meets the boy's skull, spins him sideways into the wall. Melvin snares Joe's shirt and leads him toward remittance. Five feet from the wall, he brings his weight to bear and hurls Joe at the wet dent in the sheetrock. Joe bounces hard and topples to the floor. Dazed and throbbing, he does not yet register the glass in the palms of his hands.

"Whew." With the cuff of his sleeve, Melvin swipes at his forehead. "You're right. I'm fat."

Joe lifts his face, ready for Melvin to end him. Weighing his options, Melvin licks his bloody lips. He spots his tumbler, miraculously whole, and takes two plodding steps. With the hem of his shirt, he tries to buff blood off the crystal, then gives up and shoots the dregs. The moment is lost, and Joe hangs his head. His long hair sweeps the hardwood floor. He touches the lump made with Melvin's ring and cuts his ear with the glass in his palm.

"Clean up this mess," Melvin says. "I'll go make us another drink."

Motherly Love

A husky-voiced battle ax of indeterminate antiquity, Betty Stillwell appraised Picknell with a jaundiced eye. "I see you brought your pet ape."

Ignoring her, Craig addressed the poor attorney who'd drawn the short straw. "How you doing, counselor?" Ashley Yost managed a wan smile. She couldn't have been more than fifteen years old. Craig assessed the old scorpion coiled beside her, stinger pointed straight at him. "I'm going to have Detective Picknell read you your rights, Betty."

"I know my rights. You read 'em to me yesterday."

"Yes, we did. And today's a new day."

While Pick ran through the script, Betty eyeballed Craig. "Do you understand these rights?" Picknell asked.

"Yes, you idiot. I still understand them." She continued to study Craig. "I wanna know what Sherm told you."

"Joshua Christopher, Betty—he's why we're here. Either you know something or you don't."

Betty looked at Ashley. "Aren't you supposed to do something? Object or file some happiass crapass?"

"I've been trying for the past hour," Ashley said flatly. "You don't listen."

Betty laughed. Turning to Craig, she said, "So do it already. Charge me with taking that kid."

"Why would we do that?"

"My client will not be answering that question or any other," Ashley said. "This was a bad idea, Betty. It's time to go."

"Shut up," Betty told her.

"Do not answer."

"Shut. Up." To Craig now, "You think I don't know my Sherm? He told you I took the kid."

"Where's the boy?" Pick asked.

Betty graced him with a smile. "Not so fast, Neanderthal Man."

"Why did you want to talk to us, Betty?" Craig asked.

"I wanna smoke."

"This is a non-smoking facility."

"Gi'me my smokes, and I'll tell you a story."

Craig glanced at the camera. "First, tell me why you asked to speak with us."

Something close to mirth scuttled Betty's features. Unfurling the longest tongue Craig had ever seen, she licked the tip of her bulbous nose. "How else was I gonna learn what's going on?" She glared at Ashley. "This fool doesn't know a thing."

The door buzzed, then opened, and the turnkey walked in, Betty's cigarettes in one hand, an ashtray in the other. Interrogation rooms, like Las Vegas, were anything-goes zones. Health and decency and truth were optional.

"Bless your heart," Betty said.

"Give them here," Craig told the officer.

The uniform placed the cigarettes in front of Craig, a lighter balanced on top of the box. He slid the ashtray onto the table, then left the room as quietly as he'd entered. "Neat trick," Betty said. Out came the tongue, this time pointed at the camera.

"All right, Betty," Craig said. "Tell us why we're here."

Betty pointed at the hardpack. "First a cigarette and an answer to my question."

Craig rose slowly, testing the wind. He had no desire to go down in front of Betty Stillwell and Ashley Yost. Sliding the cigarettes and lighter to Picknell first, he dragged his chair around the table. Picknell fired up the lighter. Betty inhaled deeply.

"Do you mind?" Craig asked Ashley, pushing the table aside. The young attorney scooted back to make room, and Craig situated his chair directly in front of Betty. He handed her the ashtray, and she placed it in her lap. Ashley scooted closer to her client again. "What do you want to know?"

"I wanna know if Sherm's okay."

"Sherm's great. He's getting ready to take a polygraph."

Betty flicked ashes onto the floor. Face askance, she released a jet of smoke, her eyes never leaving Craig's. "I wanna see him."

"No."

"I know what you want from me. But you're gonna have to let me see Sherm."

"No. You can't see Sherm."

She thought about this while her cigarette smoldered. Silence and smoke filled the room. When the nail was mostly filter, she flicked it at the camera. No one moved to retrieve the butt. "Did he tell the truth? Or did he confess?"

"Why would he confess? Unless he did it, of course."

She peered at the box of cigarettes on the table. "No. Even if he confessed he didn't do it. Can I have another smoke?"

Craig nodded, and Pick retrieved the box and thumbed open the flip-top. Betty put the cigarette between her lips and cupped her hands around the lighter Pick extended. He dropped the box into her lap with the ashtray and handed Craig the lighter.

"What makes you so sure he didn't do it?" Craig asked.

Betty smoked for a moment, now avoiding Craig's gaze. "I'm his mother. I know my son."

"You have no idea where the boy is. You don't know anything about any of this."

"Listen to what I'm saying. Sherm had *nothing* to do with it. I don't care what he said. It wasn't him."

Craig usually enjoyed lying, but today it serviced neither clarity nor truth. He did not doubt the Stillwells were guilty, just not of Joshua Christopher's abduction. "Why would he confess if he didn't do it?"

"So he did confess," she said peevishly. "Why am I not surprised?"

Ashley Yost shifted in her chair.

"Why would he confess if he didn't do it?" Craig asked again.

She cocked her head, the cigarette poised an inch from her lips. She lowered her hand without taking the hit. "He loves his momma."

"You're telling me he confessed to protect you?"

Ashley leaned forward and touched Betty's knee. "Don't answer, Betty. You need to stop talking."

Smiling, Betty extinguished her cigarette on the back of the lawyer's hand. Ashley jerked away hissing, her shoulders curled around the pain. Craig snatched Betty's forearm and yanked her off the chair. The ashtray and cigarettes scattered. She emitted a sharp yelp, then started to laugh. Arm around Ashley, Pick held her close as he examined her injured hand. Her open-mouthed horror seemed a conjuring to Craig, Edvard Munch's silent scream.

He dropped Betty into the chair and kicked the cigarettes against the wall. "Interview's over. Say goodbye to your lawyer."

"I don't want a lawyer," Betty said.

Ashley turned toward her client, her damp forehead glistening in the overhead light. "You're a fool, Betty. You're going to hang yourself."

"Go away," Betty told Ashley. "And don't come back."

Ashley went away. And didn't come back.

■

"Sign it." Craig held out the pen.

Betty scribbled her name to the Counsel Waiver. She might have been claiming a million dollars.

"Cuff her, again," Craig instructed Pick. Waiver and pen in hand, he rounded the table and sat down. "All right, Betty. Let's hear about mother's intuition."

Betty leaned forward in the chair Pick had seated her in. "I can't think cuffed like this."

"Tell us your story."

"At least cuff me in front so I can smoke." Unmoved Craig and Pick gazed at her. "For this I should get the cigarettes, too."

Craig stood up and turned for the door.

"All right. I did it. I took the kid. That's how I know Sherm's innocent."

The two policemen stifled yawns. Craig wandered back and settled into his chair.

"Where's Joshua?" Picknell asked.

"I'm not talking to him."

"Where's Joshua, Betty?"

She shook her head. "I'm not telling any more until I get what I want."

Craig glanced at Picknell who rolled his eyes. "Stand up." Betty stood and turned around. Pick removed the cuffs and tossed them on the table. "Sit down."

"And the cigarettes, too," she said. "Please." Rubbing her wrists, she sat down again. Pick retrieved the dented pack from the floor and put it in front of her.

Craig slid the lighter across the table. "Where's Joshua?"

Betty extracted a bent cigarette from the box and put it between her lips. The crooked tip bounced when she spoke. "I'll get to that when I'm ready." Picknell lit the cigarette. Betty inhaled. "You say Sherm confessed. But if he took the little turd, why haven't you found him yet?" She lifted her chin and released the remaining smoke. "Those pictures you found on my computer?"

Craig nodded.

"I got 'em for Sherm. Took me six months to figure out how to do it. And it wasn't cheap, let me tell you. But I got 'em."

"What does that have to do with anything?"

Betty chuckled smoke through her nostrils. "Sherm's gutless and he's stupid. I mean *really* stupid. In a thousand years he couldn't have gotten those pictures himself. Just like he couldn't have abducted that kid. He can diddle 'em and he can whack off to 'em but that's the extent of his repertoire."

Craig looked at Picknell. "How's this working for you, Pick?"

Pick shook his head. "I can't figure why she's so anxious to unburden herself."

"Why you so anxious to unburden yourself, Betty?"

"Ashtray?"

Picknell found it under the table and handed it to her.

Studying the moniker at the bottom—Herb's Towing—she ashed her cigarette onto the floor. "You have kids?" she asked Craig. He stared at her. "Then you know how it is."

"You know what she's talking about, Pick?"

"Motherly love, I think."

"Weird," Craig said.

Betty listened calmly, straightening another cigarette. In the ashtray her current one burned toward the filter. "I had no other choice. I wasn't about to lose him."

"So you supplied him with child pornography."

She nodded. "He has his needs. I have mine. But that doesn't mean I didn't have his best interest at heart. I don't know how he's going to survive without me."

Storm clouds gathered beneath florescent fixtures. The room had grown darker by the exhalation.

"You're full of shit, Betty," Craig said. "If you knew where the boy was, you'd have told us by now, that or you wouldn't be here at all."

"Don't be in such a hurry. The kid's not suffering."

Shoulder to the wall, Pick rolled the lighter deftly over his knuckles. Patience, he believed, was not a virtue.

"All right," Craig said. "For kicks and giggles, let's pretend you're telling the truth. Why did you do it?"

"I told you. I couldn't lose him."

"I'd say your plan was a tad shortsighted."

A yard of ash fell on Betty's worn shift. "It would have worked except Sherm's such a retard."

"How so?"

"Going up by the kid's house, getting himself caught like that."

"Maybe he was planning ahead."

She gave Craig a dubious onceover. "What do you mean?"

"You know, setting things up so we'd believe his confession. Making it look good. That's the thing with false confessions. They have to seem credible. You two sure do love each other a lot."

Betty ground her cigarette into the ashtray. The one she'd straightened waited. "You cops, you're all cocksure you know how the world works."

"What changed? What made you decide you had to grab a kid?"

Picknell pushed off the wall, lighter extended. On the exhale, Betty pointed the cigarette at Craig. "You look green behind the gills. You better not be sick. I catch everything."

"Something must have happened."

She nodded. "Sherm decided to move out. He went looking

for apartments. I told him what would happen if he ever tried to move out. What else was I supposed to do?"

"I'm not getting you."

She shook her head, smoke streaming from her nose. "I told him I'd steal a kid and make it look like he did it."

Craig and Picknell shared a glance. "You mean if he tried to leave you?"

Betty nodded. "Yes. And he was trying to leave me."

"But why this, why the confession? This couldn't have been in the plan."

Lowering her face, she brushed ash from her lap. "Sherm surprised me."

"Surprised you how?"

"He wouldn't diddle the kid. I was positive he would, but he wouldn't. He had to diddle the kid for the plan to work." She fluttered a hand, confused by Sherm's fecklessness. "Anyway, I made my threats, but I never would've turned him in. Nobody was ever gonna find out. And it would have worked too, the stupid putz. I know it would have worked."

Craig shook his head. "So after you abducted a child for your son to rape, you suddenly got a conscience?"

"I'm not making Sherm pay for what I did. He's my boy. You think he's bad, but he's not. He's just stupid."

"Where's Joshua?" Craig said. Betty shook her head. "Is the boy alive or dead?"

"You don't wanna know how I did it?"

Craig had endured enough of Elizabeth Stillwell. He wanted the interview finished. "Sure, Betty, tell us how you did it."

"I drove up next to the kid, opened the door, and called him over. When he got close, I dragged him inside. Nothing fancy."

"Joshua doesn't talk to strangers."

Betty giggled herself into a coughing fit. "Well," she gasped. "Not anymore he doesn't."

"Were you driving your own car?"

"It's the only one I got."

"The dogs went through your Nova, Betty. They found nothing."

"Get new dogs."

"Why Joshua?"

"Sherm likes boys better than girls."

"Why that neighborhood?"

"Because it's not mine. And because the kid was there and nobody else was."

Craig's second-hand buzz felt more like a jackhammer. "How did it happen? Paint me a picture."

Betty reached for the cigarettes. She mishandled the first, watched it disappear beneath the table, then dipped into the box for another. "I could get used to this manservant thing." She leaned into the flame, her hands wrapped around Picknell's. "A picture, huh? Okay, how about this one? Little Bunny Foo-Foo's hopping through the forest, going to a birthday party—"

"How do you know he was going to a birthday party?"

She smiled. "It was all over the news, wasn't it? He was carrying a gift. Wrapped up real nice."

"There wasn't a gift."

"Wrong."

"What was it?"

"The gift?"

"Yes, Betty, the gift. Certainly, you opened it."

For no reason Craig could fathom, Betty ashed her cigarette in the ashtray. "You really do look wretched."

"You don't know if there was a gift. You're making this up as you go."

"That's the thing," she said. "I'm just sure there was a gift. But shit got kinda confusing there for a minute. I must have misplaced it. Did you find it?"

Whistling through his nostrils, Picknell turned to the one-way window and glared at Betty's reflection. "What's his problem?" she asked. A mushroom of smoke welled from her mouth. She sucked it back in for recycling.

"So now Joshua's in the car," Craig said. "What then?"

"I told him to shut up or I'd smack him."

"Did he shut up?"

"After I smacked him."

"And then?"

"I drove over to Mount Ogden Park. It was raining, no one around. I parked up in the trees by the picnic pavilion and tied him up."

"What did you tie him up with?"

"Duct tape. I like duct tape. Got lots of it. Very handy stuff. I put some over his mouth, then made him lie on the floor and drove him to my house."

Picknell turned from the one-way and Betty glanced at him.

"What did you do after you took him in the house?"

Disdain flooded the channels of Betty's face. "Did I say I took him in the house?"

"You said you took him home."

"Right. I drove him home. I put him in the trunk and went in the house."

"Weren't you afraid someone would see you?"

"Why would I be? You know the houses around us are vacant."

"So the kid was up front and in the trunk both. And still the dogs got nothing."

"Like I say, get new dogs."

Flicking the lighter, Pick glanced up at Craig and shook his head.

"Let me guess. You went in the house and got Sherm."

"There you go again, putting words in my mouth. Sherm wasn't home. He was out looking for someplace else to live. I went inside and turned on the tube. I wanted to see how long it'd take to hit the news."

Craig sat back in his chair. "Yesterday you told us Sherm was with you. You said you watched TV together after he got home from his shift at the dog food plant."

"I lied." Betty mined for another cigarette. "I was out collecting that damned kid, and Sherm was out trying to leave me. He still wasn't home when I got there. The kid was on the news before Sherm pulled in."

Betty held her unlit cigarette out to Picknell. He ignored her. Finally, she dug into the ashtray, fished out the smoker, and used it to light the new one.

"All right, let's pretend again you're telling the truth," Craig said. "What happened when Sherm got home?"

Betty ashed. "Pretend? Is it pretend you caught him up in that ritzy neighborhood? Like I already told you, when he got home, he wouldn't diddle the boy. He had to see the boy not to diddle him."

Betty's logic was circular when it wasn't twisted, and her game was making Craig angry. "Tell us where Joshua is." Betty stared at the wall and said nothing. "I don't believe you, Betty. Nothing you've said makes any sense and it all contradicts everything you both told us yesterday. You have no idea where Joshua is."

She lifted her face, her expression vacant. "He's in the river. Probably hung up somewhere along the bank by now."

"The river? Which river?" Craig watched Betty run a shaky finger along her top lip. "Answer me, Betty. Which river?"

She licked the tip of her nose. "The Ogden. Back behind the golf course."

"You're lying."

Betty graced the men with a matronly smile. "Am I?"

The Cabin

From the air Karley could see the deputy's rig parked beside the tarmac, the evening rays winking off its windshield. The man himself leaned against his SUV, the hand at the end of his extended arm open to block the sun. Hat in hand, he tracked the plane in. Karley sat back in her seat and closed her eyes, ill with turbulence and a growing certainty. Melissa's betrayal, that she'd jeopardized Hans's career, had razed the remaining barriers between Karley and her doubt. The force of her fury had blasted them down.

"Sorry again about the ride," Short Wilson said. He swallowed back the throttle and leaned hard on the brakes, throwing the women against their seatbelts. "Going over the range is always an adventure, especially so close to a storm."

"The city owes you," Jill said.

"Nah," Short said. The two big motors thrummed as he turned the plane on the tarmac. "Find the kid, we'll call it even."

Jill was already out of her seat gathering gear. Short steered the plane onto the pad beside the SUV and began the process of shutting it down. It was his plane, a twin engine Beechcraft, leather seating for six, a cramped but nicely appointed cabin. He was a large-scale contractor (something to do with freeways, Karley recalled, though she'd missed the specifics) and used the plane for business.

"Here, let me get that hatch," he said.

"You okay?" Jill asked Karley.

"Fine." She hadn't removed her seatbelt.

The criminalist turned away, and Karley sat another minute

before releasing the buckle. Emerging from the cabin, she immediately felt better. In the contrast—the fading sun, the cool, sage-laced air—she finally registered the extent of her claustrophobia. She paused on the top stair to breathe. She'd never flown into Manila, though she'd been here hundreds of times.

The deputy removed his hat as she approached. He was a red-cheeked kid, younger than Karley, the outline of his vest pronounced beneath his uniform.

"This is Karley Nordling," Jill explained. "The cabin belongs to her family."

"Ma'am," the boy said.

"I'm sorry," Karley said. "I didn't catch your name."

The deputy's awkwardness was so familiar she hardly noticed. "Kent. Deputy Kent Lambert. I know your place if it's the one I'm thinking of. It's that in-holding, right, the one off SR 1145?"

"That's the one. It's been in the family since before my mother was born."

Deputy Lambert nodded. Dipping his head, he donned his hat.

"I think that's everything," Short said. "Gears all loaded, you're ready to roll."

"I can't say how long this will take," Jill apologized. "We'll stay in touch."

"I'm not going anywhere," Short said.

"You want us to drop you in town?" the deputy asked. He opened the driver's door. "Not much there, a café and a store, but you can find something to eat."

Short stretched his back and squinted at the ramshackle assortment of buildings a mile or so to the east. "I could use the walk but thanks. I'll keep my phone close."

"Motel in this town?" Jill asked.

"Couple," Lambert said. "For the lake tourists."

"Not for me," Short said, manning the rear door for Karley. "Comes to that I'll sleep on the plane."

The back seat, Karley discovered, was a cage—a metal grille behind, a thick glass partition in front, doors with no interior handles. Deputy Lambert slid the partition open and placed his hat on the console. A shotgun in a bracket pointed up at the rearview mirror. Lambert picked up the radio—the VIPs had arrived, he was preparing to roll. He slotted the handset and put the truck in gear.

"You received the warrant?" Jill asked. Without taking his eyes off the road, the deputy extracted a thin metal file from somewhere beneath his seat. Jill opened the lid and leafed through the documents. Finished, she placed the file in her lap then pulled out her cell phone and checked for a signal. She typed a quick text and watched it send. "We sure appreciate your cooperation," she told Lambert.

"Quite a thing." The boy shook his head. "All over the news up here. Sheriff's more than happy to help. I'm yours for the duration. We already notified the Wyoming side in case we have to go that direction."

"How far are we from the state line?"

Lambert thumbed over his shoulder. "Five miles that way."

Jill considered the spare landscape. "Where's the nearest FBI field office from here?"

"Salt Lake City. But they don't generally handle this area. Satellite offices in Lander, Casper, and Cheyenne. In Jackson Hole, too, I believe. Lander's the closest. Feds are pretty thin in this neck of the woods."

"Funny you'd finally mention the FBI," Karley said. "Sally Frye from the DA's office has been asking your people to call them since the beginning."

Jill looked back at Karley. "If Josh crossed the state line, she may get her wish."

"The receipt was from Evanston. He might've crossed a number of times."

"True," Jill said carefully. "But we don't know for sure he was in the car. Or if the crossings constituted a crime."

Lambert pushed the SUV toward the edge of town, accelerating on the narrow highway. Jill's phone rang and she checked the screen. "Hey, Milo ... What? ... No, bad connection. Come again? ... Hey, no, nope, listen, let me call you back when we get out of this gully."

Manila, Utah: Population 316, elevation 6,375. But for its

proximity to the Lucerne Valley Recreation Area, the village could never have supported a landing strip. Karley settled into her exhaustion and watched the town slip away. The sky was big here, the red and gray terra undergirding the vast blue canopy. Giant stone monuments, phallic and insistent, reached like flames for heaven. Before long the gorge would reveal itself, glittering like a pink diamond.

"Karley?" Phone to her ear Jill tapped the partition.

"Sorry?"

"How long from here to the cabin?"

"Thirty minutes," Karley said. Steering with his wrist, Lambert nodded.

"Half-hour," Jill said into her phone. She faced forward again. She didn't speak for a long time. "Pull over," she ordered, touching Lambert's arm.

There was no traffic on 44 and Lambert, braking hard, nosed the Expedition left across the opposing lane. Gravel pelted the undercarriage as the rig entered the turnout. Jill yanked the handle and disappeared into a rolling cloud of red dust. Lambert followed her from the truck. In the far distance, Flaming Gorge had finally shown itself, a tinted sky in a salmon-colored bowl. Karley slipped her phone from her jacket.

Hans answered on the third ring. "Where are you?"

"Sitting in a turnout on 44 about thirty minutes from the cabin. The police woman's on her phone. I think with Detective Craig. Something's going on."

Hans hesitated. "You need to come home, Karley. As soon as you can. You need to make them bring you home."

"What? *Why?*" Lambert, who'd left his door open, glanced over his shoulder through the windshield.

"Oh, *kjæreste*, it doesn't look good. Theo thinks it's Stillwell, but the authorities aren't telling us anything." Hans's accent was thicker than she'd heard it in years.

"*What* doesn't look good? *Tell me, Hans.*"

The air between them pinged and soughed. "The news, *kjæreste*, the TV. Search and Rescue is moving everything to the Ogden River. The police are already there setting up. They've been showing shots on TV. The river's swollen from the rain last week and the snowmelt. And it's going to be dark before long."

Karley sat very still. She understood what Hans was telling her, but she didn't feel it. She circled the possibility, Joshua dead in the river, and was absolutely certain Hans was wrong. More than anything, she wanted to ease his fear. For him, this dismay, but not for Stillwell. Not for Joshua in the river.

"Karley?"

"It's not Stillwell. He didn't do it. The authorities haven't been right about anything. Joshua's not in the river, not until they find him."

Hans didn't answer immediately. "Karley—" He paused again. "Okay. You're right, we need to wait. But certainly the cabin's out. We need you here now."

Jill had finished her call. Lambert pushed off the grille and moved her direction. Twenty feet out, they huddled.

"I'll come as soon as I can. Have you said anything to anyone about the scripts?"

"No, I need time to think. Melissa and Joe, if they've truly lost Joshua, if he's really in that river—" He let the phrase dangle.

Guileless Hans, he meant what he said, his concern even now for Melissa. "I'm glad you waited. Please don't say anything. I love you."

"I love you, too." Hans breathed into the phone. "I'm so afraid. For Melissa and Joe especially, but for you too."

The huddle broke and Jill and Lambert turned for the truck. "I've gotta go."

"Listen," Hans said quickly. "This search at the river—I know, I know—but just in case—"

"Joshua isn't in the river, Hans. They're not going to find him there. Try to believe me."

Lambert settled into the Expedition.

"That's exactly what's worrying me," Hans said. "That kind of talk."

"They're back," Karley said. "I need to get off now." Eyeing Karley through the partition, Jill pulled herself into the truck.

"*Kjæreste*," Hans protested.

"I'm okay. Really, I am. I can't explain, but you shouldn't worry about me."

Hans groaned under his breath. "I may go to the river. I need to do something."

"Be careful," Karley said. "I'll call as soon as I can." She thumbed off then gazed out at Flaming Gorge. The truck idled. Lambert had not put it in gear.

"Change of plans," Jill said.

"We're not going back," Karley said. "Joshua's not in the river."

Head against the rest, Jill gazed straight ahead. "You sound certain."

Was that relief Karley heard in the woman's voice? "I am. If we turn around now, we'll just have to come back later."

Suspicion, curiosity, Karley couldn't tell which—Jill swiveled around on the seat. "Perhaps you haven't told us everything?"

Karley shook her head. "I just told you all I know. Joshua's not in the river."

"And you know this how?"

"Are you a religious person, Jill?"

The tiny woman smiled. "I don't see what that has to do with your nephew and the river." Karley waited. "As a kid. Episcopalian. I'm not religious anymore."

"Me, either," Karley said. "But my sister Melissa is. She believes in prayer. And in personal revelation. She thinks God told her Joshua's dead."

Lambert's radio hissed. Units were needed, a disturbance at some roadhouse Karley didn't know. The deputy turned down the volume.

"Do you believe her?" Jill asked. "That God told her Joshua's dead?"

"I believe she believes it."

"Do you think Joshua's dead?"

What Karley thought mattered not at all beyond its service to the process of discovering the truth. "I have no idea. If I were still a praying person, I'd pray he wasn't. But I'm not a praying person. All I have now is instinct and intellect and a devotion to accurate data. I believe in them the way I used to believe in prayer."

She met Lambert's gaze in the rearview mirror. "And right now they're telling me it's a mistake to get on that plane before we check the cabin. What's another hour when we're already here? You guys asked me to make the trip and here I am. We all deserve a little certainty."

Jill glanced at Lambert, then back at Karley. "If it were up to Detective Craig or me, we would. But the Chief of Police pulled rank. These are the chief's orders, not Milo's or mine."

Karley smiled. "Disobey them. It wouldn't be the first time today."

Jill's gaze lingered as she assessed Karley's position. "Why the change? Why are you suddenly so hot to have us look at your sister and her husband?"

Karley had not planned for this. Even now she couldn't say why she'd invoked religion and prayer. But facing the heart of her terrible certainty, she understood there was no weapon to wield but the truth, not if she intended to prevail. "Because they're guilty."

Jill spoke softly. "Betty Stillwell confessed, Karley."

"Sherm Stillwell's mother?" Karley shook her head. The possibility was outrageous. "You must mean she turned on Sherm."

"No. I mean Betty confessed, which means we lost our probable cause. The mayor forced the chief to have the warrant revoked. We search the cabin now, you might sue us for violating your constitutional rights."

"The Stillwell woman's a hundred years old," Karley scoffed. "I saw her on the TV. None of this makes any sense."

"Who says it has to make sense?" Popping a mint in her mouth, Jill studied Karley, her open expression a leading question.

"Ah." Karley nodded. "Detective Craig wants us to search the cabin, anyway."

Jill smiled. "Even if he did, we can't enter without a warrant. Or a Consent to Search."

It was Karley's turn to smile. "The cabin's in a trust. The trust's in our names, my siblings' and mine. It's still Mom's cabin, that's the way we think of it, but in legal terms, it belongs to us. I'll say or sign whatever you need."

∎

They rolled in silence, the shadows falling longer and darker, every color leaching into twilight's common values. By the time Lambert swung onto 1145, the sun was deep below the western range, the wedge of headlight the only remaining source for shadows.

"I hear the National Foresters hate these in-holdings," Lambert said. "Access and maintenance, or so they claim, but I think it's all about control."

They were close to the cabin now, and Karley was frightened, her foreboding more acute with each passing landmark. Sufficient gray cells barely remained for her to process the deputy's words. "We maintain our own road. With an old John Deere. We all know how to operate it."

"You'd need a tractor. Especially during the winters. You come here when it's cold?"

A pair of antelope materialized at the far reach of the lamp beams, one on the yellow line, the other in the gravel just off the highway. Their eyes shined back, four green reflectors. Common fare, antelope, more hazard than fascination to anyone who spent much time on these roads. Lambert let off the gas, and Jill leaned forward. The creatures vanished mid-air. "Wow," she said.

Karley caught Lambert watching her in the rearview mirror. "You were about to say?" he asked.

"We use it year-round."

"Gets cold, well below zero. I haven't seen your place up close. Must be better than most of the old clapboard shacks the summer folks keep around here."

"Log." Karley didn't really mind Lambert's chatter. It was just so difficult to concentrate. She'd never before felt anything but anticipation on State Road 1145.

"And you're close to the lake," he pointed out. "Ten minutes by car."

Karley nodded absently. "Summers we spend a lot of time there. Our favorite spot's a little farther east, about twenty-five minutes from here."

"Rosy Pond, I'll bet. That's what the locals call it anyway. Nice little protected bay. Real pretty. Private, too."

"That's the spot."

"Good diving," Lambert said. "Out of the way. Access rough enough to keep most folks out. I used to drink beer with my buddies there. Skinny-dipped with a girlfriend once, too."

The more Lambert relaxed, the better Karley liked him. "It's a good place for skinny-dipping."

He eased off the accelerator. "There we go, up ahead on the left."

"Stay on the highway," Jill instructed. "I need to see the access before we get off the asphalt."

Karley unbuckled her seatbelt and scooted forward on the bench. Lambert steered the Expedition across the highway and onto the opposing shoulder. He stopped short of the entrance and, opening his door, toggled a switch between the overhead visors. The landscape around the truck began to pulse.

"How far in from here?" Jill asked.

"Two hundred yards to the gate," Karley said. "Cabin's at the top of the hill beyond that stand of quakies you can see there outlined against the sky. Maybe three hundred yards from the gate to the cabin."

"I'll need my gear," Jill told Lambert. The deputy leaned back inside and engaged the rear window. On his way to the tailgate, he opened Karley's door.

It was not as dark outside as it had seemed from inside the truck. Red and green under sunlight, the landscape—what wasn't illuminated by the Expedition's various lights—seemed freshly bruised, a velveteen contusion of purples. The moon had not yet risen, but the stars were out, still sparse in the navy sky. Skunk funk wafted with the sage, the aspens quaking it along. Karley's light jacket would not suffice for long.

"I need you to stay here until I give the word," Jill told her. The two police officers had emerged from the back of the truck, powerful flashlights leading the way. "Kent and I will check for tire tracks, then we'll all go up to the cabin together."

"No," Karley said. "But I'll stay behind you."

In the pulsing light, Jill's angular face appeared molten. "You have an extra flashlight, Kent?"

Lambert leaned across the driver's seat and emerged with a long, heavy flashlight. He thumbed it on and handed it to Karley.

The beam began to pulse. Reaching in, he turned it off then on again by shifting the switch the opposite direction. The beam held steady and bright.

Jill led the way, a digital tablet bright in one hand, her flashlight in the other. Karley and Lambert trailed behind. At the edge of the drive, Jill panned her flashlight. Head down, she paced the full length of the entrance, then stepped off the asphalt.

Karley at a remove conducted her own investigation, following the beam of her flashlight. Though the sun had dried the highest spots, some of the road was still damp. Water pooled in a few of the firmest depressions, but the potholes contained only mud. There was no evidence, none at all, that a vehicle had been on the road in recent days.

Squatting at one edge, Jill glanced up as Karley and Lambert approached. "Looks like we were wrong about the cabin." She studied the tread pattern on her tablet's display then the swath of ground she illuminated with her flashlight. "This isn't new." She stood up, her light still framing the impression. Indeed, the faded track had survived only because the tire had wandered through a winter deposit of gravel and clay on the shoulder.

"Is it the correct tread?" Karley asked. "The 4Runner?"

Jill nodded. "It's the tread. But too old."

"You're sure it's old?" Karley asked softly. "It rained hard. For two days."

"I'm sure," Jill said. "Nothing's been on this road for weeks."

"Is this the only access?" Lambert asked.

"The only road." Karley played her beam through the sparse timber on the other side of the split-rail fence. "But they could have walked in."

"Red mud," Jill said, mostly to herself. "This would've explained it."

"They could've gotten that mud anywhere between here and Evanston," Karley said. "They could've pulled off on 44 exactly where we did. The absence of tracks means nothing. Winters we hike in all the time." She started up the road toward the gate.

Behind her, Jill said, "Bring up the truck, would you, Kent?"

"I'll follow in a minute," Lambert said. "I should probably check in with the sheriff."

Karley was moving fast now, and Jill had to trot to catch her. At the gate, Karley placed the flashlight on the ground and sorted through her keys. Jill aimed her flashlight at the huge padlock. Karley uncoupled the links and wrapped the chain around the post, then lifted the gate off the bracket and swung it wide. "The road's accessible," Jill said. "It wouldn't make any sense for them to walk in."

"Who says it has to make sense?" Karley reminded her.

The women climbed in silence, the air cold enough to fog breath. The drive curled through the rise of the hill's natural contours. Beneath them, the Expedition's big motor telegraphed, its gear-whine amplified in the silent hollow. The women crested as the truck appeared behind them, its powerful headlamps rolling shadows through the trees and across the dark cabin. In the reddening glow of taillight, Karley hurried up the stairs and onto the deck.

"Hang on," Jill called. "We need to go in first." At the bottom of the stairs, she waited for Lambert.

Ignoring the criminalist, Karley went about the complicated procedure of opening the cabin. Liquored-up teenagers and petty thieves had long-ago inspired the fortress effect, a necessary concession to the vulnerabilities of rural isolation and occasional use. The front entrance was comprised of two heavy doors, the newer a weave of strong steel mesh. The inner door, constructed of thick, studded oak, had withstood every abuse, every attempt at unauthorized entry for better than half a century. The windows, like the outer door, were secured with heavy woven grilles.

Karley unlocked the mesh door, then turned again into the light and picked through the keys she'd borrowed from her father. "Put these on before you touch anything else." Jill held out a pair of nitrile gloves.

Lambert came up the stairs probing the long deck with the beam of his flashlight. Karley tugged the gloves on then turned back to the inner door. "Once it's unlocked," Jill instructed, "step back so we can go through first." Karley pushed the door open and walked into the cabin. "Nice," Jill sighed.

The structure's stale, dank chill was sufficient confirmation, though Karley could feel it, too, the void as raw as homesickness. She moved quickly through the downstairs turning on lights. Four bedrooms, beds neat under heavy quilts, extra blankets folded on the bureaus. Spiders had been busy in the living room, mice in the kitchen. The wide-plank floors, marred with history, echoed under the tread of Lambert's large boots.

Karley paused in the living room to check the thermostat. Fifty-five degrees, the prescribed setting, warm enough to protect the pipes from freezing. In the kitchen she lifted the clipboard from its nail, Margaret's checklist of close-down duties. "Thermostat at 55°. Main breaker on"—the first two tasks on the list. These and the other twenty-three duties were verified with the requisite check marks. Melissa's quick signature dated the visit at two weeks earlier.

"I think we can pretty much rule out the cabin," Jill said, wandering into the kitchen. Karley handed her the clipboard and headed for the loft. Two more bedrooms up top and a family room, the ping-pong table folded against the wall under the ceiling's apex. Shelves packed with games and puzzles, old paperbacks. A flat-screen/Blu-ray combo Karley and Hans had donated last summer when the boxy old TV had finally died. A second bookshelf full of DVDs, a small but growing collection of Blu-ray discs. Two threadbare hide-a-beds, a mountain of beanbag chairs, an old armoire full of pillows and blankets and sleeping bags. Beside the loft woodstove a stack of split pine.

Karley gazed down from the loft, no longer afraid of what she might find here but all the emptier for what she now knew she wouldn't. The moment felt final, nostalgic, as though she knew she would never return. Stepping from the railing, she wandered into the hallway. Both loft bedrooms were little more than dormitories, each with built-in bunk beds for six. Except for linens and minor appointments, neither had changed during Karley's lifetime. She switched on the light as she entered the second.

"Big." Jill appeared in the doorway behind her. "I'd love to have a place like this. More lodge than cabin, really. You could sleep an army."

"We have. Church groups. Big outings with friends."

Jill opened the closet and peered inside. More bedding. No Joshua. "Be good for that, all right."

"My husband and I honeymooned here."

"Good for that, too," Jill said. "How about Melissa and Joe? Did they have their honeymoon here?"

"No." Karley stepped past Jill. "Joe's never liked it here." She flipped off the light and headed for the stairs.

"Why's that?" Jill asked, following.

Karley waited for the criminalist to start down, then turned off the loft lights. "I have no idea." And she didn't. Neither Melissa nor Joe had ever explained. But Joe always seemed restless here, anxious to get back to Ogden. On rare occasion the family coaxed him to Rosy Pond, but he always remained on the bank. Not once had Karley seen him in the lake. More often than not, he refused to join them, choosing instead to remain at the cabin. His aversion, like so much else about him, was a mystery the family accepted or ignored.

Midway down the staircase, Jill stopped and turned around. "Did you know it was Joe who took the drive Friday night? Detective Craig overheard Melissa telling your parents. She said he'd been drinking, that he showed up home early Saturday morning. He claims not to remember any of it."

Karley blinked at the criminalist. "How come you didn't tell me this earlier?" Jill watched her closely and did not answer. Karley swept down the staircase and turned into the living room.

More slowly Jill trailed in her wake. "Do you think it's possible? That Joe doesn't remember?" Karley passed through the kitchen into the mudroom where a line of old coats waited on hooks. From the living room, Jill called, "Where would Joe go? If not to the cabin where would he go up here?" Karley selected an old ski parka, one of her own. On her way out, she switched off the kitchen light.

Jill stood admiring a framed photo, a large black and white on the wall beside the front door. In it the four DeBoer children lounged in a tiny rubber raft, all of them in swimming suits, no adult in sight. Not even Caleb, a preschooler, wore a life jacket. They'd all been good swimmers from a very young age, a necessary ability if you spent much time in Flaming Gorge. Good swimming skills and a high tolerance for cold were required if you grew up a DeBoer.

"Where the hell did Joe get that mud?"

"I told you," Karley said. "Joe doesn't like the cabin. He doesn't like it anywhere up here, especially not Flaming Gorge. Drunk or sober, he wouldn't come here, not unless Melissa made him."

Lambert opened the outer security door. He tapped dirt from his boots before entering again. Karley caught the door, then lingered to study her siblings and herself floating in the rubber raft.

"Your mud?" She straightened the photo then reached for the light switch. "You'll find it at Rosy Pond."

Go

Mayor Hyrum Benson stood ablaze in halogen and righteous indignation. Since his earlier press conference, he'd traded his suit for jeans and a leather bomber jacket. Spot-lit behind him, the Ogden River swirled, a phalanx of searchers working the bank. To Hans, even they seemed made for TV. The large screen broadcast the presser live and Hans's only desire was to shut the man up. In Joshua's certain death, in a five-year-old's murder, the mayor was declaring a major victory.

" ... I'm sorry, we're not yet at liberty to discuss the specifics of that information. I can only restate what I've already said, that we're certain now Joshua Christopher was put in the river sometime yesterday, probably near 1:00 p.m. ..."

But for Hans and Melissa, the family wept. On the sofa beside Melissa, Margaret leaned into Curt, while Joe, all alone, sat shuddering on the toy box. Sally, against a wall, shook her head in disbelief. Theo watched over Jared and Caleb's heads. Not once had Melissa glanced at the TV.

"That's correct," the mayor told another reporter. "The parents have been cleared and our hearts go out to them."

Theo snorted.

"We hope to locate their son very soon, tonight God willing, but the river is very high. Pine View Water closed the spillway, but it'll still be some time before—"

The screen went blank. Arms around his knees, Joe slumped sideways against the wall. Melissa placed the remote in her lap. "Please leave," she said. "There's nothing anyone can do now. Joe and I need some time together. Just the two of us."

Sally whistled softly at the ceiling. "Not now. You need people around you."

"No," Melissa said. "If you want to help, leave." She spoke like a sane woman, the voice of reason, intent on calming the panicked masses. She placed the remote on the cushion and stood. "If you won't leave, Joe and I will. We'll go far away where we won't be bothered."

Hans felt the room shift, a sensation as palpable as a plummeting temperature. The assembled, minus Joe, stared at Melissa. Cheek to the wall, Joe didn't move.

Curt released Margaret. Hands on his knees, he paused for a moment before rising to his feet. In two days' time, he'd become an old man, stiff and halting, dizzy and disoriented. Hans took a step toward him, but Melissa had seen it, too. She drew Curt into her arms. "It's okay, Daddy. This is all God's plan."

Leaning back, Curt cupped her face in his hands and kissed her on the forehead. "Such a cruel plan." He crossed to Joe and ran a hand down his back, then wandered to the sofa and reached for Margaret.

Jared and Caleb consulted in a corner, then Caleb disappeared up the stairs. Jared stepped close to Hans. "We're going to the river," he whispered.

Hans nodded. "I'll meet you there in a little while."

Jared watched Joe. "Should we really leave them alone?"

"I guess we have to honor their wishes."

Jared thought about this. "Do you think they'll be all right?"

"No," Hans said. "They'll never be all right, not ever again."

Jared studied Hans's face, then turned away and hurried up the stairs.

Margaret had begun to sob. "Hush, now, Momma," Melissa said. Weak-kneed Margaret all but hung from her daughter, Curt bracing her from the side.

Hans took a breath and stepped into the scrum. "Ativan," he told Melissa. "Bring me what you have. And a glass of water."

Melissa processed Hans's request, then passed Margaret to him.

"I've never seen her like this," Curt said.

Hans helped his father-in-law guide Margaret to the sofa. "She's in shock."

"Should we lay her down?"

Hans kneeled before Margaret and squeezed her hand. "Margaret, I want you to look at me. Come on now, focus, listen to what I'm saying." He released one hand and touched her face. When she still didn't respond, he flicked the cartilage of her left ear.

Recoiling, she clapped a palm over the ear. "Stop!"

"Lie down, sweetheart," Curt said.

"I want to go home. Please take me home." Brushing Hans aside, she sprang from the sofa. Hans followed her up, poised for the catch.

"Here," Melissa said, appearing at Hans's shoulder. She handed him a small medicine bottle.

Hans popped the lid and jiggled a pair of tablets into his palm. "Margaret, I want you to take these. They're a mild tranquilizer. They'll help." Margaret swooped in, but her fingers flailed and the tablets refused to be gathered. "Open your mouth."

Margaret obeyed, and Hans placed them on her tongue. Teeth chattering glass, she swallowed the pills. "Thank you," she sighed. She already seemed better.

"She can have those," Melissa told Hans.

Hans handed Curt the vial. "Up to two every four hours."

Tucking the pills in a pocket, Curt addressed his daughter. "Please, pumpkin. Let someone stay."

Melissa smiled at her father. "No, Daddy. We're okay. The worst is behind us now."

"I don't understand," Curt said. "Why would they make us find out this way?"

"It doesn't matter," Melissa said.

Fist mashed to his lips, Curt loosed a single sob. Finally, he put his arm around Margaret. Melissa kissed her father's cheek. She kissed her mother's. Hans helped Curt guide Margaret toward the stairs. "We'll be fine," Curt assured him. "Make sure they're settled before you leave, would you, Hans?"

"Of course," Hans said. He watched Curt steer Margaret up the stairs.

"In all my years as a lawyer," Theo said, "I've never seen the police treat anyone, not even a perp, with such callous disregard. Never."

Across the room, Melissa stood stiffly in Sally's embrace.

"I'll run you back to your car," Hans told him. "We're very grateful for your help today. I'll get you my address so you can send me the bill."

Theo shook his head. "Thanks, but, no. This one's on me."

"You're very kind."

"Kind is the last thing I am." Theo surveyed the room. "I'll get my things and wait for you upstairs." He started up the stairs.

Hans slipped past the women and made his way to Joe. Joe's back rose and fell, his shallow breathing steady. Hans sat down on the toy box and pulled Joe against him. But for their breaths, nothing moved. Gradually, the room fell silent.

It was Melissa finally who ended their embrace. "They're all gone. Everyone but you, Hans. I want you to leave now. Please." She stood so close Hans could feel her heat.

He did not look at her. "I love you, Joe." Gently, as if arranging a newborn, he returned Joe to his wall and stood. Drawing a hand from his back pocket, he produced the four scripts.

Like a lover, Melissa studied Hans's face, falling at last on his eyes. Without looking down, she accepted the scripts, then lowered her gaze and sheaved through each sheet. Smiling, she lifted her face.

"Leave us alone," she told Hans. "Go."

Hans reclaimed the four scripts and went.

Holding Out for Charity and Chastity

Hans is an excellent physician, and gentle, though in ways Melissa finds more off-putting than endearing. He has brought heartache and damnation to the people she loves, and she is not inclined to forgive him. She waits with Joe, listening to Hans and the attorney, their voices muffled, their leaving slow. Joe, her dear Joe, is gone, taken by events she could never have anticipated. He sits before her like a catatonic. Soon, very soon, it will all be behind them, the entire story finished.

That Hans has found Melissa out is interesting but no longer of any real consequence. The scripts themselves have ceased to serve a purpose. Still, she is not without regrets. The things people do, the things they must do, to make it from day to day. What begins as a small pain becomes another—how quickly it all grows unmanageable. She is surprised that Hans has violated her privacy, but there is nothing to do about it now.

Footsteps through the kitchen, then the back door closes and the house grows still and silent. "Are you ready, Joe?"

Joe doesn't move. No matter. Melissa leaves him where he is and climbs the stairs. They won't need much for their trip—a few clothes, her purse, a car. Everything else they can find where they're going.

Once upon a time she loved this house, but six years of hiding within these walls have rendered it uninhabitable. So much anger after so much love. How she misses those early days. But God giveth. God taketh away. It is a fool who resents God for doing what God does.

Because Heavenly Father would not allow it, they never played their games again, not after Joe told her his stories. A dear price

269

to pay for God's protection. But the Still Small Voice, God's will to Melissa's heart, could not have spoken more clearly.

"You make no sense," Joe would seethe. "First God wants us to rut like bunnies, then he says no sex at all."

"Don't exaggerate," Melissa countered. "We can have all the sex we want. We just can't play our games."

"And we can't play our games why?"

"I've told you a thousand times." How Melissa wanted Joe to bend her over, peel down her underpants, and whale her raw. "Self-control, Joe. It's because God wants us to learn self-control. If we sacrifice this, God will make us strong. He'll bridge the gap when you're feeling weak. That's why we can't play our games."

Joe moaned. "You make me want a drink. How about this? Every day I don't drink, we get to play any way we want."

"Joe."

"You can't tell me you're happy. When was the last time you came?"

"I come."

"No, you don't. Not hardly ever."

For this particular episode, Melissa and Joe lay on their king-size bed. She slipped a hand into her garments and pinched her clitoris until the pain calmed her mind.

"It's only temporary," she said. "You'll see. One day sooner than you think, we'll be together in the Celestial Kingdom. We'll play and play and play."

Joe laughed bitterly. "Yeah, I can see it now, me and my hundred wives. 'Melissa, you've been very bad, taking nine days to populate a six-day planet. After I finish slapping your ass I intend to make whoopee with my two new acquisitions, Charity and her little sister Chastity. Now bend over and pull up your robes.'"

Not funny. Not in the least. Joe knew celestial polygamy was the one gospel doctrine Melissa could not abide. She scooted across the bed and nestled into him.

"Please trust me." Sliding a hand to his crotch, she found him at half-mast.

He rolled out of bed and picked up his pillow. In the nursery across the hall, toddler Joshua began to fuss. "I couldn't care less about the games, Melissa. None of this has anything to do with that and you know it. Whatever you think God's telling you, you're wrong." Pillow tucked beneath an arm, he gazed back from the doorway. "I think I'll hold out for Charity and Chastity."

■

In that same bedroom now Melissa takes an overnight bag from her closet and opens it on the bed. The strafing comes earlier each day, plagues her with greater efficiency. It arrives as a pressure behind her eyes and, if she's not quick, grows radiant. Her neck seizes first and then her back, and it becomes difficult to see or move.

Feeling it now, she detours to the clothes hamper and digs to the bottom where she's secreted her purse. Since marrying Joe, she has managed their finances because he doesn't care or worry about money. She has resented the burden, the worrying alone, but has come of late to appreciate the benefits. The considerable expense has proved easier to hide than the medicines themselves. Such are the contortions when insurance can't be billed. Cancer, knee replacements, crushed vertebrae, car crashes—poor Joe has suffered them all. From Bountiful to Brigham City, the pharmacists are most sympathetic.

Melissa sorts through the bottles until she finds what she needs, Oxycontin 40mg, oxycodone 5mg. With the drive ahead, she dares not take 80, a dosage she much prefers. She fishes four 5s from the bottle of oxycodone, then returns both medicines to her purse. On her way from the room, she deposits the purse on the bed beside the overnight bag.

Coke works best, Mountain Dew, anything with caffeine and sugar. Of all Melissa's failings, her many transgressions, she pays dearest for this hypocrisy. She is not Joe, but in her need for these pills, her weakness is no less than his. She knows God's plan has many facets but is ashamed of herself nonetheless. Still, there's an order of operation, a few absolute truths. This very moment was foreordained in heaven.

She uses two spoons to crush the four oxycodones. She's read stories of people snorting the powder but is not herself yet so desperate. She licks the spoon clean, then chases the powder with soda swigged straight from the bottle. She tongues a few flecks from the counter top, then throws in the Oxycontin.

Two years ago she returned home from work to find Joe in the backyard barbecuing his temple garments on the charcoal grill. He was mostly finished by the time she arrived, a feathering of cloth on the briquettes. Peddling his Big Wheel, Joshua raced back and forth, the skin around his lips ringed popsicle purple.

"Perfect timing," Joe said. "I was about to throw some burgers on." He dropped the last undershirt onto the grill, then tossed two wadded bottoms after it. Taking a cautious step back, he squeezed a stream of lighter fluid onto the smoldering cloth. He struck a match on the big red box, and a column of fire mushroomed from the pan.

"You've been drinking," she said.

"Not a drop." He handed her his glass, and she braved a sip. Watery diet Sprite. She pressed the glass between her breasts and watched the white holiness of Joe's sacred garments shrivel brown then black. Careening about the patio, Joshua chased butterflies. "And I saved us a load of wash."

Melissa had not yet begun to cry, but her diaphragm was making plans. "You have no idea what you've done."

"Actually, I think I do." With the grilling fork, Joe stirred the smoking pile. "You'll probably want a divorce now."

"Beep-Beep," Joshua cried and rolled over her shoes.

Foot into the air, Melissa breathed through the pain, the flush of inspiration flooding her senses. How wrong she'd been to think herself abandoned. God was showing her the way. "You're a coward, Joe. Time and All Eternity. I'll never divorce you. Never. Burn your garments. Stop going to church. Drink yourself to death. But believe this: If you ever try to divorce me, you'll never see your son again, not in this life or the next."

Joe let his gaze drift to the edge of the patio where his beautiful boy cranked into a turn. "Careful, Melissa. Threats like that have a way of coming back to bite you."

∎

The seam has opened, and Melissa is tracking smoothly again, soft within herself. Their biggest problem will be a car. She crosses the living room which is dim and cloistered, the blinds now closed against the media. Had she expected anything, it would not have been this, this Frankenstein's monster made of their lives. She parts the blinds and peeks out. It is dark now, very close to dark, the streetlamps yellow on the pavement. Only one transmission van and a small clutch of reporters have resisted the river to monitor the house. Melissa thanks God for preparing the way. Even the problem with the car only troubles her a little. She is, after all, on his errand.

She strips to the skin in their bedroom. She has gained a few pounds from the sugared soda, but her breasts, she thinks, are quite lovely. From her underwear drawer, she selects a pair of powder-blue panties, silk with a lace front, and a white bra, her most flattering. She suffers a minor pang of nostalgia—she so much preferred it when her play clothes matched. She threads her legs into the panties, her arms through the bra straps and hooks the clasp at the front. Matching or not, she trusts her attire will help Joe do what he must.

They store their temple robes beneath the bed in two tiny suitcases. On hands and knees, she pulls them out and places them on the mattress. One suitcase at a time, she transfers the contents to the overnight bag—white robes and sashes, her veil and Joe's cap, the green embroidered aprons. She considers her white dress, Joe's white shirt and pants, then the overnight bag which is already full. From Joe's closet, she fetches a carry-on case and empties the overnight bag into it. She adds her white dress and Joe's shirt and pants but leaves the white slippers behind. She retrieves clean garments from her underwear drawer and places them on top of the temple clothes.

In her closet again she digs to the back. Joe's favorite is Baby Doll, short and light, but Melissa's thighs no longer taper with quite the same allure. That leaves Schoolgirl. She takes all four hangers in one fist and lifts them from the rod. There it is, the second in line, the very skirt she wore the day Karley broke their hearts. A plaid Pendleton knock-off lined with frayed satin, the pleats a little loose now. Is it possible she and Joe have not played their games since the morning of Karley's call?

She drops the three skirts and unclasps the one. The matching necktie snakes from the hanger. She was slimmer back then but not so terribly much, and, anyway, the skirt, purchased from a thrift store, was two sizes too large to begin with. She removes the safety pins she used to size it, unzips the side, and steps into the opening. The skirt is snug, but she is able to zip it. She returns to the closet for a simple white shirt with a collar and fitted tails. She takes care with the buttons, then turns up the collar and retrieves the tie from the floor. Cinching the knot, she returns to her drawers for blue kneesocks she's never thrown out. Keds with laces, blue with white soles. Very Schoolgirl indeed.

Finished with her own things, she pauses over the suitcase and listens to the ringing in her ears. Like the opioid itch, the ringing is a side effect. She does not mind, even pleasures in the scratching, but the ringing is an annoyance to be endured.

Back in her closet, Melissa locates the garments she purchased many months earlier, a man's bottom and top still sealed in their bags. She places them in the suitcase, then steps into Joe's closet and begins sorting through his belts. The hanger is a jumble, and it takes her a moment to realize the one she wants is missing. She rifles Joe's pants and finds it there, threaded in a pair of jeans.

She coils the belt into the suitcase, zips the lid closed, then luxuriates for a moment in the massaging of her nose. Draping her purse over a shoulder, she picks up the suitcase and carries it all from their bedroom. She has solved the car problem, or very shortly will, once she locates her cell phone. She puts the suitcase on the floor beside the kitchen table, her purse on the table itself. The purse is a chaos of medicine bottles, and she cannot locate the device. Their landline is bugged. She dare not use it. Scanning the kitchen, she wonders where her phone is. She's not thought of it in two days.

"My," she says. Then she takes the stairs to the basement. Joe has moved from his perch on the toy box. He now sits on the edge of the sofa. "It's almost time to go," she tells him.

His gaze tracks slowly over her outfit. "What?"

"Everything's ready. We'll be leaving as soon as the car arrives." She continues into his office.

"Where are we going?"

"You'll see." On the desk Joe's phone is connected to its charger. She unplugs it, then checks to make sure it is on. She does not have Bishop Furthington's number, but the ward directory is upstairs with their phone books.

Joe is standing when she returns to the family room. "What are you doing?"

"Everything's going to be fine, Joe. You'll see." She crosses the room and starts up the stairs.

From the base of the stairwell, Joe says, "I'm not going anywhere. Not with you."

She stops two steps below the landing, bends over, and straightens her socks from the ankles up. The socks reach to the bottom of her thighs, and one at a time she folds a cuff into each. Righting herself, she peers over her shoulder. "Just this one last time. This one more place and you'll never have to go anywhere with me again."

Her vulgar tricks mean nothing to Joe. He's neither aroused nor angry. Still, Melissa sees the dawning—the woman might be crazy, his hollow gaze says, or she might be something else. He isn't quite sure he wants to know. He isn't quite sure he has a choice.

Melissa takes the final stairs to the backdoor landing. On the parking, illuminated by the floodlight above the garage door, Caleb's Jeep awaits them like a magic carpet. *"Caleb?"* she calls, but the boy is not here, so she opens the back door and slips outside. Triggered by her movement, the porch light flashes and she skips down the steps and rounds to the driver's door. Theirs is a family governed by habit, that, or God has procured extra keys. Caleb's or God's dangle from the ignition.

"Mrs. Christopher?" A reporter waves from the bottom of the driveway. Melissa closes the Jeep and hurries back inside.

In the kitchen Joe says, "Tell me where we're going."

She hands him his phone, then takes a new bottle of Coke from the fridge. "I will when we're on our way." Joe flicks the phone, and it clatters on the floor. Melissa consults the clock. "It's 9:36. We have a drive ahead of us. I'd use the bathroom now if you need to."

Joe takes a deep breath. "What have you done with Joshua?"

She places the soda on the counter and reaches for his face. She out-waits his recoil, then approaches again and this time he allows her to touch him. "Poor Joe. You really don't remember, do you?"

Joe closes his eyes. He really doesn't remember.

"Take the suitcase to the Jeep and wait for me there." Melissa caresses Joe's cheek then withdraws her hand. "I'll drive."

Joe picks up the suitcase and turns for the back door. Melissa sweeps through the house and finds it in the living room, Joshua's favorite stuffed toy, the Pooh Bear. She presses it to her nose and inhales.

Outside, Joe waits in the passenger seat. Melissa passes him the Coke and the Pooh Bear, then scrambles immodestly into the Jeep. The woven seat-cover is abrasive beneath her thighs. Joe presses the Pooh Bear to his nose and inhales.

Melissa secures her purse behind the seat. Working the clutch and the accelerator together, she starts the motor and shifts the stick into reverse. She gives it a nudge and lets gravity take them. The house is luminous inside and out.

The reporters are wrong to think she won't hit them. They scatter like leaves in a gale. Braking, she wracks the Jeep into first, and a large camera lens bumps expensively against her side window. She pops the clutch and pins the accelerator. Fat wheels spin and grab.

"Tell me now," Joe says. He clutches the Pooh Bear.

Rushing a yellow light, Melissa swings onto Harrison and the short boxy Jeep sways into alignment. She smiles at Joe as she shifts into third.

"To Joshua, of course. He's waiting."

Rosy Pond

Karley and Deputy Lambert stood side by side, the beams of their separate flashlights shining down the rough access. The tracks crisscrossed—two tracks, four tracks, two again. Placing her feet with care, Jill stepped off the hardpan. Ten yards from the asphalt, she squatted. She brought the bright tablet close to the rut and illuminated the tracks with her flashlight. She looked back at Karley. "You were right. These are the same as the 4Runner's."

Karley let her gaze drift long. Three-quarters of a mile from where she stood, Flaming Gorge was visible in its invisibility, a black absence without reflection. Miles beyond the lake's far shore smoke-glow marked the mines and refineries that provided what industry the region enjoyed. Rosy Pond, the tiny bay, lay secluded ahead at the end of the 4Runner's tracks.

"How far in to the lake from here?" Jill asked.

"Little under a mile," Lambert answered. The deputy's earlier banter had given way to a pensive wariness. He hovered near Karley.

The idling Expedition threw high-beam toward the lake. Jill pushed herself upright, and the shadow she cast vanished at the rim. She panned her light through the sagebrush, then stepped left over the tracks and started back. "I'm walking," she said. "Is there another way to get the truck in?"

"No," Lambert said.

"How rough is it? Can you stay to the side of the road?"

Lambert thought about this. "Most of the way. There's one stretch on the hill that's a little dicey. Steep and full of boulders."

Jill nodded. "I'm sorry, Karley, but this time I need you to ride

277

with Deputy Lambert. Kent, the headlights will help me so try to stay close. If you have to cross the road, talk to me first."

Hands buried in her ski jacket, Karley returned to the Expedition. The truck rocked as Deputy Lambert climbed in. He cleared his throat, then engaged the front wheels and shifted into 4-high. Karley, beside him, stared straight ahead. Flashlight beam bobbing, Jill weaved down the road toward the gorge.

"I have a brother," he said. "Eighteen months younger." He put the truck in gear and steered left, leaving the macadam for the soft undulations adjacent to the dirt road. "Rumor has it my mom wasn't too pleased to be pregnant again, not so soon after having me." Sagebrush swept the undercarriage. "Funny how different we are. Here I am, a cop. Him, he can't hold down a job. Goes from one girl to the next. Always in trouble with someone."

The Expedition crept along behind Jill. Each time the criminalist stopped to examine something, Lambert stopped as well. "Thing is," he went on, "I know him like a twin. Maybe it's our closeness in age. Sometimes—he might be a hundred miles away—I'll get this feeling. Like he's in trouble. And I'll know just the kind of trouble, too. I've been right more times than wrong. He's a problem, but man I love him. When we're together, we don't even have to talk. I can't explain it better than that. But I'm guessing you get what I mean."

Karley glanced at the deputy but kept her own counsel.

Lambert picked his route carefully, steering around boulders, piles of smaller stones. He walked the truck over passable outcroppings and rocks the size of basketballs. High off the ground, the undercarriage cleared everything but the sagebrush and the rims of the steepest gullies. "That's how you knew?" he asked eventually. "That we'd find the tracks here?"

"My family loves Rosy Pond," Karley said. "But none of us loves it more than Melissa."

"Isn't the 4Runner her husband's vehicle?"

"Yes. But my sister was driving it. And I'm all but certain she was alone."

Lambert fell silent. They'd dropped over the edge of a wide streambed, the deepest gully yet. The nose dipped severely, the undercarriage scraped, and Karley braced a hand against the dashboard. The shallow runoff flowed toward Rosy Pond. At the bottom the truck leveled out then started up the steep other side. The pitch frightened Karley, but Lambert seemed unconcerned. The wheels began to dig and he backed down the hill. Truck idling in the stream, he opened his door and stepped onto the running board. To Karley, the incline looked like a vertical wall.

Lambert closed his door and shifted into 4-low. "Put your seatbelt on."

As Karley did as he asked, Lambert backed the truck until it tilted downhill. Karley expected him to rush the bank, but he swung right instead, into the densest foliage. Slowly he cut a path through the brush, never gunning the motor. On occasion the wheels seemed to lose purchase, but the truck itself never stalled. Karley sank back into her seat like an astronaut. Dim straight ahead, obscured in headlight, the stars awaited her arrival.

Cresting the bank, Lambert said, "When you say your sister was alone, does that include your nephew?"

Karley closed her eyes.

When she opened them again, Jill Grafton was waving from the road. Lambert circled in and parked, the rig's headlights aimed at the criminalist. Behind her the road dropped off the hill into the streambed Karley and Lambert had just crossed. It curved up the banks on both sides of the water.

Karley climbed down from the Expedition. Jill raised a hand, and Karley ignored her. She rounded the truck but stayed off the road. "I need you to drop the tailgate," Jill told Lambert.

Karley stayed to the uphill side of the embankment, cautious in her movements because she'd forgotten the flashlight. More than once loose earth threatened to send her tumbling. Near the road, however, the footing was better but the night was also darker. Unable to see much of anything, she turned around and watched Jill and Lambert begin their descent. Behind them the truck's headlights shined across the gully, illuminating almost nothing at the bottom. The small criminalist and the deputy, silhouetted against the light, tracked left and right scattering debris down the incline.

"Shit!" Jill yelped.

"Whoa!" Lambert said.

Karley, reaching, scampered into the cascade. Sand and stone washed over her ankles, but she managed to stop Jill's slide. A flashlight skittered past them and stopped on the road. "You okay?" Karley asked. She helped her up.

"Fractured ego," the woman grumbled. She brushed herself off, then stepped cautiously to her flashlight, which she panned across the road. Three feet from the far shoulder, the beam settled on a protrusion. The mouth of a boot—four inches of battleship gray—poked like a stovepipe from the mud.

Four inches of rubber ten feet away observed in distorting light. It wasn't much, but Karley was certain, couldn't have been more certain were she holding the boot. Hans had given the pair to Joe, part of a gag gift he'd assembled because Joe had requested a snowboard for Christmas. Karley herself had procured the boots, then Hans had strapped loops of hemp rope to a plank and presented the whole to Joe at the family Christmas party. The real equipment was already secreted at Karley and Hans's house, purchased by Melissa months earlier. Joe and Hans, Jared and Caleb and Joshua had taken the contraption to the foothills for a session of mutual mockery. Joe had thrown the broken board away, but the boots he'd kept.

"It belongs to Joe," Karley said.

Jill was skeptical. "You can't hardly see it."

"It's his boot," Karley said. "I bought them myself at Smith and Edward's."

Lambert moved along the shoulder surveying the road. The mud told a story even Karley could read. The snaking ruts, still a foot deep, had folded in on themselves. Behind the boot a long hillock of churned soil appeared ready to slough off the slope. Karley was amazed the 4Runner hadn't slid off with it. She was amazed the truck wasn't still stuck in the sludge.

"Come with me," Jill instructed Karley.

Karley followed the woman fifty yards up the hill to firmer ground. Stepping where Jill pointed, Karley crossed the road. Jill moved slowly, examining the bank. Across the road Lambert illuminated the boot. In the side light, the ruts seemed even deeper than they were.

"Still think it's Joe's?"

From three feet away the boot was unmistakable. "Yes," Karley said. "Most Wellingtons aren't lined. The ones I bought were. With the same red stripe at the cuff. Size ten. Pull it out, and I'll show you. The size is stamped in rubber on the heel."

"Later," Jill said. "But you're right about the brand and the size. We identified both from a print we found in the 4Runner." She produced a fluorescent flag from her bag. Kneeling, she reached long and staked the wire in the mud beside the boot. "Driver was lucky," Jill noted to Lambert. "Another few inches a back wheel would have left the road."

Karley studied the impressions. "How do you know it was a back wheel."

Jill drew lines with her flashlight. "Front wheels are there, see, near the center of the road. Back wheels started to dig and the rear end faded downhill. Driver braked and got out to lock in the hubs. Manual hubs on that older-model 4Runner. That's when the boot came off. Maybe it was too stuck, maybe whoever left it was in too big a hurry to care. Whatever the reason, it got left." Jill aimed at the tire tracks near the center of the road. "Driver engaged the front drivetrain and pulled straight out. These tracks are the back wheels coming around. Never would've made it without four-wheel drive. Lucky the boot didn't get buried. Truck went right over it."

"But not the tires," Karley observed. She could see it now, the drama as vivid as if she were watching it happen. "She was on her way out when she got stuck."

Jill nodded. "Headed out." She glanced at Karley. "You're holding pretty tight to the 'she' stuff."

"The husband's truck," Lambert said. "Now his boot."

"His night away," Jill added. And a receipt in the pocket of Joe's sweats, Karley thought. The sweats Melissa had worn when she'd stepped into Joe's boots and driven to Rosy Pond in Joe's truck. When Karley said nothing, Jill gestured to Lambert. "Let's move on. I'll keep Karley with me for a bit."

The deputy toed into the hillside and climbed a few steps. "The final drop's maybe a quarter mile ahead," he called back. "From there the road's the only way in."

"We'll decide what to do when we get there." Jill hoisted her bag and continued up the shoulder. "Going to have to rethink a couple things."

Karley followed a few yards behind. "Such as?"

"Carwash," Jill said, though mostly to herself. As they climbed from the gully, the ground firmed beneath them. At the top Jill stepped into the road and moved out between the tire tracks. Lambert made a three-point turn, then inched in behind the women. The SUV's brights bounced beyond the horizon. Jill studied the road and said nothing more.

Karley's ski jacket was old but warm, and she draped the hood loosely over her head. She had traveled this road often in the dark but had seldom walked it, day or night. She was glad for the exertion. Secluded in her hood, she breathed in the lake and struggled to pierce the darkness.

■

"I wish," Melissa said, "Mormons did like those guys who burn their dead."

"Buddhists," Karley said. "Hindus. Pagans."

"How do you know so much about pagans?"

Naked and alone, fifty feet from shore, they clung to inner tubes. Beneath the horizon moon Melissa's shoulders and face and the tops of her breasts were smooth and white and young.

"Remember?" Karley said. "I'm a witch."

"How could I forget?"

On the bank near the water, a fire burned brightly in its ring. They'd sneaked from the cabin as the others slept. The property's old yard truck had a manual transmission, and Melissa, new to driving, had jerked them all the way to Rosy Pond. They'd laughed so hard they'd wet themselves, which was another excuse to skinny dip. Their swimming suits were dry, their shorts and underpants wet. They needed something dry to wear back to the cabin.

"So why do you wish you were a pagan?" Karley asked. At

nearly fourteen, she liked the idea. Fairies and nymphs, mermaids and elves were right up there with the boy bands she loved.

"Not a pagan, you dork," Melissa said. "I just want my ashes sprinkled here on Rosy Pond."

"Ashes don't resurrect," Karley reminded her. "Only bodies buried facing east."

"Not true," Melissa disagreed.

"Uh-huh," Karley teased. "You remember how they buried Grandma and Grandpa Willard? Toes pointed east so when Jesus comes, they can stand right up."

"Like the vampire in that one movie. Remember how he stood up without bending his knees?"

"Like he had a pole up his butt."

Funny stuff. Giggling, Melissa splashed water in Karley's face. Karley dipped beneath the surface and came up firing. "Kind of strange though," she said a moment later.

"How so?"

"The way they dressed Grandma and Grandpa Willard before they buried them."

"They always do that. So they'll be ready to meet Jesus at the Second Coming."

For reasons Karley had never articulated, the memory of her grandparents' funerals still bothered her. The strange clothes more than the corpses that had worn them. "Do you really have to wear all that stuff when you go through the temple?"

"*Get* to wear it," Melissa corrected her.

"Weird," Karley said, unapologetically. "That green apron? With all those fig leaves stitched into it? And that funny hat?"

"You wear them when you get married, too."

Karley's first period had arrived but a few months earlier and with it new growth in her breasts. She was self-conscious about her appearance, especially around boys. "How embarrassing," she said. "To have to wear fig leaves over your privates at your own wedding."

Melissa laughed. "It's an apron, sweetheart. And it's just symbolic. You're wearing a dress underneath." Karley's teeth had begun to chatter, her lips to blue. "Besides," Melissa added. "By the time your wedding day comes, keeping your privates covered will be the furthest thing from your mind."

Karley pushed the inner tube away. Treading water, she said, "Nasty girl."

"Tell me you haven't thought about it."

"I have no idea what you're talking about."

"I've heard it hurts the first time."

Karley kicked then dived, mooning Melissa before she slipped beneath the lake. Twenty feet away she surfaced, head back, then sank and resurfaced to clear her hair. Arms looped through both tubes, Melissa swam to her.

"Mom gave me the talk," Karley announced. "After I *finally* got my period."

"You're one to complain. I got mine when I was eleven. That's two extra years of cramps for me."

"Two extra years without the talk for me."

Melissa hooted. "'Sex is for the man, babies are for the woman.'"

"'Sleeping Giant,'" Karley crowed. "'Don't wake the Sleeping Giant.'"

"And the cow."

"Oh, *baby!*"

"'God gave us *intercourse* but only in marriage. It's the glue that binds a husband to his wife. He gave women this very powerful gift, Melissa—'"

"'So men will marry us.'"

Together, Melissa and Karley sang, "If the milk were free, *why would he ever buy the cow?*'"

"'Mahana, you ugly!'" Karley rasped.

"'Come down from that tree,'" Melissa added.

This last a quote from *Johnny Lingo*, the tackiest Mormon movie they'd ever seen, sent them into a fit of hysteria. Karley lunged at Melissa, and they both went under, their slippery bodies writhing. Out of air they popped up reaching for their inner tubes.

"Poor Dad," Melissa coughed.

"Nothing but the missionary position for him," Karley giggled.

Melissa slapped at her. "Ewww! Now *that* grosses me out."

"No blow jobs either."

"*Karley!*" Melissa squealed. Her voice echoed off the basin walls. "For gosh sake! *You're only thirteen.*"

"Fourteen. Almost."

"Well, *stop* it."

The bright night settled around them then. Silent, they turned in the water and watched the sky. "I'm cold," Karley said eventually. "I'm not as fat as you are." She expected a pinch, another slap at least.

Instead, Melissa drew her in by the forearm. "Not yet. Not until you promise me something." Her breath was warm and sweet on Karley's face, her expression serious. "Promise me you'll find someone just as good as you are, a boy who'll take you to the temple. You have to make it to the Celestial Kingdom, Karley. We just have to be together forever. I can't imagine dying and never seeing you again."

Karley grinned. She leaned over and kissed Melissa on the lips. Nose to Melissa's, she said, "No one's as good as I am. But I'll meet you in the Celestial Kingdom even if I have to marry a toad."

Melissa laughed. "Promise?"

Karley rolled to her back and kicked for shore, the inner tube floating above her. "*Promise!*" she cried. "*I'll marry a toad and meet you in the Celestial Kingdom!*"

■

Karley stood with Lambert at the top of the final hill, the Expedition idling behind them. Rosy Pond glinted some seventy-five yards beyond Jill, the water finally visible in the headlights. "Bring it down," she called. "Park right here where I'm standing. Karley, you'll need to stay with the truck while we search the landing."

Lambert opened the door. "Wanna ride?"

"If it's okay, I'd rather get in at the bottom."

Lambert reached into the Expedition and emerged with the long flashlight. He carried it to Karley, then without a word climbed into the truck and closed the door. Karley waited beside the road as the rig crunched past her, Lambert's flashlight dark in her hand. As instructed, the deputy parked near the base of the hill. He turned off the motor but not the headlamps, the broad flat landing now bathed in directional light. Rosy Pond lapped the stone lip, its churning amplified by the basin's swooping contours. Good for diving, Lambert had said. Karley could hear it all, past and present.

Below her, the officers canvassed the landing. "Got some boot prints," Lambert called. "Quite a few right here."

"Mark 'em," Jill answered. Then ten seconds later, "The 4Runner was parked here I think."

Karley turned away from the road and crept laterally across the rocky face. There was little sagebrush here, little foliage, the ground mostly porous stone. She followed the contours knowing what she sought and finally the grade sloped into the ravine. Hidden at its nadir, she slid down the incline using her free hand for balance. Shaped like a football, the landing ran some 500 yards along the bank, a hundred yards deep at its widest. Karley picked her way down the final steep grade shifting Lambert's dark flashlight from one hand to the other.

On the level she stood still and tracked the officers, their voices now diminished by position and distance. Rosy Pond was still fifteen feet below her, one final descent to make. Cut by ancient seas and scathing winds, the lower lip lined the landing like a bottom step, a fortuitous outcropping carved millions of years earlier. Some 300 yards from where Karley stood, a natural staircase joined lip and landing.

She crossed the landing, flashlight off, unconcerned about being seen. In the open she could hear the voices more clearly. "…the truck closer," Jill was instructing. "Stay to this side."

"Have you seen Karley?" Lambert asked a moment later.

"What?" Another short silence. "She's not in the truck?"

Karley crept along the ledge, stopping and starting, searching for the best route over the edge. The wall here was more sheer than she remembered. Finally, she turned around and crawled backwards off the landing. Behind her the water lapped at the lip. She wondered how far she would fall if she missed.

Not far, it turned out. The flashlight clattered, but she managed not to yelp as she bounced off a boulder and skidded. She lay flat on her back and breathed. Her ankle hurt worse than her chin, the former a twist, the latter a scrape. She touched her face. Sticky but not bleeding. She found the flashlight and stood up slowly, testing her ankle.

"Karley!" the officers called. "Where are you? Karley!"

She hurried along the edge, limping at first, then moving with greater ease. The dark shapes she passed were familiar to her— large abutments, massive boulders, campfire rings made of smaller rocks. The landing above cast a shadow beyond the lip where the surface of Rosy Pond waved gently in headlamp.

Close now, the family's spot just ahead, she thumbed on the flashlight. The fire ring had survived the winter, and she circled it, illuminating the interior, then aimed the beam at each separate rock. Sweeping circles, she widened her search.

"There she is!" Lambert called. *"Down by the water."*

Karley closed her eyes and breathed into memory, then opened them quickly. She crept toward the lake, the beam held close, and ten feet from the water found it. After all these years, the engraving appeared new, the ring of names scored into soft stone. *Curt Margaret Melissa Karley Jared Caleb. The Eternal Family DeBoer.* With a chisel they had each carved their own name after Curt had inscribed the title. She switched off the light and gazed out across Rosy Pond.

The officers approached, calling her name. "You need to learn to mind," Jill said.

Lambert shined his light on Karley's face. "You hurt yourself."

Karley ignited her flashlight and illuminated the engravings. Melissa's wedding ring, placed carefully at the center, spangled light across the sandstone lettering. She lifted the beam and showed them Rosy Pond.

"Right there. Not far from the lip. That's where you'll find Joshua."

She Might Never Let Go

Like the headlights that guide them tonight, God kept Melissa on the pavement when nothing but omnipotence could. Now, two nights later, Joe sits silently beside her, Joshua's Pooh Bear in his lap. His resignation simplifies matters, but it saddens her all the same. When the time comes, God will help her find him.

The state line is not far ahead, Evanston just beyond. Melissa prefers the scenic route through Ogden Canyon, up over the pass at Monte Christo to Highway 89. But it is dark outside, and there is Karley to consider. By now she has seen the cabin. She will lead the authorities to Rosy Pond. She will think all is lost, but once this is finished, she will know for herself God's truth. She will have her confirmation, and, her faith restored, they will all be together, Melissa and Joshua and Joe, Karley and their brothers and parents, an Eternal Family in the Celestial Kingdom.

Traffic is lighter than it was Friday night, the cheap alcoholics and gamblers and perverts having returned to Utah and its enforced prohibitions. Melissa reaches behind the seat and hauls her purse onto her lap. The Jeep's dome light is broken, so she's resisted until now. The weigh station at the outskirts of Evanston approaches, the light bright enough to read labels. Driving one-eyed, she sorts through the bottles. It takes her a moment to find the right one. She fingers out an oxy, reconsiders and takes two. Chewing them up, she swings her purse behind the seat.

When she glances at Joe, he is studying her nethers. The business with her purse has tugged up her skirt revealing her powder blue panties. The pills are a paste in her teeth now, and she reaches back and locates the Coke. Bottle between her

289

thighs, she breaks the seal, then unscrews and removes the cap. By the neck, she one-hands it, swishes and swallows, then takes another sip. She places the bottle against the steering wheel, six inches from her pudendum. It has been years since she's offered Joe anything of the sort.

Joe runs his tongue along his bottom teeth, then cocks his head and peers at her face. Between the slits, his hateful gaze is black with raw desire. "I should slap the shit out of you," he says.

There it is. Melissa presses the heel of her thumb to her pudendum and slides her nail from anus to clitoris. Then with the hem of her skirt, she wipes soda from her thighs, recaps the bottle, and places it behind the seat. Ahead The Bluff rises from the desert. Joe releases the mechanism and reclines his seat. Melissa takes the exit.

The Bluff. It is everything one expects from a Wyoming truck stop right down to the lotto and porn and liquor store. Once, however, it was a quaint little establishment with plank floors and a penny-candy aisle with the best chewing wax known to man— soft little bottles and straws filled with syrup, giant lips you could wear over your own.

A fleet of eighteen-wheelers idles in a dirt lot on the far side of the complex. Drivers wander the aisles between their trucks, giant travel mugs in hand. Closer in, every pump serves a semi. Two rigs wait their turns. Over here at the unleaded pumps, however, the lot is all but empty. Dropping the keys in her purse, Melissa opens the door and gets out.

When the tank is full, she replaces the cap and closes the little hatch. The pump offers a receipt, and she tells it *No*. She has no memory of accepting the one Karley found in Joe's sweats. She assesses his profile through the rear side window, then hurries across the lot to the convenience store. She's never entered *The Room* but has always been curious to see what the fuss is about. Her hourly bump has straightened the squiggles, and she notes a mild thrum of excitement.

One-stop shopping. Four men peruse the racks of magazines and DVDs, another two wander the liquor aisles. A massive person of indeterminate gender looms behind the sales counter. Melissa can see she has dressed appropriately—her anatomy is covered in eyes. It's a lot to take in, and she stands for a moment absorbing all the labels. Barely Legal, Teen, Housewife, Secretary, Nurse, Mature, Amateur, Granny, MILF. Asian, Black, Latina, Redhead, Blond, Brunette. Dildo, Group Sex, Masturbation, BDSM. Hardcore, Softcore. Leg, Ass, Breast, Foot. Oral, Anal, Double Penetration. Pissing, Panty, Fisting, Piercing, Tattoo, Taboo, Cream Pie. Girl on Girl. Gay. Schoolgirl.

Melissa fans through magazines one after another. She is fascinated and aroused but mostly disoriented. Men harbor hungers she's never imagined.

"I have a double sleeper." She feels his hand on her butt. "And a hundred bucks in my billfold." Re-shelving the magazine, she turns slowly toward him. He is swarthy and wrinkled, vested in leather, somewhere between fifty and seventy. He leans in. "And my friend over there has another hundred just to watch."

Melissa glances at the friend—wiry and balding, his white beard streaked with coffee and tobacco juice. "One thousand. Each."

His smile fades. "Bitch," he whispers. "You ain't worth no two grand. You ain't worth two hundred."

Melissa steps around him, and he watches her go, then ambles back to his friend. Joe's Smirnoff is on a shelf near the register, but she chooses Glenlivet instead. Scotch Single Malt Whisky, 12 Years Old, $42 even. She grabs two fifths and places them on the counter. Hands planted on the slab, the clerk stares at her. Melissa produces a credit card and places it beside the bottles. The clerk looks from the card to the men across the room, then reaches up and taps a sign overhead. *No Soliciting.*

Laughing the two men make for the door.

"I.D.," the clerk tells Melissa. She opens her wallet and holds it up. "Take it out." She extracts her license and hands it over. The wo/man looks at the card, at Melissa, at the card. Scowling s/he hands her the license. "Little boy by your name went missing down in Ogden. Heard it on the news."

"Me, too," Melissa says.

"Related?"

Melissa nods. "Probably. Lots of us Christophers in Utah."

The clerk rings up the whisky and runs the Visa. "Not so fast, I need to see that signature." Melissa returns the card to the counter.

She signs the receipt, then waits while the clerk verifies her signature against the card. The clerk puts the bottles in separate sacks, then combines the two into one. "Hook elsewhere," s/he says, sliding the bag across the counter. "And don't never come back here again."

Outside, the two men are waiting at the corner of the convenience store. Striding long, they hurry out, angled to intercept. "Hey, *bitch*," the big one calls. "Come to help you put those bottles in your box."

The Jeep is not far from the convenience store, and Melissa steadies her pace and pretends not to hear them. Through the windshield, she sees Joe sit up in his seat. His door swings open, and the men halt their pursuit. Melissa opens the driver's door and looks back through the hinge crotch.

"Lookee there," the big man says. "Got herself a pretty boy. You are a boy aren't you, girl?"

"And rich, too, hey, Hank? Pussy that expensive, he's gotta be rich."

Without a word, Joe closes his door and walks toward the men. Hank has it right, Joe is desperate but not in a way these men can imagine. Dropping her purse on the ground, the bottles on the seat, Melissa watches Joe circle in. She is almost to him when Hank takes a swing. Joe is not unfamiliar with fat men and violence, and he easily dodges Hank's punch. Wiry takes a running kick and misses altogether. By the arm, Melissa pulls Joe toward the Jeep.

They have nearly made it when Hank catches up—he snares Melissa's hair from behind. As her head snaps back, Joe sees what has happened. Fat Hank never has a chance. Melissa falls on her ass, but she hears Hank's expulsion, the sound of a highway blowout. Joe stands over the man deciding where to stomp. Melissa scrambles to her feet and grabs him by the arm and drags him again to the Jeep. She hooks her purse off the concrete, shoves everything from her seat. Joe climbs in his side, then starts to get out, and Melissa snatches him by a sleeve. He tows her halfway across the center console before he realizes she's attached. He looks at her, at Hank and Wiry, then climbs back into the Jeep.

Melissa steers the Jeep around the two men and rolls through the exit. She takes the ramp shifting hard and prods the Jeep up to speed. Motionless beside her, Joe radiates like yellowcake. Leaning sideways, Melissa mines for the bottles. She offers one to Joe, and after a moment he takes it. He holds it to the windshield and reads the label, then stares at Melissa for a long time. Settling back in his seat, he slices the seal. "Don't mind if I do," he says.

■

Two nights earlier Melissa could not have imagined she would ever drive this stretch again. Joe had failed God's test, and she feared him beyond redemption. Joshua, buckled safely in his booster seat, had been dead for a number of hours.

Now Joe lips measured nips from the bottle with more restraint than Melissa has anticipated. She's not sure she likes his newfound self-control. "Not the Stillwell woman," he thinks aloud. "Not her son." He looks at Melissa. "Neither of them?"

"No."

Joe raises the Glenlivet then lowers it without drinking. "Was it me?"

"Yes."

He tilts the bottle and pulls.

As they pass the first sign announcing Exit 39, Hans's BMW streaks past them. Melissa jerks her foot off the accelerator, afraid Hans has recognized Caleb's Jeep. His car fades onto the exit, then spins right onto 414. Melissa coasts up the ramp tracking its taillights. They recede at a high rate of speed. Under the light at the stop sign, she hauls out her purse. Hans's race to Karley means only one thing. She has found Melissa's wedding ring.

Joe says, "So everything you told me was a lie. Everything we told the police. You made the whole thing up?"

Melissa throws back the pills and chases them with Coke. Stowing the bottle she lets out the clutch. "To protect you, Joe. To protect us both. It was the only way."

"He was already gone. No wonder I don't remember."

"You never remember anyway."

He is silent then and Melissa is relieved. It is not yet time to tell him the rest. The highway tonight is less treacherous than Friday and not only because the roads are dry. Friday from dawn until ninety minutes into Saturday she did not take a single pill. This was not God's command but her own sacred offering. She knows what is real, what is fake. For God and herself, she kept it to the real.

■

Notice the dash clock: 12:37 a.m., barely Saturday morning. Melissa glances in the rearview, but the darkness obscures him. Joshua hates long drives, but he loves Rosy Pond. "We're here, baby," she tells him. "You've been so patient."

The road to the landing is slick and sloppy. She was right to choose the 4Runner. But the manual hubs are difficult to turn, so she has waited to see if they can make it without four-wheel drive.

"Look at that. The road's washed out." She puts the truck in park. The problem, she sees, isn't the road itself but a slide from the hillside above it. She sets the parking brake. "Stay here," she tells Josh.

The rain is really pounding now, harder than she thought. The wind is blowing, and she's forgotten a jacket, though she scarcely registers the cold. Standing to the side, she studies the problem, then steps into the mud to test its depth. She doesn't sink far, but Joe's boots are loose and she must secure them by hand as she backs from the slide. She surveys the road for another ten seconds, then squishes back to the truck.

"Okay, pal," she says, getting in. "Let's see if I'm right."

She backs halfway up the gully and offers a prayer, then releases the brake and gives it a push. The tires hit mud, and the 4Runner, rising, floats rudderless into the stew. Melissa nudges the gas, and the back end fades as the tires begin to sink. She eases off, the wheels spin and catch, and she's sure she's made a mistake. But fifteen feet from the slide's far side, the tires touch solid ground. The transmission drops, and the 4Runner emerges. Melissa nudges them up the gulley's far bank.

Her seizing body flashes hot and cold, and she steers to the landing dreaming of pills. She parks at the rim near the staircase and leaves the motor running, the headlights aimed at Rosy Pond.

"I am yours," she tells God. "I will do as I'm told. But please, Father, please help me now." She breathes through her mouth, fighting the panic, the first she has suffered since leaving the house. "Thank you for giving us Rosy Pond. In the name of Jesus Christ, Amen."

She toggles the switch and the rear window scrolls. She gets out and drops the tailgate. Joe's large nylon athletic bag is waiting with the scissors. She unzips it on the tailgate, then cuts a series of slits in the fabric. Strap around her neck, she tosses the scissors in the truck and lifts the tailgate home.

Unpredictable, the things that come to one's rescue. When she lifts Joshua from his booster seat, he stays folded at the waist and knees. It's just the reminder she's needed: This is not Joshua, God has welcomed him home. He waits with Heavenly Father in the Celestial Kingdom for his parents to find their way to him.

She could navigate this path with her eyes closed. Fearless now, Joshua wooden against her, she descends the natural staircase to the lip. Their place is not far from the water's edge, and she feels her family, even Karley and Joe—they have all come to say goodbye. She has forgotten a flashlight, but the headlights suffice—she locates the engraving with ease. She places Joshua on the ground beside it and drops the bag on the lip.

In the dim illumination, the surface of Rosy Pond is pocked with rain and wind caps. Wet to the skin, she brings her hand into light and examines her wedding ring. Sticking the finger in her mouth, she slavers it slick then works the ring over the knuckle.

The names are indistinct but the circle is obvious, *The Eternal Family DeBoer*. Kneeling, she places the ring at its center. Then she unzips the bag, gathers Joshua in her arms, and presses her nose to his neck. Even in death, he smells like Joshua, and she allows herself to breathe him in. She places him on the bag and works the folds around him. From a neighboring fire pit, she selects a round stone and lugs it back to Joshua. She arranges it in the bag beneath his knees, then works the zipper to his chin.

In the oblique light, he appears quite alive. She closes the fold and zips him in.

On her feet again, she sheds her wet clothes—she takes care to keep them together. The bag is heavy, but she refuses to drag it. Stooping she slips the strap over her head. Joshua bumps on her hip when she brings herself upright. The stone sinks to one end, and the strap slides on her shoulder, abrading the skin at her clavicle. She shuffles to the water's edge.

Five feet from the lip, the lake is thirty feet deep. Melissa has measured it with a string attached to a lead weight. She swings the bag to the front, and it settles against her thighs. The weight on her neck pulls her chin toward her chest. Mustering her strength, she hoists Joshua to her belly, then again above her breasts. She waddles two steps into the lake. A third will send her off the ledge. She hears nothing, not even the rain and wind.

Like falling, they enter with hardly a splash. The strap by design remains around her neck. Kicking, she tries to swim them from the bank, but the bag is heavy, difficult to steer. It floats for two seconds, then sinks beneath the surface. Angling for the deep, Melissa follows it down. She can admit it now, Joshua tethered beneath her, she can acknowledge what she harbors in her most essential self: She hates God. She hates him like she has never loved anyone, not Joshua, not Joe, certainly not herself. Curled around Josh, she spins slowly toward the bottom.

She might never let go.

Day Three

"My Faith is gone!" cried he, after one stupefied moment. "There is no good on earth; and sin is but a name. Come, devil; for to thee is this world given."

—*Young Goodman Brown,* Nathaniel Hawthorne

Thursday

4 DAYS AGO

"It rained all day," Joshua announced. "I hate it when it rains all day."

Melissa placed her wallet in the tray beside the microwave. Fifteen minutes earlier in the clinic lot, she'd chewed up four oxys before starting the Outback. She was already feeling much better. "Oh, I'm sorry, baby." She picked him up and saddled him on a hip. He wrapped his legs around her waist.

"That's okay. Billy came over. We played Harry Potter."

"Was it fun?"

"Kind of. When's Billy's party?"

Melissa carried him to the calendar. "Right here." She put a finger on the day, a week from Saturday. "And here's where we are today."

"How many days is that?"

"Let's count. Start right here. This is tomorrow."

"One," he began. "Two, three, four, five, six, seven, eight."

"Right. Eight days. Do you think you can wait?"

"No. I wish it was tomorrow."

"Me, too, honey. It's hard to wait." Melissa kissed his nose and put him down. "Where's your dad?"

Josh opened the fridge. "Working. What's for dinner?"

Joe had not started dinner. On Melissa's workdays, he usually cooked. Reaching over Josh, she lifted the Coke from the top shelf. "What sounds good?"

"Coke. Can I have some?"

"No, Josh. Coke has caffeine. And lots of sugar. You know you can't have Coke."

299

"Dad lets me sometimes." Closing the fridge, he glanced at his mother. Too late, he'd seen his mistake.

"I guess that's what dads do," Melissa said. "How about tater-tot casserole?"

Bulging his tongue through the prized gap in his teeth, he showed her the rest of his chompers. "How about hotdogs?"

"How about tater-tot casserole?"

"Okay," he grumbled. "But I want hotdogs tomorrow. Can I watch TV?"

Melissa poured Coke in a glass. "You can watch one of your DVDs."

"But when can I watch *Aliens*?"

"Never," Melissa said. "That's a scary movie. And it's gross. People get killed. Heavenly Father doesn't like us to watch shows like that. He says no R-rated movies."

"Did you hear him say?"

Melissa smiled. "Sure I did, God told me in my heart. But that's why he gives us general authorities too. So we know how he expects us to live. The general authorities say no R-rated movies. God told me what they said is true."

"Dad watches them."

"Joshua."

"What if I pray, and he says it's okay?"

Melissa laughed. "Go watch a DVD. One of your own. And tell Dad I'm home."

Sag-shouldered, he trudged to the stairwell. He had a flair for drama, that kid. Coke in hand Melissa wandered down the hall into the master bedroom. Joe'd not run the wash—another bad sign—and she pulled a pair of pajamas from the hamper. She stripped to her garments and stepped into the bathroom. Renal retention, another opioid side-effect. She thumbed through the *Ensign* and waited for her bladder.

In the bedroom again, she pulled on the PJs. Through the heat vent, she could hear sexy little Ariel plotting her Disney defloration. What to do about her fishy little tail? Melissa sighed. There was just no winning.

When she walked into the kitchen, Joe was hunched over the

table addressing an envelope. He copied the address from the letter beside it. Melissa opened the freezer and selected a pound of ground beef, a bag of frozen peas, the tater-tots. "Tater-tot casserole?"

Joe didn't answer. She studied him for a three count, then gathered from the pantry a can of Cream of Mushroom and another of corn. He occasionally drank while watching Josh, though only twice had he drank himself drunk. She couldn't always tell if he'd opened a bottle, and his demeanor now told her nothing. "What's that?"

Dropping the pen, he picked up the envelope. Melissa paused her preparations to watch him lick the flap. "You forgot to put the letter in."

"No, I didn't." He glued down the flap. "I printed this copy for you."

Melissa sipped her Coke. Joe hadn't been drinking, she was sure of it now. He'd written the letter sober, that was the point. He'd made her a copy, that too was the point. Finally, he looked up and she settled against the counter. "Why do I get the feeling I'm not going to like this?"

Joe smiled and not unkindly, though there was no joy in it either. "Because you're inspired, Melissa. Your feelings always mean something. It's the way your God talks to you."

He'd made such remarks many times in anger, but today she sensed no derision. Foreboding creeping, she kept her distance and refused to look at the letter. "What does it say, your letter?"

"Read it."

"Uh-uh, no."

Ariel sang below them. The automatic icemaker hummed. Cubes rattled into the bucket. "I'm finished," Joe said.

In the face of all things blatant: "Your liver will be most grateful."

"That's not what I mean."

Precisely.

"I wanted to believe. I wanted it more than anything. I tried, Melissa. You know I tried."

She scraped at her thumb with a fingernail, then ripped off the cuticle with her teeth.

"Look what it's done to us."

She glanced at the letter.

"I'm worn out. I can't live by doctrines I don't believe in. I'd rather not live than go on living like this."

Melissa rolled her eyes.

"Pathetic, huh? Well it's true. I'd rather die and never wake up. To be honest, sweetheart, I think that's pretty much how it is, anyway."

Melissa stared at him. She didn't understand his words, not a single one. He'd railed against God and the church for years, but he'd never said anything like this. "You're divorcing me? Is that what this is?"

"Melissa—"

"Because you can't divorce me. Not if you have any intention—"

"I don't want a divorce." He picked up the letter and scanned it, then raised his face and met her gaze. "But your thing with God, Melissa. It's sick. You've chosen him over me. Why would you do that?"

"Because he never lets me down."

"I love you, Melissa. But it's fading."

Melissa folded her arms and spoke calmly. "You don't love me. You don't even love Josh. The only thing you love is booze."

Joe sighed. "Okay," he said. "How about this? You choose me over God and I'll stop drinking."

She turned her back to him. "You've given up drinking a thousand times. You give it up every time you're hung over."

"Oh, I could give it up, Melissa. I'm not as addicted to booze as you are to God."

On tip-toes, she retrieved the Excedrin from the medicine cupboard and shook two oxys into her hand—Joe hated caffeine; he never touched the bottle. When she turned around, he was proffering the letter. "Read it." Brushing past him, she palmed the tablets into her mouth. She swept her Coke off the counter and took a long pull. "Read it, Melissa."

Spinning toward him, she snatched the letter from his hand, wadded it up, and tossed it beneath a chair. Joe toed it into reach and picked it up then un-crumpled and smoothed it on the table.

"Membership Department," he began. "Church of Jesus Christ of Latter-Day Saints ..."

May __, 20__

Dear Sirs:

This is to inform you that I hereby resign my membership in the Church of Jesus Christ of Latter-day Saints and request that my name be stricken from its records. This demand is made freely and with a full understanding of the consequences of this action. Please be advised that I exercise my right to permanently remove myself from the Mormon institution under guarantees contained within the U.S. Constitution. As a free agent, I choose to follow my conscience. Religious freedom is my right and my demand.

I insist that official proof, under cover of a letter notifying me that my name has been removed from the records of the Church, be sent to me forthwith. The official record shall show that the only reason my name has been removed is because I requested it as an act of resignation. I will not be a target of the harassment and humiliations your institution has historically inflicted on internal critics (apostates you call them) and those who attempt to resign. Indeed, I will proceed with legal action against the Church if anything is done to libel my good name or the name of my family. If we suffer any loss of reputation, I will first go to the media, then I will sue.

Be advised, should any representative of the LDS Church attempt to contact me, I will consider it an invasion of my privacy and an attack upon my agency. Again, I will go to the media, then I will seek a restraining order. I will not participate in any Church court or trial, for I have done no wrong.

If in two weeks' time I have not received satisfactory proof that the Church has honored my demand, you can expect to hear from my attorney.

Very Truly Yours,
Joseph Andrew Christopher

"I'm starvin'," Josh said. "When's dinner?" Pooh Bear dangling he stood in the stairwell doorway. He looked at his father then at his mother. Melissa opened a bottom cupboard and worked the frying pan from the stack. It slipped from her hand and clattered on the floor. Trembling, she retrieved it and set it on the stove.

"Tell you what, buddy," Joe said. "I have to run to the post office. How about you ride along? When I'm finished, I'll buy you whatever dinner you want."

Joshua grinned.

"No," Melissa said. Her voice echoed in her head. She put the hamburger in the microwave and pushed defrost. "I'm making tater-tot casserole. No one's going anywhere."

Joe mussed Josh's moppy hair. "The main post office, that's where we're headed. The others are already closed."

"Hotdogs?" Josh asked.

"Get your shoes on. Go grab your raincoat." Josh ran to find his shoes and jacket.

Melissa dialed on the burner, then turned to face Joe. "What do I have to do?"

He ran his fingers through his hair. "Excuse me?"

In her moment of need, oxy had forsaken her. How had God let it come to this? "How do I choose you?"

Joe didn't believe her. He studied his letter and tried to decide. "Let me be who I am."

"If I do that—if I let you drink, if I don't talk about God, if I don't bother you about the church, if we go back to our games—will you not send that letter? Ever?"

Joe's features softened. "No."

The microwave beeped and Melissa's left eyelid twitched. "If you mail it, you'll lose me forever. You'll lose Josh."

"Yes. We'll no longer be sealed in the temple and I won't have the priesthood. Our eternal family will be dissolved. We'll be left with nothing but this life to live. We'll have nothing to believe in but our earthly family. Imagine the relief."

Dragging his raincoat, Josh clicked into the kitchen. "I can't make this shoelace stay tied," he said.

"Bring it here, pal." Shoelace flopping Josh padded to Joe. "You did a good job on this one."

"Yeah. But it was hard. And I'm hungry."

Finished with Josh's shoelace, Joe pushed to his feet. "Well, let's hurry." He retrieved his keys and wallet from the tray and secured them in his pockets. When he turned for the envelope,

Melissa was holding it. "Melissa," he warned. She lunged for the door and he blocked her exit. "Don't be childish. I'll just print another one."

"Mom's in her pajamas," Josh noted. "Do we have to wait for her to change her clothes?"

Melissa double-gripped the envelope, but before she could rip it, Joe had her by the wrists. "Give it to me," he whispered.

She struggled to free herself, but Joe held tight. "Let go!" she wailed. *"Let go, let go."* Joe took his opening and spread her wrists. The envelope slipped from one hand.

Suddenly, Josh was between their knees, his face pressed to Melissa's thighs. "Stop it!" he muffled. "Stop it, now!"

Bending, she tried to bite Joe's hand. He dropped her left wrist and spun a 180, pinning her arm in the pit of his own. He pried back her thumb and extracted the envelope, and she sank her teeth into the flesh of his triceps. Growling, he lurched and Josh lost his balance. He landed on the linoleum floor. Joe cupped his triceps and glared back at Melissa, who'd stumbled into the counter. Hand clamped to her mouth, she could taste Joe's flesh and the chemical tang of deodorant. Rolling his arm, he tugged up his sleeve. He palmed the wound and showed her the blood, then waved the envelope like a victory flag.

Wide-eyed, Joshua lay at Joe's feet, his fingers in his mouth. "Here we go, pal." Joe gathered him into his arms.

"Leave him."

A pair of red crescents bloomed on Joe's sleeve. He patted his pockets for his keys and wallet, his memory misplaced in the fracas.

"Leave him here."

Joe brushed a wisp of bangs from Josh's eyes. "You still wanna go for a hotdog?" When Josh didn't respond, Joe rubbed his back. "You ready? We can leave now if you still want to go." This time Josh nodded and Joe started for the back door.

"If you mail that letter, there will be nothing left. You'll lose him forever. In this life and the next."

Joe stopped but did not look back. "Do whatever you're going to do, Melissa."

Over Joe's shoulder, Josh stared at her. "Go with Daddy now," she told him. "Everything's fine."

"Better than fine." Joe triggered the garage door. "We're going to Arctic Circle for a foot-long. Then after dinner I'll take you to my favorite store. It has shelves and shelves filled with all kinds of bottles."

Joshua lifted his hand. Melissa lifted hers. "Whoee, what a downpour," Joe said. He opened the storm door. "Get ready to make a run for it."

The empty fry pan ticked on the stove. Joshua's raincoat lay abandoned on the floor. On the yellow-flecked linoleum, a drop of Joe's blood pooled in a crown of red jewels. The window hummed as the truck's headlights scrolled. Melissa turned off the burner, then closed her eyes, and prayed until she felt God's gentle touch. She listened to the strains of the Still Small Voice. She listened for a very long time.

She picked up Josh's coat, draped it over a chair, and wended down the hall to their bedroom. She opened her purse and found the script, blank except for Hans's signature. She studied the white trying to remember the name—what was the name of that medicine? She rubbed her nose and massaged her eyeballs. She changed into jeans and a sweatshirt.

In the kitchen, she lifted her wallet from the tray and placed it with the script on the counter. The pen was on the table where Joe had left it. Poised over the script, she again closed her eyes. She'd done her homework—why couldn't she bring up the name?

"A little help?" she asked. Then like Joseph Smith she began to transcribe God's scripture. *Seconal.* Pen to paper she waited for the rest. *100mg. #100. One capsule 3 times daily for epilepsy. Joseph Christopher. Today's date.*

She checked the box allowing for generic then creased the script and put it in her wallet. She punched the garage opener on her way out the door. Her keys were already in the ignition.

■

They crest the final hill, the junction just below them, and see flashing lights on the highway far ahead. *Hans,* is Melissa's first thought, pulled over for speeding. But the timing is wrong, and these lights are moving. They speed toward Rosy Pond.

Joe sips his whisky and watches the show. "Are they looking for us?"

"For Joshua."

Joe nods. "That's what you said. 'He's waiting.' At the cabin?"

Coasting in, she applies the brake. "No, not the cabin. Rosy Pond."

Joe swirls the bottle, then puts it to his lips. Melissa takes the right onto SR1145. "In the Pond?"

She nods.

"Did I put him there?"

"Do you think you did?"

Joe stares straight ahead. "I hate the lake. I'd never leave him there."

"Your mother was waiting."

"My mother's worm food."

"She was waiting all the same." Melissa could use another bump, but the cabin's not far now. "No, you didn't put him there. I did. I put him there for all of us."

Joe takes a sip. "Was I there?"

"No, Joe. I did it alone."

Joe has been drinking for longer than an hour, but except for this boldness, he shows no intoxication. But he's taking the whisky more freely now, and she trusts he'll be close by the time they arrive. Shifting in his seat, he leans against the door and gazes across the cockpit. "And he was already dead when you put him in?"

"You know he was."

"Because I did it. I killed him, but I wasn't at Rosy Pond."

"Because, Joe, if he'd been alive, there wouldn't have been any reason to put him in."

Joe raises the bottle and toasts Melissa's dodge. He exhales a vaporous breath. "You dotted your I's. You crossed your T's."

"Your I's. Your T's. And God wrote this story."

"Well." He nods. "He I'ed and T'ed Josh right off the page."

"No, Joe. You did that."

Rolling down his window, he spits into the night and Melissa leans harder on the gas. She doesn't know how much longer she can evade him. He rolls up the window and looks at her. "So how did God manage that book in the gutter?"

Changing her mind, Melissa brings out her purse. One medicine at a time, she holds the bottles to the speedometer. She can scarcely see the words. Finally, she finds the Oxycontin, a twelve-hour dose she needs every six. "Quite a habit you got there, Molly." Joe offers the whisky. "A swig to wash it down?"

Molly Mormon is Joe's favorite derision, and Melissa deems its use a promising sign. She swallows the tablet dry. "The book was easy." Tossing her purse, she locates the Coke. Joe waits while she swishes some down. "It happened just like I told the police."

"Not quite," Joe says.

Tedious minutia with no obvious point of entry. Should she start with the carwash she visited before daylight? Or with him at 6:00 a.m. still passed out on the basement sofa? The load of laundry she did while he slept, those damp, dirty sweats, one sock clumped with mud? Should she tell him how she nearly slid off the road or about hiding the boot in a bag? Showering and dressing, the trip to Walmart for the book and to throw the boot away? Or that she'd had to collect the scissors from the 4Runner before she could wrap Billy's present? It's all one thing, a single moment, and she hasn't the strength to unwind it.

"I put the book on the street just before I called Nat. I drove around the block and braked near the curb. I didn't even get out. I set the book in the gutter and continued up the street."

"Huh." Joe nods then tilts the bottle. "Pretty brave. What if someone had seen you?"

"No one did and no one would have. God made sure of that."

■

Proof?

Picture Friday evening. See God do what God does best. See Melissa outside in her wet backyard icing her nerves in the rain. She has believed God's plan would be accomplished by now and doubts she can endure much longer without a pill. But the cold has helped, and she returns to the house and descends again into the breech. Head tilting severely, Joshua lies across

Joe's lap. Joe sleeps sitting up on the basement sofa. The room reeks of urine and feces.

The landline rings and Melissa picks up the handset. Brian MacMillan, which likely means Nat. She returns the device unanswered to its base, then bends low and lifts Joshua into her arms. Joe doesn't move except to breathe. She carries Josh upstairs and lays him on the kitchen table and continues into the bathroom. She stoppers the tub and opens the spigot, then returns to her son in the kitchen.

Beginning with his feet, she removes his clothes—socks, pants, shorts, shirt. She wets a clean dishcloth with warm water and at the table takes him by the ankles. As she did when he was new, she lifts his legs and carefully cleans his bottom. She tosses all but his shorts down the stairwell, then carries his underpants with the washcloth to the bathroom and swirls them in the toilet. The tub is full, more water than he's allowed. She closes the spigot and returns to the kitchen.

When she releases Joshua into the water, his perfect little face floats to the surface. She slips a clean washcloth from the rack and studiously washes his body. He's still warm in her hands, and she caresses his everything. She must imprint his essence into the clay of her memory.

She longs to linger but hasn't the time, so she yanks the plug and starts the shower. The spray takes the soap, the drain the water, and she shuts off the spigot and whips a towel from the bar. She unfurls it on the bathmat and plucks Josh from the tub, then shrouds him with a second towel and lifts him off the floor. She carries him to his bed, drying as they go. Lifting his head, she finger-combs his hair. She threads his stubby appendages into the holes of his underclothes, then steps to the closet for a top and pants. Before she can choose, the doorbell rings.

She glances over her shoulder at Joshua's Pooh clock. 8:48 p.m. What, she wonders, has God up his sleeve now? She straightens Josh's body, nests his head in the pillow, and tucks the covers around him. First collecting the towels, she turns off the light and closes his bedroom door. From the toilet, she gathers the underwear and washcloth and flushes the waste down the drain.

She uses the towels to wrap the soiled items and carries it all to the living room. Crossing to the door, she spies the dirty cup and makes a note to collect it later. The bell rings again as she swings the door wide.

Nat MacMillan. Melissa likes Nat. Once very recently, they shared a pair of sons. Melissa opens the storm door smiling.

"Gosh, Melissa, I hope I'm not disturbing you too late." Nat frowns apologetically. "I left a message. The lights were on. I wouldn't barge in on your Friday night except Billy's having conniptions."

Melissa's smile widens. "You're perfect. Come on in. Is Billy okay?"

Nat hurries inside. "Billy's fine, and now I'm mortified. You didn't answer the phone. I bet I caught you in the middle of something."

"Oh, heavens, don't you worry a bit. I was trapped in the bathroom washing Josh's hair." Melissa shows Nat the wad of towels, then opens her arms to reveal her wet clothing. "Kid was asleep on his feet. I was just about ready to check for messages."

Appearing relieved, Nat nods then grins. "Friday night, kid's in bed. Joe's probably waiting with bells on."

"We'll see," Melissa says, returning the grin.

It's Nat's cue and she takes it with grace. "So it turns out Brian has to travel next weekend. We're hoping to move Billy's birthday party up a week. To tomorrow, actually. I know it's short notice. We're not planning anything big, just Josh and Billy, our kids. Cake and ice cream, a few games."

Melissa tries to remember. "I don't think we've got anything tomorrow. Let me peek at the calendar. You want a soda or something? Juice?"

"Oh, no. Thanks. Billy's got his nose squished to the front window. You know how they are at this age." Nat's hand flies into the air. "*Oh*, I almost forgot! I promised to pick up a Harry Potter game he left when he was over yesterday."

Melissa suffers a second's indecision, then realizes what this is. In a flash she sees it all the way to the end and is grateful to God for his gifts. Turning, she beckons Nat to follow. "Billy has quite a thing for Harry Potter."

"You have no idea. We finished the first book two weeks ago. Since then it's 'Harry Potter this, Harry Potter that.' Billy Harry Potter."

Nat waits in the doorway while Melissa checks the kitchen calendar. Caleb's matinee date with Josh. She hasn't washed the table but can't smell Joshua. "Tomorrow looks great. What time?"

"Does eleven work? Sarah has a soccer game in the afternoon."

"Eleven's perfect." Melissa deposits the towels on the table and turns. "Does he have all the Harry Potter books?"

"He has one and two. But Brian and I bought him three and four, and the kids are giving him five. I know he'd love either of the others or even one of the movies. Don't spend much. Paperback's plenty."

Melissa takes Nat's hand and leads her down the hallway. "I'll see what I can find." Outside Josh's door, she lowers her voice. "We'll try his bedroom first."

"Oh, gosh," Nat whispers. "You think it's in there? Billy can wait until tomorrow."

Melissa squeezes Nat's hand. "Believe me. We couldn't wake him now."

Nat follows her uncertainly into the room. The hall fixture illuminates their search. Almost immediately Nat spots the game near the bookshelf. She points, Melissa nods, and Nat sneaks past the bed. She packs up the pieces while Melissa studies Josh. Nat joins her near the door, and together they admire him. "I should've combed that mop," Melissa whispers. "By morning, it'll be nothing but tangles."

Nat gusts through her nose and pats Melissa's arm. Melissa lingers with Josh for a moment longer, then follows Nat out and closes the door. "Clichés are cliché for a reason," Nat says.

"Excuse me?"

"Sleeping children and all that. Clichés are cliché because they're true."

"Oh, absolutely," Melissa says. "Watching them sleep is what keeps us from killing them."

Nat throws her head back and laughs without sound. This is the way the women bond, by making jokes at their own expense. "Something like that," Nat agrees. Melissa has guided them back to the front door. "So 11:00 o'clock?"

"He'll be ready." Melissa opens the door and follows Nat onto the porch. "I'll give you a call before I send him."

Hood draped over her head, Nat descends the porch stairs, Billy's game tucked under her arm. "Go get in bed with that cute husband of yours. Watch a good movie or something."

"Listen to him snore is more like it."

Nat giggles down the walkway.

Door closed, Melissa grips the knob from behind and presses her shoulders to the wood. Chin on her chest, she hungers for a pill. Where was she? Josh to dress, dirty clothes to the wash. Harry Potter shirt for the party. Towels on the table—Melissa touches her wet front—and these to the washer, too. Then find Joe's boots and a pair of dry sweats. God is correct—Joe's clothes will do just fine.

Poor Nat.

Poor Billy.

"Good one," she tells God. Then she releases the knob and rocks off the door and misplaces her legs in the process. She hits the floor, and the piano strings hum and the photos sway with their frames. She closes her mouth and the other sound stops. She remembers what she was doing. Laundry, she thinks. Comb Josh's hair. She staggers to her feet, retrieves the dirty cup and weaves toward the kitchen rechecking God's list.

Old Fool

The road to Rosy Pond was a pulsing serpentine of flare glare. It glowed medieval, a torch-lit pilgrimage to the Red Sea. Observed from a truck doing seventy miles per hour, it flowed like molten lava.

"You've been busy," Craig told Sheriff Smith. They'd been passing flares for a quarter mile. Ahead, a state cruiser blocked the highway.

Nodding absently, Smith eased off the gas and rolled down his window. The highway patrolman slid off the hood of his car. "Howdy, Doug."

Patrolman Doug rested his hand on the roof. "Sheriff." He nodded at Craig.

"How's traffic?"

The right side of Doug's face glowed red. "It's a pig derby."

Smith chuckled. "Any sign of the Feebs yet?"

Doug shook his head. "They've not yet graced us with their excellence. Forest Service got here fast though."

"Land or sea?"

"Both," Doug said. "Heard the boat buzz in about forty-five minutes ago."

Craig leaned forward. "You happen to know if a guy in a Beemer came through?"

"As a matter of fact," Doug said. "An hour ago maybe. Doctor insignia on the bumper. Said he was the husband of the woman they got down there. Checked out, so I let him in. That okay?"

"Fine. Thanks."

Stepping back from the truck, Doug touched his hat. Smith

313

raised a hand and released the brake. Rolling up his window, he steered around the cruiser, then nudged them to thirty-five. "Year doesn't go by we don't lose a few folks to the lake. Forest Service got this ES grant last year. Side-scan sonar. Good stuff."

They rounded the final bend, and the world lit up, two dozen rigs at least. Hans Nordling's BMW cooled on the shoulder. Smith weaved through the rally and parked near the congestion at the entrance to a dirt road. He opened his door.

"How do you want to do this?" Craig asked.

The sheriff looked back. "Not interested in pissing around the perimeter, Milo. If there's any paving to do, I'll do it. Just tell me what you need. When this is all finished, you can say nice things about my deputies and me, and we'll call it even."

He rocked the vehicle getting out, and Craig remained where he was, too ill to make himself move. Finally, he lifted the latch and lowered himself to the asphalt. The hazy desert stank of cordite. Behind him, a flare sputtered and hissed, sputtered and coughed, sputtered and hissed and coughed and died. Someone popped a new one and dropped it beside the dead casing. Craig turned toward the beat of a distant rotor but was unable to locate the helicopter. He hoped it wasn't the media.

"That's our ride," Smith said when Craig joined him at the entrance. A pair of headlights weaved up the hill.

The helicopter was close now, somewhere behind them, hidden by the hills to the southwest. Craig still couldn't see it, then abruptly there it was, a deafening roar overhead. It tracked the line of flares toward the lake, then, blinking, banked and circled back.

"Turbo jet," Smith said.

"Government issue," Craig agreed.

"I should have been FBI."

Their ride had arrived, a muddy Expedition with a light bar. Smith wandered away to consult with the driver. Two hundred yards east, cops popped flares on the road, then scattered for the helicopter's landing. Its cyclone touched ground and the flares spun away. God in his burning bush. Big Brother hovered while experts chased flares. Shaking his head, Craig watched the circus. He hoped the diver was inside the aircraft.

The helicopter landed and two passengers emerged. They passed a bag to a welcoming cop, then hoisted two more and moved toward the vehicles. Smith and his deputy stepped close beside Craig and watched the FBI come. "Which field office you boys from?" Smith asked.

The FBI was dressed down for the occasion—jeans and North Face jacket on the older agent, a dark peacoat on the younger. "Salt Lake," the older agent said.

"Smith, Sheriff." He extended his hand.

"Special Agent Tinkerton. This is Rob Anders. Former Navy SEAL. Does a lot of SARs. We've used him a number of times."

"Not FBI?" Smith said.

"No, sir," Anders said. "Contract work's as close as I come."

Contract work. Craig studied the man. Body of a sprinter, face of an analyst, black head shaved and shaped like a bullet. Anders looked as though he could manage a little contract work.

"This is Lieutenant Craig," Smith said. "Ogden City Police Department."

"We spoke on the phone," Craig said. "You guys move fast."

Tinkerton was of average size, maybe fifty, with the open face of a Mormon bishop, which Craig suspected he might very well be. The FBI loved Mormons almost as much as the CIA. Loyal and obedient, authoritarian to the core. Full of conspiratorial obsessions. The agent smiled. "Like I told you on the phone. We were ready for your call. We've been watching this case since it started."

To Anders, Craig said, "Nice of you to join the party."

"Glad to help," Anders said. "We got a location on the body yet?"

The deputy answered. "Boat started with the towfish about forty-five minutes ago. When I left to come up, it still hadn't pinged anything promising."

By herd consent, they set out for the truck. "Word on the parents?" Tinkerton asked.

"No," Craig said. "We have camera footage of them leaving their residence, but no one's seen or heard from them since. They left their cell phones behind. Recovery team found both devices in their house."

The deputy scrolled down the rear window of his Expedition

and began loading gear. "Tell you what," Smith said. "You three ride down with Deputy Lambert. I have a few things to do here. Kent, once you get 'em unloaded, come back for me."

"Sure thing," the deputy said. He took Tinkerton's bag and stowed it in the truck.

"Any ideas?" Tinkerton asked Craig.

"You mean the Christophers? None. Got an APB out. Mostly, we're hoping they'll use a credit card. If we ever get a peek."

"Subpoena?"

"Not the snag." Craig looked at his watch. "One-thirty a.m. Monday morning."

Nodding, Tinkerton produced his phone. "You have the information with you?"

"No. The ADA's running point."

Tinkerton swiped through his contacts. "Get him on the phone."

"Her."

The FBI put the device to his ear. "Say again?"

"The Assistant DA's a woman. Mary Turner."

Tinkerton smiled. "Good old Mary. I love that woman. Get her on the phone. Let's see if we can light a fire."

Anders looked back at the helicopter and laughed. "That's right. FBI knows how to light fires."

■

In the floodlit atmosphere above Rosy Pond, bats darted helter-skelter, hunting easy prey. Red rock refracted the radiance across the lip where Craig had been standing for the better part of an hour. The water appeared its own conflagration, an illusion as mesmerizing as the real fire in the pit twenty yards to his east. The boat trolled slowly, its wake riffled satin. Back and forth, it motored across the bay as though powered by its bright cycloptic eyeball. Despite his misery or maybe because of it, Craig found it rather beautiful.

From behind him, a new light panned across the water, then Lambert's truck started down the hill. Fifteen feet away Jill Grafton flashed a photo of Melissa Christopher's wedding ring. She shot another from a different angle, then stepped back and flashed a third. "You're breathing's labored," she said. "I can hear you from here."

"I'll survive," he said. The staggered closing of the Expedition's doors echoed across the bay.

"What's the weather supposed to be?" she asked.

Tinkerton answered. "Clear until Wednesday."

Jill nodded. "I'm thinking we wait until sunup to pull that boot. I'm getting tired of working in this dark."

Tinkerton consulted his watch. "Three hours until daylight? Let's wait. Won't make any difference."

Jill placed the camera in its bag and kneeled down beside the DeBoer Family Shrine. "Snazzy ring. Big rock, princess cut. All I got is this skinny gold band."

"How is Cheryl?" Craig asked, though mostly as a test. He wasn't convinced he was really here.

"Pissy," Jill said. She stripped an evidence envelope from a bundle of the like. "Says she's tired of sleeping in our big bed without me."

Tinkerton peered at the criminalist, then looked away.

"Boy's mother wasn't mincing words," she continued. "Don't know what she was saying, but she certainly said it loudly."

"Forensic psychology 101," Tinkerton said. "You throw your wedding ring away, you're throwing your marriage away. Or your husband."

"Uh-huh," Jill said. What she meant was nuh-uh. She picked up the ring and admired it in the light. "The sister, Karley, seems to think otherwise."

"Really?" Tinkerton said. Not a question. Mr. FBI knew what he knew.

Jill secured the ring in the envelope and labeled it with a Sharpie. Bending slightly, Craig stretched his body. His skin felt prickly, his innards panicky. Jill glanced up from the envelope. "Gonna make it?"

Above them, Sheriff Smith and Deputy Lambert appeared at the rim of the landing. Their shadows extended to the far side of the bay. "Anything?" Smith called down.

"Nada," Tinkerton answered.

"Got some coffee here," Lambert said.

"Whoa," Jill said. "I don't like the way you look, Milo."

Craig turned toward the fire. In the flickering light, Hans held his wife. Together, they watched the eyeball on the lake. Handsome people even in despair. Firelight did them justice. "Think I'll walk over and have a word with the Nordlings."

"You're really starting to worry me, Milo."

"Where's Anders?" Smith called. He'd started down the staircase.

"Over here, walking the bank," Anders hailed from the darkness to the east.

"You want Lambert to carry your stuff down?"

"I'll come up," Anders answered. "I'm thinking we might do better if I just go in and look myself."

"May I intrude?" Craig asked the Nordlings. He'd paused outside the ring of boulders. Hans turned his head. Karley stayed with the boat.

"Pull up a rock," Hans said. Craig rounded the ring and eased himself down. Hans studied the detective for a moment longer, then returned his attention to the lake. "You're getting sicker. Did you take the medicine I gave you at the river?"

"I did," Craig said. "And I brought the rest with me. It's probably too soon to notice any improvement."

This time both Nordlings looked his way. In the firelight, he could see Karley had scraped her chin. "You should have gone to the hospital for tests," Hans said.

Karley slipped Hans's embrace and took a step toward the lake. "*You're too far out,*" she called.

Voices conferred on the water. "*You talking to us?*" one returned.

"*Yes. You're too far out. He's nearer the bank. In front of the engraving.*"

In their silence, the boatmen seemed to be weighing her claim. "*The tide pulls pretty hard toward the lake. We need to work it backwards from the channel in. We do it that way so we don't miss something.*"

Karley stepped over a boulder and walked to the water's edge. "*Do it differently this time.*"

Another clipped conference. "*Ma'am?*"

"*Roy,*" Sheriff Smith called. "*I appreciate you got your ways but maybe this once?*"

"I'm getting ready to go in," Anders hailed from the landing. "Give me a minute and I'll work the bank."

"*Yeah. Let him work the bank,*" Roy called. "*It'll take us another hour to get there.*"

"*Roy.*" Smith again. "*I think you oughta do what the lady asks.*"

Pause. "*Shit. All right, all right. We're coming.*" The eye panned slowly toward the bank.

Karley backed herself to the fire ring. "*You're getting close now. Right in there somewhere, yes.*"

Craig shifted his butt and nearly fell off his rock. "I'm truly sorry for putting you through this hell."

She glanced in his direction, then back at the boat. "You didn't put me through anything."

"Still, I can't help notice how certain you've been about all this. Joshua's location, your sister." Karley tracked the boat, but Craig could see she was listening. "You're sure Melissa isn't covering for Joe?"

"Yes. Joe had nothing to do with it. Not with Joshua's death."

Craig's illness smudged his every thought. He could barely locate the edges. "You don't think she was trying to protect him? Wives do that for husbands, husbands do it for wives. It happens all the time. She has a history, right? She hid Joe's drinking for years."

"Yes," Karley said. "But she was protecting herself, not Joe."

"Her wedding ring," Craig pointed out. "It makes sense as a punishment or an act of rage. If Joe—"

"No." Karley looked at Craig. "She left the ring for Joshua. And for me."

"For you?"

Without answering, Karley turned back to the lake.

"Do you think he was alive when she put him in?"

She shook her head.

"How do you know?" Again she refused to answer. "Do you think it was an accident?"

"Yes," Hans said. "It had to be an accident. Melissa would never hurt Josh on purpose."

Craig nodded. "Accidents happen. Children drown in

bathtubs. They play with loaded guns. They swallow lethal doses of household cleaners."

"They take lethal doses of medicine," Hans said. Karley lowered her gaze to her toes.

"Oxycodone would do that," Craig agreed. "I saw her take some Saturday."

Hans lifted his chin, and Craig wondered if he'd known. "Yes, opioids would do it. But not as quickly or efficiently as Seconal."

In the bloom of Hans's dismay, Craig caught the scent of self-judgment. The doctor clearly knew more than he was saying. "Of course, none of this explains why Melissa hid the body. If it was an accident, why did she fabricate such an elaborate story?"

"You don't know my sister," Karley said.

Dropping both hands, Craig held tight to the boulder. He had floaters in his vision. Hans watched him struggle, then squatted in front of him. He turned Craig's face into the better light, then pressed two fingers to his neck. *"Lovely,"* he whispered.

Craig gazed up at Karley. "Do you know where they are?"

Karley didn't understand. "Who?"

"Melissa." Craig panted. "Joe."

She spun toward him. *"What do you mean?"*

Hans stood up. "We need some help over here. And water, I need drinking water."

"What do you mean?" Karley demanded again.

"They disappeared. They drove away in your brother's Jeep. They've been missing for hours."

Jill arrived first, Smith right behind her. "What's the matter?"

"Tachycardia—his pulse is racing. Dehydration, the illness, I suspect. He needs an IV and a hospital now."

Thank God, Craig thought. Death by dehydration sounded so much nobler than death by old and stupid.

"Dehydrated?" Jill demanded, rifling through her gear. "How can he be dehydrated?"

"The chopper?" Smith asked Tinkerton.

"Yes, yes!" Jill exclaimed. She passed Hans a liter of bottled water. "Get the chopper *now.*"

"Okay, Milo," Hans said. "Take a sip of this. Good. Now I'm

going to lower you to the ground and recline you against this boulder here."

Smith hurried in to assist Hans.

"This is Tinkerton," the FBI barked into his phone. "I need you to bring the chopper."

"Tell him to bring oxygen, too," Jill said.

"And a paramedic," Hans added. "With an IV pack."

Smith's foreshortened body seemed to sway in Craig's vision. "Here, put this behind his head."

"*Yo!*" a voice called from the lake.

Hans lifted Craig's head and tucked Smith's jacket into the gap, then passed him the liter of water. "Start taking this in. You're going to be okay."

Jill's face appeared three inches from Craig's. "Can you see me, Milo? Can you hear me?"

"I could," Craig said, "if you backed up a little bit."

"*Yo!*" the voice called again. "What are you guys doing over there?"

"Got a problem here, Roy," Smith told the boatman. "What you need?"

"Your diver. Where the hell is he?"

"I'm here," Anders called. "Suiting up."

"Well, hurry!" Roy bellowed. "I think we may have found the boy!"

Three feet from Craig, the fire found pitch and the explosion launched a fountain of red embers. One landed on the boulder beside his head, but no one but Craig seemed to notice. He started to get up, and Hans forced him down, then brushed the ember away.

"You old fool," Jill whispered. She touched Craig's face.

Karley tucked her hair behind her ears and gazed across the fire at Hans. "Will he die if you don't go with him?"

"*Yes!*" Jill said.

"Thanks for the encouragement," Craig groaned.

"You're not going to die, Milo. We'll start an IV before you take off. That'll hold you to the hospital. Rock Springs is only a few minutes by air. The paramedic will take good care of you."

"Please," Jill pleaded. "What if you're wrong?"

"Stop, already," Craig told her. "I'm gonna die of embarrassment before I die from anything else."

From the lake Roy said, "Okay, we're anchored. Forty-seven feet."

Karley rounded the fire and stopped over Craig. "Thank you," she said.

He could now hear the helicopter, could feel it through the rock. He mustered a dry-lipped smile. "Really, I'm sorry about all of this. About putting you in the middle."

Squatting beside him, Karley squeezed his hand fiercely then stood and strode away.

"I'm going with you," Jill said.

"No, you're not. Ogden needs you here to bring the boy in."

Jill's hand was on his face again. "How could you let this happen, Milo?"

Craig closed his eyes and enjoyed his friend's touch. He pretended it could save him.

Witness

The gate is locked, the chain snugged tight and shackled through the fourth link so the padlock hangs against the post. Textbook. Margaret would be proud. Melissa unlocks, unshackles, swings the gate wide. The road shows Karley's visit, two sets of tracks, one for her arrival, the other for her departure. Melissa carries the lock to the Jeep and climbs in.

Joe clutches the bottle by the neck. "They'll come back you know. They'll figure it out and come after us."

Melissa puts the Jeep in gear and rolls through the entrance. She stops and sets the brake. "It won't matter. By then, we'll be gone."

She gets out again and walks the gate to its bracket, a giant cargo bolt with a grooved head the size of a dinner plate. She lifts the bar into the channel and threads the shackle through the fourth link. She tugs the lock to be sure the notch is seated.

Again in the Jeep, she drives them up the hill, noting as they crest that Karley has broken a rule—light shines from a back bedroom into the quakies behind the cabin. She parks near the porch and leaves the Jeep running. The digital clock glued to the dashboard tells her it is 1:06 a.m. Even with their stop, they've made impressive time.

"Joshua's at the lake," Joe says. "Why have you brought me here?"

His question, Melissa knows, is disingenuous. A trip up Weber Canyon means only one destination to Joe and the family. That it's taken him so long to ask about the cabin is proof he's known all along. "To tell you a true story."

"Maybe I don't want any more stories."

"Believe me. You want to hear this one." She turns off the

323

motor but leaves the headlights on. On her lap she assembles her purse and the second Glenlivet, then opens her door. "Bring the suitcase."

Joe examines his bottle in the backlight, and Melissa notes it's more full than empty. "I think I'll stay put."

She removes the keys from the ignition and extracts the Coke from between the seats. "Fine. You rest. You'll need your energy anyway. I've been a very bad girl."

Joe pretends to stick a finger down his throat. A waste of imaginary bile. He'd never on purpose hurl single malt Scotch. "If it's fucking you're after, you should have stayed with those guys at The Bluff."

Melissa slides from the Jeep. "I'll build us a fire and get the bed ready."

"Get a lobotomy while you're at it."

She hips the door closed and hurries up the stairs. She hopes he won't wait long. Stooping, she deposits her load on the porch, then unlocks the two doors and switches on the deck light. Legs straight, she presents her ass to Joe and gathers her things off the porch. She looks back in time to see his bottle sail in. Geysering Scotch, it bounces off the cabin. She drops her load and scampers after it, manages to catch it before it rolls off the porch. An inch of Scotch remains at the bottom, soapy bubbles bright in amber. Repenting her assumption about Joe hurling Scotch, she carries it down the stairs.

He glares at her through the open window. She proffers the Glenlivet, but he doesn't take it, so she reaches inside and balances it in his lap, then gives it a little pat. In Joe's hostile gaze, she sees God's will fulfilled. She takes the stairs swishing, snatches her purse off the porch, and hurries into the cabin.

The rooms are cool but not uncomfortably so. Flipping on lights, she crosses to the kitchen. It's time to mix Joe a drink.

∎

Witness. Go forth and preach the gospel. For Melissa so loved the world.

Friday she returns from work to find Joe on the basement sofa, tumbler of Smirnoff sweating in his fist. The bottle itself is wedged between the cushions. Curled on Joe's lap, Joshua gapes at the television. He's oblivious of Melissa's arrival. Transfixed, he watches *Aliens* while Joe snoozes through the carnage.

"*Get away from her, you bitch!*" Ripley snarls and Momma Alien complies. With Ripley available, she has bigger fish to fry. The movie is nearly finished.

Melissa quietly withdraws and hurries up the stairs. In the kitchen, she half-fills a Pooh cup with Coke and carries it to her bedroom. She retrieves from her garment drawer the medicine she's hidden and opens the bottle in the master bathroom. The internet has told her how many to use—fifteen for an adult of average size. Shaking badly now, she places the bottle on the toilet and returns to the dresser for the Pooh cup she's forgotten. She carries it to the bathroom and places it on the vanity then turns for the secobarbital. Hand or eye, she couldn't say which, but she misses, and the pills go flying. She chases the capsules and returns them to the bottle, then climbs again to her feet.

Where was she? Fifteen. She pours a likely batch into her hand and counts them onto the vanity. She puts the extras back in the bottle and twists on the child-proof cap. The pills look like candy against the vanity's green marble.

Not even prayer will still Melissa's hands. One by one she separates the capsules and dumps the powder into the Coke. Odorless, says the internet. Flavorless, Melissa hopes. The particles clump on the surface then sink. She squeezes each end then checks every part to be sure she has emptied them all. She opens the toilet and tosses the empties. Once dissolved, they will flush without a trace.

Spoon to stir. Melissa returns the secobarbital to her garment drawer and carries the Coke to the kitchen. Thunderheads roll at the bottom of the cup. Changing her mind, she slips a straw from the package and uses it instead. The cloud drops a funnel, the soda sizzles. When she stops stirring, the medicine is all but invisible. She puts the cup on the table by the living room sofa and leaves the straw beside it.

In the master bathroom, she unspools a wad of tissue, drops it in the toilet, and flushes. When she steps from her room, Joshua is frozen in the hallway staring through his dark bedroom door-way. "Hey, baby," she says, and he shrieks then starts to sob. She swings him off the floor and squeezes him tight. "I warned you it was scary."

"I couldn't stop watching."

"It's okay. It was all just pretend."

"I want Pooh."

Melissa flips on his bedroom light. Pooh is on the floor beside the bed, and she bends over, Joshua clinging, and holds while he grabs his bear. She carries him and Pooh to the living room. "Can we snuggle for a while?" she asks. Josh sniffs and shudders as she settles into the sofa. Head nestled like a baby's in the crook of her elbow, he presses his knees to her ribs. "How was Daddy today?"

"He felt yucky." Hiccup.

They both know what yucky means. "What did you two do all day?"

"Watched movies." The shudders come less frequently now, and he seems to have stemmed the crying. "We played some games, too."

His hair's getting long, Melissa will have to cut it, maybe tonight after they've eaten dinner. She fingers his bangs from his eyes. "What games did you play?"

"Go fish. Harry Potter. Dad let me have Dino-Bites for lunch."

"Wow. Dino-Bites." Is this, Melissa wonders, what jumping from an airplane feels like? "Looks like today's your day for special treats."

Diaphragm dancing, Josh exhales. *"Aliens* wasn't special."

Melissa slips the straw into the Coke and gives it a little stir. "No. But you'll like this." He looks up and she shows him the cup.

"What is it?"

"Coke, baby."

"You said I can't have Coke."

She smiles. "I know. And you can't very often. But this one time, I'm going to let you. I want you to drink it all. It'll make you feel better."

After his date with *Aliens,* he's a little suspicious of parents offering treats. He wipes his nose and waits for assurance.

"Come on." She stirs the Coke again. "Sit up now." Josh hesitates, then sits up quickly. Such unprecedented offers must be seized before they're lost. He takes the cup in his dimpled hands. "Drink it all," she says softly and steps into air. "When that's gone, you can have more if you want."

Joshua puts the straw in his mouth and sucks. He pauses, nose wrinkled, and takes a breath. Clutching the ripcord, Melissa rockets toward earth. Joshua bites down on the straw and empties the cup.

"More?" she asks, and he holds the cup out to her. "Slide off."

Josh obeys and Melissa gets up. She takes the Coke from the fridge and places it on the counter. Then she crouches in the corner behind the kitchen table and wraps her arms around her legs. Back to the wall, she squeezes until her arms threaten to pop from their sockets. She relaxes her grip, then does it again. And again and again and again. Finally, breathless, she pushes to her feet. At the counter, she splashes a little Coke in the cup and forces herself back to the living room.

Joshua sits upright on the cushion, his short legs extended, his heels hanging off the edge. Hands on the sofa, he props himself up. His eyes are as glassy as Pooh Bear's. Sinking in beside him, Melissa deposits the Coke on the end table. "Here, baby." She pulls him onto her lap, and Josh slumps sideways against her. She retrieves the Coke and puts the straw to his lips. "Here's a little more. Drink it down."

Josh doesn't respond so she shakes him. He lifts his head, but it wobbles like a top and flops backwards on his slender neck. One-handed, she catches him and, cradling his head, brings the straw to his lips again. This time he accepts it and begins to suck. Coke dribbles from his mouth. Melissa places the cup on the table and holds him tight against her. So much secobarbital, such a small body. His breaths are already shallow and apneic. She reclines him across her lap and rests his head on the arm bench. His eyelids droop, but Melissa sees pupil. She presses two fingers to his neck. Her hands, she notes, have grown oddly steady. His pulse is weak, but she feels it flutter. She measures the beats and watches a large bubble form between his lips.

Scooping him up, she rolls from the sofa. In the kitchen she awkwardly pins him with one arm and opens the medicine cabinet above the fridge. The glass vial of holy oil is where it always is, at the side near the front within easy reach. She closes the cupboard then curls and lifts Joshua. Eyes closed, she receives his chemical exhalation. She kisses him on the lips, then descends the stairs to the basement.

Joe sleeps slouching, gripping the empty tumbler, Melissa's husband For Time and All Eternity. He twitches and the tumbler springs from his hand. It rolls off the cushion and drops to the carpet. On the day they were married in the Ogden Temple, their unborn children were sealed to them forever.

Forever means forever.

Aliens has returned to its menu. Melissa finds the remote and switches off the TV, then turns and faces the sofa. Joe's hand flops out, palm up on the cushion, his fingers curled like a dead spider's legs. A bubble like Josh's suspires between his lips. The child hangs limp in Melissa's arms.

"Joe," she says. "Wake up now, Joe. Joshua needs you."

■

He pushes roughly through the big front door and slams it. Melissa drops the spoon in the sink. The empty pill casings are hidden in the waste basket. The ice melts in its tray on the butcher's block. She carries the green plastic tumbler from the kitchen. Joe sways on the living room's giant rag rug. Extending the suitcase and the empty bottle, he drops them both to the floor.

"Tell me how I did it."

Melissa hands him the tumbler, which he receives without recognition, then picks up the suitcase and unzips it on the dining table. Setting the belt aside, she lays out their white clothes, first stripping Joe's garments from their factory plastic. When she turns around, his hands are empty. She locates the drink on the old Philco radio.

"Put these on and I'll tell you." She shows him the garments.

"You're out of your mind. Get those away from me."

She steps closer, and he snatches the garments and throws

them. She bends over and picks them up. "This is a sacred night, Joe. It's important we dress appropriately."

"You sick crazy bitch."

This, too, she accepts as God's plan. Folding the garments, she returns to the table and places them on Joe's temple clothes. She loosens her tie but does not take it off. Slowly she unbuttons her blouse.

Joe's teeth shine white between his parted lips. Both shoelaces are untied and his shirt is torn from his adventure with the boys at The Bluff. "How did I do it?"

Tugging her tails from her skirt, she pines for the security of her garments and temple clothes. She hopes before they're finished God allows her to put them on. She picks up the belt and tests its heft. The buckle, cast in bronze, is sharp and heavy. How wrong she was to believe Joe could change. Or to think God intended he should.

■

"Joe," Melissa says. "Wake up now, Joe. Joshua needs you." When Joe doesn't respond, she lays Josh on his lap then kneels down and leans low, her ear to the child's nose.

He breathes.

"It's time, Joe. *Wake up.*" Melissa slaps him, and his eyelids pop open. Lids drooping, his head lolls back. She slaps him again, this time harder, and his head bobs into alignment. "Bless him." She holds out the vial of consecrate oil. "You have to save him before it's too late." Joe squints at the vial of consecrated oil. *"Do it!"*

Joe glances down at Joshua in his lap. "What?"

Melissa presses the vial into his hand. "Put it on. *Bless him.*" He shakes his head and flings the vial, and Melissa scampers after it. "He's dying!" she yells.

This time Joe seems almost to rally. Slipping his hands beneath his son, he lifts him, an offering. Josh's legs and arms and head sway loose, and Joe gives him a gentle shake. Joshua takes a deep breath and releases it slowly. His jeans darken at the crotch, his bowels evacuate, and the room floods with the stench of his leaving. Holding him aloft, Joe appears to fall asleep.

And Melissa pulls the ripcord.

"Now," she commands.

She jerks Joshua from Joe and thrusts him in his lap. She unscrews the vial and puts it in Joe's hand, then squeezes his fingers to help him grip it. She must lift Joshua's head to present the crown. Together they pour the oil into his hair. It is clumsy work, and the vial is mostly empty when she takes it from Joe's hand. She caps the little bottle and drops it on the floor. Joe's eyes are closed, his mouth gone slack.

"Anoint him." Melissa wrangles Joe's hands and holds them on Josh's head. Their son's tiny face disappears. *"Say the words."*

"Nuh," Joe says, fighting to lift his eyelids.

"Joshua Joseph Christopher," Melissa begins. "By the power of the Holy Melchizedek Priesthood and in the name of Jesus Christ ..."

"Josh," Joe mumbles. His eyelids flutter. "By the 'chizedek Priesthood and in Jesus, I anoint you ..."

Though not word perfect, the anointing is close. She lifts Joe's hands from Joshua's face. Joe has begun to weep. "Now, seal it, Joe, say the words." She returns his hands to Joshua's face. "Say Joshua Joseph Christopher, by the power of the holy Melchizedek Priesthood and in the name of Jesus Christ, I seal this anointing ..."

Joe wags his head and continues to weep but tries to do as he's told. "... seal this 'nointing and give you blessing—"

"Tell him to live. Bring him back. Say the words." Plummeting, Melissa waits for her parachute. *"Now, Joe,"* she cries. *"Say it* now! *Command him to live!"*

Opening his eyes, Joe finds death in his lap. "Live?" he whispers. He looks up at Melissa. "Live?"

"Live!" she screams. *"Live, Joshua. Live ..."*

"Live," Joe says, and then he is wailing too. *"Live, live ..."*

∎

"... live," Melissa tells Joe. She unfurls the belt and carries it to him, and this, too, he accepts without seeing what she's given him. He grips the leather strap, and the buckle hook snags in a loop of the rug. Melissa places herself directly in front of him.

"You killed your son with unworthiness. It was a test from God and you failed."

Joe's eyes drift away. Cranking his head, he pops his neck and spies his Scotch in the process. The rag rug puckers, and the buckle tears free as he takes three steps to the Philco. He quaffs deeply, then brings the tumbler aloft and squints at the whisky through the colored plastic. "*Nasty* old ice."

Melissa unzips her skirt and lets it slip to the floor. Joe watches from afar, his gaze turned inward even as his eyes come to rest on her panties. Slowly, he begins to nod. He returns the tumbler to the Philco. "I thought it was a dream."

"It wasn't a dream."

"You put what in his Coke?"

Still stuck at the beginning. Has he not heard a thing? "Secobarbital."

"Secobarbital." He looks at the floor and shakes his head. Melissa wanders toward him. "You held him in your arms and watched him die."

Melissa has already told him all this. "I held the straw to his mouth and made him drink. I made sure he got every drop."

Joe's head snaps up. "You killed him. Your son. *Our son.*"

"No, Joe. *You* killed him. *You* held him and watched him die. Your *son.*"

Joe catches her with the back of his hand, and she cross-steps sideways and her feet leave the floor. She lands on her side and slides to a stop. More stunned than injured, she crawls to a chair and pulls herself upright.

"A worthy man could have brought him back." She turns around and faces him. "All you could do was *kill* him."

Joe strikes her open-handed, and she staggers against the dining table but this time keeps her feet. "That's right, Joe." She bends over the table, spreads her arms wide, and elevates her head to make it an easy target. "I watched him die in your arms. I gave him poison and watched him die because you were too weak to do anything about it. Someone had to save him. He had to die before he turned into you."

The buckle sinks into Melissa's hip and opens her to the bone.

She leans hard against the table, her palms on the surface. The second strike wraps around her waist and tears her belly above the navel. She has blood on her hands, feels it warm in her knee-socks. On her belly and down her thighs.

"You don't have it in you, Joe. No wonder your father hated you. You couldn't even kill your mother right."

"You crazy fucking bitch," he whispers. This time the belt curls under her right arm, and the hook punctures the side of her breast. A spritzing red mist speckles their temple clothes. The next strike bounces off her skull, and for an instant she is no longer sensate. Her stiff legs noodle, her face hits the table, and the rest of her slides to the floor. Joe whips the belt, and it streaks away. Glass shatters where it hits the far wall. Still conscious, Melissa points a finger and laughs. Joe grabs her by the tie and drags her around the room. Instinct takes over, and she fights to fill her lungs. Then duty restores her, and she goes limp on his lead.

"God damn you to hell!" By the neck he dangles her torso in the air. He shakes, then releases, and her head bounces hard. He falls on top of her, and she takes his weight. They have achieved a meeting of the minds. He jerks the tie to the back of her neck, and the knot sands painfully over her ear. Teeth to teeth, he stretches the tie tight and decides at last to get serious.

A peculiar thing to peer into your husband's eyes as he gives himself to your death. A peculiar thing to feel such gratitude. Melissa can't recall ever loving him more. His heart beats with hers, and his strained face quivers, the tears that flow freely flying. The tie crushes her throat, but she does not struggle. She has seen this moment consecrated by God and regrets only the temple clothes.

Joe struggles above her, spittle swaying, his lips forming words she can't hear. She can't smell him either, but she feels his hot breath. The voids in her vision focus her gaze. Joe's eyes widen slightly, and his face grows still. Melissa sees what's coming and panics. The pressure loosens and blood rushes to her head. Joe rolls to his back on the floor beside her, and she nearly passes out. Together, they gasp for a full two minutes, then Joe finds his elbows and props himself up. He gains his feet barely and, with the heels of his hands, squeezes his head at the temples. He stumbles a step and stops.

"Loser," Melissa rasps.

But Joe's had enough of killing her. Nothing she says will bring him back now. He lifts his face and bellows at God—his rage comes and comes and comes. Empty at last, he staggers to the Philco. Melissa rolls her head backwards and tracks him upside-down. He picks up the tumbler and turns toward her swirling ice.

"I really wish you'd married Ezra Reinholt." He toasts the air and winks at Melissa, then drains what remains in his tumbler. Dropping the glass, he bumps through the kitchen doorway. The ice tray hits the wall. He returns a moment later throttling Glenlivet. Palming walls, he wends past Melissa and pinballs through the turn at the hallway.

■

She does for Joe what he cannot do himself. It is the way it has always been. She removes his clothes and drapes them over a chair. He is gone now, with Joshua. They are together waiting for her. Joe's body is young, a lovely body, and Melissa feels how much she has missed it. At the resurrection, it will be made whole again, no longer plagued by temptation and weakness. Her body too will be perfected, made slender and beautiful beyond earthly measure. God and Goddess, they will make up for time lost. Their offspring will populate planets.

Joe weighs more than Melissa, and she's tired and injured. She must roll him like a baby. She straightens the garment top around his torso, then works the bottoms up his thighs. She shakes out his temple shirt, now wrinkled from storage, and threads his arms a sleeve at a time. Aligning buttons, she begins with the collar and works the flaps closed to the tails. She feeds his feet into the white pants and pulls them into place. First affixing the clasp, she zips the zipper then tidies the tails in the waistband. She ties the white tie around her own neck then slips it off and over Joe's head. She turns down the collar and cinches the knot, buttons the corners, sharpens the crease.

Then, by the arms, she pulls Joe to a sitting position. His heavy head and spineless back make it nearly impossible to keep him upright. She shuffles around him and kneels on the bed so she can brace him from behind. She drapes the robe over his left shoulder, then catches her mistake and moves it to the right. On the day of their resurrection, he will call her sacred name as he did on the day they were married. Robed on the right, he will bring her through the veil into the Celestial Kingdom.

She eases Joe down and crawls to his other side, toes snagging in the folds of her long temple dress. She untangles herself, then ties Joe's strings and tugs the robe into place. Its white pleated front is painted with blood because the tear in her scalp won't stop bleeding. She has bled through her garments and dress as well. In places, her own robe is scarlet.

She drapes the green apron over Joe's front, then reaches beneath him and pulls the ties through. She secures them at the front and adjusts the fig leaves, then threads the sash beneath his torso. She ties it at the hip then finger-combs his hair and rubs a bloody smudge from his cheek. Arranging the cap, she revisits an unruly cowlick then ties the string to his robe. She aligns his head then gets off the bed and stands for a moment assessing her work. His feet are bare, but God will understand. She straightens his legs and draws his heels together, then combines his hands on his stomach.

She gathers his clothes and carries them to the living room, the Glenlivet beneath her arm. Packing his things with her own in the suitcase, she catalogues the mess they have made. The table and the floor are an abattoir, a drip-spattered Pollack on a canvas made of cabin. The blood is Melissa's offering, her atonement. Even now, she sheds it freely.

Toting the Glenlivet, she recovers Joe's tumbler, then continues to the kitchen. In her purse, Grace waits in the form of a pill. It is sacramental, this preparation, sacred in its own way. She dumps the remaining capsules on the knife-scarred counter, then one by one empties them all in the green tumbler. She considers the two bottles, the Coke and the Scotch, unable to make up her mind. It is not the sin but the taste that troubles her. She fears she will gag up the Scotch. But Joshua and Joe await her decision. And Karley will be here soon.

She uncorks the Scotch and half-fills the tumbler. Stirring the solution, she sorrows for her family. They may never in this life understand. Her offering will confuse them. They will fear her beyond salvation. But later, together in the Celestial Kingdom, they will all look back and laugh at the pain.

Nose plugged, she swallows eight times, the mixture a trail of blaze down her gullet. At the sink, she refills the glass and chases the Scotch with water. To her surprise, the sensations begin almost instantly. A wave of nausea rolls from her belly, up through her chest and into her throat. Anchored against the sink, she forces it down, then breathes through her mouth as she consults the clock.

3:39 a.m.

She finds Joe still dead on his side of the bed. His hands have slipped apart. Dizzy now, she sits down beside him and drags her feet onto the mattress. She tucks herself against him and straightens her robes. She has forgotten to turn off the overhead light. She drapes the veil over her face, then frees Joe's hand from between their bodies and laces her fingers through his.

Witness.

God is wise. With her blood, her body, Melissa has sealed her covenant.

She breathes in and out, and her red veil ripples. God and family gather her in.

3:51 a.m.

3:51 A.M.

At 3:51 a.m. ex-Navy SEAL Rob Anders broke the surface of Rosy Pond. He removed his mouthpiece and pushed his goggles to the top of his hooded head. His powerful flashlight, attached at the hip, glowed phosphorescent beneath the surface. Shoulder dipped, treading fiercely, he crawled heavily to shore.

Lambert and Tinkerton stepped cautiously into the pond testing for the edge of the drop-off. Fighting for buoyance, Anders rolled his heavy cargo onto the shallow ledge. The two officers caught it by the handles and hauled it onto the lip. Water streamed through slits in its nylon skin as the bag itself collapsed.

With Tinkerton's help, Anders dragged himself from the lake. "Took you a while," the agent said.

"Weighted." Anders shrugged out of his tank.

"Should've winched it up."

"Not on my watch," Anders said.

Kneeling beside the bag, Jill Grafton studied Karley. "Maybe you should go wait over there." Karley gripped Hans's hand and pressed her cheek to his biceps. Neither Nordling moved. With a sigh, Jill located the tab and drew down the zipper three inches. She zipped it closed and tried again. Karley released Hans's hand and moved a step closer. "Sand," Jill said, settling back on her heels.

Smith and Lambert illuminated the bag with their flashlights. Water lapped the hull of the Forest Service boat. Karley kneeled down beside Jill.

"Hand me that satchel, would you, Kent?" Jill pointed, and Kent fetched the satchel. Eyes on Karley, she removed a pair of surgical scissors. "Do you recognize it?"

337

Karley didn't answer. She reached for the zipper, and Jill snapped, *"Don't."* Karley put her hands in her lap.

"It's Joe's," Hans said. "We play racquetball sometimes. He carries his things in it."

Jill addressed Karley. "You can't touch him. Do you understand? If that's a problem, you need to go over by the fire and wait. I'd prefer you did that, anyway."

"No," Karley said. "I have to be here."

Head shaking, Jill bent over the bag again. She made a small puncture and began working the scissors parallel to the zipper. Chrysalis-like, the husk revealed its prize, a tiny ear first, a cheek and a neck, a hand and a hip, and two duck shoes. Jill put down the scissors and split the skin wide.

Joshua lay on his side, his feet touching a stone no larger than his head. An irregular pink lividity mottled the macerated skin of his otherwise dusky face and hands. Cold emersion had preserved the ocular fluid. Through the slits, Hans could see the whites of his eyes. He was not a coroner but was certain all the same that the child had not died in the lake. The little body looked much too serene to have drowned.

Karley had begun softly to weep.

"He didn't drown," Jill said.

"No," Hans said.

"Let's get the M.E. down here," Smith told Lambert.

Jill picked up the scissors and got to her feet. Hans could see she was trembling. "Take your time," she called after Lambert. "I have a few things to do first."

"Good work, Roy," Smith called to the men in the boat.

"He's in there?"

"He is. You're done here. Much obliged."

Roy cranked the motor as his partner drew anchor. Face in her hands, Jill Grafton stood motionless. Hans watched her until he felt Karley stir.

"Ma'am," Smith said.

Jill lowered her hands and turned. "Ah, shit."

"Stop her!" Tinkerton said. Legs crossed, Karley rocked Joshua in her arms. Hans stepped between his wife and the officers. "Put him down," Tinkerton ordered.

"Ma'am," Smith coaxed. "You really have to put him down."

Hans squatted in front of Karley. Head tilted maternal, she caressed Josh's face. She smoothed his wet hair and cried. "Kjæreste. We have to put him down now."

"He's so cold," Karley said.

Tinkerton pushed in roughly, and Hans pistoned to his feet. By the lapels, he plucked the agent off his feet and threw him onto his back. Furious, Tinkerton scrambled up, but Anders was already there. Arms locked around the agent, the diver pulled him back.

"*Lambert?*" Jill yelled. She'd joined Hans's vigil above Karley.

"What's up?" Lambert called down from the landing.

"Wait for the Nordlings. They're on their way up."

"Let go of me," Tinkerton told Anders. "I'm all right. Let me go."

"I'll be in my truck," Lambert called.

Hans kneeled next to Karley. "Here." He slipped his hands beneath Joshua. "Give him to me." Leaning, clinging, Karley finally let Hans take him.

"Where?" Hans asked Jill.

"Not in the bag," Karley pleaded. "Please not in the bag." Flailing to her feet, she stripped off her parka and spread it on the lip. Jill nodded, and Hans placed the body on it. Gaining his feet, he took Karley's hand. Above them, Lambert had started the Expedition.

"Please," Jill said. "Deputy Lambert's waiting."

Close overhead bat wings soughed while distant now, far beyond the basin, the Forest Service's powerful outboard thrummed.

Karley turned first. Together, she and Hans crossed the lip to the staircase.

■

They were 500 yards from the asphalt when Deputy Lambert's phone began to ring. Karley lay curled on the backseat with her head in Hans's lap. The improvised road rocked the truck, and Hans braced them both with a hand on the ceiling.

"Lambert." The deputy listened to the caller for a time

without speaking. "Yes, sir. I'll drop 'em off and be right back." He tossed the phone on the passenger seat. "Ma'am?"

Karley didn't respond. "What is it?" Hans asked.

They'd reached the asphalt, and Lambert stopped the truck. He looked back at Hans through the open slider. "Melissa and Joe were in Evanston about four-and-a-half hours ago. They made a couple of purchases with a credit a card."

Karley sat up. "They're at the cabin."

Lambert nodded. "That's what Jill seems to think. I'm on my way back to fetch the FBI. Sheriff wants me to get the keys from you."

"I'm going," Karley said.

"No, ma'am. That's already been decided. Just the keys."

Karley settled against the seatback and gazed out the window. "They're in the pocket of my parka."

"You're sure?"

Karley nodded. "Yes. If you don't believe me, call Sheriff Smith, have him check."

Lambert, embarrassed, glanced away. "No, that won't be necessary." He got out and opened Hans's door.

Hans slid off the seat and reached back for Karley. "Do we need to wait?"

Lambert shook his head. "I wouldn't think so. You're welcome to though. You could wait here or get a room in Manila." A flare sputtered. Face flickering, the deputy watched it die.

Karley took Hans's hand. She'd begun to shiver. She was wet from holding Joshua. "No. Our family doesn't know yet. We need to get back to Ogden before anyone notifies them."

Lambert climbed into the Expedition. "I'm very sorry for all of this," he said. He hooked the handle then, pausing, addressed Karley without meeting her gaze. "If you don't mind me saying, I think you're incredibly brave." Then he closed the door, put the truck in reverse, and backed into a three-point turn.

Cops turned their heads as Karley and Hans passed. Hans clicked the remote and the BMW sounded, its lights flashing on and off. Karley closed herself in, opened the glove box, and removed the small ring of keys they kept there for convenience. Hans steered from the shoulder and weaved through the fleet, flare and bar light strobing the interior. An eighth of a mile later, the final patrolman touched the brim of his hat. Hans tracked the trooper in the rearview mirror, then gave the BMW its head.

■

The cabin shined brightly through the trees. Hans swung the gate wide and returned to the car. Thirty seconds later the BMW emerged from the hilltop copse. Rectangular light planked the gravel parking, made stumps of tall-standing timber. Passenger's door open, Caleb's Jeep threw dim headlight, its battery all but dead. Hans parked beside it, and without a word he and Karley stepped onto the gravel.

At the front door, he placed a hand lightly on her shoulder. Gripping the knob, she looked back at him. She lifted her chin and stepped aside, and Hans swung the door open. He smelled it before he saw it, the metallic reek of death. Hand over her mouth, Karley pushed past him.

The rag rug lay curled and heaped against the wall, a Scotch bottle protruding from the folds. Placing his feet with deliberate care, Hans stepped around his wife. Near the center of the room, he squatted—the pool of blood was larger than his open hand. A streak of the same rived the room in two. Reading the violence, he tracked it to the table, where Karley stood clutching a tartan skirt. She stared down the hall into Melissa and Joe's bedroom, then bunched the skirt to her face.

Hans stood up, stepped over the pooled blood, and moved toward the hallway. In the corner of the room, a heavy-buckled belt lay snaked against the baseboard. Karley put the skirt in the suitcase and rounded the table. With Hans, she examined the belt. The blood-tarnished buckle, hinged back against the leather, showed hair on its angry hook. Not far from the belt, a framed photo of Margaret's parents lay on a bed of broken glass.

Hans stepped back, and Karley tucked herself against him. The light from the bedroom slanted across the hallway. Hands in Karley's hair, he monitored her rapid breaths as he gazed through the door at what she'd already seen. Melissa, dressed in white, lay on the bed, a hand hanging limp off the mattress. Scrimmed beneath a blood-soaked veil, her head tilted to the left. Joe, at her side, lay mostly obscured.

Karley lifted her face, and Hans brushed her lips with his own. Mouth and nose, they breathed each other in. Then, fingers trailing, he left her slowly. Before entering the bedroom, he paused in the doorway. Karley turned away and stepped carefully into the kitchen.

For an instant, she mistook them for dried rodent droppings, each one near the size of a pencil eraser. The floor was covered and the counter as well. She tiptoed across the old linoleum to the medicine bottle on the counter. A bloody print obscured the label, but she could still read enough of the script. Secobarbitol, 100mg. Dr. Hans Nordling. Joseph Christopher. Epilepsy.

Item by item, she catalogued the rest: Glenlivet Single Malt Scotch on the butcher's block, Melissa's yawning purse beside a jug of Coke. A green plastic tumbler on its side in the sink, an ice tray on the floor in a slurry of actual rodent turds. In the window's reflection, she found herself. She touched her lips, then her neck at the throat. She found her heartbeat and held it.

When Hans appeared in the doorway, she was ready. They gazed at each other in the window's reflection. "Both of them?" she asked.

"Yes."

She turned from the glass, from the pill casings and Scotch, from the purse, the vial and the green plastic tumbler. Taking Hans's hand, she led him through the living room. At the heavy front door, she lifted the old photo from its hook. She touched each face, then stepped past Hans and hurried across the porch and down the stairs. The warning chime chimed until Hans closed his door. Karley held the photo in her lap, her hand on the cool glass.

"Drive fast," she said.

Afterward

"Had Goodman Brown fallen asleep in the forest and only dreamed a wild dream …?"

—*Young Goodman Brown*, Nathaniel Hawthorne

One Bump

His daughter, Kim, has grown into a remarkable woman, smart and lovely, reminiscent of a young Theresa. Hourly, Craig protests her doting but only because he feels guilty. Twice in two weeks, she's flown in from Seattle where she's an employment attorney with a yen for spanking bosses.

"Bigots and sexists and gropers are plentiful," she assures. "There'll be windmills to tilt at when I get back."

Nearly two weeks earlier, when she'd walked into his room, Craig mistook her for Theresa's ghost. "Am I dead?" he asked.

"Close enough," she answered. "You're in a hospital room in Rock Springs, Wyoming."

Three days at the hospital, another two in Ogden before she was convinced he could manage a few days without her. A week in Seattle to put her life on hold, then this return for a genuine visit. Now, beer in hand, she glides in from the kitchen to answer the ringing doorbell. She opens the front door and grins up at Picknell, who ducks as he steps inside. To Craig's surprise, Jill has come along too.

"Come 'ere, Sasquatch," Kim tells Pick then she pulls him down and kisses him on the cheek. Picknell turns his head which surprises Craig because the man doesn't own a neck.

Feet up, Craig sits in his Barcalounger, four dead soldiers on the TV tray beside him. He shows Pick the one he's holding. "Beer?"

Pick taps his watch. "On the clock."

"Me, too," Jill says. "And I'd love one."

Kim hurries off to aid and abet.

"Sit," Craig tells his friends.

345

With all the misgiving of a wild buffalo, Pick considers the various chairs in Craig's living room. Settling for the sofa, he tucks himself in as Jill crosses the room to the rocking chair. Kim returns with two bottles and hands one to Jill. When she proffers the second, Pick puts up the good fight then accepts it with a grin. "The mayor has it right," he says. "'Evil is powerful, and we're easily deceived.'"

"Was that an admission?" Craig asked.

"Oh, no," Pick says and Jill shakes her head. "*We* screwed up, the department, by focusing on the Stillwells. He's so horrified with our incompetence, he's not renewing O'Neil's contract."

Craig nods. "Yeah, I saw the article in last night's paper. If nothing else, he's predictable."

"Worse than predictable," Jill says. "The Christophers have been vanquished from official memory. It's all about the department and Betty Stillwell and family values now."

"Speaking of which, I understand you attended the funeral."

Jill's face falls. "Yes. Sad. Very sad. Triple funeral. Private event, just family and old friends. I take that back. I'm not an old friend and neither is Sally Frye. But the real surprise was Theo Evans."

"Theo Evans?"

"I know. He even cried. I think they were actual tears."

Craig shakes his head. He sips his beer. He listens to Jill's sad account. "I'm glad you went," he says when she's finished. "When I get a chance, I intend to visit the cemetery."

Pick hoists his empty bottle. "May I have another?"

Craig sets his own empty on the TV tray. Kim studies Jill who rocks and ruminates. "Make that four," Kim says and pads to the kitchen.

"So, anyway," Pick begins.

Craig raises a hand. "Wait 'til we all have our beers." Kim shimmies back with two beers in each hand and passes them around. "Okay," he says. "Let's hear what you came to say."

"It's like this: You're a prick. And if you don't change your mind, I may just never forgive you." Pick offers Kim an apologetic shrug, and she returns him a placid smile.

"That's why you're here? You made an appointment to call me names?"

Jill and Pick share a glance. "Seriously, Milo," Jill says. "Resignation aside, when are you coming back?"

"Not that we don't admire some good seppuku," Pick adds. "But you *are* coming back, aren't you, Milo?"

Placing his beer on the tray, Craig lowers the foot bench. Just shy of seventy, his body no longer recovers as quickly as it did even a few years earlier. The Christophers, the illness, he's not been the same since—he feels it in every movement and breath. Sipping their beers, the others watch him rise. Of the many things he won't miss about police work, Pick and Jill are not among them.

He shuffles to the kitchen and from the cupboard removes the Jack Daniel's he bought after Theresa's death. He doesn't own shot glasses, so he fingers four mugs and carries them with the bourbon back to the living room.

"Criminy," Pick moans.

"Ooh," Jill coos. "How did you know Jack's the one man I sleep with?"

"One bump," Craig says.

"Fine. One bump," Pick says. "Then you're retracting this retirement bullshit."

Craig winks at Kim. She winks at him. "After you take me to the cemetery, how about I buy you all dinner?"

"Criminy," Pick says.

Jill holds out her mug.

Craig swigs from the bottle, then pours.

Expatriates

2 YEARS 8 MONTHS LATER

Karley hears Leif stir, and her milk lets down. Quietly, because Hans is sleeping, she slips from beneath the duvet. She unsnaps her nightgown as she crosses the room.

Street light casts softly through the arched window. Leif's tiny limbs wriggle in their wrap. He has not yet remembered he owns a voice. Karley lifts him from the cradle and nuzzles him in. More asleep than awake, he gums his fist, and she must guide him to her nipple.

At the window, she rocks gently on her feet and watches snow fall over Byfjorden. The water in the harbor is calm. Fishing boats float steady on their moorings. Bryggen is quiet, all of Bergen is quiet, this great old city at 2:00 a.m. Narrow cobblestone roads, small shops, the ancient fish market. This loft of theirs near the waterfront sits high above it all. The building belongs to them, a gift from Hans's mother. It's nearly 200 years old and gorgeous.

Leif swallows and breathes, sucks and swallows and breathes. His left hand clenches and opens on Karley's breast. She takes it in her own and examines the fingers. She must trim the nails before he scratches himself.

"It's snowing," Hans says.

She turns from the window. "Yes. I'm sorry I woke you."

"You didn't. I've been awake."

Karley settles on the bed and shifts Leif to her other breast. Engaged now, an expert already, he rolls his face to receive the nipple. Hands behind his head, Hans watches Karley open the folds of Leif's blanket. She loosens his gown and slips a finger inside his diaper.

"Wet?" Hans asks.

Karley leans to the night table and tugs loose a moist wipe. "Messy."

Hans gets up and from the changing table collects the necessary items. He spreads a changing pad on the bed. "You're crying."

Head down, Karley watches Leif nurse, his skin and her own almost translucent in this light. She caresses his cheek with the pad of her thumb. "It's nothing. Hormones."

But Hans knows better. Their recovery has been incremental, excruciating, two-and-a-half years of growing new skin.

"He's dropping off," she says.

Hans receives the small bundle and holds it to his chest. He can smell his wife in his son's sweet breath. He lifts him to his shoulder and paces patting. With a burp cloth, Karley dries her eyes and her breasts, then buttons her nightgown. Hans adjusts the reading lamp to its lowest setting and lays Leif on the changing pad. Fat and complacent, the baby sleeps through Hans's ministrations. His pink eyelids twitch, his tiny lips pout. He purls softly through his nose. Finally, Hans wraps Leif snuggly in a blanket.

Karley pulls back the duvet. "I'm not sleepy. I'd like to watch him for a while."

Hans carries him to her, and she places him on the bed. She curls herself around his body.

"Light?" Hans asks.

"If it won't bother you."

He gets into bed and, opposite Karley, curls around their son. Their knees kiss, and he runs a foot down her shin. With the burp cloth, she dries her eyes again. "Have you made up your mind about the university?"

Hans thinks about her question. "I'd like working with medical students. The teaching would be good."

"You should do what makes you happy," she says.

"I could be happy at the university." Leif takes a shuddering breath. "How about you? Could you be happy with me there?"

"Yes. So long as it's what you want. And we're here together."

"You're still happy here?"

Head propped on her hand, she studies his face. "I'm happy." As proof, she has almost stopped crying.

"Someday you'll be ready. You'll want to show Leif where you came from."

Karley blots a dab of spittle from Leif's lip. "Maybe. Yes. Someday."

"We could still go to Jared's wedding. Caleb will be home. Your parents would be thrilled."

Karley smiles. "For now, I'd rather they come here. Yesterday in an email, Mom mentioned they're thinking about it. When they pick Caleb up from his mission."

"I'd like that." Hans's gaze slides past her and out the window. "It's really coming down out there."

"Skiing will be good. You should call your mom."

Hans reaches over Leif and cups her hip. His fingers caress the swell of her bottom. The radiator ticks. Hans yawns. "Maybe I will. It'd be nice to see her. I'll call tomorrow."

"Today," Karley says. "It's already today."

"Today." Smiling, Hans closes his eyes. Beneath their window, a car bumps over cobblestone. Receding, it turns the corner and is gone. The baby sighs, and Hans opens his eyes. Together, he and Karley listen to Leif breathe.

Outside, snow gathers deep on window ledges, in the sectioned frames of each pane. It is winter in Norway and Sunday. The mornings are dark until ten.

The Nordlings, Leif willing, won't rise until dawn.